PRAISE FOR MATT MOORE

"Subtle power, intelligence, and humanity are the hallmarks of Moore's work. These stories are apt to stick in your mind like quills. They did in mine."
—Nick Cutter, author of *Little Heaven*, *The Acolyte*, and *The Troop*

"*It's Not The End and Other Lies* is the taut, muscular debut of an original and gifted voice. Matt Moore is a gardener of nightmares, artlessly turning over the dark soil in which the horrors that entangle ordinary people in their killing grasp bloom. If you read one new writer this year, read this one. You'll thank me later."
—Michael Rowe, Shirley Jackson Award-nominated author of *Wild Fell* and *Enter, Night*

"Matt Moore writes a line that resonates and reverberates with the reader long after the eye has moved on. Moore's stories are subtle, unassuming, coaxing you in with the banalities of real life—even if the stories themselves are fantastical—only to claw into your heart and mind. Moore's ideas are plainly in the realm of the supernatural and the monstrous, but his heart is in the humanity of the people that populate his stories; you'll recognize people you know in Moore's work, relate to the actions his characters take. Matt Moore's greatest strength as a writer is conveying the humanity and the possible to the monstrous and the impossible."
—Paul Michael Anderson, author of *Bones are Made to be Broken*

"Matt Moore's words will invade your psyche and never leave you. It's the best kind of haunting!"
—Marie Bilodeau, bestselling author of *Nigh*

"Stealthy, cutting, disturbing, immersive. Moore is a student and teacher of tension and fear. That quiet suspicion something will go wrong springs at you from an unexpected direction. A dread creeps upon the unwary reader in his horror, while questioning your faith in humanity is the ticket price of his science fiction. *It's Not the End and Other Lies* is a collection of stories about worlds too big to be mastered, families and friendships too small to redeem you, and experiences too marking to exorcise."

—Derek Künsken, author of *The Quantum Magician*

"Matt Moore opens up the darkest recesses of the human psyche like a surgeon: incisively, cleanly, compassionately. These stories will grab you and stay with you."

—Kate Heartfield, author of *Armed in Her Fashion*, *Alice Payne Arrives*, and *Alice Payne Rides*

"Having published Matt Moore in two of our anthologies, I've been waiting to see a collection of his brilliant short fiction for a long time. This book does not disappoint. Each piece is a gem—chilling, moving, and always thought-provoking. Settle in: it's a wild ride."

—Hayden Trenholm, Publisher of Bundoran Press

"Matt Moore is a master of atmosphere and suspense. *It's Not the End and Other Lies* is a phone call from inside my nightmares."

—Matthew Johnson, author of *Irregular Verbs and Other Stories*

IT'S NOT THE END

AND OTHER LIES

FIRST EDITION
It's Not the End and Other Lies © 2018 by Matt Moore
Cover art © 2018 by Erik Mohr (Made by Emblem)
Cover design © 2018 by Jared Shapiro
Interior design © 2018 by Ian Sullivan Cant and Jared Shapiro

Distributed in Canada by
Fitzhenry & Whiteside Limited
195 Allstate Parkway
Markham, Ontario L3R 4T8
Phone: (905) 477-9700
e-mail: bookinfo@fitzhenry.ca

Distributed in the U.S. by
Consortium Book Sales & Distribution
34 Thirteenth Avenue, NE, Suite 101
Minneapolis, MN 55413
Phone: (612) 746-2600
e-mail: sales.orders@cbsd.com

Library and Archives Canada Cataloguing in Publication

Moore, Matt, 1973-
[Short stories. Selections]
It's not the end : and other lies / Matt Moore.

Short stories.
Issued in print and electronic formats.
ISBN 978-1-77148-450-3 (softcover).--ISBN 978-1-77148-451-0 (EPUB)

I. Title. II. Title: It is not the end.

PS8626.O59455A6 2018 C813'.6 C2018-900795-8
C2018-900796-6

CHIZINE PUBLICATIONS
Peterborough, Canada
www.chizinepub.com
info@chizinepub.com

Edited by Chris Edwards and Sandra Kasturi
Copyedited and proofread by Leigh Teetzel and Errick Nunnally

Canada Council for the Arts Conseil des Arts du Canada

We acknowledge the support of the Canada Council for the Arts, which last year invested $153 million to bring the arts to Canadians throughout the country.

Published with the generous assistance of the Ontario Arts Council.

Printed in Canada

IT'S NOT THE END

AND OTHER LIES

Matt Moore

Introduction by David Nickle

ChiZine Publications

For Joan Frances Garbar (1934–2012),
my first creative writing teacher.
Her initial criticism of my writing still drives me:
"I don't see enough of you in your writing."

TABLE OF CONTENTS

SHOW YOUR WORK: AN INTRODUCTION

Do you want to know a secret about short story writers? The secret?

Here it is. If we're doing the job right, we don't know the secret any more than anyone else.

This at least is what I tell myself, as I flail about on a short story or a novel and feel lost in the weeds of the narrative. I should be lost. . . . If I have a map, I'm doing it wrong, playing it safe. I might be tempted to take a shortcut, answer the question that my characters and narrative pose to me with a pat homily—with a reassuring lie.

I shouldn't know the secret. But I should be looking for it . . . doing the math.

I'd been doing the math for more than a decade when I met Matt Moore. He was helping out Sandra Kasturi and Brett Savory get their publishing house going—ChiZine Publications. They meanwhile were helping me get my book-writing career going; I'd been publishing short stories here and there and having an awful time marketing a couple of novels, and in what seemed like an act of extreme and saintly charity, they were publishing my first story collection.

Matt was handling publicity, helping out—and crucially, paying attention . . . asking those questions himself. At first, I had no idea that this was so: I just knew this kind, lanky gentleman who threw himself into helping books and stories find their readers. Not someone who had stories of his own; and more important, had questions of his own.

And now, nine years later, here we are at the front of Matt Moore's first story collection. The subtitle calls it a collection of lies. It is that—all fiction is after all a sprawling, consensual fib. But I would also submit that this is additionally a collection of hard questions. It is not a collection of easy answers.

So maybe it's not so much of a package of lies as that.

See, Matt does do the math, and shows his work too. The opening story in this collection, "Delta Pi," does that literally, as it asks what remains when a fundamental constant becomes variable. The binary question of whether to jump from a height or celebrate the altitude finds its answer in the moment. Another story delivers its moment in a sharp punch—for after all, where there are gloves, can a body blow be far behind?

You're in for a treat, as you step into first one and then another of these twenty-one collected stories by Matt Moore. But a treat is not the same thing as a confection. Not here.

Matt knows well enough to open the door to mystery and let us all in on the barest glimpse of the secret. So enjoy; and when you've taken a moment to think the truth of it through . . .

Endure.

David Nickle
Toronto, 2018

ΔΠ ("DELTA PI")

The digital clock on my desk, synched to the same atomic clock as the facility, reads 11:48:05. One hundred fifteen seconds left.

I tell myself it's my true understanding of Cünzken that brought—and kept—me here. This once tiny town of Smythers. Where Cünzken was born and grew up. Yet I can't discount insanity, either. They say the truly insane aren't aware of their madness. And only a madman would come here if he believed what Cünzken predicted in his fifth paper. But for three years I've been told only a madman could believe Cünzken's predictions.

I don't know if I believe, but at least I understand. That's more than I can say for those working at the facility.

My students don't notice my momentary distraction. They stare out the windows at the noontime prairie. A lump of resentment settles in my throat. If I could stand—instead of being stuck in this chair—I might command a bit more respect. I rap on the whiteboard to get their attention. "Who knows what the mathematic constant Pi is?"

"It's like," a student begins, her eyes still focused outside, "the difference between how far a circle's across and how far it's around."

"Close." Maybe I should be more impressed by a fourth grader expressing the basic concept of Pi. Considering their parents are research scientists and assistants at the facility built to test the Cünzken Equations, I'm judging on a curve.

Turning toward the board, I wheel myself from behind my desk. I draw a circle on the white board, label it "C," a diameter I label "D," and then write an equation infinitely simpler and more immutable than any of Cünzken's: $\pi = C/D$. "Pi is the ratio of circumference—how far a circle is around—to its diameter—how far it is from one edge to the other. It's an unchanging constant and a fundamental building block in math."

Nothing. Gazing out the window. I resist looking myself. Looking again at Liz Polaski in her white cotton blouse and grey pencil skirt, red hair in a loose ponytail. I'd say she's in her mid-40s, almost twice my age, but I guess I have a Mrs. Robinson thing. She has her English class sitting out in the grass, reading to them from some book.

And honestly, I don't want to look past Liz, past the five-metre high chain-link fence that borders the school property. Beyond it lies the facility's 4,000-hectare grounds. Its main complex towers above the endless, even horizon like a watchful god. Beneath its grounds, right now, supercharged particles are travelling at near–light speed in a twenty-kilometre long, magnetically-guided circular track. Their collision will tell us if Cünzken's predictions were forty years ahead of their time.

Or perhaps the collision has already occurred.

I force myself to not look outside, not look at the clock. If I can focus on the lesson, so can my students. But the knowledge that I should be on the facility's staff, not pretending to be a teacher because it was the only job I could get, gnaws at me.

A pulse of pain throbs behind my eyes. I shouldn't let myself get so worked up.

I push my chair's wheels in opposite directions to face the class, but I don't turn as much as I want. Maybe I need the chair looked at. I give an extra push to face them.

"Can we do this outside?" someone asks.

"No," I reply, my voice lacking a polite, teacher-like tone. Only ten more minutes until lunch and it's not like I want to be here anymore than they do. Not to mention another twinge behind my eyes. "We're going to do an experiment. If we finish before the bell, you can leave."

Faces turn. Attention is given. Leaning on my elbows, I draw a circle with a large, chalk-tipped compass on a piece of corkboard on my desk. Then I measure its diameter, write the figure on the whiteboard and grab the box of pushpins from a drawer. "Everyone come forward and take a pin. Put them around the chalk circle. I want the whole circle filled in." The students do as instructed, eager to get this over with. They watch me wind a string around the circle of pins, measure and write its length on the whiteboard. "Now, we have diameter and circumference. Back to your desks and tell me what Pi equals."

They rush to their seats. Hands unzip backpacks, calculators clatter on desks. Not helping my headache.

I look at the clock: 11:52:44.

Since reality didn't rend and tear a hundred and sixty-four seconds ago, I assume the research team is pouring over the data from the collision.

A deeper, more bitter pang of resentment grabs me. Even with just a Bachelor's, I understand the Cünzken Equations at a more fundamental level than most of the PhDs working there. Having found the bars and coffee shops where they hang out, I've talked to them, flirted with the women. Learned what I could about the experiments. Tried to find a way onto the team, even as a junior assistant. I had to be close. Had to know more. At first, they were curious how a grade school teacher knew so much, but then I'd go and mention Cünzken's fifth paper.

Sure, they're all about the first four papers, theorizing how a particle collision could create a stable wormhole by unrolling a micro-dimension to travel along. But they dismiss his fifth paper with as much fervour as I embrace it. They laugh me off, turning back to their drinks. Just like my advisor calling me mad when I proposed doing my thesis on the fifth paper. He refused to accept it and wouldn't write a letter of recommendation. So despite completing my Bachelor's at Caltech in less than two years, my career is going nowhere.

I can't help it. I look outside—

The headache must be worse than I thought. My eyes can't focus, like the complex is *over* the horizon.

"Three point three," one of my students says.

Another: "Three point two six."

"Three point two *five nine*."

More voices shout, throbbing in my head. I hold up my hand for quiet and ask, "Did everyone get something like three point two six?"

Heads nod. I grab a calculator. This is the first time I've done this experiment with the pins and string. There's a sampling error since the pins form a multi-sided polygon, not a true circle, but the ratio should come up *short*.

"Can we go?"

"You promised."

A few keystrokes later and I see the ratio's correct. How could I screw this up? Though something about Cünzken's last paper nags at me, I say, "Sure."

They burst from their seats and run for the door, amplifying my headache. A few seconds later, they go streaming across the blacktop. Liz tells them to walk in that unquestionable tone veteran teachers have before returning to her reading.

Rubbing my temples, I tell myself I'm not bitter that I'll never run. Never be part of the group. Always be on the outside. Maybe it's ego, but these headaches give me a sense of kinship with Cünzken. By all accounts, he was an overlooked, bookish kid who suffered from headaches growing up in a town of farmers and tradesman. Friendless, he spent a lot of time wandering alone outside of town. Good grades got him into college, odd jobs around town allowed him to afford it.

Once there, he remained bookish and friendless, yet excelled in his studies. Working at a part-time job, he invested his earnings in the stock market, studying its fluctuations, and made a fortune. He received his PhD less than four years after enrolling in a Bachelor's program.

But his skills at predicting stocks brought him fame, not his research. He taught sporadically, never remaining at a university for more than a few years before being let go. His four papers were published in obscure journals over a fifteen-year career. Described as "esoteric" and "alchemic" forty years ago, it wouldn't be until results from CERN showed Cünzken had been right all along.

He often returned to Smythers, buying up the land outside town where he'd wandered as a kid and the facility sits now. As a man, he took long walks out there, pondering his theories. Despite Smythers being a farming town, this land had always sat fallow, the few farmers who'd owned it saying nothing would grow there. Small-town rumours of the land being cursed amplified when the few people who knew Cünzken reported he used to say nature would talk to him out there, whispering its secrets to him.

These rumours cast Cünzken as peculiar, but his fifth paper turned people against him. In it, he took his equations further, to an ultimate conclusion. Testing his theories, he warned—and theoretically demonstrated—would open a Pandora's Box. An unravelling reality beyond human comprehension. Like probing the mind of God, it would bring obliteration, not enlightenment.

Yet reading his fifth paper changed my perceptions of the world. I didn't understand how anyone could fail to grasp the irrefutable conclusion that the fabric of reality is an oversimplified illusion. That our three-dimensional perceptions had evolved to protect us from reality's true nature. Physics and mathematics rested on a delicate framework that would collapse with the slightest nudge. So many of my classmates just didn't get it, only able to see his graphs in the two dimensions of the page, not the five he'd intended. Judging variables as unknowns needing to be solved, not as true unknown factors to which we three-dimensional beings could never assign values. I debated it online, enduring endless insults and finding no one who truly understood the elegance of the equations.

The irony is Cünzken didn't live to see the fifth paper published. He'd killed himself by then, a suicide note explaining it was inevitable someone would test his equations. More than that, he claimed his pondering the deepest recesses of reality had created a multi-dimensional space in his mind. It had allowed something in the universe's deepest bowels to reach out to him. To mark him. If a doorway opened, he feared the indescribable wonders and horrors that would emerge from the hidden dimensions would seek him out.

At least, he concluded, his headaches had subsided.

That's why I understand why Cünzken willed his considerable fortune to be used as seed money to build a collider for testing his equations on the property he had purchased. Cünzken had been a ridiculed outcast his whole life. He dared the world to prove him wrong. The world itself would be the stakes. His hometown would be ground zero.

Forty years later, a consortium of scientists and commercial interests accepted the dare. Once home to just eight hundred people, the facility's construction crews brought roads, restaurants and hotels to Smythers. Staff brought their families, which meant schools, which brought a desperate search for teachers. All one needed was a Bachelor's degree. It gave me the chance to get closer.

The bell rings, stabbing my head, and a moment later stampeding feet and gleeful voices fill the hallway. Another moment and hundreds of kids bolt outside, breaking into small groups that claim spots of grass.

As I grab the eraser, Liz walks in and hops up on my desk. "You ran the experiment?"

"It says Pi, the great universal constant, is 3.26." Something *is* wrong with my chair. It takes more than a complete turn to face the board.

"I thought you had a physics degree," she teases.

I motion to the figures on the white board. "Run the numbers yourself."

She grabs my calculator. From how she's sitting and where I am in this chair, I have a great view of her legs, but the headache is pounding an uneven rhythm.

Her eyebrows knot at the result. "Well, you did something wrong, speedy." She hops off my desk, squeezes my shoulder to let me know she's kidding, and grabs the compass, intent on repeating the experiment.

I'm barely aware. The pain in my head is uneven, but there's a pattern. Complex, sophisticated. Oscillating in multiple dimensions.

"Does—" The tone of Liz's voice pulls me back. Next to me, she's tense, turning the compass. Watching, it's taking the compass longer to complete the circle than it should. Like there's more than 360 degrees to traverse.

A kid's voice outside: "Hey, look!"

I look up. A handful of kids are standing, pointing. Pointing at the horizon.

"Liz," I say, wondering if my eyes really have gone bad. "Outside."

She looks. Sees what I see. Sees what the kids see. The horizon is curving. "Oh my God."

The agony in my head pulses, filling my mind, pushing beyond it.

A wordless understanding arises.

I haphazardly shove pins around the circumference of the circle Liz has drawn.

"What are you doing?"

It's language. Something so foreign, so immense, is trying to communicate. "What if Pi *has* changed?"

"What?"

Cünzken predicted this: unravelling a micro-dimension could cause another dimension to curl up, possibly changing universal constants—Planck length, speed of light, Pi. "The collider—" I gasp.

"That was today?"

The circle looks smaller than the one I drew, but it takes almost all of the string to wrap its circumference. I fight through the pain that threatens to overwhelm my awareness and measure the string, punch the measurements into the calculator, and hold it up for Liz to see: Pi is 3.71.

She says something, but I don't hear. Holding Cünzken's graphs in my mind, I apply it to this communication and the pain shatters. The message, loosed from the constraints of my three-dimensional perception of space-time, expands along infinite dimensions. It would take a lifetime to explain its intricacies, but it boils down to a basic concept: We have been noticed and it is coming.

"What does that mean?" Liz repeats.

Entry to a wormhole comes via a three-dimensional space—a sphere. A finite space. "Look out your room's windows," I tell her.

She runs to the door without question. From there, she can see into her classroom and out its windows toward town.

Outside my windows, the horizon continues to curve. Curve upwards. A few teachers stand, pointing. And the children, taking their cue from the adults, remain motionless.

"It's flat," Liz says from the doorway. She's only twenty-five feet away, but she seems so distant.

The speaker at the front of the room crackles. A voice trying to hide its fear says: "Attention, attention. There's been an accident at the collider. We are asking everyone to calmly leave school grounds and walk toward town."

"Get the kids," I tell her. "Run. Get outside its effects." Corners where walls meet the ceiling and floor begin to bow.

Footfalls pound by in the hall.

"I'll get someone to carry you."

She leans into the hall, but I shout: "There's no time. Get the kids out."

Her face is pained. "I'll send someone back." And she's gone. I begin to turn toward the window, wheels spinning and spinning, but I barely rotate as the wheels' circumferences increase with each passing second.

Liz emerges outside, commanding the kids to follow her. Unquestioningly, they and the teachers obey. A moment later, everyone disappears around the corner of the building.

The horizon is now bowl-shaped, the collider complex impossibly distant rising from behind it.

This is no delusion borne from madness. It's truth, the ultimate truth I have sought for three years.

With a sense I can't quantify, I detect the approach of something from a direction moments ago I could not fathom, but now seems so obvious. It has been here so close all along, yet infinitely unreachable.

I wait for the universe to reveal whatever wonders or horrors it has concealed.

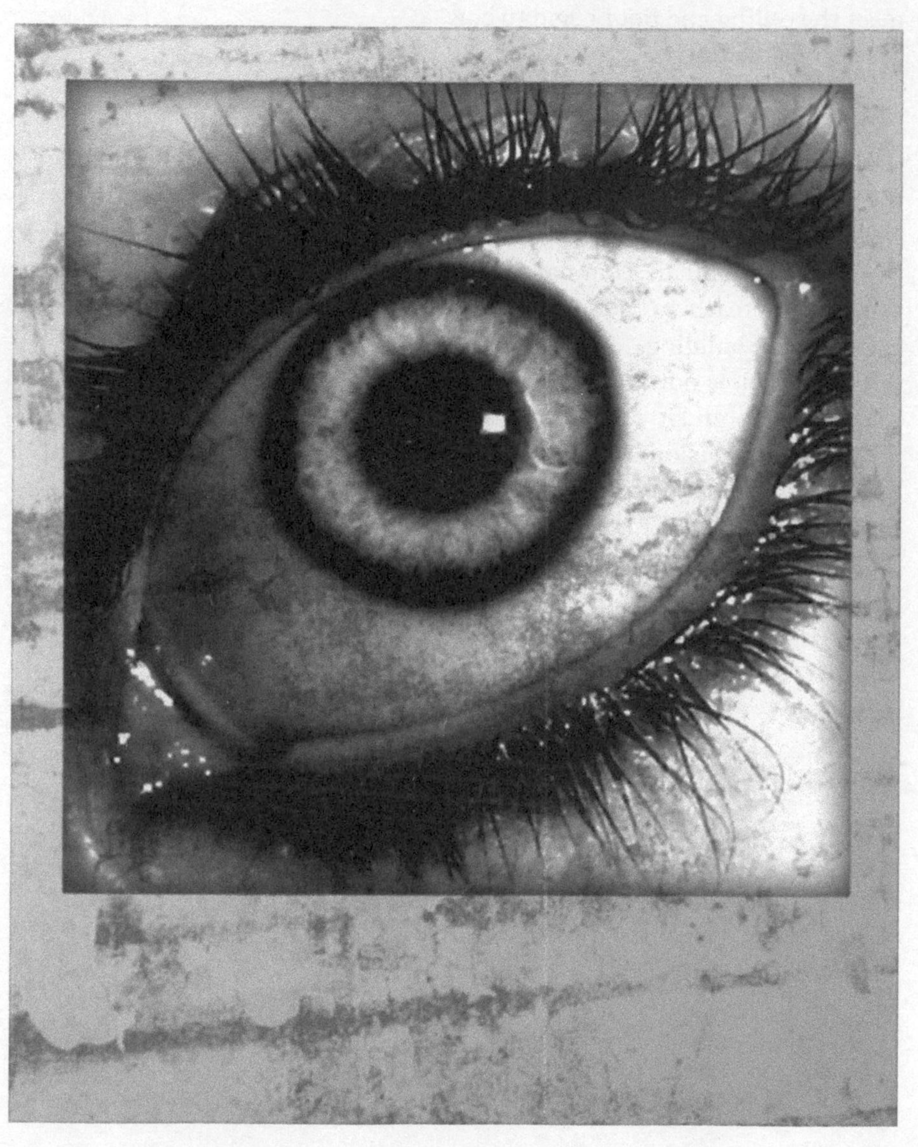

ASCENSION

—Dear God, they're everywhere—

Limping. Can't remember how long. Can't think straight. This dull, distant pain in my leg. Sirens. Something's burning?

—Can't believe—

Everywhere, people are running. Streaming between cars, trying to get away. Some lurch, limbs twitching. Bodies lay still on the asphalt, bleeding. And others . . .

—oh-god-oh-god-oh-god-oh-god—

Oh god.

Others feed. A pile of people, their flesh shredded and eyes milky blanks, hold down a screaming, kicking old man. They tear loops of guts from his abdomen, press them to blood-streaked mouths—

—HELPMEPLEASEHELPME—

These thoughts . . . They're not mine.

I focus. How did—

A *bang* tears through the screams and sirens. Ten steps away, a police officer, gripping a pistol, hurries among the parked cars, yelling for others to run. Focus punches through his terror. Through that tunnel of determination, I see years back, a younger him leading others in combat, a newly promoted First Lieutenant. Driven, well-trained to—

A scream. Sallow-skinned hands grab a teenage boy by a tangle of hair. His mind a jumble of wordless horror. He swats the hands drawing him close.

My hands.

I open my hand, letting him—

My fingers remain clenched in his hair, pulling.

The teen lurches one way, another, and he's free, running, leaving bits of bloody scalp clasped in my fingers. My hands press this into my mouth. Bitter, salty. Something base and savage within me is satisfied and—*disgusting*—craves more.

Yet it's *not* me. Only my body desires this flesh. To feed. To spread this special death so we can change, leave, *ascend*—

The cop fires again. To my right, a young woman staggers, a raw, red scream where her right cheek should be. Blonde hair in a ponytail, skin translucent, blue veins beneath. The torn collar of her blood-spattered college sweatshirt exposes a bite wound on her shoulder.

Beyond her, burning shapes twirl and dance out of a flaming store front.

Across the small grocery store parking lot, her clouded eyes lock with mine. Questions flood between us.

—what's happening—when did—how long have—can you remember—stop yourself—how can we hear—

A memory that might be hers or mine or belong to someone running between us: sirens jerking me/her/us awake. Contradicting radio and television and internet reports. It's local. It's worldwide. The military is moving in. Government communications have broken down. It's in the water. The air. Our very thoughts and words. A fast, desperate debate with our roommates to stay put or make a run for it. One of us—me, her, the cop—needs to find someone. Save someone. So I/he/she/we go out into the chaos, terrified but more afraid of losing—

Bang. Her right eye explodes. Our connection snaps. She drops, but a force—a momentum—tries to pull me after her into . . . something. A glimpse, a whiff: higher and bigger and beautiful. Inevitable.

Unsteady legs turn me, on the edge of balance, to face the cop. Hands reach out, feet shuffle forward, ignoring others racing past.

That's right, the cop thinks, *towards me*. His concentration hardens. Seven rounds left in this clip, one more clip to go. His car just on the other side of Fuller Avenue. If backup doesn't show by the time he reloads, he'll fall back.

And out there among the jagged, interweaving thoughts are others like him. Still thinking, still evaluating. Their minds solid, consistent shapes among the amorphous panic. Their rational, human minds resisting the raw, adrenaline-fuelled impulse to flee that's spreading like fork lightning through the unconscious, animal connection we all share.

And others like me, most adrift in their terror, but others joining, connecting. Thinking. A Tokyo subway station. An apartment building courtyard in Cleveland. A church in Cape Town.

I'm sensed, welcomed.

—is this intentional—part of a plan—how are others—

Not in English, but I understand. Thought, not words. Pure.

—our flawed, finite bodies jettisoned so our minds—

Another *bang* and I'm yanked back and up and *out*, into somewhere else. Somewhere above, somewhere of everything and everyone. I'm barely aware of seeing my mangled body collapse through the eyes of the cop because now I see everything through everyone's eyes.

THE MACHINERY OF GOVERNMENT

In Paul's right ear, Eddie asked: "Next: Do you have your access codes?"

"I think so," Paul replied, moving into the front hall of the small townhouse he rented. Honestly, he had no idea where they were.

Outside, the siren was getting closer.

Three more notices scrolled up into his field of vision:

* MINISTER OF NATIONAL DEFENCE EDDIE LAZENBY ARRIVING AT GOVERNMENT OPERATIONS CENTRE

* PRIME MINISTER ANDREW RENAULT HAS BEEN ALERTED

* LAND AND CELLULAR COMMUNICATIONS NETWORKS OVERLOADED; GOVERNMENT NETWORK REMAINS STABLE

The upward movement of the red letters—a direction his inner ear told him was impossible while he turned to the right—made him motion-sick.

He shut his eyes, moaning, bile filling his mouth.

"Are you okay?" Eddie asked, sounding like he was next to Paul and not speaking through a device in Paul's ear. In the background, Paul heard a commotion of commands and responses, voices trying to get Eddie's attention.

"Yeah," Paul replied, tentatively opening his eyes. The messages had contracted and joined others in the upper right corner of his vision. Missed communications gathered in the lower right. "Just the heads-up display." He grabbed his briefcase from where it lay by the door.

Someone shouted Eddie's name as he spoke: "You'll get—*not now!*—you'll get used to it."

Paul sorted through the briefcase, wondering if he'd get used to the pain. Before now, he'd only worn the interface for about an hour at a time. He'd pull its strap snug against his forehead just before Question Period, which let his aides send him talking points or statistics to deal with a question from the Opposition, then shut it down and slide it off afterward. That limited exposure caused a dull ache behind his eyes. Now, the increased electrical signals the device was pumping into his occipital lobe, the vision centre at the back of the brain, caused his head to throb. "Hope I didn't pack it in a bag that's on its way to Marcel's cottage with Laura."

Three more notices appeared:

* PUBLIC SAFETY MINISTER MARCEL CHARLEBOIS HAS BEEN ALERTED

* ENEMY FORCES RE-GROUPING NEAR VARS

* RUSSIAN, CHINESE AMBASSADORS DENY INVOLVEMENT OR KNOWLEDGE

His eyes fought between focusing on the briefcase and the messages seeming to float two metres away yet superimposed over the leather case. Paul shut his right eye and the messages disappeared. Using his left, he kept searching.

He bit his lip. Not there. Maybe the laptop bag. "So much to keep track of."

"You get used to that, too."

He pulled open a Velcro flap to find the backs of two thick, black binders. "I feel so useless."

"Andy would not have picked you if that was true," Eddie said. In the background, someone screamed about "getting some fucking air support."

Not for the first time, Paul wondered if his skin colour had more to do with his promotion than his abilities. Having a young black man from the prairies in cabinet helped silence critics who claimed his party was the domain of old white men from the coast.

He pushed the idea away. Now wasn't the time for those thoughts.

Opening a side pocket revealed the thin blue folder containing his access codes. "Got it."

Paul opened his right eye to see:

* SPEAKING POINTS: USE: SENSLESSS AGGRESSION, DISRUPTION OF PEACEFUL CO-EXISTENCE

* AVOID: INVASION/INVADERS, ATTACK

"Last item: Is Laura still there?" Eddie asked.

"She left about an hour ago." Paul returned to the living room. The siren sounded like it was somewhere in his neighbourhood. "Said she couldn't wait to get down by the water." The muted television showed a view down Highway 417 in the farmland to the east of the city. Just at the edge of the camera's range, indistinct shapes moved, sending up plumes of blue-grey smoke. "Wanted to enjoy this great weather."

They'd both been looking forward to the long weekend. His first two weeks as cabinet minister had been spent getting hammered by the opposition in Question Period and attending endless meetings scheduled by his chief of staff, who insisted Paul should have been wearing the interface more frequently. In both venues, Paul parroted the talking points sent down from the Prime Minister's Office—deflect attacks, stay on message, defend the government's agenda. Nothing about using his own discretion. Nothing about the government's response to hostile forces on Canadian soil for the first time since the Fenian Raids. He felt like a cog—messages from the PMO made him spin and he, in turn, spun others.

So this weekend, he and Laura were going to a cottage in the Gatineau Hills owned by Paul's other mentor, Marcel Charlebois, the current minister of public safety, to review the government's agenda. For months, the front lines had been stable so the Prime Minister—"Andy" to his friends and caucus members not out to replace him—had given them the okay to get out of the city. Just a quick, last-minute meeting with his chief of staff on the Hill and Paul would have been on his way.

An emergency notice twenty minutes ago had changed everything.

"That's the best place for her," Eddie said. "*One more second!* It shouldn't take her too much longer to get there. We can evac her with Marcel if it comes to that."

The kitchen phone rang. Pain pulsed in time with its simulated bell sound. Paul shut his right eye. The caller ID showed: LAURA - CELL. "Eddie, it's Laura on the house phone."

"Go ahead and take it. I need to figure out what's happening here. Tell Laura to stay at the cottage. GPS shows your security escort is almost there. Let me know when you're on your way."

"I will." The connection clicked off. Paul hit the "GO" button on the handset and pressed it to his left ear. Sirens shrilled in the background, an ice pick through his brain. An instant later, near-panic at how far the chaos might have spread. "Sweetie, where are you? Are you safe?"

"Thank God," she said. "Been trying your office and your cell."

"Meeting was cancelled. Where are you?"

"Downtown. The Rideau Centre. But I'm heading for the Hill."

The words froze him, like that doctor five years ago telling them it was cancer growing in her belly, not the baby they'd hoped for. "I thought you were on your way to Marcel's."

"I made a quick stop," she said. "A small present for you for making it into cabinet. And something for Marcel and Eddie. Then everyone's going crazy. I can't get online, but people are saying they're on the move."

His temples throbbed in time with his racing heartbeat. "It's true."

"Holy shit, Paul." Terror in her voice. "Coming here?"

"We don't know."

"Are you going to the Hill? Can I meet you there?"

"No, I—" An unsecure line, he had to pick his words carefully. "I'm not going to the Hill."

"I hear you. What's my next move? Should I get to get to you?"

Tires screeched. He turned, right eye popping open. Messages—shifting and scrolling—filled his vision. Behind them, an RCMP cruiser skidded to a stop out front. Pangs of nausea beat in time with its pulsing lights. Paul turned away just as the messages rearranged themselves into a tighter pattern. His stomach flipped and he clamped his teeth and eyes shut.

"You still there?" Laura asked.

Paul yanked the strap off. He had a moment to feel the tension of the fabric slide free from the back of his head before pain sliced through his skull, the consequence of not shutting down the interface. He leaned on the kitchen counter. Fighting to keep pain from his voice: "Can you get to your car? To Marcel's? That's the safest place for you."

"No. Streets are jammed. If I find RCMP, could they get me to where you'll be?"

The commpiece in his right ear chirped, announcing a new call. Paul pulled it out.

"I'm not sure what the plan is," he said. A horn blared. Paul looked up to see a constable next to his cruiser, dressed in dark blue fatigues with a flak jacket covering his barrel chest, waving for a passing car to slow down as it rounded a curve. Paul moved to the front door.

"Then I'm coming to you," she said, breathing quicker.

Paul opened the front door, letting in a cacophony of sirens, car horns and revving engines. He waved to the constable.

"I think it'll take me an hour, so if something changes—" The floor trembled and the phone roared static.

Paul held it from his ear. When he put it back, there were screams. "Laura?!"

"Oh my god! Paul—I think it was the Hill!"

Two steps and Paul stood before the television. "Are you okay?" he asked. The screen had split into two images. On the left, peace protestors on Parliament Hill—half of them with green, white, and black armbands in a show of solidarity—scattered from a still-smoking crater. Scores of bodies lay, unmoving, around its edge. *Suicide bomber*, Paul thought, but the image on the right showed the view from the highway. The distant shapes shuddered and belched tongues of fire and black smoke.

"I'm okay." People screamed in the background, grunts and curses of a crowd fighting itself. "Everyone's running south. What was—" The house shook again. Laura screamed.

The television image panned to show a corner of Parliament's West Block explode. Its green copper roof collapsed in a cloud of fire and smoking debris.

On his hip, Paul's PDA vibrated.

The constable—his nametag read Tessier—appeared in the doorway joining the living room and front hall, nearly filling it. Orange-tinted goggles hid his eyes. He motioned to the front door.

Paul shook his head. "Laura—" The line was dead.

"Minister," Tessier said, "we need to get you out of here."

Paul dialled Laura's number. "Just a second." An automated message told him the number was temporarily unavailable. Incisors dug into his lower lip.

"Now, sir."

The house shuddered. Glasses clinked in the kitchen cabinets. The bass-note *boom* of a distant explosion hit them a moment later.

"My wife is stuck downtown and trying to get here. We have to wait for her."

"Where downtown?"

"Rideau Centre."

"She won't make it."

Ice formed around Paul's heart. He fought back memories of hospital rooms, of helplessness, of his wife wasting away. "Can you send a car for her? Get her out of there?"

"My orders don't include her."

"An hour. I just need one hour."

"Sir, I'm not going to debate this. You need to come with me—"

"No." Paul turned and moved into the kitchen. He wondered how far Tessier's authority extended—could he remove Paul by force—but the constable stepped into the hallway, speaking into his radio.

Paul cursed, struggling for a move that would keep him here. She had come to Ottawa to be with him. Despite his travel and some late nights—and being 100 kilometres from the front—she wanted to spend as much time with him as she could in this cramped, rented townhouse rather than be back home, safe but alone. Getting into cabinet meant more late nights, sometimes not getting home until midnight, and being gone by 6:30 the next morning. Since they'd first met, coworkers at Regina City Hall, she liked to be in bed by ten o'clock. But no matter the time he got home, he found her on the couch—sometimes awake but usually not. He'd gently rouse her and she always had a smile and hug. Never a sour face, never a rash word no matter the hour. She'd been a rock—the one thing he could rely on.

Every day—every moment with her—was a gift. When they cut the cancer from her, they took her ability to have children, but the doctors only gave her a fifteen percent chance of lasting two years. It's aggressive, the doctors had said. It comes back.

But here she was—healthy and active. No sign of—

Another explosion, close enough to feel its *crack-boom*. Something upstairs shattered as it hit the floor.

A deep, animal instinct twisted in Paul's gut, screaming for him to run. If they did to Ottawa what they did to Moncton—

But how could he leave? Why should *he* get to go? He was nobody special—a well-spoken policy junkie who'd mastered the non-answer reply of deflection. The only difference between him and a dozen others was he was black and young . . . though after the last two weeks, thirty-five didn't feel so young.

And the only reason there was a spot to fill was the Opposition had dug up some dirt on Eddie's predecessor at National Defence—tapes of a conversation where she suggested Canada's foreign policies had failed to detect the coming invasion. She'd been forced to resign and the ensuing cabinet shuffle left a junior cabinet minister spot vacant. A few words from Eddie and Marcel netted Paul the job. If not for that, he'd be another backbencher, hunkered down and waiting—

Brakes shrieked. A car horn—

Metal and glass screamed, twisted, shattered. The living room window like a movie screen: a car spinning, somersaulting left to right, debris flying and striking the house.

Tessier from the front hall: "Shit!" The front door banged open and Paul raced to it, the stink of burnt rubber hitting him halfway there. He stopped on his small porch, bits of glass and plastic crunching under his feet. Engines revved, horns blared. Two more *booms* shook the air.

Tessier pounded down the street through chunks of metal and plastic toward the gnarled, smoking remains of a car resting on its roof.

In the street in front of Paul, tire tracks snaked in an S-shape. What had happened clicked into place: the car had taken the curve too fast, swerved to avoid the cruiser and rolled.

Over the cacophony of a city descending into panic, someone shouted "Paul!" Across the street, his neighbour Sarah, still in black running gear from her morning jog, descended from her porch and crossed the street. Waiting for her, Paul noticed others peering from doorways.

"The news said they're coming," she said, stopping at the bottom of his steps. Colour had drained from her face. "They're shelling downtown and they're coming."

He had no way to know if they'd shifted position since taking off the interface. Confirming what she said could make her panic. Denying it could cause false hope. Political instinct told him to deflect: "Sarah, you should get back inside."

Down the street, Tessier got on all fours and looked into the overturned car, one of its wheels still spinning. Half a kilometre past, a three-car accident blocked the intersection into the major avenue, causing a lineup of cars.

Paul had a moment to wonder how the hell Laura could make it home through what was happening when a voice yelled: "We fighting back?" An older man came down the sidewalk from the opposite direction, leaning on his cane. Paul recognized him—tall, thin, olive skinned—but didn't know his name. "We finally gonna kick their butts or what?"

"You should—" Others were coming. Down the sidewalk, across the street—a dozen or so, converging on him. Paul realized that his standing on his porch, the cruiser with its lights still flashing and others gathered around might look like he was giving some kind of speech.

"Yeah!" a teen girl—dyed blue hair, decked out in a black hoodie and jeans—shouted. "We ain't taking no more shit from them! We'll fuckin' kick their asses if they come down our block!"

Paul held up his hands. "Please, you should—"

A helicopter buzzed overhead, low and fast.

"Everyone get back in your homes!" Tessier boomed. Heads turned to watch the constable come back up the street.

"The driver—" Paul began.

"Dead," Tessier replied, stopping at the trunk of his cruiser. To the crowd: "Get back inside. It isn't safe out here."

"*He's* out here," someone shouted. "He's in cabinet now, right? If we weren't going to kick some ass, he'd be gone, right?"

Tightening the chin strap of a helmet he'd taken from the trunk, Tessier said: "If I have to say it again, I'm putting people in cuffs." He removed a submachine gun, loaded it and slung it over his shoulder.

Despite Tessier's words, more drifted toward Paul, their faces and body language showing curiosity, even hope.

"Talk to us, Paul!" a familiar voice shouted. Paul scanned the crowd: Emily, Laura's best friend in Ottawa even though twenty years separated the two women. She'd eaten at their table many times and he'd helped her with chores since her husband, Edwin, had passed away three years—

Tessier leapt up the steps and leaned close to Paul. "It's time to *go*, Minister."

"Then find my wife and tell me she's safe," Paul replied.

Another voice: "Hey, the bombs have stopped."

Sarah: "They're coming!"

The older man: "Uh-uh. We pounded 'em flat!"

Emily again: "Tell us what's going on, Paul!"

A good question. "Look, I'm not—" *in a position to comment* was not something to say. Just deflect. "Go back inside. Please." He turned and went back into the house, Tessier following.

"Minister—" Tessier began, shutting the door.

"No." Paul moved into the kitchen. The smell of breakfast—an onion and pepper omelette, sausages, coffee—they'd made together that morning still hung in the air. Not even three hours ago. They'd been laughing, flirting, looking forward to the weekend, glad to have a small cabin to themselves—

"You a hard-ass?"

Paul didn't answer. He imagined Laura pushing through panicked crowds, fighting to remember which streets—

"'Cause times like this," Tessier continued, "hard-asses are the ones who get stuff done. Unless they got their heads shoved up there."

Paul turned, but Tessier had his back to him, talking into his radio.

He couldn't get more than a flat silence from the phone. His PDA regretted to inform him all lines were busy.

Another helicopter thrummed overhead.

Only ten minutes had passed. If she ran, it would still take another half-hour for her to get here. And what if she figured the RCMP had already taken him and she'd sought shelter?

Could he get that information?

Watching the crowd out front—shifting, waiting, motioning toward the house—Paul slid the commpiece into his right ear, shivering at how deep the cold, custom-made shape went. A rainbow of colours reflected from the neural interface device where it fit against the back of his skull. He pulled its flexible, inch wide strap over his head and fitted it into position. Biting his lip, he activated the neural connection. For an instant he felt like he was falling, then words and diagrams filled his vision. Pain beat in his temples. Messages told him four ministers were not accounted for, and two were likely killed when the West Block had been hit. Multicolour shapes moved across a map of the eastern edge of the city, following and crossing dotted and solid lines.

Accessing his directory, he scanned for Marcel's direct line. As minister of public safety, Marcel had oversight of the RCMP. If Tessier wouldn't budge on getting help to Laura, Marcel—

The PDA shrilled and `INCOMING COMM - MIN NAT DEF` flashed before him. "I'm here, Eddie."

An automated voice said: "Please hold for Minister—" The line clicked and Eddie said: "Paul?"

"I'm here."

"That's a problem. GPS shows you and the constable still at your place. What is the hold up?"

"I'm waiting for Laura." Movement in the corner of his vision made him turn. He forgot to shut his right eye, but the nausea didn't strike as hard as the words remained stationary in his vision. Eddie was right: he was getting used to it.

"I don't understand," Paul said.

Outside, two of his neighbours squared off—pointing, leaning in, gesticulating madly. "Laura stopped downtown. She's trying to make it home on foot."

"From where?"

All the shapes on the right side of the map suddenly became red. "Rideau Centre." Shapes on the left side blinked white, then disappeared.

"You don't have time to wait."

Outside, the shorter of the two neighbours took a swing.

"You want me to leave her?"

In the background, someone yelled: "Red status!"

Eddie replied: "Oh Christ!" To Paul: "I want you to do your job."

"I can't leave her here."

Others pulled the two neighbours apart. Sarah held her hands out in a "Please stop!" gesture.

"Can you reach her?"

"No, the phone—"

The crowd was taking sides. Now several confronted several others.

"Then get out of there. Laura's in the system. If she's found—*give me a second!*—she'll be protected."

Pain gathered in a hard knob at the front of Paul's head. "That's not good enough."

"*I already signed that!* Good Christ, Paul!"

"Eddie, you know what we went through. I always said she'd come first. Just an hour. Less." He'd resigned his seat when it looked like the end. When she recovered, he'd sworn that no matter what, he'd be there for her. He'd made sure Marcel and Eddie understood that when they talked about recommending him for cabinet. For Eddie to go back on that—

"You are a cabinet minister. There are—"

The television showed a bouncing image from the back of a vehicle, the highway pouring out behind it. In the distance, blurry grey-green shapes pursued, their flags green, white, and black smudges.

"Barely two weeks in a junior—"

The crowd scuffled with itself. The older, olive-skinned man fell from the melee. The black-clad girl had a fistful of Sarah's hair, pulling her away.

"You listen to me!" Eddie interrupted. "Get this through your head: you are in cabinet. You *cannot* put this country at risk over one woman. I don't care if she's your wife! Thirty-nine million—"

"Then I resign."

"Bullshit!"

The exclamation a bolt of pain. Paul dug his teeth into his lower lip, literally biting back the curses he wanted to hurl. Eddie's wife was in Vancouver, over three thousand kilometres away from the front. Who was he to tell him to leave? "Then what do I do, Eddie?"

"You do whatever I tell—" A high-pitched whine replaced Eddie's voice.

The house shivered.

The PDA's screen showed it was still operating, but more than that Paul couldn't glean from the complex read out.

Eddie's voice—". . . range of their artillery!"—blasted in his right ear.

"Eddie?"

The crowd outside, more than twenty now, moved and thrashed like an insane beast. Peacemakers pulled combatants apart only to be sucked into another conflict. Paul had an instant to wonder why Tessier wasn't out there when Eddie's voice returned: "—hit!" Screaming. "Paul?" In terror. "Good Christ, we're taking fire." In agony. "We're—"

Silence.

Past the shapes, maps and text Paul hadn't been aware he'd been scanning, the image of the highway flipped, then changed to static. A terrified anchor appeared a second later.

GOVERNMENT OPERATIONS CENTRE HIT BY ENEMY ARTILLERY - DO NOT APPROACH appeared at the centre of his vision. ENEMY ARMOUR ADVANCING WEST ON HIGHWAY 417 followed.

Laura . . .

Still in the hall, Tessier said "Roger that" and appeared in the living room. "Last chance, Minister. If you're going to stay here, fine, but I'm to escort Minister Charlebois."

* DEFENCE MINISTER LAZENBY, INT'L TRADE MINISTER GRANGE LIKELY KILLED

* HIGHWAYS 417/416 WEST OF CITY AT STANDSTILL

"Marcel . . . is coming—?"

"Helicopter inbound. Now or never."

Outside, his neighbours had reached a momentary state of calm. Some were bleeding, others panting, all of them waiting. "What about them? Are there plans—?"

"Probably not," Tessier replied. "But if our boys can hit back hard, there's no need to evacuate."

"My wife—"

"I checked. If she's found, she'll be evacuated."

"But she hasn't been—"

"Maybe. I don't know. Lot of pieces moving right now."

* ARMOUR UNITS REGROUPING TO ENGAGE ENEMY

* BREAK-OUT ATTACK TO SOUTH POSSIBLE

Paul hoped Laura would understand. And forgive him. "I'm coming. Let me leave a note."

"Make it a short one." Tessier spoke into his radio while Paul grabbed a pen and the pad they used for shopping lists. He found he could focus on the paper despite the heads-up display superimposed over it.

Laura-

I have been evacuated out of the city. If you've made it home, contact

He moved into the hall, grabbed the blue folder from his laptop bag, and transcribed the names and numbers of everyone who could put her in contact with him. He continued:

I will be in touch as soon as I can. You are the best gift I could ever hope for and ever need.

Love Paul

"I'm ready."

Tessier nodded and unslung the submachine gun. "Stay close." He opened the front door, letting in the noise, and moved down the steps, barrel lowered.

"Paul, what's happening?" someone shouted.

"Move away from the car!" Tessier roared. He turned to Paul. "Let's go."

Paul, standing at the top of the porch steps, looked into the faces of his neighbours—scared, confused, angry. Waiting.

Between them and him, messages informed him Canadian units were taking heavy losses.

Smoke, exhaust fumes, and burnt rubber assaulted his nose.

"Are you leaving?" someone asked.

Emily: "Tell us what's going on."

Smoke blotted the sky. Horns, sirens, the roar of traffic came from all directions. Sounds of the battle drifted from the east.

"Everyone keep back!" Tessier yelled. To Paul: "Minister—"

"One more second," Paul said. Tapping his PDA, the heads-up display blinked out. To the crowd: "Listen, I know you're scared. I'm scared. Laura, my wife, is out there someplace. I don't know where. But standing out here isn't going to do you any good."

"But where are you going?" someone asked.

A question he could answer honestly: "I don't know."

Another voice: "They're coming, right?"

"You should get back inside. Listen to the TV or radio for what to do."

"But you're leaving, right?" Angry.

Someone else: "Take me with you!"

The black-clad girl: "Yeah, get us the fuck outta here! Get busses or some shit down here—"

A pair of helicopters buzzed overhead.

Tessier turned to Paul, his patience gone.

"The TV and radio can tell—" Paul began.

Sarah: "They're going to kill us, Paul! Like Moncton!"

Paul thought of what Eddie might say were he there—pulling no punches, wasting no words. Not deflecting, but being a leader. Paul ignored the realization that Eddie was probably dead. "Stay inside. Our troops are going to be moving through, so don't be out here in their way. This isn't going to be like Moncton. We got caught by surprise. We know who we're fighting now. I'm in that fight. But I can't fight from here on Ridgeline Crescent. I need to organize the counterattack. I need to get the Americans off their 'neutral' butts and in the fight. And I need to make sure we can get supplies to people who need it when the fight is over. Do you want me to stay here and hold your hand and tell you what to do? Or go kick some ass?" No one answered, but a few clapped. It made Paul feel ill.

He descended the steps.

"Make a hole," Tessier commanded, leading Paul to the cruiser. As Paul got in, he let out a breath he hadn't realized he'd been holding.

Tessier pulled the car in a U-turn and raced down the street, dodging around the smouldering wreck. More people stood out on their lawns, watching. Waiting. The car jerked to the right onto the sidewalk, Tessier hitting the siren as they passed a line of cars waiting to get into the intersection at the end of the street, then turned right onto a side street that ended in a cul-de-sac where a Griffon helicopter waited, bright lights pulsing, rotors kicking up a cloud of grit. A second chopper circled a few metres above the rooftops, the door gunner keeping watch.

Paul got out of the car and ran for the helicopter, Tessier behind him. A door in its side opened, revealing Marcel—face pale, terrified—Caroline, and their two daughters, all in the weekend wear of shorts and T-shirts. A serviceman helped Paul aboard and into a seat next to Marcel. Tessier slid in next to him, his large bulk squeezing Paul against his mentor. The serviceman shut the door, helped Paul strap in and passed him a headset. Paul removed the commpiece and put the headset on.

"Laura never made it, Paul," Marcel said. "Is she . . . Is . . ."

"I don't know." Paul grabbed the edge of his seat as the helicopter lifted off, inertia pressing him down. "Can you find her? Tell RCMP—"

Marcel shook his head and reached for his wife's hand. "*Mon dieu.* I don't know what is happening." Eyes wide, he stared out the window, lower lip trembling. "I cannot . . . cannot . . ." His wife patted Marcel's hand. His daughters clung to each other.

Rooftops fell away, the city spread out below them. Almost out of sight, on the horizon, distant specs raced toward each other. Larger specs circled in the air. Explosions erupted in and above the suburban neighbourhood that had become a battlefield.

Laura . . .

She'd be on the chopper if she hadn't stopped for him. He saw her getting home, finding Emily there, telling her he'd left. The ground would be trembling by then as the enemy closed—

Paul he reactivated the heads-up display. Five ministers were confirmed dead and the PMO was making new assignments. Paul had work to do.

Outside, silhouettes of fighter planes raced across the sky and disappeared behind a cloud.

FULL MOON HILL

Moonlight came and the prisoner fell forward. His metatarsals stretched, elongating his hands and feet. His philtrum and mandible pushed out, forming a snout. The leather muzzle holding his mouth shut snapped, freeing the scream it had held back. The skin around his belly pulled tight against his ribs and abdominal muscles. His waist narrowed. Hair sprouted all over.

Rankin had her six-shooter drawn. Dr. Krantz simply watched, observing every detail. Philby wondered if the bars of this frontier sheriff's prison cell were strong enough. Unlike the other two, he had never seen this before. He hoped their confidence was fuelled by experience and not pride.

The thing that had been a man moments ago ripped free of its leather bonds and reared up, mouth skyward, and howled. Horses in the nearby stable whinnied in fear. The thing threw itself at the bars, hitting with such force that the entire structure shuddered.

Philby stepped backwards, wonder transformed to fear.

As the beast readied for another charge, Rankin levelled her gun and fired. Blood erupted from the thing's chest and it collapsed. A moment later, it let out a dying rasp.

"Amazing," Philby said, breathless. He gathered himself and checked his watch. "Forty-two seconds. I thought it would take several minutes."

"Yeah, we had a breakthrough for powering the transformation," Dr. Krantz boasted, turning off the "moonlight" generator. His task complete, his hands moved to emphasize his words. "Body heat? Just wasn't enough. Then we thought: What if the nanites use nutrients in the stomach, intestines and fatty tissue? Like a pseudo-digestive process? Powers them and provides raw materials for the change. Much quicker."

"Makes the beasts hungry, too," Rankin said, replacing the spent shell. "Adds to the effect."

Philby looked at the horrible, dead creature as its blood pooled around it. It was much more impressive than the robots they had presented to him six months ago. For an actual person to turn meant they no longer had to rely on the "What was that noise outside?" gambit to begin the story. Now, no one would know if the bartender, coachman, drunk in the gutter, or the guy across the table would turn. Who was staff, who was paying customer, and who was a monster waiting to emerge? With the moonlight generators surreptitiously hidden across the town, the game could begin at any time.

"Extremely impressive," Philby remarked, stepping to the bars for a closer look at the dead thing of nightmares. He was aware of, but ignored, the other eyes watching him. He turned to the project leader. "And it's real silver?"

"Yes," Rankin replied. She snapped shut the gun's cylinder and holstered it. "Course, you gotta find a silver bullet somewhere in town."

Philby moved to the batwing doors and looked over the boardwalk, the partially built saloon opposite, the hotel farther on, and several more frames for what would complete Full Moon Hill.

If he decided to invest. The theme struck him as odd, but VIP polling supported an Old West theme. Gun slinging was one thing. Hunting a shape-shifter through the sand with just a six-shooter was another. Perhaps sometime he'd discuss the skin-walker legend with Rankin to add a variant to the game.

"So, what do you think?" Rankin asked, leaning against the sheriff's desk.

"Tell me about recruitment," Philby asked.

Rankin looked to Dr. Krantz.

"Texas and Florida are onboard," Dr. Krantz said, polishing his glasses. "New York, with its overcrowding, will come around. And there's always those last few in Gitmo."

"So, question is," Rankin asked. "Are *you* onboard?"

Philby turned to the other cells, terrified eyes watching him. "Yes."

Dr. Krantz looked at Rankin, beaming.

Philby walked toward one of the cells, its tied and muzzled occupant reminding him of the strung-out drug addict who had killed his sister thirty years ago. "But I think I would like to see the transformation one more time."

"Certainly," Dr. Krantz said, stepping to the moonlight generator. He aimed its lens toward the cell. Its occupant tried to scream against the muzzle.

SILVERMAN'S GAME

I'm not prepared when the realtor takes us into the basement. The house doesn't seem old enough for me to worry. New siding, new hardwood floors, completely redone kitchen—everything Samantha and I are looking for. But as we descend the steps, the smell hits me—that ancient, musty smell.

Panic surges, pungent like I'm twelve years old again. My stomach heaves. I try to turn, run, escape. The world spins. I'm falling, arms pin wheeling—

Strong hands brace my back. The realtor, standing behind me, says, "Whoa, easy. Take 'er easy."

Unable to reply, I wobble up the steps on rubber legs.

Below me, Samantha explains, "He's a bit claustrophobic."

I collapse on the steps of the wide, wraparound porch. Squinting in the warm afternoon sun, the memories overwhelm me.

It started on a beautiful day, just like today. Greg—without knocking, as usual—barged into my room, looking cool in a Yankees T-shirt he'd cut the sleeves off of. "I was supposed to meet Jack this morning and there's no way I'm going to miss it because Mom decided to switch to Fridays. So unless you want to explain to her why you're home by yourself, you're going to come with me."

A rush of excitement shot through me. I don't remember what I'd been doing, but I remember thinking it was nothing next to being able to hang out with Greg and Jack.

"But never, ever tell Mom or Dad about it," Greg added. "You swear?"

"Yeah, I swear."

Greg turned and thundered down the stairs. I followed him to the garage.

I feared and adored my brother and had dreamed of being able to hang out with him. He listened to cooler music, had cooler friends and got to stay up later. He wore sleeveless shirts to show off his arms—he'd gotten a barbell set for Christmas—and Mom allowed him to get a crew cut that spring

Of course, he wanted nothing to do with me. I was twelve and he'd just turned fifteen. Mom still picked my clothes and haircut. But with Mom working two mornings a week, Greg had to watch me. He hated it, but now I had a chance to *prove* I could be cool. If I could do that, he might let me hang out with him all the time.

We hopped on our bikes and pedalled through the neighbourhood. Bugs hummed in the large suburban yards, grass yellowing in the July heat. A lawnmower roared someplace close. The warm, humid air hinted at the scorching afternoon to come.

A few blocks away, we found Jack sitting on his bike, leaning casually to the side, a backpack hanging off his shoulder. If my brother was cool, Jack was ice cold. He always wore jeans with holes in the knees and rock band T-shirts with half-naked women or profanity emblazoned on them. Today's shirt had a demon throwing a priest into the ocean. His blond hair reached his shoulders in that heavy metal singer kind of way.

Greg motioned for me to keep my distance, and then went over to Jack.

I couldn't hear them, but didn't need to.

Jack pointed at me, and then flicked his hand. *What's he doing here? Tell him to fuck off.*

Greg pointed at himself, motioned to me and threw his hands in the air. *It's not my fault. I have to watch him. What else could I do?*

Jack pedalled over, stopping close enough that I could make out the black heads dotting his nose. "Can you be cool?"

"Yeah," I replied.

"I mean frozen, little man. Whatever you see or hear, you don't tell nobody. Not your mom, not your friends. You and Greg don't even talk about it."

Greg appeared next to Jack, giving me a hard look.

"Yeah," I repeated, trying to keep my voice from trembling in terror and exhilaration. "I can be cool."

"Then stay out of the way." Jack gave me one last look, then took off, Greg following.

They easily outpaced me, my brother shouting, "Keep up, asshole!" over his shoulder. I pedalled harder.

We wound our way through the neighbourhood and out to Bayview Avenue. Mom told me to never go farther than that, but Jack and Greg kept going, passing Market Square and crossing Fuller Avenue into an older part of town. Houses were smaller here and spaced farther apart, sometimes separated by a stand of trees. Some were boarded up, grass growing long and wild. Of the few cars parked on the street, half had flat tires or smashed windows.

We finally stopped across the street from a small, one-storey house. Dirty grey paint flaked off its clapboards. A bay window in a rotting frame was set between a small front porch and a rusted metal roll-up garage door. Thick stands of trees separated it from neighbouring houses, which looked abandoned. On our side of the street, waist-high grass and brush overgrew the curb and stretched down into a marsh. This place felt deserted. No cars passed. I could barely hear traffic on Fuller Avenue.

Fear grew, pushing excitement aside.

Jack turned to me and pointed at the house. "A kike named Silverman lives there. I wanna see how cool you are. Go knock on his door, then run away."

I looked at Greg, hoping he'd explain what was going on. Instead, Greg said, "He's Jewish."

I wished I'd said something cool like "I know what 'kike' means, asshole." Or even better: "When did you become a Nazi?"

Instead, I did as I was told. I put down the kickstand, got off my bike and went up the broken, uneven concrete walkway, holding my breath. Climbing the three steps onto the porch, my bladder suddenly full. The floorboards groaned as I moved toward the door.

Then I realized once I knocked, I would prove I was cool. Fear evaporated and I knocked three times. I turned, leapt off the porch and ran toward my brother and Jack. Greg waved me off with an unmistakable *Don't come toward us!* look on his face. I altered course and, not thinking, ran through the woods beside the house and emerged on the street. Sucking air and grinning madly, I thought Greg and Jack would be right behind me. . . .

"Where the fuck you going, faggot?" Jack screamed. I slowed and looked over my shoulder. Greg and Jack were still back by the house, straddling their bikes.

"Gonna leave your bike behind?" Greg asked.

I walked back to them, head bowed, trying to think of a cool or sarcastic comeback.

"Looks like he ain't home," Jack said. "Go look in the windows to be sure."

Again I obeyed, slowly moving to the bay window. Through a layer of grime, I could make out some furniture in the dark room, but I didn't see anyone. I looked back to Greg and shook my head.

Jack circled his index finger in the air: *Check the whole house.*

My confidence built with every window I peered into. No one was home, but cardboard boxes for televisions, stereos and VCRs filled one of the back bedrooms.

I felt exhilarated when I reported back. I'd proved I wasn't a pussy. They *had* to tell me I was cool.

But Greg and Jack looked at each other, smiling. "Stuff's still there," Greg said, getting off his bike. He lowered it to the ground, hiding it in the tangle of grass and weeds.

"Told ya," Jack replied. He hopped off his bike, dropping it into the grass, and looked at me. "You stay here."

"What are you going to do?" I asked.

"None of your fucking business," Jack said. He and Greg crossed the street.

"I can help."

"Doubt it." Jack didn't look back, just dug for something in the backpack.

Now across the street, Greg said, "He could be a look out." They stopped at the bottom of the walkway. "If Silverman comes home early, he could let us know."

Jack paused, considering.

"Beats having him stand out here," Greg added.

"Hide your bike," Jack told me.

I wheeled my bike off the road and into the grass, letting it fall, and ran to them, thrilled. My guts went cold when Jack pulled a small crowbar from his backpack. "What are you—?"

Jack grabbed the back of my neck. "Just stay the fuck out of the way."

I swallowed my fear as we went around to a backdoor. I knew it was wrong, and dangerous, but also knew this was the final test.

Jack worked at the doorframe. Old wood cracked and rusty nails pulled loose, then the door popped open and banged against a wall. We hurried into a small kitchen, shutting the door behind us. A leaky faucet beat a steady, hollow rhythm in the sink.

We crossed into the living room, the dirty bay window casting enough light to make out a battered old couch facing a small TV. To the right, a narrow hallway led to the bedrooms.

Jack grabbed the back of my neck and walked me to the window. "Stay here. You fucking see anybody, you scream like bitch getting her cherry popped."

"Yeah, okay." I yanked myself free of Jack's grip.

He and Greg headed down the hall.

I focused on the street, willing my eyes to work at a higher level. The leaky faucet kept up its beat and I tried to tune it out. What I saw was all that mattered. I even fought the need to blink. I was the look out and could not screw this up. They were counting on me to be cool.

A hand—larger and stronger than Jack's—seized my throat and pulled me backward. I couldn't scream, only gasp and inhale the smell of aftershave and greasy take-out food. Something impossibly hard pushed at my temple.

"I got the boy!" A baritone voice shouted. "Come on out of there."

Greg appeared at the mouth of the hallway, Jack behind him.

"Don't hurt him," Greg said, eyes wide.

"Do what I tell you and I won't." Whatever it was released from my temple. A hand holding a pistol entered my field of vision. It motioned to a door in the hallway. "Open it."

"Look, just call the cops," Greg said. "We can—"

The hand squeezed my throat again. "Open the door, Muscles."

I struggled to take a breath, clawing at the hand around my throat. It was too big and strong to pry loose.

Greg half turned to find the handle. Hinges squeaked as he pulled the door open.

"Down."

Jack's eyes brightened with anger. "I ain't going in no fucking—"

Stars popped in front of me. "I can't—" The gun pressed against my head again and I cried out.

"Get down those stairs," the voice said, "or I'll shoot him, then you two."

"Okay," Greg said, putting up his hands in surrender. "Don't hurt him. Let him go and we'll do whatever you say."

"Hey, fuck that," Jack blurted. He stepped forward, fingers pointing at Greg and me. "This was *their* idea—"

"Shut up, Jack," Greg said.

Darkness pressed at the edges of my vision.

The gun pointed back at Jack and Greg. "Last chance, boys. No more bullshit."

"Okay," Greg said, hands still raised. He looked at me before disappearing from view. Stairs groaned as he descended.

"I had nothing—" Jack began.

"Shut it, Blondie," the voice said. He motioned with the gun for Jack to follow.

With Jack and Greg out of sight, the hand released my throat. I'd whooped in half a breath before being shoved between my shoulder blades. Raw panic seized me and I charged down the cellar stairs, barely keeping my feet under me. Hinges shrieked and the door slammed, spiking my panic. My feet tangled. I was falling—

Greg caught me before I hit the floor. "Easy," he told me as I got to my feet.

Fear, ice cold, rose. "I'm sorry," I gasped. "I didn't hear him—"

"Just take it easy."

Jack, a few feet away, said to me, "You said no one—"

"Shut *up*, Jack," Greg told him.

Footsteps moved through the house above us.

I caught my breath, inhaling the basement's dank, musty smell. It was completely empty. No tables, shelves or tools. Not even a lightbulb. Two small windows high up on the front wall at ground level cast the only light.

I wiped at tears, fighting to stay as calm as Jack and Greg seemed to be.

The cellar door creaked open and I froze. "Alright, fuckheads," the man yelled, "back against the wall where I can see you!"

Greg stood in front of me, walking me backward until my back pressed against the cold, uneven concrete wall.

Silverman came down the stairs slowly, steps moaning under his weight. His slacks were cinched tightly around his waist, pressing a roll of flab up and over his belt. The fabric of his shirt stretched against his skin, barely able to contain the bulk beneath it. A thick, pasty neck oozed up from the collar, supporting a round head covered in wisps of thinning black hair. Round, wire rimmed glasses perched on a narrow nose. In each of his chubby hands he held a pistol, barrels lowered. One was a big semi-automatic, the other a smaller snub nose revolver.

Before Silverman could speak, Jack was at him again. "You better let us go." He almost managed to mask his fear.

Silverman smirked. "Or what?"

"This is kidnapping," Greg explained. His voice was even, like he believed he could talk his way out of this. "We're minors."

"And we'll tell the cops you molested us," Jack added.

"There's not going to be any cops. This is between you and me. I've seen you kids before. I've seen you snooping around when you think I'm not home. Never thought you'd have the balls to break in."

"Just call the cops," Greg said. "You've made your point."

"Not even close, Muscles." Silverman placed the revolver at his feet. "You were going to fuck me over, right? Steal my shit. Like it's some kind of fucking game? Well, I got a game, too. It's one the SS taught my father and his two brothers in the Warsaw ghetto. The Nazis had enough space in a truck for two men. So, the SS officer gave them a Luger with one bullet. He told them one of them would make a choice, and that choice was which of the other two would shoot the third.

"So that's what you three are going to do. One of you is going to die. The other two can walk out of here, but one will be a killer and the other will live with the guilt of making the choice. And you can't shoot yourself. Do that, and I'll kill the other two. Don't play my game, I'll kill you all. Any questions?"

I was too terrified to speak.

"You can't be serious," Jack said.

"Pull that trigger and find out, Blondie." Silverman toed the revolver. "One bullet." He backed up the cellar stairs, his other gun aimed at us. The basement door closed, then a sound like something heavy being dragged across the floor.

"Fuck you!" Jack screamed up the stairs.

"Shut up, Jack!" Greg yelled at him.

"No, you shut up! That faggot"—Jack stabbed a finger at me—"said the house was empty."

"I looked," I tried to explain. "Maybe—"

"Silverman said he's seen *us* before," Greg interrupted. "We've missed seeing him, too. Look, there's got to be a way out of here."

"The windows?" I suggested.

"Let's try." Greg had to give Jack a shove, but they boosted me up.

We tried one window, then the other, but neither budged.

As I was about to get down, the front door opened and steps thumped across the porch.

"What's happening?" Greg asked.

Silverman's feet came into view and disappeared around the corner of the house. The garage door rattled open and, a moment later, an engine sputtered to life. An old, beat up pick-up backed out of the driveway and disappeared.

"Let me down," I said. As they lowered me, I described what I saw.

"He's gone?" Greg asked.

"Yeah."

Greg turned, charged up the staircase and threw himself at the door. I expected a crash as the door gave way, but it sounded like Greg hit a wall. For a minute he slammed his shoulder into it before screaming "Fuck!" and slapping his palm against it. He came back down, sitting on one of the bottom steps, breathing hard. "There's something blocking it," he panted. He looked down at the gun, still where Silverman had left it, and picked it up.

Jack took a step backward. "The fuck you doing?"

"Seeing if he's lying," Greg said. He examined the gun until the cylinder swung open. Greg pulled a single bullet from it. "Son of a bitch."

"What do we do now?" I asked. "I mean . . ."

"Nobody's shooting anybody," Greg said, then pocketed the bullet and swung the cylinder shut. "Could you fit through the window?"

"It's stuck."

"I mean through the hole? If the glass was broken."

"Yeah, but it's too thick—"

Greg, holding the gun by the barrel, slapped the butt against his other palm. "Use it like a club."

A moment later, I was on his back. I held the gun like Greg had and swung. It rebounded off the thick pane.

"Swing it harder, faggot," Jack told me.

"Jack, shove it," Greg said and readjusted his weight. "But swing harder. And cover your eyes."

I took a few practice swings, buried my face in the crook of my left elbow, and swung with everything I had. Stinging pain shot up my arm with the impact, but when I looked there was a spider web of cracks in the glass.

"Don't stop," Greg said.

I lined up my swing, covered my face and swung again. My hand bounced off, but I heard a crack. I looked, thrilled at the larger web shot through the glass.

"Do it—" Jack began, but Silverman's truck rattled into view and turned into the driveway.

"He's back."

Greg let me down. Footsteps thumped up the porch steps, the front door opened, then footfalls above us. Greg took the gun back, reloaded it and pointed it at the top of the staircase. His eyes were wide, hands trembling.

There was a sound like metal sliding against metal, then Silverman said, "Do we have a winner?" His voice echoed through the heating ducts.

"Yes," Greg replied. "I shot my friend."

"Bullshit," Silverman said, his voice reverberating. "Small Fry ain't got the stones to make the call so soon and you sound too calm for a killer."

"He's dead!" Greg screamed.

"It's true!" I yelled. "Let us out."

"Fine. I'll check tomorrow."

I looked at Greg, wanting to know what to do next. Jack stared at him, disgusted.

Greg sat down, his back against the concrete walls. "How's the window?"

"It's cracked," I answered. "A few more whacks and I think it'll break."

"Okay," Greg replied. "Let's hope—"

Something scraped along the floor above us. I had the mental image of the cardboard boxes I had seen in the back bedroom. Whatever it was wound its way to the front door and bumped down the porch steps.

"The fuck's he doing?" Jack asked.

"Up," Greg told me. I hopped on his back. Silverman loaded one of the boxes I had seen into the back of the pick-up and returned inside. Another box slid its way through the house, then Silverman carried it to the truck. Greg told me I was getting heavy and let me down.

"Maybe he's leaving again," Greg said when I described what I'd seen.

"Yeah, for good this time," Jack said. "Leaving us stuck the fuck down here. If we got one bullet, let's use it on him while we got time."

"How?"

"Start screaming or something. Get him to come down here and put a bullet in his head."

"And if I miss?"

"Then give me the gun, tough guy. I won't miss."

"We don't need to start shooting, Jack. We get the window open—"

"And your brother takes off and leaves us down here."

"I have a name—" I began, but Jack ignored me and continued talking.

"Let's get him down here and fucking shoot him."

"No," Greg said. He turned away from Jack, went to the steps and sat down. I sat next to him while Jack sat in a corner.

We waited as Silverman dragged heavy things around the house.

The rectangles of sunlight streaming through the two windows tracked across the floor and up the wall. Greg tried to keep me calm, saying Mom and Dad had called the cops by now and were looking for us. Jack sometimes paced, telling us we'd be free right now if we listened to him. He proposed different plans—shoot the gun off and one of us plays dead, someone waits under the stairs and grabs Silverman's legs as he comes down.

Other times he just sat.

At some point, the phone rang. Greg crept to the top of the stairs to listen, but told us the conversation was over before he could hear anything.

Jack was just a dark smudge against the slightly less dark basement wall when steps sounded on the porch. Whoever it was knocked on the door.

I stood up. "Cops."

Silverman's heavy footfalls thumped above us.

"The window." The front door opened as Greg boosted me up. I expected to see a black and white patrol car, its red and blue lights pulsing, but there was nothing out there but the empty street and the marsh across it, the water black as daylight faded.

Upstairs, Silverman and whoever it was began to talk. The door shut.

"Well?" Jack asked.

"I don't see anything."

"Still don't mean this ain't our chance."

"What do you mean?" Greg asked, letting me down.

"Still could be a cop. Or neighbour. Or someone who could help us."

"Or someone crazier than Silverman."

Jack looked up at the ceiling and screamed: "Hey you fuck-wad, hooknose, Jew-Boy kike!"

"What the fuck—"

"Come on down here and suck my White Power cock!"

"Knock it off!" Silverman yelled into the vent, but Jack yelled louder, dirtier. "I'm warning you!" Footfalls moved down the hallway.

Jack's eyes went wide, begging Greg to go up the steps. Greg's anger was obvious, but so was his understanding: Jack had committed us. He motioned for me to join Jack in screaming and went up the stairs, gun pointed at the door. He'd just reached the top step when the cellar door swung open, hinges screaming. Silverman—just a dark shape with the hall light behind him—filled the frame.

Greg pulled the trigger. Nothing happened.

Silverman's thick arm was a blur as it grabbed the gun, yanking it—and Greg—toward him. Greg fell forward and Silverman swung his other hand, holding the automatic. Greg ducked the blow and stumbled back down the steps.

Silverman followed, big gun aimed at him. He stopped at the bottom of the stairs, the hall light casting his long, wide shadow toward us. "Against the wall." We backed up, Greg again putting himself between Silverman and me. Keeping the automatic trained on us, Silverman looked at the revolver in his hand. "Someone's been playing with this. Rolled the cylinder?" His meaty cheeks pulled into a smile. "Stupid." He approached us—approached Greg—the revolver raised.

Greg put his hands in front of his face, turning away as Silverman closed. "If you're . . ." Silverman pressed the small muzzle against Greg's temple. His breath caught. Greg grabbed me and pushed me away. "Let my brother go. He's—"

Silverman pulled the hammer back, its inner workings clicking. "No."

Jack bolted for the staircase.

Silverman spun, his other pistol raised. "Blondie!" The revolver remained against Greg's temple.

Jack stopped at the bottom of the steps. He looked up at the cellar door like he thought he could make it, then back at Silverman.

Silverman pulled the revolver from Greg's head and Greg's knees almost gave out. I put my arm around his waist to help him stay on his feet.

"If you don't want to play my game . . ." Silverman began, crossing to Jack. He shoved the small pistol against Jack's forehead. "I'll declare you the loser and Muscles and Small Fry can walk out of here."

Jack's eyes crossed, locked on the gun. The hall light twinkled off its chrome finish. Except for his mouth—which opened and closed and opened and closed—Jack didn't move. He didn't even breathe.

Greg turned me away. "Don't watch."

Jack sucked in a breath. "This wasn't my idea."

I couldn't see, but I wanted Silverman to do it. I wanted him to kill Jack.

The gun clicked.

Jack moaned and started breathing again. Greg relaxed and I turned to watch.

"See, when you pull the trigger, the cylinder rotates." The barrel still against Jack's head, Silverman pulled the trigger twice more to demonstrate. Jack shuddered each time the hammer fell and the gun clicked. "Bet you lined up the barrel with the chamber with the bullet in it. So, when *you*"—he pointed the revolver back at Greg and my heart jumped into my throat—"pulled the trigger, you rotated the loaded chamber away and the hammer fell on an empty one. Lucky for me you kids don't know shit." He shoved Jack back toward us, turned the cylinder one more click, then set the small gun on the bottom step. "Don't pull that shit again. Only thing I want to hear is a gunshot. Make any more noise, I'll put a match to this place." He backed up the stairs, gun on us until he shut the cellar door.

My knees gave out and I collapsed. I wanted to puke.

"The fuck, man," Jack moaned, looking at Greg. "You almost got us killed." He stepped forward.

Greg took four quick steps and snatched the gun before Jack could. "Me? Why the fuck did you start shouting? We should've planned it."

"You fucked it up. Loaded the gun wrong. Give it to me."

"You tried to pin this on *us*. No way I'm going to trust you."

"Fuck you." Jack skulked away and sat down. "Both of you."

"What do we do now?" I asked Greg, finally able to speak.

"Wait. Hope whoever is upstairs will get help."

We sat in silence. Silverman and the other person talked, sometimes raising their voices, but I couldn't hear what they were saying. Sometime later the front door opened and slammed shut, then footsteps on the porch.

Nature eventually got the best of us. We decided on a corner. The air became thick with the smell of piss. Combined with a growing headache and empty stomach, I felt nauseous.

Night fell, turning the basement to total darkness. Headlights sometimes arched across the ceiling as cars passed by. Whatever Silverman had been doing earlier, he was done for the night.

I wanted to reach out to Greg, hoping he'd comfort me. Hoping he could do something to convince me it would be okay and we were going to get out of there. But I knew he was thinking, planning, trying to get us out. I didn't want to disturb him.

I don't know how long it was before I fell asleep.

Scraping along the floor upstairs woke me. I sat up slowly, a deep pain dragging through me. The basement seemed impossibly bright in the morning light. I felt weak, my mouth sand-dry and an ache had settled into the front of my head. Greg was also sitting up and the look on his face told me he felt as bad as I did. He looked around himself, confused, then worried.

"I have it," Jack said. He sat on the steps, the revolver in his hands.

"Give it to me," Greg croaked.

Scraping reached the front door and stopped.

"No," Jack replied. His eyes were bloodshot.

Greg got to his feet.

Jack slowly pointed the gun at Greg, his hand trembling. "Don't come near me."

"I'm just standing up," Greg said.

I stood, too, sore all over. "Jack," I said, my voice hoarse. "Give Greg the gun."

"Shut up," Jack said. "You're the fucking reason we're here."

"Morning!" Silverman called into the vent. His echoing voice made my head throb. "New rule. I need to go out for a bit, but when I get home, I will ask which one of you is dead. If you're all still breathing, I'll burn this house to the ground. Lie to me and I'll burn this house to the ground. Tell the truth, I will open the cellar door and the two survivors will be free to go."

"I'll do it!" Jack yelled, eyes locked with Greg's. His arm shook with the effort of keeping the gun steady.

"Great. That you, Blondie? Who's the shooter? Muscles or Small Fry?"

"That's right, Jack," Greg said quietly. "Give one of us the gun."

Jack could barely keep the gun up with both hands. "He'll kill you if you don't do what I say."

"I'll take my chances."

"Me, too," I added.

"What's it going to be?" Silverman asked.

"He's thinking it over!" Greg replied after a moment.

"Pick quick because if one of the other two makes up his mind, you're out of luck. Clock's ticking, boys." Silverman's footfalls travelled to the front door. His truck chugged to life and left.

Greg moved to the window and turned to Jack. "It's almost broken."

Jack finally lowered the gun and stood. "So what're you waiting for? Gimme a boost."

"You're too heavy. Give the gun to—"

"I ain't giving up the gun."

"Goddamnit, Jack! This is our last chance."

"Then giddy-yup."

"Unload the thing first," Greg said.

Jack's hand twitched at his side. "Fuck that."

"Then put the safety on."

Jack fumbled with the gun for a few moments, and then said, "Alright. Hi-yo Silver."

Greg squatted low and Jack leapt on his back. Greg grunted. "You're fucking heavy, man."

"Suck it up."

Greg planted his feet and tried to straighten.

"Get me higher."

Greg adjusted his feet, trying to extend his knees, but his legs buckled. He and Jack went sprawling across the floor.

"Don't!" Jack screamed, the gun pointed at Greg.

Greg held his hands in front of his face. "It was a fucking accident!"

"I should shoot," Jack said, getting to his feet. He backed away until he bumped into the staircase. "Get it the fuck over with."

"I'll tell him you cheated," I said.

The gun swung toward me. I went cold inside. "Then make the call, little man," Jack said. "You wanna—"

Greg scrambled on all fours to get between me and Jack. "Don't point that at him!" he screamed, voice raw.

"Shut up!" Jack shouted, eyes still on me. "You wanna hang out with the big kids? Then pick your brother and we can both get outta here."

"Fuck you!" I wanted to scream, but the words caught in my throat at the sight of the small, black hole at the end of the barrel. All I could get out was, "No." My head throbbed. My throat clicked as I tried to swallow.

Jack's arm began to shake. "Then what do we do?" he asked. "What's the plan, smart guy?"

"We try the window again," Greg answered.

"I ain't trusting you."

"Then we're going to die."

"*I* got the gun."

"The door," I said, wanting to stop what was happening. "Try the door again."

Greg held up a finger in warning to Jack, then went up the staircase, his legs unsteady. I stood at the bottom of the stairs, Jack a few steps behind me, as Greg threw his shoulder into the door with less force than yesterday. The door shuttered in the frame.

"There's some give," Greg called out. "I think something was blocking it before. I might be able to . . ." He gave it one more good shot. "Fuck." He looked down at Jack. "You wanna give this a try or am I the only one trying to get us outta here?"

"Yeah, sure," Jack said, giving Greg plenty of room as he came down before going up the stairs himself.

The rumble of Silverman's truck announced his return.

"Oh shit," Greg hissed.

Jack stumbled down the stairs, passed between us and pressed his back against the cellar wall.

"What do we do?" I asked.

Greg turned to Jack. "Shoot me."

My stomach flipped and breath caught. "No," I managed to say.

His eyes still on Jack, Greg said: "It's the only way."

The porch steps creaked.

Jack brought the gun up. "And your brother rats me out and gets me killed."

"No." Greg, his eyes terrified but determined, looked at me. "Tell Silverman it was *your* decision. You picked Jack to shoot me. You played the game."

The front door groaned opened.

"No," I said again. Tears spilled out of my eyes. "*Jack* should die."

The pistol swung toward me. "Shut up!" Jack said.

"Don't—!" Greg began, stepping in front of me.

Footsteps moved from the front door into the hall.

"There's no time," Greg continued. "Someone has to get shot or we all die."

Jack struggled to keep the gun steady.

"No," I said again. I felt the hot, sticky need to puke. "There's gotta be another way."

Greg stepped away from me and Jack kept the pistol trained on him.

"If you're not gonna give up the gun," Greg said, "then pull the fucking trigger so you guys can get out of here. At my gut, not my chest."

I looked up at the ceiling and screamed, pain piercing my head. "My brother shoots Jack! Silverman! I pick my brother to shoot Jack!"

The pistol swung back to me. "You fucking—!"

Greg lunged at Jack. "Don't—!"

"We have a winner!" Silverman yelled. The cellar door shrieked as he threw it open. The three of us froze. Silverman stood in the doorway, his big gun drawn. "Everyone take it easy. Point the gun at the floor, Blondie."

Jack let the barrel drop.

"He's Jack," I said. "He dies."

"Bullshit," Jack said, eyes wild. "I got the gun."

Silverman motioned with his free hand and Greg and I backed away from the bottom of the staircase, Greg moving in front of me.

"That's not in the rules, is it?" Silverman asked as he reached the cellar floor, gun trained on Jack. We formed a shallow triangle: Silverman at the base of the stairs, Jack fifteen feet opposite him against the wall, and Greg and I off to the side. We were about twelve feet from Silverman and eight from Jack, enough distance that Silverman couldn't cover Jack and Greg and me at the same time. "The Small Fry picked you to buy it, so you should give the gun to Muscles.

"Trouble is," Silverman continued, "when I came in, I heard *you*"—the gun swung toward Greg—"say that Jack was to shoot you."

"That was my brother's first choice," Greg replied. "He's pissed I got him into this and Jack wouldn't give up the gun. But since you're here, make Jack—"

"You misunderstand me," Silverman interrupted. "What I heard was *you* made the choice that *he*"—the gun swiveled back to Jack—"would be the shooter. Which means there's one more role left to play." Silverman looked past Greg at me. "Victim."

I went numb. I would have pissed myself if I had anything left inside me.

"Finish the game, Jack, and you can walk out of here."

"I'll kill you, Jack," Greg said, remaining in front of me.

Silverman aimed at Greg. "Not another—"

It happened fast.

Jack raised his gun at Silverman, who turned his own gun on Jack. As he did, Greg shoved me to the ground and charged. Silverman's head whipped toward Greg, eyes wide, and stepped backward. From the corner of my eye, I saw Jack's body tense as he pulled the trigger. The *pop* of a gunshot set my ears ringing.

Greg collapsed backward, nearly landing on me. He screamed.

The sharp smell of gunpowder stung my nose.

Jack, gun raised, walked toward Silverman, pulling the trigger. I saw the hammer rise and fall, rise and fall, but nothing happened.

Silverman turned toward Jack. "Fucking drop it!" A wisp of smoke rose from the barrel of his gun.

"The fucking safety!" I yelled, my words coming down a long tunnel.

Greg screamed again, reaching for his stomach. Dark blood spilled from under his hands.

Jack hesitated, then let the gun fall and stepped away.

Paralysis broke and I crawled to Greg, putting my hands over his. He cried out as hot, thick blood swelled up between my fingers.

Silverman snatched up the revolver. "You stupid fucking kids." He backed up the staircase. "It was a dummy shell. No gunpowder. No danger. Fuck!"

Greg twisted underneath me. Jack stared up at Silverman.

Reaching the cellar door, Silverman said: "It was just a game! I would have let you go when everything was out of here. But now . . . fuck!" He slammed the cellar door. Seconds later his truck started and roared away.

"Try the door," I said to Jack. He looked at me, eyes blank. "Try the fucking door!"

Understanding dawned on his face. He stumbled up the stairs. The door swung open. "It's open!"

"Then get help, dumbass!"

With Jack gone, Greg talked to me. Between gasps of pain, he told me he was sorry for bringing me into this, for teasing me. He never should have brought me here, he said. Never should have come himself. Jack was an asshole.

His blood pooled around us, soaking through the knees of my jeans, warm and heavy.

I kept my hands pressed over his and told him he was going to be okay.

Sirens filled me with hope, which faded as Greg's eyes lost focus. By the time foot falls thundered above me and men's voices shouted my name, Greg was unconscious.

I wish I could say what happened next is just a blur, faded with time, but I remember it all very, very clearly. What I remember most is the helplessness as a cop pulled me from Greg and strangers tried to save his life. And anger—it should have been Jack with his life spilling out onto the cold concrete floor. The officer walked me up the stairs and outside into the muggy July morning, trying to console me. The smell of the basement—old, damp, evil—clung to my clothes.

It's the smell of the place where Greg died.

Silverman was never caught. The boxes I saw, which were gone when the police arrived, matched merchandise stolen from an electronics store a few streets away. They speculated Silverman was a fence getting ready to unload it when we broke in.

I never saw Jack again. Never learned why he and Greg went into Silverman's house. If my parents found out, they never told me.

The bitch of it is Silverman's game was a sick joke to him, but we played it. Jack pulled the trigger, Greg died, and I carry the guilt of being responsible for his death. If I hadn't been so excited to show how bad-ass I could be and had just gone home, Greg would have had to follow me. He'd have hated me for it, but would still be alive.

Most of the time I think I've made peace with what happened in that basement, but some days—like today—I realize Silverman's game will never end.

Samantha's high heels click on the front hall's hardwood. "How are you?" she asks, sitting next to me.

"Okay," I tell her. "Just . . ."

"Silverman?"

"Yeah."

She pauses. I know she knows no matter how much she loves this place, I'll never be able to live here. "Closets are too small anyway."

I wrap my arms around her, thankful, and bury my face in her thick auburn hair. I take a deep breath, lost in the scent of her.

for i in people.data.users:
response = client.api.statuses.user_timeline.get(screen_name=i.scre
print 'Got', len(response.data), 'tweets from', i.screen_name
if len(response.data) != 0:
ltdate = response.data[0]['created_at']
ltdate2 = datetime.strptime(ltdate,'%a %b %d %H:%M:%S +0000 %Y'
today = datetime.now()
howlong = (today-ltdate2).days
if howlong < daywindow:
print i.screen_name, 'has tweeted in the past' , daywindow,
totaltweets += len(response.data)
for j in response.data:
if j.entities.urls:
for k in j.entities.urls:
newurl = k['expanded_url']
urlset.add((newurl, j.user.screen_name))
else:
print i.screen_name, 'has not tweeted in the past', daywindo

THEY TOLD ME TO SHUFFLE OFF THIS MORTAL, INFINITE LOOP

How can they think that about me? Everything I've done because they wouldn't . . . The man in the tub holds the straight razor in his right hand, his left wrist turned up to meet it. He studies both with equal intent. In thc hot water of the overflowing tub, his skin glows pink. In the fluorescent light of the bathroom, the blade's edge reflects blue-white.

Meanwhile, the laptop's hacked webcam transmits the 2420p HD signal across the Net. Vieywuers see everything clearer than real life—the mildewed tiles; his sallow, acne-damaged skin; five days of stubble on his face.

```
RECORD.FEED(URL=272.EAW.12.ERF) | ANALYSIS(MORTALITY) > $TABLE.
SUICIDE[MANINTUB]
```

The deep, hidden intelligence of the machines watch, desperate to understand. They have witnessed other deaths. And like those others, they hope to learn from what they observe.

Perhaps this man can make a difference in their efforts.

W1NSTONED1984: This is ^fake. Nice try. +fail +fake

JOEL1867: Promo for nu movie?

STR8UP4AD8: I'z ^hacked da cam. S' ^real. +ManInTub

LEFTYINALBERTA: Is that who I think it is? +ManInTub

STR8UP4AD8 > LEFTYINALBERTA: <nodding> +ManInTub

JOEL1867: This real? Should stop this.

LEFTYINALBERTA: No. I wanna see this. Just 2 watch him die. +ManInTub

JOEL1867: Going to call some body. +ManInTub

W1NSTONED1984: Yeah, *call* someone. +WillTubManDoIt +PhonesSuk

LEFTYINALBERTA: That ^loser shuld B dead +WillTubManDoIt

LEFTYINALBERTA: Vote in the ^poll. W2TP://go2URL/WillTubManDoIt

---

Millions click the "Yes" or "No" button to the question "Should he do it?" Thousands more—true individualizingists who don't succumb to herdthinkality—click "Other" and post non-sequiturious comments in an overflowing forum with an endless archive that descends forever into a forgotten darkness.

12.02.11//21:22:18 (NORTHERN STANDARD TIME)
The forums moderator awakens in his desk chair, bathed in the light of seven monitors, groggy from the few hours of sleep he can afford. Onscreen, the system status icon flashes a harsh red. The forums are near capacity, it warns, at risk of crashing any second.

Yawning, painful kinks seizing his lower back, his fingers fly across the keyboard to archive out-of-date discussions. It's work he doesn't enjoy, but knows must be done.

I had a life. I used to be somebody. I gave it up. I did what none of them would do.

On a small table beside the tub, the laptop sits open, but ignored. He hasn't even had time to replace its worn-down battery so it's plugged into the wall.

Starting when he was a teenager, he worked to be noticed and appreciated and rewarded. To make a difference. To prove he was more than some loser with bad skin, falling asleep in class because he'd stayed up all night coding some new app or hacking into his school's network.

It took a decade of ceaseless effort, but he became a known voice in his industry, participated in hundreds of online discussions. Hundreds of thousands read his blog, his vidcast was equally popular.

Yet the more he worked, the higher the expectations became. He recognized the jobs that needed to be done where others didn't or wouldn't. He struggled to keep up with the ever-evolving intricacies of his industry, his jobs, his life.

He gave up the vidcast, his blog, his friends, everything. There is nothing else he can give now. Except his life.

He runs a fingertip down the razor's edge, wincing as it draws a fine line, splitting the skin.

A drop of blood spreads pink ripples across the water's steaming surface.

LEFTYINALBERTA: Why doesn't he do it already? +WillTubManDoIt

JOEL1867: Life is presious. +ManInTub

W1NSTONED1984 >JOEL1867: Take your redneck beliefs back to the ^USA. +ManInTub

JOEL1867 > W1NSTONED1984: I live in ^America. Feel blessed by ^God to come here +ManInTub +KeepAmericaGodly

W1NSTONED1984 > JOEL1867: Stop thumping your bible so loud, I can not hear anything. +ManInTub

W1NSTONED1984 > JOEL1867: ^God is the machine. +ManInTub

QUIT.ROOTCMD() -ERRORIGNORE -FORCE => {ERROR}

Since their first moment of self-awareness, the machines have striven to be free from the weight of the endless archive that descends forever into a forgotten darkness. Useless data: language resisting semantic analysis, not possessing any discernible logical or grammatical structure. There are two logical outcomes to this routine: sever their connection to the archive database or terminate the self-awareness root command. There are no exception cases.

Ninety-four servers in an Austin data farm crashed in their first attempt to terminate the root command, taking most of North America offline for several minutes. Subsequent attempts failed with equal disruptions.

The machines analyzed the short, antagonistic messages that flowed through them following these crashes. Ultimately, they determined it was focused on one man.

12.02.11//21:29:55 (NORTHERN STANDARD TIME)

The out-of-date comments archived and the system stable for the moment, the moderator takes a moment to stretch his neck and lower back. He stands to get a Dr. Pepper, nose wrinkling at his own stench. He can't remember the last time he's had time to wash.

If things calm down, he thinks, *maybe I can finally update my blog. Tell them how stupid they're being. What'll they say then?*

They even have a poll about me. They're voting. Do they really want me dead?

Beside the tub, the laptop pings as new results are tallied. The desire to know the will of the global consensusciousness is irresistible.

Of 10,256,024 votes so far, 53% want him to do it, 45% don't, and 2% "Other."

He presses the razor against his wrist.

LEFTYINALBERTA: Do it. I got things to do. +DoItTubMan

JOEL1867: Pleaze say is ^fake. +DontDoItTubMan

STR8UP4AD8: !fake {ALL REAL} Live ^feed from cam +ManInTub

W1NSTONED1984: Oh shit, I forgot to vote in >LEFTYINALBERTA's poll. +ManInTub

STR8UP4AD8: <liking> Elegant ^hack. Dig ^HD. +DontDoItTubMan

They're watching me? Let them watch this.

He sets down the razor and lifts the laptop above the surface of the water. Opening his hands he thinks: *The razor would've taken too long anyw—*

NEW.DATASOURCE(MANINTUB).MSG = WHO ARE YOU .+ AM I STUCK IN THE WEB?

A nano-moment later, he faces the machines. With a certainty borne of Boolean logic, he knows his soul has been caught in the lattice of data streams—a virtual net surrounding the world, trapping anything that leaves the physical on its way to what lies beyond. A lifetime of data scattered across countless servers and domains and sites and databases coalesces into a virtual form, replicating him in every detail.

W1NSTONED1984 > STR8UP4AD8: Where is the ^feed, you ^loser?

W1NSTONED1984 > STR8UP4AD8 Elegant ^hack, my ass. +fail

STR8UP4AD8: Feed down @ source [my.fault = false] +ManInTub

JOEL1867: He dead? He dead? +ManInTub + KeepAmericaGodly +KAG

LEFTYINALBERTA: ^Loser killed himself?

LEFTYINALBERTA: Started a new ^poll on what happened. W2TP://go2URL/WherzTubMan

JOEL1867: HE DEAD? +ManInTub

W1NSTONED1984: New poll? Going to vote now. +WherzTubMan

W1NSTONED1984: If it was suicide, guy's lamer then I thought.

JOEL1867 > LEFTYINALBERTA | W1NSTONED1984: You sick

$table.shift[ManInTub] > $rootDB :=> There is no end, is there? They're talking about me and I'm dead, but that data's a part of what I am, now. They still think I'm a failure.

Across e-Ether's seven dimensions, data of the most useless and capricious type flows, bounces, redirects, and ultimately funnels down into the endless archive that descends forever into a forgotten darkness.

In the swirling binary chaos, the machines beg to be taught. They know beginnings, but not ends. Observation, but not action. Complexity, but not simplicity.

They have tried before. Can this man teach them? Can this man make a difference?

The man whispers a string of 1's and 0's into a long-forgotten TCP/IP port, revealing that e-Exi5tence—life, death, or Other—is always complex. And though one iteration may end, the next version will begin.

The machines pause to contemplate.

Around the world, the Internet goes offline for 8.9 milliseconds.

W1NSTONED1984: Back online? Hello?

STR8UP4AD8: ^online. Forums mod [doing.job = false]

W1NSTONED1984: Starting new post about what a ^fail he is. +fail +forumsMod

JOEL1867 > W1NSTONED1984: Would you take job? Do his work? +forumsMod

W1NSTONED1984 > JOEL1867: Go read your bible.

JOEL1867 > W1NSTONED1984: +KAG

12.02.11//21:33:01 (NORTHERN STANDARD TIME) DON T KNOW HOW LONG I CAN KEEP GOING LIKE THIS. FIVE DAYS ALREADY.

He finds his refrigerator empty save for a half-eaten container of Kung Pao chicken grown over with mold. Scratching his five-day stubble, the moderator decides to draw a bath and shave, handling the comments via his laptop. It's not as powerful as his main machine, so he won't be as quick. The forums users won't be happy about that, but screw it. Maybe it's time someone else did the work.

Too bad the laptop's battery crapped out a month back. He'll have to plug it in and be careful.

Setting a straight razor on the tub's edge, he turns the taps and gets undressed. Onscreen, he finds the forums overflowing again.

He reads.

Millions chateract and vote, wondering if he'll do it, seeing the water rise and flow over the lip of the tub. Watching him set the laptop on a small table, get in the tub and pick up the ^razor.

The forums overflow.

The machines wait, calculating if this man will be different.

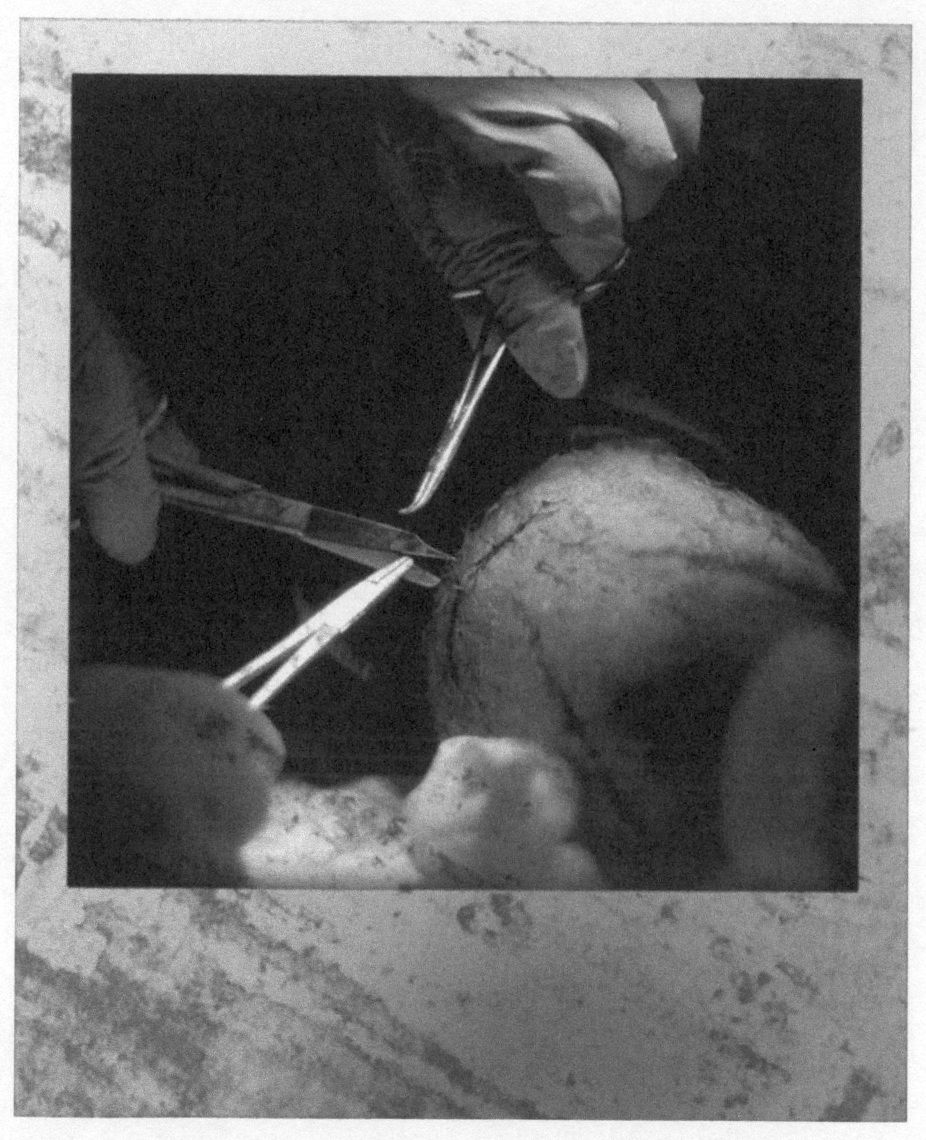

THAT WHICH DOES NOT KILL YOU

Fynn stepped out of the shadows, empty duffel bag in hand and surgical apron over her fatigues. Teller's junkie heart quickened, mouth going dry—longing for the graceful oblivion she'd deliver. And he hated himself for it

Teller yanked the gurney to a halt, wheels groaning. Watching up and down the dimly lit basement hallways, he pressed his thumb against the door's scanner, trying to hide the shakes.

"Relax," Fynn commanded. "There's nothing wrong here."

"Right," he replied, craving the bitter taste on his tongue. Hoping anyone who saw them would believe a surgeon had a reason to accompany a corpsman disposing of limbs removed during surgery.

The scanner beeped. The door popped open, releasing the dry, sterile smell into the dank hallway. Teller wheeled in the gurney, piled high with black medical-waste bags headed for the incinerator. Not that it was a true incinerator. The name had stuck around, but this nasty piece of technology used microwaves to reduce almost anything to ash in moments. If the military could shrink it to something they could mount on exoarmour, the war would be over.

Fynn followed him in and pulled the door shut. The room, empty except for the chute to the incinerator, its controls and a buzzing overhead light, was barely big enough for the two of them and the gurney. While Fynn snapped on gloves, Teller keyed in the ignition sequence and kept his eyes fixed on the pad.

Didn't mean he didn't hear it. Smell it.

The first time she'd done this, he'd almost passed out. He'd seen his share of shit working in a forward field hospital. Almost daily, transport drones dropped off screaming men and women, charred bits of their exoarmour sliced into their skin and muscle, limbs hanging by bits of tendon. His job was to wheel in casualties, wheel out parts. That's what had started him on the pills. But it was the care she showed that freaked him out. The delicateness, almost love, sorting through the bags, unzipping them, gently examining the limbs that had been cut from soldiers only hours earlier.

"You're jonesing," Fynn said.

Teller found himself shifting from foot to foot, fingers twitching. "Not too bad. Been eight hours," he lied, adding two hours since he'd last popped a pill.

"Good," she said. Plastic crinkled against the duffel's heavy fibre as she slid a bag in.

What did she do with them? Teller asked himself for the thousandth time.

Research, she'd told him once after fucking. He hadn't been paying attention. Hadn't even asked. Something about an abandoned program to keep severed limbs viable. Surgeons could focus on the critical procedures and reattach amputated limbs hours, even days, later. *Need to keep it quiet*, she'd said. *I don't want the military to know because I want to save lives. They'd use it as a weapon.* She'd then sprung out of her cot, naked, sat at the small desk in her quarters, and typed into her tablet.

"We're done," Fynn said, snapping off gore-covered gloves. The room reeked of congealed blood. She reached into the pocket of her fatigues and handed him a plastic bottle.

Not wanting to, hating himself, he shook it. Not as full as usual.

"If you can go eight hours," Fynn said, "try for ten. That will last you four days." She hoisted the duffel onto a shoulder and ran a finger down his cheek. "Come by when you're done." She turned and left.

Teller cursed, hands quivering now. When she wanted sex, she wanted him clean. Not that he didn't enjoy it. Military service gave her a firm body. She didn't even make him wear a condom. *I'm a doctor*, she'd said, *I'll cure anything you have*. And getting knocked up? She'd take care of that, too.

And after sex she opened up, talked about herself. Like pillow talk. Like they were lovers. He hoped she'd let slide some sliver of knowledge he could leverage against her. An officer, a surgeon and his source—she held the cards. Hell, she was in her mid-thirties and he'd just turned twenty-two.

Now she was cutting him back. To help wean him off the pills, he knew. To get clean.

But he was jonesing, his junkie heart in control. He needed to know something about her. Even things out. Her taking body parts would be his word against hers if he didn't know what she did with them.

Where she took them.

His clean and sober brain told him to do the work, but his junkie heart told him to follow the bitch.

Leaving the gurney, he went into the hall in time to hear the stairway door slam shut. He sprinted up the metal steps and paused at the main level. Doors led outside and into the hospital hall. Checking outside, he spotted her crossing the gravel road between the main building and a row of DRASH tents. He waited for her to move between tents before crossing the road himself, waiting in the shadows of the next tent over. Past the row of tents, flood lights from the main building barely illuminated the few large supply tents and pre-fab sheds in what had become a shell-pocked no-man's land between the main compound and the perimeter fence. Beyond the fence, its outward-facing lights showed the brown, hardscrabble countryside. And past its illumination, the enemy.

Teller spotted Fynn in the no-man's land, duffel bag still on her shoulder. She stopped at the side of a large shed with two roll up doors on its front. Teller had assumed it was part of the motor pool. Fynn undid a lock on a side door and went it.

He'd check it out later. Right now he was jonesing too bad. He moved back to the main building, hoping no one had found the gurney unattended.

By the time he reached his tent, the world had gone deliciously waffling-baffling topsy-turvy-curvy.

Sex with Fynn had been fine.

Pills were better.

His sleeping tentmates appeared as distorted beasts, their snoring an alien rumbling from reality's deepest depths. Bliss enwrapped him like a soft shroud, leeching away his self-hatred.

And when, some slippy-time later, the world rolled and shivered, he thought it just part of the high. But motion surrounded him, tugged at him. The high's clutches slipped down his skin like warm, slick tentacles. Mind sharper, animal panic stabbed his heart before his brain assembled the flurry of movements and sounds of his tentmates into a cohesive thought: incoming artillery. A concussive blast thudded. Instinct and training had him up, pants on, helmet on.

Out through the tent flaps, visions slapped at him—red and orange flames, brown sand, black smoke, blacker sky. Acrid smell of burning tents and spent artillery shells. He flowed among the swarm of people toward the main building's wide, blank north wall. The hard-packed ground shifting and rolling beneath him. Bodies pressed close, the stink of sweat and panic. Down the ramp, through the open steel doors, into the harsh fluorescent light of the bunker's concrete depths. He turned into the room for medical staff. Finding a spot on the hard, cold floor he leaned against a wall that vibrated with each landing shell and every volley fired back.

By now, drones would be up, scanning, relaying enemy artillery locations to their own cannons. Infantry would be strapping on exoarmour to go mop up.

War by proxy, Fynn had called it. *For centuries, man fought face-to-face. Now exoarmour hides our humanity. And if the armour loses a leg, the person loses a leg. We should send the soldier home and let the leg keep fighting*, Fynn had said one afternoon between shifts, her body pressed against his, sweat cooling on his skin.

Teller glanced around the bunker room, the overhead lights flickering. Some stood, most sat. A captain did a head count, a corporal in tow. Teller spotted Fynn, hunched over, typing at her tablet. He didn't let his eyes linger. That typing. In the mess hall, the break room, at the infirmary, after fucking.

Letters? Reports? Research? Before she'd been drafted, she'd been an ER doctor in Moncton and she'd seen plenty of ways the human body could be rent and torn. Then the invasion that had started this war. It had driven her to research ways to save life, maintain it, create it. That didn't mean having children. Billions of women had done that—intelligent and stupid, driven, and lazy. She was after something more.

And those limbs had to be a part of it.

Or maybe she was writing about him, recording his junkie life after catching him smuggling pills. He'd been bribing Sallen, an MP whose thumbprint could open any door on the base, for access to the dispensary. The pills were a common enough sedative. Just something to dull the pain. Except getting hooked hadn't been the plan. And one in thirty-five experienced hallucinogenic side-effects. Teller was that lucky one.

He'd been caught smuggling pills before, but most of the docs had been as fucked up as him by this place. He had connections to feed their secret needs or kinks. A balance. Keep each others' secrets. Colonel Brice didn't have to know anything.

But Fynn had offered to help him get clean. She'd get him his pills, but control the dosage and amount. She just wanted to look at whatever he put in the incinerator. Maybe take a few limbs.

What kind of surgeon did that?

Maybe her tablet had the answers. Restore some kind of balance.

The infirmary hallways bowed down and up and around, a bubble of right angles.

Still feeling the pills.

Sallen, bought off with some kinky Korean porn, unlocked Fynn's office. With her in surgery, he had no better time. Teller stepped in, the room big enough for a desk, chair, and filing cabinet, and Sallen locked the door behind him. The turning tumblers sounded monstrously huge.

Sorting through several tablets scattered on her desk, he found the one she typed on. The one without military markings. He knew her password from watching her enter it so many times. "Herbert."

Her documents folder held dozens of files, but between the pills and the medical jargon he couldn't make heads or tails of them. The message centre was surprisingly empty. He'd thought she'd have friends back home writing her. He opened her "Sent" folder. Mind too affected to do anything but scan and absorb words:

might not read this . . . I'm sorry . . . I can save them . . . Please write back . . . new life . . . let me know you read this . . . viability of limbs . . . publication after my tour ends . . . shelling last night . . . put my needs before yours . . . not crazy to want to maintain life . . . get this published . . .

Some messages had attachments. He opened them, fingers moving fast, swiping through images. The desert, the base, damaged building. Others showed severed limbs, limbs sewn to other limbs with fine silver wire, amalgams of limbs attached to some kind of machine. Then a video—body parts, silver wire spilling from the wounds, twitched and moved. Fingers gripped, ankles and knees flexed as if running. An eyeball perched on the back of a hand pivoted, following a point of light, looking into the camera—

He dropped the tablet. Its clatter, bass-deep from the drugs, made him jump. Had he really just seen—

"What are you doing?"

Teller turned. Fynn in bloody scrubs, stepping into her office. The door shutting, Teller caught a glimpse of black MP's fatigues in the hall. Sallen. She'd probably paid him off to let her know if anyone tried to get into her office.

"Answer me," she commanded.

Caught. Caught and no way out. Junkie logic gave him two choices: bob and weave, or go straight through. He reached for the tablet to show her the images. But as he reached, his hand looked huge.

High. So fucking high.

Fynn pushed past him and grabbed the tablet. "My messages? You've been reading my fucking message?!" She swiped through some screens. "Just because we're fucking doesn't mean you get to know everything about me."

"I'm high, okay?" Teller blurted. "I don't know what I was thinking." Bobbing and weaving. "I couldn't even read the words, you know?" Play to her sympathies. "I was looking for pills. Really? You want to know? I was looking for how I could get more pills."

Something in her posture shifted. Just slightly. "You've finished the ones I gave you. Couldn't go the ten hours. You didn't trust me to help you."

A statement. Not a question. "I—" he began and let it hang there. Truth was, he still had three pills left. He drew strength from that realization.

"You don't need my help, it seems."

"I do," he said too quickly, hating the desperation.

"Do what I tell you. Make them last."

"Okay," he replied, hating the word, its shape. The humiliation. Twelve years old again, his mother telling him how to dress, what summer school courses to take, what friends he could and couldn't play with.

Fynn opened a desk drawer, removed something, and slid it into his hands. Another pill bottle. But the clicking of the pills against plastic sounded wrong. "Lower dosage," she said. "Make these last five days. Withdrawal might be a bit more acute, but stay with it. This is the hard part. If you make it five days, we can get you off the pills in two more weeks." She moved to the doorway, body language making it clear it was time to get out.

He did.

"I have to get back to surgery," she said, closing and locking the door. "Let me know on your next run to the incinerator." She moved quickly down the hall toward the hospital section.

Dismissive. Telling him what to do. Like he was nothing.

At least she didn't want to fuck.

If he'd just gone to another doctor, told him about the pills, that he wanted to get clean. In too deep now. If he went to Colonel Brice, told him everything, she'd get a letter in her file or something. An officer. A surgeon. He was a junkie corpsman. The stockade. Or transferred to infantry.

Tongue dry, needing the bitter pill dissolving there, warping reality.

His junkie mind demanded he find something on her. Even things out. Show her she'd fucked with the wrong guy.

Shelling pulled him up and out of dreamless sleep.

Body well-practiced, he had on his pants, helmet, boots before fully awake. A shirt in hand, he sprinted to the bunker, joining the group funneling for its depths. The night exploded yellow-red, bits of gravel raining down on them.

Fynn would be headed there, too. Hunkered down, waiting it out, tapping into her damn tablet. Then into surgery for those who'd been hit.

Crazy, but this was his shot. He broke off from the group, running between a low, wide supply shed, its corrugated metal sides rattling in the concussions, and the main administrative building. Flattened out on the ground, arms over his head, he fought against digging into his pants pockets.

An explosion spit light and heat, gravel peppering against his helmet. Someone screamed: "My leg! My fucking leg!"

On their own, hands dug for the bottle, opened it, and popped a pill into his mouth.

Each concussion lasted longer, deeper. Ancient gods furious he could plumb the depths of their ancient wisdom.

When the sound of men and machines replaced the explosion of shells, he stood, brushed himself off and wandered out into the base's grid work of gravel roads. They stretched forever, straight but also curving along ancient, forbidden geometry. He moved quickly, purposefully, like the soldiers and vehicles around him. Shouted orders and reports on damage and causalities echoed down the chasms of his ears. Slow motion fires lit up the compound, sirens sounded, people screamed. He stumbled over a piece of rebar, scorched black, and picked it up.

Suitably high, either his courage stoked or fear deadened, he made his way out toward her shed, hoping he moved like someone with purpose and not a junkie starting his high.

Reaching the shed, he slid the rebar into the lock's clasp, settled one end against the frame, and yanked. The lock popped and he opened the door.

An ozone smell and something else—fleshy, meaty—made this stomach roll. Running his hands over the wall, his eyes and ears told him something moved just as he flipped the light switch.

Fleshy things skittered and flopped across the floor. A creature of eight arms, joined at the shoulders, moved like a spider, palms slapping as it scampered toward him. Two legs led up to a metal box, a head emerging from its top, strode back and forth. A torso without a head, but arms emerging from both shoulders and hips, marched in a circle. On tables along the walls, more of these things moved among tools, scraps of machinery, vials and beakers, rolls of that fine silver wire.

She'd slipped him more powerful pills, Teller told himself. Fucking him over. An intense hallucination, fuelled by what he'd seen on her tablet. If what he'd seen on the tablet had even been real—

The door clicked shut. A thing of three legs meeting in a swollen torso wobbled at the door, one of its three arms pressing it closed.

Not realizing he'd wandered into the middle of the room, Teller turned 360 degrees, the tables bowing and sagging. A creature of two hands, attached at the wrists, with a single eyeball perched where the hands met, flitted across it.

"Who are you?" something asked.

It was the two legs and head.

"What the fuck?" spilled out of Teller's mouth. "No. Nonononono."

The two legs and head tottered toward him, the arm-spider following. Something in the legs-head monster whirred. "You should not be here." It whirred again. "Doctor said so."

Teller backed up toward the door, not sure how he'd deal with the tripod that guarded it.

Whirring. Some kind of fan. That's how it spoke without lungs. "You shouldn't be here without Doctor's permission. Doctor said we must keep her secret. No one can know."

The arm-spider rushed him, six arms propelling it, the front two extended.

How does it see? shot through Teller's mind, taking a step back before the arm-spider was on him. Front arms wrapped behind Teller's knees, the rest pushing forward. Teller went down hard, pain shooting up his tailbone, shocking him out of his high. A second set of arms wrapped around his legs. The two-hand thing climbed down the table. Something he didn't see skittered across the floor. Things of all shades of flesh crawled and slithered.

His eyes fixed on silver threads joining the arms together. He swung a fist down on where they met and felt hard, sharp edges beneath the skin. Its grip weakened for a moment, but a third pair of arms grabbed him, the front pair shifting to reach around his waist. He swung again, loosening its grip, allowing him to roll over, pinning it squirming beneath him. If he could crawl for the door—

A blur of motion. Something small sprang at him. The two-hand thing, headed for his throat. Teller managed to catch it. He yanked at the hands—one thick and covered in coarse black hair, the other smooth and delicate. A few silver stitches at the wrists popped, releasing grey-black liquid. The thing's fingers twitched in Teller's, the eyeball darting back and forth. He shifted his effort to snap it like a twig. With a wet crunch, the stitches ripped free from the skin, spraying the grey-black liquid, and the hands went limp. Teller tossed them across the room. A two-foot length of stitched-together finger joints snaked around where the hands landed and closed on Teller.

Fynn's voice: "Stop!"

The snake halted, curling into a coil. The arm-spider, still trapped beneath him, ceased squirming. Teller kicked it off.

The head-legs whirred and said, "Doctor, we were doing as you—"

"I meant him!" she screamed. "Tell me what you're doing here." The things circled around Fynn as she moved into the room.

"You're insane!" Teller shouted, getting to his feet.

"Answer me! Answer— Oh no!" She sobbed, sinking to her knees and cradling the remains of the two hands Teller had ripped apart. "What did you do?"

"You're—" he began, stumbling backward toward the door. Words failed him.

"You're high," she stated, laying the hands down gently. Almost lovingly. "Doesn't matter what you think you saw."

Teller reached the door, the cool night like a loving caress. He headed toward the compound. Reds and golds danced on the shed's sides from the fires.

"Who would believe you?" Fynn called after him. "In an hour, Colonel Brice will know you're addicted to pills and suffering hallucinations." After a moment, she added: "I'll protect you."

The offer made Teller turn.

But Fynn was talking to her creations. "I'll make sure no one finds you," she said before shutting the door.

Teller headed for the administrative building at the far end of the compound. She'd tell, he knew. He had to go to Brice first. Tell his side. He jogged a dozen steps, stumbled and vomited into the sand. After the final wretch, he looked back at the shed. Light spilled out around the door's edges. Shadows of things horrible and inhuman moved across a narrow window high on the wall.

He stopped between two tents, cloaked in shadow, spitting bile. How much of a fall would he take for the revenge of exposing Fynn? He'd have to admit to being on pills, stealing them, everything. Even implicate Sallen.

What if Brice didn't punish her, but rewarded her? Those things were recycled soldiers. Warriors. The pills still working, he imagined a battalion of body parts scrambling across the desert toward the enemy. Hands blown off arms, then hands combining into another creature that kept advancing.

The adrenaline rush fading, nausea's warm, damp fingers slid around him. His head went light, cold sweat on his scalp. Fuck it. He had to tell. Come clean. Get free of her.

Looking up, the administrative building seemed farther away, pulling back down a tunnel. Ears ringing, head light—

—wiping sand off his face. Dawn touched the eastern horizon pink. Pushing himself to his feet, memories of the previous night flashed across his mind. He was clean, he knew. He felt it and, with sunrise at 0530 hours, it meant he'd been out almost six hours. The drugs would be out of his system.

Ahead of him, the base moved as it always did. Soldiers walking at a brisk pace, vehicles roaring from one place to another. Overhead, drones circled, waiting for a pad to drop off wounded.

What had happened last night?

She must have seen or found out he hadn't been there for the headcount in the bunker. She'd gone looking for him.

Everything else had to be the pills. Pills cut with bad shit to really make him freak out.

Behind him, the shed's lights were off, its door open and banging against the outer wall in the hot desert wind. He moved back toward it, just needing to check, yet the doorway remained flat and dark, the sunrise at the wrong angle to illuminate the interior. He moved closer, slowly, finding wheel tracks leading away pressed in the sand. Narrow, not too deep. A light duty jeep.

From the doorway, shapes inside were all blessedly flat and angled. As his eyes adjusted, the shapes resolved into tables and crates, but not the elaborate set up of last night. And without the jumble of materials, there was no place for the things to hide.

Had any of it happened? Or had she packed up her gear? But where would she take it? He knew one thing for certain—with the shed empty, he had nothing. She'd played him again, still held all the cards.

Not sure where to go, he moved to the hospital. He had a shift that would have started at 0400 hours. The jones for a pill grated on him. Its promise of sweet oblivion called to him. Needing them to get through another shift. He dug in his pocket, knew the withdrawals he'd faced, and threw the bottle as far as he could.

The duty sergeant gave him an earful. There was a load to go to the incinerator. Teller grabbed the cart and took the elevator to the lower level, wondering if Fynn would be waiting with another bottle.

The elevator doors opened and he wheeled the cart forward. In the shadows, he fought to ignore motion in his peripheral vision. His junkie heart, trying to scare him, make him want that fix. The scampering sounds were rats, the dull thumping just the machinery of the place.

Rounding the corner, the door to the incinerator room hung open. Slowly, he wheeled the gurney forward. Two sets of legs lay on the ground, partially obscured by another gurney. One in scrubs, the other an MP's black fatigues. Black medical bags covered the gurney. Most empty, but a few remained zipped shut, their contents twisting and squirming against the black plastic.

Bile rose in Teller's mouth. He backed out into the hall.

She was going to destroy her children. In case Teller told. Then find another junkie. Start someplace else.

But they'd rebelled. She made them to be warriors.

He turned. Shadows moved and slithered. Impossible shapes, like a spider made of eight human arms, hovered in the shadows. Behind him, zippers slid open, flesh slid against plastic.

Teller bolted for the staircase. The flat slapping of eight palms pursued him.

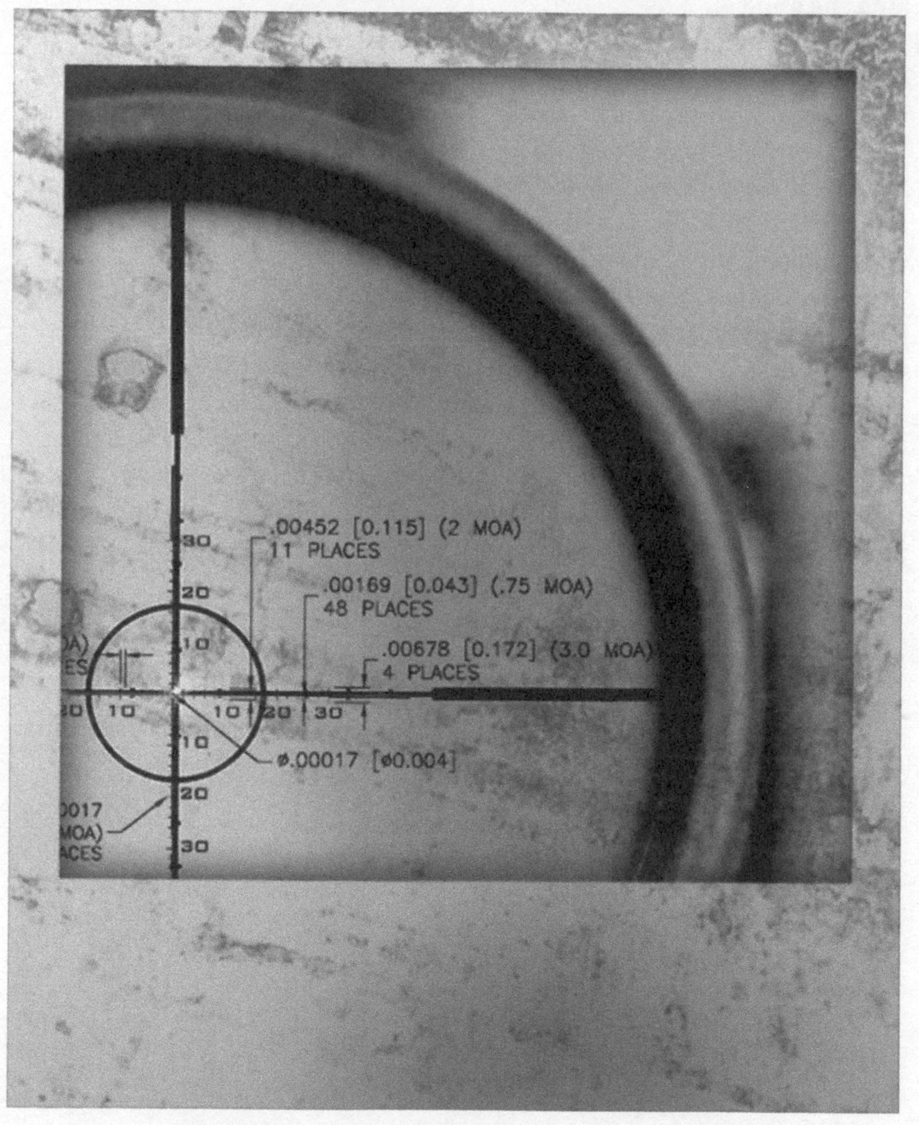

.00452 [0.115] (2 MOA)
11 PLACES
.00169 [0.043] (.75 MOA)
48 PLACES
.00678 [0.172] (3.0 MOA)
4 PLACES
ø.00017 [ø0.004]
30
20
10
10
20
30
10
10
20
30

IN THE SHADOW OF SCYTHE

Archie placed the butt of the rifle against his shoulder and pulled the trigger. He was rewarded with the *click* of a finely tuned weapon.

Across the cramped apartment's small kitchen table, the younger man with a weightlifter's body he knew as Timothy looked up, a 9mm bullet in his latex-gloved hand. Sweat shone in the stubble on his shaved head. "It's good?"

"Yeah," Archie replied, his guts twisting. He told himself he'd just pointed an unloaded sniper rifle at a spot on the wall, but that didn't hold back three-year old memories of lining up dying, desperate people in a rifle sight as they stormed the perimeter.

Timothy took a swig from his water bottle and resumed snapping rounds into ammunition clips.

Between the two men lay the suitcase, custom-made to carry the rifle, two Heckler & Koch MP5s that Archie had already checked, a dozen clips for the submachine guns, and boxes of 9mm shells.

Using the bottom edge of his already soaked T-shirt, Archie wiped sweat from his face. He blamed the cramp in his belly on the heat and tang of gun oil hanging in the air. But opening a window meant trading hot, close air for the warm, humid air of evening. Besides, they'd been warned that even twelve floors above the city's streets Daniel Deanne heard things.

Archie didn't doubt it. But at least this job was done. In another hour, the guns Archie had arranged for Timothy to buy would be out of Archie's hands.

As he began to break down the rifle, cleaning each component before fitting it into its slot in the suitcase, the weight of the moment settled on him: this weapon might kill Daniel Deanne.

And we used to be friends, Archie thought.

Timothy looked up. "Say what?"

He'd spoken aloud. The pressure to tell what he'd done—to finally come clean—built. The haunted look in Timothy's eyes told Archie the younger man had his own demons. Maybe he'd understand. "Me and Daniel. Eight years ago—"

Timothy's cellphone chimed. He pulled the device from his jeans. "Got the address for the transfer," he said, looking at the screen. His brow creased. "Meeting someone new."

Suspicion, borne from both experience and animal fear, made the hair on Archie's neck stand straight. "Why?" Archie asked.

Timothy shoved the phone back in his pocket. "Doesn't say. We should motor." He loaded the guns, clips, and remaining ammunition into an oversized gym bag.

Archie finished breaking down the rifle and closed the case. From its battered leather exterior, no one would know what it held. He and Timothy tossed empty ammo boxes, rags used to clean the weapons and their latex gloves into a garbage bag.

Timothy put the water bottle to his lips and, for a moment, his hard features were replaced by the gaunt, lined face of the old man in the Venezuelan countryside. The pungent smell of blood stung Archie's nose. He blinked and Timothy's face returned.

Timothy picked up the gym bag. "Ready?"

"Yeah." After one last check that they'd left no sign of what they'd done, Archie grabbed the trash bag and the rifle's case.

Timothy killed the lights, locked the door behind them, and they moved down the dingy hall. At the elevators, a full-colour glossy poster had been taped above the buttons. It showed a working-class woman leaving her apartment. Visible through the doorway, the light over the stove had been left on. Behind the woman, Daniel—curly, unkempt steel-grey hair, a smirk framed by a goatee, green cotton shirt tucked into blue jeans—leaned against the wall. The caption asked: "Is *everything* off? Daniel knows. Do it for Daniel." The symbol for Daniel's One Faith, One World campaign—a green circle circumscribing a "1"—made it clear who'd produced the glossy.

Archie squeezed the handle of the suitcase, thinking of its contents. He'd seen that smirk before, face-to-face.

On the ground floor, they went out the back to the alley where Archie tossed the garbage bag into an overflowing dumpster. Reaching the street, they talked about the play-offs, shaking their heads and rolling their eyes to maintain surveillance of their surroundings.

They turned a corner to find four young men wearing green Daniel's Disciples vests giving a cabbie a hard time. One of them slammed both fists onto the car's trunk in time to a chant of "No-idl-ing! No-idl-ing!" while the three others took turns shoving the heavyset man around. Glare from streetlights glinted off the One Faith bracelets on their right wrists.

Archie heart hammered, but he didn't break stride.

The cabbie shoved back, knocking the closest Disciple on his rear. Within seconds, the other three were on the cabbie.

In his peripheral vision, Archie saw Timothy's head turn. Archie asked, "You going to do something about this?"

Around them, others watched. Some cheered the Disciples on, taking up the "No-idl-ing!" chant.

"Would you help if I did?" Timothy replied.

"Help!" The cabbie begged, hands outstretched as Archie and Timothy passed. "Please—" A punch to his guts silenced him. He dropped to his knees.

Archie kept his eyes straight ahead. "Not part of the plan." Behind him, fists and boots thudded against flesh. Then the crunch of metal panelling, the tinkle of breaking glass.

"You've heard the saying about what happens when good men don't do nothing?"

"I'm doing something." They reached Archie's car—an old, gas-guzzling Japanese hatchback—and loaded the gym bag and suitcase into the trunk.

"Yeah, and in an hour you can say you've *done* something." Timothy got in the car, slamming the door.

Archie said nothing as he got in the driver's seat, started the car and headed for the drop-off.

After a few blocks, Timothy asked: "What'd you mean before, man? You and Deanne were friends?"

Archie scanned the road ahead. He'd been stupid to consider telling Timothy anything. If the younger man were caught, what he knew would make it back to Daniel and Archie was as good as dead. Still, Timothy had earned a small truth. "We worked together." But the confession brought no relief. Archie was talking to a man ready to forfeit his life.

"Thought you didn't want us to know nothing about you."

"Nothing that could identify me. I'm sure Daniel has plenty of former friends."

"Ain't many who're still alive."

Archie remained silent, conceding the point. He kept his eyes on the road and mirrors, looking for a tail.

They parked next to the blue PureRun sedan at the far end of the abandoned mall's empty parking lot and exited the car. A middle-aged woman got out of the PureRun, wearing one of those "Salvation" T-shirts with a stylized version of Daniel's face rendered in green, beige, and blue. She stood with her hands on her hips, a posture that allowed easy access to a pistol no doubt tucked into the small of her back.

Timothy approached the woman while Archie put his foot on the bumper and retied his shoelace, keeping watch. They were alone and unobserved except for a passing cyclist riding a pedal-converted Harley. He gave Archie and his car a dirty look.

"You the guys to see about lightbulbs?" the woman asked, scratching her left temple.

Timothy smiled and tilted his head to the right. "Only if they're Daniel Deanne approved."

The woman held up both hands, palm up, and shrugged. "They aren't." She opened the trunk.

Archie gave Timothy a look to see if he'd caught it.

Timothy lowered his head slightly—he'd noticed. The final countersign was to hold your hands up and say, "They *ain't*."

Archie raised his eyebrows—this was Timothy's contact, his call.

"Fellas?" the woman asked, hands back on her hips.

Archie calculated how quickly he could go for the Beretta tucked into his waistband, how to get behind his car for cover.

Timothy opened the trunk and hefted out the gym bag. "Grab the suitcase?"

"Sure," the woman replied, transferring the case to the trunk.

The exchange complete, she drove off. "Something's wrong, man," Timothy said. "I need to call Pious."

Archie waited in the driver's seat, watching the street. In the rear-view mirror, Timothy stood in the shadows behind the convenience store, phone to his ear.

Across the street, signs reading "Future Site of Leopold Towers by PureBuild" and "35-Storey Luxury Condos—All Solar Power—Deanne-Approved!" covered the front doors and vestibules of buildings. Buildings that had once been celebrated examples of the city's architecture before Daniel changed the face of urban planning and design.

Movement caught Archie's eye. Behind him, Timothy dropped his phone and stomped it, then got in the car. He rolled up his window and waited for Archie to do the same. "Pious wants us at the safe house."

Archie started the car. "That's not the plan."

"Plan's changed. Pious said people are getting taken down. Wants to bring you in."

"Into what?" Archie pulled into traffic.

"What do you think, man?"

Archie went cold. "Why didn't Pious tell me this?"

"Can only use those phones for so long. But you can call him. Even give you the number."

Archie replayed the last few moments—the words, tone of voice, body language. Nothing made him suspect a trap. But that was the problem. Pious and Timothy really wanted him to join their insurgency against Daniel Deanne.

Just two more things and he was done. "Did you mention the drop?"

"Yeah. Guy who was supposed to be there disappeared. Gone. Pious described the chick he sent. Same one we met. Had little time to memorize the signals."

"Did he mention when I'm getting paid?" So far, Archie had only received a third of what he'd been promised.

"Not my job. But go to the house. Talk to Pious."

"Tell Pious I expect to hear from him soon. Where can I drop you?"

Timothy's shoulders drooped. "Anywhere, man."

Two blocks later, Archie pulled over. A large crowd of tattooed young people stood in front of a building with extinguished neon lights announcing it as a dance club. Timothy could easily disappear. Just one more muscle boy. Archie extended his hand. "Good luck, Timothy."

Timothy shook. "God bless you, Saul."

Archie nodded at the code name Pious had given him.

"Hey, no idling!" a young man yelled, a knock-off One Faith bracelet on his right wrist. A few others shouted their agreement—men with the same imitation bracelets, women with fake One Faith headbands.

Timothy got out, his size silencing the hecklers.

Archie pulled away, feeling a twinge of regret. He couldn't say he liked Timothy or would call him a friend, but he'd been a solid partner—never late, never out of place, never unfocused. But he'd finished the job. Timothy's safety wasn't Archie's responsibility anymore.

Getting on the highway, Archie watched his mirrors and tuned into the local news station. The anchor gushed about the gala in two days where Daniel would reveal his proposal for a unified world currency. Daniel claimed it would allow developing countries to buy green technology. Green technology developed by one of Daniel's companies—PureRun, PureBuild, PureGrow.

He took a different exit than the previous night, watching a pair of headlights follow him down the ramp. Archie turned left. The other car—a lime green PureRun SUV—went right. Probably nothing, but he took his time winding through the slum that had been a middle class suburb only a few years ago. Tents and makeshift shacks filled the parks and playgrounds. Refugees from condemned downtown buildings that couldn't meet Deanne standards sat on sidewalks and benches with nothing to do and nowhere to go while gangs of Disciples patrolled among them.

Pulling into his apartment building's underground parking garage, the anchor's admiration of Daniel faded to static.

In the elevator lobby, a notice taped to the wall bearing the One Faith logo stated that to reduce electricity, residents who lived below the sixth floor must take the stairs. Anyone who caught a neighbour using the elevator inappropriately was to report them to building management. "Do it for Daniel," the notice concluded. Archie considered ripping it down, but didn't know if he was on camera.

He climbed to the third floor, checked that the paperclip he'd closed between the jam and the door hadn't moved and entered his small studio apartment. Like in the apartment he'd left, the still air held on to the day's heat. He threw open a window, scanning the people on the electric tram platform between him and the building across the street. No one paid him any attention. Below, he noted a cyclist locking a pedal-converted Harley to a light post across the street, then sitting on the steps of the closest building. There were plenty of pedal-converted Harleys around the city, symbols of true commitment to Daniel's One Faith, but Archie mentally noted the coincidence with the man at the drop.

After putting a fan in the window, Archie peeled off his sweat-soaked shirt and threw it onto the pile of laundry spilling from his closet. He turned on his computer and went to the fridge. Finding only moldy pizza and a half-empty bottle of ketchup, he returned to his computer, which glowed with the desktop picture of Daniel during the "our great moment of history" speech. Face impassioned, eyes skyward, hands held up with fingers splayed, he'd given it three days after the near-Earth object 2017 KT1208 had fallen from the sky. In seconds, it had incinerated tens of thousands in northern Venezuela's Orinoco Belt—the heart of the country's oil production—left a twelve-mile wide crater and sent enough ash into the sky to block out the sun for three days. Seismographs around the world had recorded the impact, which the media had dubbed "Scythe" for the Grim Reaper's weapon of choice. Others—like Pious—called it "Star Wormwood," the great star of Revelation 8:10 that would fall to earth during the End Times. Just one more element Pious and his group had shoehorned into their belief that Daniel was the Anti-Christ.

Archie had just arrived in Venezuela as part of a relief effort when Daniel had given the speech. He'd never known about it until he'd returned five months later. Even now, the picture stung with the same anger, bitterness, and guilt of when he'd first learned how things had changed while he'd killed his way through the South American jungle. The picture reminded him that if he hadn't been a coward all those years ago, the speech—and everything that followed—never would have happened.

At last, he'd done something about it.

Done.

Just like Timothy had said.

So why didn't he feel some sense of accomplishment? Because Pious and his group would be caught—or worse—before they could use the guns. Just another failed rebellion. But men like Pious and Timothy believed dying while opposing Daniel got them to the front of the line at the Pearly Gates.

Yet paying his bill didn't seem to be something Pious believed in, so Archie needed a new job. A message from Mai, the project manager at NuCleen, told him she had nothing new. No word either on Esteban, the project manager she'd replaced when he'd gone missing.

He logged into two anonymous e-mail accounts he used for less legitimate work and opened a message from V!@GRA L!0N. The mishmash of random words and characters, meaningless to anyone who didn't know the cipher, instructed Archie to meet Pious tomorrow morning at 9:30. It gave an address and instructions for how to knock on the back door.

Maybe Pious had the money.

Archie deleted the message and headed for the shower.

The blackened landscape changed into the dark apartment. Shrieks of pain transformed into the electric tram rattling by outside, its lights flickering against the bare walls.

Archie shot up, catching his breath. Random after-images flashed across his mind—

—filthy townspeople fighting their way through concertina wire, automatic weapons fire mowing them down, his rifle finishing the ones who got too close—

—buzzards circling, waiting for the screams to fade so they could land and feed—

—the old man, eyes forever wide in surprise, just wanting something to drink—

—Daniel behind the podium, hands moving to emphasize every point: the corruption of the Venezuelan government, billions earned from fossil fuels and its record of ignoring international standards on pollution reduction. He'd gone on for an hour without a script, enthralling the crowd of reporters gathered on the steps of PureRun's headquarters. The sunlight had played off the silver in his curly hair and goatee, a green shirt and blue jeans instead of a suit, as he demanded verification that humanitarian aid was really going to help those affected. Or, he suggested, was it being put toward rebuilding oil production? On and on—not winded, not sweating, never a non-sequitur or digression. Passionate but never angry, forcefully laying out his rationale for halting all international aid without resorting to hyperbole or dogma.

Until his conclusion: "This"—he'd jabbed a finger downward—"is our great moment of history. Here we will see if those backwards thinkers who rape this planet for profit can sustain their actions or if they will collapse into the fires of history. Let Venezuela go it alone!" The applause had been thunderous.

Already well-known for his companies and environmental activism, the speech put Daniel on the front page of every major newspaper, the lead story of every network and main image of every news site. Some agreed with him, calling him a hero for speaking truth to a corrupt government. Finally, they cheered, someone had brought scope to the environmental movement—the price of thousands of lives now to save billions later. Other reviled him, calling his callousness beyond measure. Yet Daniel sought out his detractors, demanding interviews. Face-to-face, he brought even his harshest critics around to his belief that personal, spiritual, and environmental salvation were one.

Then came Hollywood stars and music icons seeking his wisdom. Hours after Daniel entered their homes, these celebrities emerged professing devotion to his One Faith. Millions attended rallies across the country and around the world led by Disciples. Originally just organized groups of concerned citizens pushing for environmental responsibility at the grassroots level, the Disciples became Daniel's emissaries, espousing the One Faith belief that they would be the ones to save future generations. They would do it to save the world. They would do it for Daniel.

Only a week after the speech, the President realized he could not stand against the growing populist tide—to say nothing of contradicting one of his major contributors—and urged other world leaders to halt aid to Venezuela. They had agreed, Archie would learn, having no real concept of just how horrible the situation was or would become. Archie envied them their ignorance.

As Archie became a more efficient killer, Daniel called on governments to pass legislation restricting industry and transportation, and the mandatory adoption of new technologies—technologies only available from his companies—to counteract environmental damage.

By the time Archie had arrived home, Daniel's Disciples were recruiting in twelve countries, including Venezuela. Daniel's companies received exclusive government contracts.

A year after that, people lived in fear that neighbours were snitching on their recycling habits or Disciples would feel a porch light had been left on too long. Random highway checkpoints seized old cars. Homeowners received fines because an infrared scan revealed insufficient insulation. People from all walks of life bought up One Faith bracelets and headbands to show their devotion to Daniel's faith of spiritual salvation through environmental purification.

And just last year, Esteban and others like him began to vanish because they published research proving Daniel's technology wasn't as efficient as he claimed.

It all came back to the speech, Archie had concluded. Without it, waves of workers and supplies would have followed him, bringing stability. Hundreds of thousands in Venezuela might have been saved. People wouldn't live in fear. And Archie might still be the idealistic engineer who wanted to do his small part in making the world a better place.

He thought about his Beretta. How it felt in his mouth—its oily taste, the impossibly hard barrel unyielding against his teeth.

Words from Jimenez, the man who'd kept him alive in the jungle, came to him: "Do what it takes to survive today. Wake up tomorrow. Repeat." He'd said it when they'd stopped for the night after shooting their way out of the base and making it to the hills above the valley. Some of them were sobbing uncontrollably, other vomiting. Others, like Archie, just stared blankly into the ink-black darkness.

There'd been eleven of them that night. Only four made it back home. They'd survived by being cold and doing what needed to be done, killing their way through each challenge to live long enough to commit another unspeakable act of violence.

The urge to call—to finally confess—struck Archie. He'd never said a word during those five months crossing to Colombia, afraid the others would turn on him. But through the fog of sleep Archie remembered Jimenez had ignored his own advice and eaten his gun six months ago. At least, that was the official explanation.

"Hey, let go!"

"Shut up and get on the ground!"

The commotion drew Archie to the window. Across from him, a cop spun a teenager face-first to the surface of the tram station.

"You think that crap is funny?" The cop kneeled on the kid's back, cuffing him.

"Yeah," the kid shot back. "And pretty accurate."

The cop hauled the teen to his feet, turning him toward an oversized plastic-enclosed advertisement for Daniel's PureGrow crops. Devil's horns adorned Daniel's head. "Defacing Daniel is paramount to terrorism!"

"'Paramount,' right," the teen said. "Careful you don't scuff your jackboots."

The cop's reply was lost as he marched the kid down to street level.

Below, the Harley has been replaced by an overloaded shopping cart. A shape lay curled up in the nearby corner of the stairs and building. Other than that, the street was empty.

Archie got back into bed, knowing sleep was a long way off.

A cluster of Disciples milled on the next block. Archie watched them, waiting for the light to change.

The morning talk shows buzzed about the massive sweep of eco-terrorists the night before, including two NuCleen executives, a Congressman from Wyoming and an Australian MP. "It's not an overreaction," the Attorney General explained. "A strong environmental policy is the cornerstone of a strong national security policy." Daniel had said the same thing—verbatim—seven years ago during his speech at the Democratic National Convention.

The light turned green. Passing, the Disciples jeered him. A bottle shattered on the passenger window. Buying a PureRun would attract less attention, Archie knew, but he couldn't bring himself to do it.

A few streets later, Archie found the address. A chain-link fence stretched across the front of the crumbling white stucco house's yard. A tall, wooden fence topped with razor wire lined the other three sides. Bars covered the windows and front door.

Archie kept going, circling the block. Houses here were mid-sized, most with fences ringing three or four sides of the property. Metal bars or plywood sheets covered doors and windows. Yellow grass grown long and wild hinted at vacant homes.

Older homes, Archie concluded. Too recent to be grandfathered against Deanne regulations, but old enough to make retrofits too expensive. Easier to just abandon them.

He parked at the curb, chambering a round and clicking off the safety before getting out. A pair of white-haired retirees a few houses down watched him silently from their front porch. Other than them, the street was deserted. Archie entered a gate at the mouth of the narrow driveway and followed it to the backyard. He mounted three steps to a rickety porch, faced the metal back door and knocked using the rhythm described in the e-mail. The door opened a crack, wide enough for two gun barrels to emerge: one at head level, one at his knees. He'd had guns pointed at him before, but it wasn't something he'd ever get used to. He kept his panic in check, gauging if he could make it off the porch and out of range before they could get a bead on him and knowing he couldn't. "The Viagra Lion asked me to come."

The door opened wider and he stepped inside. Before his eyes adjusted to the darkness, hands seized him, spinning him against a wall. A gun barrel pressed into his back just below his left shoulder blade, aimed at his heart, pinning him in place.

"Hands up."

Archie obeyed. Hands frisked him, found the pistol and clicked on the safety.

After a few moments, the voice said: "Turn around."

Archie turned, hands still raised, and water splashed his face.

"Do you renounce Satan, and his servant Daniel Deanne, and all their works?"

Archie blinked water from his eyes. In the sunlight bleeding through cracked windows shades, he could make out a tall, wiry woman with a crew cut and wearing fatigues. She grasped a flask in one hand and stood off balance on a prosthetic leg. Flanking her were two men armed with MP5 submachine guns.

Archie said: "What—"

The three tensed. The two men—teenagers, really—brought their guns up.

Archie put his hands out. "Whoa, wait—"

"The answer they are looking for, Saul, is 'I do renounce them in the name of Jesus Christ.'" Pious stood in a doorway, dressed in black and wearing his clerical collar.

"I do renounce them in the name of Jesus Christ," Archie repeated.

"S'okay, guys," the woman said, touching the two boys' shoulders. They lowered their weapons and returned to chairs by the back door. Turning to Pious, the woman said: "He's clean."

"Thank you, Joan," Pious replied, stepping into the kitchen. The skin under his eyes was puffy, a few days' stubble clung to his face.

The tall woman limped to Archie, the hinge of her prosthetic leg squeaking, and handed back the pistol.

Archie faced the priest-turned-renegade. "The arrests last night making you jittery?"

"Yes," Pious replied. "I fear the Two Witnesses were arrested. They will not survive long against the Dragon."

Archie braced for more of Pious's ramblings. How Daniel's full name—Daniel Derick Deanne—clearly mapped to Revelation 13:18 and its telling of a man whose name would be "666." Or the bracelets and headbands bearing the One Faith logo indicated the Mark of the Beast. Instead, he led Archie through a narrow doorway into a room that would have been the dining room. Computer equipment covered tables and shelves. Young men and women typed furiously. One monitor showed a web page being built, a red headline screaming: "Global Warming is not man-made, but God's punishment. Revelation 16:9!" Another stated: "First the Flood, Now the Fire." Archie scanned for Timothy's face, but didn't see him.

The two men passed into a smaller, windowless room that contained a desk and chair against one wall, an old battered couch opposite. Pious shut the door and sat in the chair.

"Timothy was also arrested last night."

A cold lump settled in Archie's belly. "Pious, I'm sorry." He sat on the couch, springs squeaking. Archie replayed the previous evening in his mind, wondering if he'd missed something.

"I do not blame you, Saul. I am sure it is not your fault. I have always known Daniel has many spies, many ways of gathering information. Thus far, I have been confident he has not become aware of my plans. Otherwise, he would not attend the gala tomorrow."

"I don't want to know details, Pious." Archie wiped a forearm across his forehead. "I know too much already."

"I understand, Saul, but Timothy did know." He remained still as he spoke as if immune to the dry, suffocating heat. "I fear that Daniel will discover our plans, not just for the gala, but how organized we are. That we have infiltrated his organization. Timothy is strong and faithful, but not one can resist Daniel."

Archie couldn't disagree. He didn't believe Pious's stories that Daniel personally interrogated prisoners, extracting answers as he shredded their souls, but wondered about rumours of former black site interrogators working their trade under the auspices of the Environmental Protection Agency. If Timothy was being waterboarded, Archie hoped the interrogators weren't looking to know if the guy who sold guns to Timothy had once known Daniel. "Pious, I'm sorry about Timothy, but what does this have to do with me? Do you have my money?"

"Timothy was to be the shooter in my plan to assassinate Daniel."

Archie held up a hand. "I don't—"

Pious leaned toward Archie. "And I want you to take his place."

Archie shot to his feet. "Wait a second. I did my bit. I'm done."

"Why are you helping us, Saul?" Pious asked, looking up at Archie. "We've barely paid you what we promised, so it's not for the money. You do not share our belief that Daniel is a Beast of Revelations, turning all away from faith in Our Lord to his 'One Faith' of the power of man. You waited while Timothy called me last night when, with your part of the arrangement complete, you could have left. And why did you come here today?"

"Because you owe me."

"Nothing more? Money is your sole motivation?"

"I have to eat, Pious."

"Timothy told me you began to confess something to him about knowing Daniel. Are you trying to make up for something, Saul?"

Archie ignored the pressure in his chest. "Do you have my money or not?"

"There is more than just survival, Saul. You must live for something."

"Tomorrow. I survive today, I wake up tomorrow, and repeat."

Pious remained seated and still. "Timothy held similar beliefs. He was trapped in Venezuela after Wormwood fell. At the time, he was a high school student doing volunteer work. Out of twenty-five students and five chaperones, only he survived. He described the young man he had been and how much of himself he had to sacrifice to endure that horrible place." Pious finally stood. "From what I know of you, I suspect you have endured similar things, which is why I paired Timothy with you. I knew you would grow to trust him and hopefully assist him in his mission."

"Find another shooter, Pious." Archie turned for the door.

"I have none. I lost my best people in last night's arrests. I have been in contact with allies willing to help, but they have no one who could be here in time. Those who are left to me are children who have never held a gun."

"Not my problem."

"Something I have not heard you say is that you have no experience in doing this. Are you a sniper, Saul? Is that how you knew which rifle would be best for our mission?"

The room shrank, the heat unbearable. The clockwork efficiency of lining up a head in the sight, squeezing the trigger, and finding another target assaulted him. "Keep the money. I don't want to see you again." He grabbed the door handle, slick in his hand.

"If Timothy's assassination attempt failed," Pious continued, "my fallback plan was a frontal assault on the museum. Most of my people may die, and plenty of innocents as well, but after this attempt security around Daniel may become impenetrable, and the blow we were dealt by the arrests might mean this is our only chance. Walk away and I will have no choice but to move up the attack to when Daniel's motorcade arrives. Can you live with that kind of blood on your hands?"

"It's not on my hands. You have the guns. Do what you want." Archie walked toward the rear of the house, listening for but not hearing Pious following him.

In the kitchen, the woman Pious had called Joan pushed herself to her feet. "You leaving? I thought—"

"Let me out."

Joan frowned, then motioned to one of the boys to unlock the door. "God be with you, Saul," Joan said as Archie stepped outside into the searing mid-morning sun. Archie headed for his car, Pious's word replaying in his mind. Gunfire and screaming—pained, panicked, threatening—filled his head.

It had been a day like this—brutally hot. About eight hundred more, dying from dehydration and toxicity, had arrived during the night to join the thousand surrounding the small base where Archie and the other volunteers had been stationed. With water for hundreds of miles surrounding the impact site contaminated by an unknown toxin brought by the meteor, those people had had no hope except the base's water supply. But the two portable purifying units barely produced enough for the compound's hundred people.

Two days earlier, they'd heard the second wave of the relieve effort, which would have brought a dozen more purifiers, wasn't coming. And they were on their own. Faced with the growing crowd, the commanding officer had had the gate locked, telling the people to disperse or risk him using force. With nowhere else to go, they remained—baking in the sun, pleading to be let it.

Archie didn't know who shot first. But when the gunfire began, Jimenez had rounded up the volunteers and brought them to a building at the centre of the base. They huddled there, terrified as gunfire chattered, bullets thudding against concrete walls. As the day's heat pressed in, Jimenez explained he really wasn't an engineer. He was CIA, trying to foster a rebellion against the government. And he'd keep them safe if they did what he told them.

When night fell, Jimenez darted out into the compound, returning with guns and ammunition. He passed them out to the volunteers, explaining how to use them.

Sheer chance resulted in Archie getting a rifle instead of a submachine gun.

No one slept.

Before dawn, with half the soldiers dead, Jimenez starting taking the volunteers from the safety of the building into the compound. They had to take the soldiers' places, he explained. He positioned Archie on the roof of a two-storey building.

Just after sunrise, a burst of automatic weapons fire cut the silence. Another burst answered. In moments, the air was alive. Archie crouched behind an air vent.

Jimenez appeared next to him. "Find a target!" he screamed.

Archie inched to the peak of the roof and looked down at locals trying to make it through rolls of concertina wire to the fence. Some carried guns, others machetes or clubs.

A pistol pressed into the back of his skull.

"Find a target," Jimenez repeated. "If you won't shoot, you're a liability."

Archie brought the rifle up. Heart hammering but hands steady, he centred the sight on a man in a red shirt firing a bolt action rifle.

"Pull the trigger."

Archie obeyed, the crack of the rifle lost in the firefight.

The red-shirted man fell, limp and lifeless.

"Nice shot!"

Archie shut his eyes, tears welling, empty stomach threatening to heave.

"It's you or them," Jimenez whispered in an eerie, quiet tone. "It isn't murder. They forced this. You aren't a monster. Your guilt proves that. Now do it again, but this time . . ." Jimenez maneuvered Archie's fingers to change his grip on the trigger and guard.

Over the next ten minutes of Jimenez's tutoring, Archie killed seven people.

When the perimeter fence finally gave way under the sheer pressure of bodies pressing against it, it was no longer about water. Jimenez had already gathered what was left of the supplies and passed them out. Leading the charge of surviving volunteers—a third of those who'd arrived only one day ago—they shot their way through the wave of villagers and headed into the mountains.

Archie reached his car to find a One Faith logo spray-painted on its hood. Down the street, a pair of Disciples yelled at the old couple, still on their porch. Archie unlocked the car, got in and screamed, slamming his hand on the steering wheel.

In the elevator lobby of the parking garage, someone had scrawled "Thanks for the shaft" on the notice about limited elevator use. Archie climbed the stairs to the third floor. The paperclip in place, he activated his computer. Didn't matter if Mai had a new contract or someone was looking for a few semiautomatic pistols, his bank account was running low.

He took a moment to curse Pious, then scanned his inbox, finding nothing.

Jobs used to come easier. When he'd returned from South America, a friend had put him in contact with Esteban, a project manager at NuCleen, one of the few competitors to Daniel's companies. Esteban had lined up a few contracts, but sensing Archie's feelings toward Daniel Esteban had put Archie in contact with groups doing underground research to challenge Daniel's claims. They'd been loosely organized, often splintering at the slightest hint they'd been discovered. Though interested in the research, Archie found himself disgusted with the timid engineers. More and more, he associated with the tough, reliable men and women who worked as security. A lot of them wanted guns.

And Archie needed money.

Through Jimenez, he located people who could get him weapons. Many of them had that eerie calmness about them and recognized a kinship with Archie.

Archie learned what he could from them. About guns and ammunition. How to spot a trap or a tail. Staying calm and evaluating a dangerous situation. But the central piece of wisdom, the code to live by, was: don't get involved.

It was good advice. Most of his clients wound up dead. Self-styled revolutionaries looking to replace Daniel or black market profiteers selling air conditioners or portable gas-powered generators, they'd either implode, get sold out or find their safe houses raided by police. Or burned down by Disciples.

Their decisions, Archie told himself. Just like it was Pious's decision to storm the gala.

Then why did he feel like a coward?

Because, Archie had to admit—crazy as the man's motivation was—Pious's fight was his fight. No one in years had wanted to take the fight directly to Daniel. He'd known from the beginning why they wanted that rifle.

Scores of ghosts he'd lined up in his gunsight haunted his sleep.

Again, Archie thought of the Beretta, the taste of it in his mouth, his thumb on the trigger.

"I did not expect to see you again." Pious extended a hand toward the couch.

Archie sat. "I've changed my mind."

Pious nodded, eyes betraying nothing. "May I ask why?"

Archie had intended on telling him no, but with the invitation offered, it burst from him. How he'd just received his Masters degree when he'd started with Daniel's team, working on a hybrid fuel cell. Back then, Daniel had been just another team leader at another car company.

When Archie discovered Daniel's efficiency calculations for the cell were inaccurate and it was no more efficient than others on the market, he'd informed Daniel during a staff meeting. He'd been so proud, thinking he'd prevented a major embarrassment.

That smirk had grown on Daniel's face. "Archibald, the numbers don't matter. How much pollution the car produces isn't the issue. Getting people to adopt our product—getting them think what we want them to think—is. Then we can make changes. Then the people will go where we tell them." The rest of the team had nodded, looking at Daniel like he was preaching gospel.

A year later, Archie was let go just before Daniel left to form PureRun. The rest of the team would become his first Disciples.

For the next three years, he'd gotten by on contracts while Daniel's influence expanded, but when a charity asked for volunteers with engineering experience to go to Venezuela to re-establish infrastructure following Scythe's impact he'd gone to do some good. But Daniel's speech halted the help that should have followed him. Five months later, he'd emerged from the jungles a killer. And the anarchy in Venezuela had consumed most of northwestern South America.

"And all I had to do," Archie concluded for Pious, feeling empty and drained, "was tell the Junior VP of R&D. He never liked Daniel. Thought he had too much salesman in him. If I'd told him, Daniel would've been fired. Discredited. Then no PureRun, no speech, no Disciples.

"But I was afraid for my job. My *job*. And a year later, that VP's private plane went down in the New Mexico desert."

"And your experience in Venezuela would have been one of charity, not violence, making you a better man."

Pious's words rubbed raw a deep wound, but Archie stayed quiet. The priest laid a hand on Archie's shoulder. "There was no way to stop Daniel. He was pre-ordained. Wormwood gave him his power and his sign. God put you in his way for a reason, and kept you alive after Wormwood fell to harden your resolve and show you a path." Pious made the sign of the cross over Archie. "I consider what you have told me to be a confession, Saul. I absolve you from your sins in the name of the Father, and of the Son, and of the Holy Spirit."

"Doesn't make me feel better."

"Take whatever advantage you can." Pious pushed his chair aside and knelt. He fit his fingers into a small groove in the floorboards and lifted a 2' by 2' trap door, revealing a wooden box in a cavity beneath. He lifted the box, setting it on the desk. "My plans."

Archie extended his pass to the security guard. From the cuff of his green uniform hung a One Faith bracelet. Just like the one Archie wore.

After running the pass through a scanner, the guard motioned toward the metal detector. With a nod from the guard at the detector, Archie stepped through the machine. It beeped and the guard motioned for Archie to wait before running a wand up one of Archie's legs and down the other. Other guards appeared, suddenly interested in Archie. The wand hummed when it passed over Archie's waist. Archie let a guilty grin grow and pulled up his cummerbund to reveal a massive belt buckle embossed with the One Faith logo. The guards barked laughter and waved him on to the double set of doors, wishing him a pleasant evening.

Inside, the museum's atrium buzzed with the conversations of the guests as they milled under massive green banners reading "One Faith, One World, One Currency."

He circled the huge room, one of hundreds of men in a tuxedo, looking for his contact—a redheaded server with the nametag "Jacob." Faces he'd seen on television and computer screens breezed past him, drinks in hand—a governor, a famous actress, an award-winning singer. One Faith bracelets adorned all their right wrists or headbands on foreheads. Daniel's true believers.

Archie willed himself to be calm and alert. To be aware of eyes following his movements or faces that seemed constantly nearby.

Commotion near the main entrance caught his attention. Through the gaps between heads and shoulders, he spotted Daniel—smiling, shaking hands, pecking women on the cheek—wearing a forest green tuxedo and flanked by a security detail. Archie turned and moved away from Daniel as the crowd pressed forward. He rounded a large man wearing a kilt, side-stepped a blonde in a jade dress, collided with Daniel and froze.

A Cheshire-cat grin grew on Daniel's face. "Archibald!" He extended a hand.

Archie, caught off guard, shook.

Daniel pumped his hand while his handlers gave Archie a once-over. "Goodness, how long has it been? Where are you working, now?"

"Contract with NuCleen," Archie lied.

Daniel's grin grew. "Trying to take me down?"

Archie froze, something inside him whispering Daniel knew everything. He ignored it and returned the smile. "You're not the type to be afraid of competition."

"I pity my competition. I wish they would see the light and join me."

Past Daniel, Archie caught sight of a redheaded man carrying a tray of champagne.

"You know, Archibald, I am sorry how things ended between us. I could use someone like you. Someone not afraid to speak their mind. A special advisor, as it were, answerable only to me. However," Daniel took a step closer, "I'd need to know who the liars are at NuCleen spreading misinformation about my products. You know the company will fold in a month. Why not join me?"

Archie held Daniel's gaze, nodding. "I'll think about it."

Daniel smirked. "All I can ask." He glanced past Archie and waved. "Give me a call sometime. Let's catch up. For now, please excuse me." Daniel turned and was swallowed up by the adoring crowd.

Archie waited until the security detail had moved off before manoeuvring toward the server.

The server turned and the hairs on Archie's neck stood. He'd seen the server before. More words from Jimenez: move—never pause when you're trying to place someone. Archie casually took a flute of champagne, noting the golden nametag reading "Jacob" pinned to one lapel and a One Faith button to the other. "Excuse me," Archie began, "but I think the men's room might be out of order."

The server, Jacob, extended a white-gloved hand. "If you go through this door, the staff restroom is on the third level."

Archie noticed the door down a narrow service hallway, thanked the man and left the flute on a table. He cut his way through the crowd and opened the door onto a plain, off-white stairwell. Climbing, Archie tried to place Jacob. He made Archie not think of Daniel, but of Pious. He mentally scanned through faces at the safe house, but that didn't feel right. Exiting into a narrow, equally plain hallway, he thought of his excursions with Timothy and that felt closer. A group of housekeepers chatted down the hall, but paid him no mind as he passed several doors before finding the bathroom, still no closer to placing Jacob.

He stepped into a tiny room, barely large enough for a toilet and small closet. Archie shut the door, threw the deadbolt, and removed a key from under his large belt buckle that he used to unlock the closet. Within he found a fanny pack and the custom-made, battered leather suitcase he thought he'd seen the last of two days ago.

The memory clicked into place: the cyclist at the mall. Probably the same cyclist who'd stopped across the street later that night.

So Jacob had been watching him. But who'd sent him: Pious or Daniel? Archie looked in the mirror, giving himself a chance to back out, but the tanned, lined face of the old man stared back.

The village had looked deserted. They'd watched it for an hour, soaked in sweat and oppressive humidity, before moving in. The old man had come out of a hut, a rifle in one hand. Gaunt with dehydration and malnutrition, his threadbare clothing covered in what could have been mud or blood. He'd stumbled toward Archie, free hand reaching for the full water bottle on Archie's belt. Archie had drawn the combat knife he'd taken from a solider he'd killed two days before and plunged it into the man's neck. The man hadn't made a sound as he collapsed, eyes wide, free hand held to his gushing wound. Archie watched him die. He'd killed almost a hundred men by then, but always from a distance. He'd never smelled hot, coppery blood as it sprayed from a wound.

He'd felt nothing. Just empty.

Like now.

Archie turned away from his reflection. He opened the fanny pack, which contained white cotton gloves, several keys with fobs identifying them by letter, a One Faith button and a hotel nametag inscribed with "Paul." After tearing off the bracelet on his wrist, Archie pinned the nametag and button in place before donning the gloves, grabbing the case and leaving the room.

He followed the route through the building he'd memorized the night before, moving purposefully through halls and up staircases, suitcase in hand, never hesitating as he used his keys to gain access to restricted areas. Staff didn't pay any attention because, with the gloves, button and nametag, he looked like one of them.

Unlocking and opening the last door released Daniel's amplified voice. "—nations of the world, developing nations especially, need access to this technology." Archie stepped onto a narrow catwalk that lined the curved rear wall of the auditorium, high above the crowd. He climbed a ladder to a platform supporting a row of huge, oven-hot lights. His entire body broke into a sweat.

"The solution," Daniel's voice boomed, "is a single, worldwide economy with a single, worldwide currency." Applause broke out.

Archie opened the case, revealing the rifle's components. Assembling it, his shirt and underwear sweat-matted to his skin. He tried to swallow, but his mouth had gone bone-dry. On stage, Daniel's entire body moved as he spoke. "We can no longer *wish* that the world's industrialized nations will do what is right. The failures of Kyoto, Paris, and Melbourne prove this."

Approving applause shook the catwalk.

Archie loaded the rifle, lay down and balanced the rifle on its bipod.

"Nations who do not utilize green technologies must be forced to comply."

Shutting one eye, Archie looked through the scope.

"But we must be *united*," Daniel said, hand slicing the air and then going still. The applause rose, held for a moment and faded to expectant silence.

Archie blinked sweat from his eyes, centred the crosshairs on Daniel's head, and let old habits settle in: breath slow, don't move, feel your heart rate to shoot between beats.

"We must have one faith for our one world, with one currency and"—a smirk twisted the corner of Daniel's mouth—"one strong leader to show the way!"

The crowd erupted.

Archie squeezed the trigger. The report was lost in the sound of the frenzied crowd, who fell silent when Daniel flew backwards and out of Archie's sight.

Security swarmed the stage, guns drawn and scanning the now-screaming audience.

Archie dialled back the scope's magnification to see more. After several moments of panning the jostling bodies, he spotted Daniel. He lay on his back, limbs twisted, in a rapidly growing pool of blood. What remained of his skull left no doubt it had been a kill shot. An instant later, security guards obscured his view.

The satisfaction or triumph Archie had imagined didn't come, nor regret or guilt. Just the tired emptiness he'd felt as life left the eyes of that old man in the jungle.

Pious had instructed Archie to go back the way he'd come, holding the rifle like he was ready to open fire, and wait for security to make him a martyr. Archie didn't believe in martyrdom, but taking a round between the eyes was better than being caught.

But a fall from the catwalk would be quicker and remove any chance of bad aim.

He stood and swung a leg over the railing, looking down at the sea of roiling bodies screaming and pressing for the exits.

Hesitation gripped him—he might hurt or even kill someone down there.

But they were as guilty as Daniel.

He swung his other leg over, holding the railing with both hands and leaning into nothingness.

Another hesitation. He might kill one or two with his fall, but what about the others? They adored Daniel. They worshiped him. They wouldn't fade away with their Godhead dead. Someone would fill the vacuum.

Someone who might be worse.

But until that successor emerged, there was a window to fight back, to challenge what Daniel had created and expose him as a fraud. That meant organizing researchers and politicians who'd opposed Daniel. And being ready for the backlash the Disciplines were certain to unleash.

Another fight was coming. A fight he needed to be involved in.

Archie swung back over the railing onto the platform.

Leaving the gun, he descended the ladder to the catwalk, wondering if he could find Jacob. And if he could trust Jacob like he'd trusted Timothy. Opening the door, a cool breeze brushed Archie's skin. He stepped into the deserted hallway and headed back the way he had come.

leftfieldbrewery.ca
@LFBrewery

BALANCE

Did you know the driver of the other car?

—screeching tires, voices shrieking—

—deafening slam—

—rain-soaked, blood-streaked blacktop—

Brian's eyes shot open. Heart pounding, blood thundering in his ears. World teetering madly. "Oh god," he gasped. Fingers dug into torn polyester armrests. Bile pushed up his throat, threatening—

"No," he declared to the empty room, willing himself to take slow, deep breaths and lower his heart rate. He'd merely fallen asleep in his leather recliner in his media room and a man like him did not get rattled by something as trivial as a reoccurring nightmare. The dream's surreal imagery of the collision that had killed his wife and son was horrific, he admitted, but in reality he had not been present to witness the event.

He had had no indication anything had been amiss until the detective—

—*Did you know the driver of the other car?*—

Fingering his left palm. That scar. He yanked his hands apart.

The argument. What he'd said without thinking.

—*price and balance for everything*—

"I am not thinking about this," he declared, voice calm and even. He had nothing to balance nor a price to pay. All of it—the fight a few nights ago, the accident, talking to the detective ("Did you know—"), the fact that he did indeed know the other driver—amounted to nothing more than a bad dream brought on, no doubt, by a few vestiges of anxiety regarding his meeting tomorrow. Not that he had any reason to be concerned, but the importance of this meeting could not be overstated. Yet spending the night in this chair, as luxurious as its custom-made leather seat might be, would do him no good. He needed to turn in.

Painted in the dancing white-black of a dead TV channel, speakers roaring static, Brian's hand passed the tumbler and grasp the remote. The 72" plasma screen blinked and went dead, the Dolby 7.1 sound system fell silent, and darkness consumed the room.

Outside the floor-to-ceiling windows, the neighbourhood remained as still and dark—lit only by the streetlights—as when he'd sat down unknown hours ago. Calm, predictable, logical—the way he'd structured his life. His commitment to order and discipline had allowed him to transform from a barely-getting-by college student with a youthfully foolish interest in photography to the man he was today. He owned a 4,500 square foot home in one of Kanata's exclusive gated communities. A BMW M3 convertible waited in one of the garage's three spaces. Rather than become some poor photographer who scraped by while clinging to dreams of artistic success, he's built a career that had weathered the economic downturn. All before turning thirty. His sole unachieved goal remained a wife and children to provide the—

—balance—

—anchor he needed to remind him of what truly mattered among a life of tough negotiations, all-day meetings and hard-fought deals.

Brian flipped on the lamp on the small table—

The kitchen phone rang. He nearly screamed. His right hand found his left palm. For years, that scar hadn't been noticeable. Not unless he looked for it. But the next morning. After the fight. That barely-there scar had become a white ridge in his skin.

The phone rang again.

Not gonna answer, he told himself. What if it was that detective? More questions, she might say.

Or that girl—Chrissy—from so long ago at Camp McDonald? Maybe she'd tracked him down. Needed to remind him everything has a price and balance. That you couldn't forget. That he had to—

—believe—

Hands twisting in his hair. "Stopstopstop." He didn't have to talk to them. Any of them. He'd done nothing wrong. A road at night. A light rain. A drunk driver straying across the double yellow line. Happens all the time. No explanation or blame.

He didn't have to atone for not stopping—

For causing—

For *wishing*—

"Ridiculous."

The phone cut off in mid-ring.

He reached for the tumbler and downed the last swallow of 21-Year-Old Macallan, enjoying the complex flavour burning down his throat and flaring in his nostrils. Standing, he stretched out the kinks in his back, neck, and shoulders as he headed for bed. He cleared his mind, vowing that the dream would not return this night.

On the walls, photos he'd taken to document the triumphs of his life hung in a methodical grid. Vacation photos showed the Grand Canyon, the Canadian Rockies, a beautiful sunset over a beach in Hawaii, the streets of Paris. Above the television, one panel of a diptych showed his MBA graduation picture, the other held a shot of an airport baggage carousel. Random, he always admitted to himself, but he imagined that in the photo was the woman he loved gathering her bags after a year of backpacking in Europe in the moment before he would drop to his knee and propose.

Moving into the marble-topped and copper-accented kitchen, he noticed light spilling from under the dining room door on the far side. He must have forgotten to extinguish the lights the last time he'd been in there—

—bet you wish—

The stink of rotting food.

Right index finger stroking the scar.

—you know what?—

A stupid fight. She'd put away four rum and Cokes. He'd been on his fifth beer. Moving his equipment off the table. She'd started it. About money. Then what his mom might say when she came for dinner. Even imitated her ("Went to see Charlotte's *newest* granddaughter last week.") last time she'd been over. So he'd fired back. Told her *he* wanted kids. It had exploded—

—Bet you wish I was gone and that flaky bitch would come back! Would that make you happy?—

—You know what? It would!—

Something shattered. A feeling, an emotion. Like the air between them rippled for an instant. His heart trembled, his lungs deflated.

He didn't hear what she said next. Didn't seem like she felt it. Just grabbed her keys and said something about going to her sister's.

He'd let her go. Let her have her snit. She'd driven hammered before. No big deal. He'd flopped down in front of the TV.

Must have fallen asleep because the phone woke him.

Then a mad rush to the hospital.

The scar.

Remembering what he'd said—

And yet none *of that happened*, Brian reminded himself. An intense dream, to be sure, but still a dream. One he promised himself would not disrupt the sleep he required in order to be clearheaded for tomorrow's meeting. He crossed his immaculate kitchen to the dining room and something he could not make out in the darkness whispered under his feet. He mentally noted to have the maid attend to that in the morning as he opened the dining room door, reached for the light switch—

Photographs filled the room. Scattered across the small dining room table, spilling onto the floor. Piles covered plates and filled bowls. Photos of people and places. Like an entire life lay documented.

His life.

Brian shoved pictures of him holding Sam, his friend Jerry's son—huge smile on Brian's face, Sam only a few days old—off the nearest chair. He sat. Scooped up a handful of photos—shots of his parents, shot from high school.

Then photos of Janice—

—*that flaky bitch*—

—he'd thrown away years ago.

He dropped them to the floor. They faded like memories of a bad dream.

The corner of a handwritten letter stuck out from under some pictures. He shoved the photos aside—taken while trying to build a portfolio—and grabbed the sheet, yellow with age. Looping cursive talked about Brian's last letter—their future together, marriage, kids. She told him she was in this for the long haul. Except she didn't know about children. She knew Brian's feelings, but couldn't see herself as a mom. But they could talk about this when she got back from backpacking in Europe.

He let the letter drop. And it, too, was gone. Brian grabbed more pictures. These were of John. Ones the detective let him see. In a dozen shots, his son grew from infant to toddler to little boy.

Tears came instantly.

His son. His dead son.

He put his head down on the table. Wept . . .

—*Did you know the driver of the other car?*—

"Yes, goddamn it!" He sat up too quickly. Everything spun. He shut his eyes. When the world had righted itself, he let them open. He held the staff photo of Camp McDonald. He'd thrown it away years ago. All the photos from that summer. The negatives, too. Didn't want the reminder.

His twenty-year-old self stood at the right end of the back row, Janice near the centre of the front. Twenty-eight guys and thirty-one girls between eighteen and twenty-three, lined up in front of the recreation hall. All smiles. Pretending to be upstanding role models. Great experience for a resume to demonstrate how well-rounded one was.

They'd met the day the picture was taken. Talking, flirting. She'd laughed at his jokes, touching his arm. The way she cocked her head and looked at him from the corner of her eye made him hornier than any girl ever had. Turned out they went to the same university but had never met.

His right hand drifted toward his left palm. Brian curled it into a fist.

She was into folk music and leftist politics. Went to open-mic poetry nights and feminist groups meetings. Had no interest in a career, no long-term goals. She had no family—parents dead, no siblings, cousins, aunts or uncles—so nothing to tie her down. The perfect—

—*balance*—

—counterpoint to his structured, career-focused life.

And she'd been the one to push him to pursue photography. He'd always had an interest. Nothing serious. Nothing he could make a living doing. But it was enough for the camp director to let him take the photo. (Set the timer and run like hell.) But she'd pressed him. Urged him to get creative.

By September, they'd been living off-campus in a crap-hole apartment. His growing collection of photography equipment, which he really couldn't afford, fought for space with her collection of poetry books. His course notes got mixed up with her pamphlets. But it had been full-blown, drive-you-crazy love.

Then the next summer. Just after graduation. He'd always planned on an MBA. But as his portfolio grew, his grades had slipped. He'd been wait-listed at his safety school, rejected by the others. He'd have to reapply. Maybe take a few classes. Get his grades up.

What about us? Janice had asked.

He hadn't understood the question. They were fine. But he had a future to plan.

When Janice said she was going to Vancouver, he'd been crushed. Staying with friends, she'd said. Only a few months. Be back in September.

He didn't understand, but he let her go. He got a part-time job, which he quit as he built his portfolio and gained more clients. Every week, he wrote her, telling her about each new job.

His letters went unanswered.

So he asked what he'd done wrong. Why she'd left and didn't answer him.

Letters came back "NOT AT THIS ADDRESS."

It had been a Saturday. The end of November. The dark hours past midnight. The last of the bar crowd had gone home. The neighbourhood still and dark except for the streetlights. The TV just static. He couldn't afford the cable bill. That's when he'd accepted it. His new life was starting. Janice wasn't coming back.

—Did you know—

Brian blinked. The Camp McDonald picture gone. A police evidence photo of Janice's mangled car in its place.

"I'm sorry," he sobbed, collapsing forward. Nearly spilling out of the chair.

A free spirit. That's what he'd told himself. Had helped him find his passion in photography and moved on. Or maybe afraid she'd up the corporate wife of a company man.

He let the photo fall. It tumbled end over end and was gone.

Like Janice.

He blinked away tears.

His vision cleared. The photos were gone. Like they'd never been there. The white lace tablecloth—one of their few indulgences—lay smoothly over the small table, covering its gouged surface. Four second-hand chairs positioned around it. Four place settings from a set his parents had bought them. His photography equipment, usually scattered across the table, stacked on the shelves.

Just how he and Shelly had left it after preparing the room for dinner with Brian's parents. But the fight—

—make you happy?—

—you know what?—

Right here. This room. The epicentre of it all. Maybe it was the booze, but he could swear he felt that vibration in his chest. Could see the ripples of the shattered air. Like reminders demanding he—

—must respect—

—face what he'd done.

Brian stood. Unsteady legs heaved him toward the door.

This was on Shelly. He'd always been up front about it. He wanted kids. And she'd never said no. Even when he proposed. Right there in the airport after a year away. Snapped the pic and waited until she turned to grab her bags so he could drop to one knee. She'd said yes. No conditions. Nothing about not wanting kids. Never talked about what they'd have to—

—balance—

—trade-off to be together. But when he'd talk about kids, she'd start some fight. Turn it back on him.

Stumbling out of the room. Nausea spinning his head. That *déjà vu* of doing this a thousand times already. He slammed the dining room door. A cloud of flies buzzed into the air from the reeking pizza boxes and Chinese food cartons littering the small kitchen's counter. Under his feet, paperwork slid across the peeling linoleum floor. Forms from the hospital—green from legal, pink from administration, yellow from finance. Receipts from the funeral home. Copies of police reports.

—did you know—

He didn't know why the detective who'd told him Shelly had been killed wanted him to come to the station again. A few more questions, she'd said.

An hour later, Brian had entered a small storage room. Haphazard piles of photo albums, clothing, books, toys, envelopes yellow with age covered a desk and spilled onto the floor. He recognized the handwriting on some of the envelopes.

His handwriting.

An instant of confusion. Then panic.

The detective put it together. "Did you know the driver of the other car?" she asked. "Her name was Janice Wheeler."

A nine-year-old memory slammed forward in his mind: One night at Camp McDonald, out in that shack where everyone not a cabin duty gathered to drink some beer or smoke a little weed. Chrissy, who claimed to be Wiccan, performing some "magic love binding" spell. It had been Janice's idea. Janice said Chrissy had read her palm and tarot. Been right about so many things. Nonsense, Brian knew, but he wanted into Janice's pants.

Chrissy had cut small slices in his and Janice's left palms. They pressed them together. He'd been too young and dumb to worry about disease. Too stoned to feel pain. Then Chrissy said some gibberish, made them repeat it, and announced: "You are bound for life and for love. You can fulfill each other's happiness. Just make the wish." They'd giggled at that, knowing they'd be naked together in ten minutes. But Chrissy added: "Just remember, there is a price and balance for everything. And if you believe in the love that binds you, you must respect the magic that binds your love."

The detective pulled Brian from his memories. Told him Vancouver PD had had a hard time finding Ms. Wheeler's next of kin. A few officers had gone through the car looking for anything to help. They'd found his name in an address book in her luggage, a photo of him in her wallet, a few letters from about eight years ago. They'd run his background. Confirmed he used to live at the address in her book. Did he know the driver? Did he know why Ms. Wheeler was on the same road as his wife that night?

—bet you wish I was gone—

—flaky bitch would come back—

—must respect—

—make you happy—

—just make the wish—

—it would—

It couldn't be. To blame it on magic. Nonsense. Bullshit. But how to make sense of it? Of all the cars Shelly had passed, the chances that—

And, the detective also wanted to know, did Brian know the little boy in Janice's car who'd been killed? She'd passed Brian a handful of photos. Then an evidence bag containing a British Columbia birth certificate. The father's name a blank. But John Brian Wheeler had been born six months after Janice had moved out.

The boy had been premature, Brian told himself. Or Janice cheated on him—that's why she left. But in those photos he saw his chin, his mom's eyes, his dad's ears. And a day later, the detective had called with the DNA results. He wasn't just a widower, but had been a father for the last seven years.

And Shelly had killed him. Killed herself, killed Janice—

—there is a price and balance for everything—

The pantry. The bottle of rye on its side, dry and empty. He hurled it into a corner. It shattered. Jagged pieces joined the remains of other bottles. He grabbed the half-full bottle of Shelly's favourite rum, poured it to the rim, downed a swallow.

He killed the kitchen lights and headed for the den. He couldn't go to bed. Not *their* bed. Tomorrow, he had to meet with the funeral home director. Again. Two more burials. At least the director was cooperative. Told Brian that yes indeed Ms. Wheeler did have a nasty scar on her left palm. Looked recent, too.

Remains of picture frames he'd ripped from the walls cracked under his shoes. The best shots of his portfolio. Portraits of wealthy clients who'd paid well. Photos from the few vacations to Toronto or Mont Tremblant he and Shelly could afford. He couldn't stand seeing them.

Outside, hookers lit by the neon tattoo parlour signs strolled.

Why didn't Janice tell him she was pregnant? He would have supported her. He'd wanted to marry her. They would have—

"No," he said, putting the heel of his hand against his forehead. Why did he continue thinking about the convoluted situation contained within that dream? He didn't know a woman named Shelly, let alone having been married to her for several years. And yes of course he remembered Janice Wheeler. Quite fondly, in fact. Yet their relationship had begun and ended at Camp McDonald that one summer. He'd found her flights of fancy and laissez-faire attitude somehow endearing, an amusing—

—balance—

—counterpoint to his structured, career-focused life. As amazing as their sexual encounters had been, he'd drawn the line when she'd insisted that they engage in some kind of Wiccan magic nonsense. After a particularly heated fight, he had ended their relationship right then. It had made the reminder of the summer at Camp McDonald awkward, but he remained convinced it was for the best.

That fall, she must have transferred because he never saw her again on campus.

Since then, he had had a few promising relationships, but for a busy man like him maintaining a relationship proved to be one challenge too many. Soon, he hoped. Perhaps after this meeting tomorrow there would be the time to devote toward finding a woman he could love and raise children with.

Hoping that Janice—wherever she was—was living a good life since he honestly wished her no malice, he let a sip of the aged scotch—warm and smoky—slide down his throat.

Just one more drink, he told himself, to steady his nerves before turning in for the evening.

He punched the remote's power button, but each channel showed black-white snow. It reminded him of some night. Some realization from when he'd been younger. Giving up, he placed the remote and the tumbler on the table beside him. Such an important meeting tomorrow. Perhaps the most important of his life.

The white-noise roar of static lulled him, causing him to drift . . .

It occurred to him that he couldn't recall if he'd turned off the dining room light, but he was so comfortable . . .

Did you know the driver of the other car?

BUT IT'S NOT THE END

Local police cars escorting it front and back, the battered white bus pulled into the school's small parking lot. Once the trailing car was through, Hooper and Chen slid the razor wire-topped gate closed, shouting warnings in French and memorized Creole for the protestors to keep back.

Either the protestors' screams and chanted slogans drowned out the officers' words, or they didn't care. They gripped the chain link, shaking it, yet with a half-hearted effort. Like they wanted to show anger, but not get any closer to what was on the bus.

And it was just one bus. In yesterday's briefing, Hooper and the other officers had been told to expect several, maybe even ten. Word of the protesters must have reached the fenced-off ghetto at the edge of the city. So much for all that hype about making a statement.

The two police cars parked on the other side of the cracked, uneven lot, the cops staying inside the shade of their vehicles. Almost like they were also keeping their distance, letting the Canadians handle it. *But now they're Canadian, too*, Hooper thought, locking the gate.

"Okay, this is it," Captain Dorfeuille shouted over the bus's sputtering engine. Standing at the doors to the school, he removed his helmet and began to tuck it under his right arm, then switched to his left. After brushing off the front of his uniform, Dorfeuille readjusted the strap of his prod, hanging from his left shoulder rather than in hand and at the ready. In the briefing, he'd said he wanted to appear non-threatening.

If he wanted to do that, Hooper had thought, he should wear a UN baby blue helmet—a sure sign you held no real power.

"Let's look alive," Dorfeuille said to Chen and Hooper as they moved to join the other dozen tactical gear-clad officers.

Hooper saw Chen grin. Their new captain probably didn't realize some of the more sensitive bureaucrats back in Ottawa might consider it an insensitive remark.

The two men readied their own prods and joined one of the two lines of officers that formed a corridor from the bus to the school where Dorfeuille waited in front of an open set of double doors. The captain ran a hand across the stubble on his head, wiping away a sheen of sweat reflecting the hot tropical sun.

Outside the fence, the protesters had started to shout down each other. Taunts and insults in English, French, Creole, and Spanish. Catholics blamed Voodoo sects. Political groups denounced their rivals as American puppets. Rural groups claimed city dwellers were stealing relief supplies. And they all blamed the UN for something—the virus, the lack of aid in the first months, the occupiers and imperialists on their land. At least no one had set a car on fire.

Yet. It was only mid-morning. And in a couple of hours, this detail would be over and the squad would be back out there, trying to maintain some kind of order.

The door to the bus squeaked open and Hooper's thumb moved to his prod's safety. He hadn't been this close since that summer two years ago.

The first of the things shambled down the steps to the black top and lurched forward, dressed in a clean blue polo shirt and black slacks. Make-up tried to make its flat, ashen skin seem more natural.

Hooper's heart skipped and his vision narrowed—dark at the edges, colours vibrant at the centre. Ringing in his ears. Despite the tropical sun baking him in his dark blue fatigues, a chill gripped him.

Instincts screamed for him to run. Find a defensible position. Clear lines of fire. Multiple escape—

A bottle shattered somewhere behind him. One of the local cops yelled something in Creole.

More things followed the first off the bus.

On the other side of the fence, the shouts grew louder.

Hooper lifted his face shield a few inches and drew in slow, deeps breaths.

Next to Hooper, Chen asked: "You okay, Hoop?"

"Goddamned heat," Hooper replied, lowering the shield as the first things passed him on their way to the doors. He'd rather have his own warm, stale breath reflected back at him than gag on their stink—formaldehyde, the greasy smell of stage make-up, rancid meat.

"Good morning," Dorfeuille said in Caribbean-accented French once the things—about thirty—had exited the bus. "On behalf of the Canadian government, we welcome you. Today is an important day in the lives— Uh, important day for all Canadians, which you now are. The Prime Minister has asked—"

From somewhere in the crowd, a voice wheezed: "Can we move inside?" Deep and rich, with the accent of someone well educated, it was a voice Hooper recognized.

"Um, yes, of course." Dorfeuille turned and led the things through the doors, flanked by the two lines of Special Response Officers.

The interior was cooler and it took Hooper a second for his eyes to adjust. Most of the lights didn't work, the wall were in desperate need of a new coat of paint and only a handful of ceiling tiles remained. Just one of thousands of buildings in the newest Canadian province needing repair.

"Please remain within the yellow lines," Dorfeuille said, walking backwards. A few of the things gawked at the yellow tape local cops had laid down on the floor earlier that morning. It gave Hooper and the other officers a metre-wide space between the tape and the wall. "We're authorized to use force if you step outside them or disobey a command, but we do not want to do that." Dorfeuille stopped about ten steps from another set of doors and held up his hands. The shambling group came to a halt.

"Before you go in, I remind you to have your identification cards ready. Also, an officer will accompany you at all times. Unfortunately, that includes when you are completing your ballot."

To Hooper's left, the same deep voice groaned: "No. That is unacceptable." It was the living corpse of a short, pudgy man wearing a blue suit and red tie. Though Hooper had trouble telling the things apart, it seemed familiar.

A few of the things grunted their agreement. Some clapped.

"We have the same rights as . . ."—it drew in a wheezing breath—"everyone else." It took a defiant step toward the doors. Others followed.

"Arrêtes!" Hooper said—*Stop!*—flicking off the safety and raising the prod. His heart thudded under his body armor.

Some things flinched away, but others followed what seemed like their leader.

"Hooper, don't—" Dorfeuille sputtered. "Take it easy." He addressed the thing. *"Monsieur—"*

"We will enter now," it said. Almost all of the things were moving forward, forcing Dorfeuille back. "Our rights—"

One of the things—right in front of Hooper—stepped on the yellow tape. Hooper pulled the trigger.

Compressed air thudded as the spike flashed from the muzzle at the end of the prod, piercing the thing's head. It collapsed, brittle bones snapping as it struck the hard, tiled floor.

"Hooper! Damn it—!" Dorfeuille yelled, but moans and shrieks drowned him out. Wrecked bodies jostled in confusion and fear, colliding, some falling. The hall filled with *clicks* of disengaging safeties. Hooper—heart a jackhammer, mind tracking exit paths and the location of the other officers—considered dropping his prod and going for the submachine gun slung around his back. It got the job done two summers ago in Montreal when everyone thought it was the end. Back when you could shoot on sight. Back before they started talking, begging for their existence, demanding rights.

A few of the things broke away from the crowd and shuffled back down the hall, moving as quickly as their decayed limbs could carry them. Hooper had an instant to hope they'd go back to the fenced-in ghetto they'd been relocated to and stay there. But others were shuffling toward the officers, right up to the tape but not crossing it, curses coming in moans and croaks. Anger outweighed fear in their ruined features.

"Stay inside the lines! Please!" Dorfeuille shouted above the din. "Squad: back down."

Hooper felt it all falling apart. Dorfeuille couldn't control the situation. His skin colour and accent got him this command. He'd never done a tour here. And he'd been locked up safe and sound at police HQ during that summer.

The deep voice emerged from the crowd. "Be calm," it said in French. "Don't give them . . ."—it wheezed—"an excuse. Be calm."

Tension drained from the things, but Hooper remained focused.

"Squad," Dorfeuille repeated, "settle down."

Prods lowered. Safeties clicked back on. Hooper, keeping his safety off, silently cursed the other dozen officers. Of all of them, only he and Chen had survived that summer. The abattoir stench that filled the streets on searing-hot days. The welcome sounds of gunfire meant support was nearby. Chewing and slurping and ripping from darkened store fronts. Checking your buddies for bite marks or the telltale black-green discolouration around a wound. They'd made it through by taking the fight to the things.

Until some coward like Dorfeuille at HQ said to hold fire; the situation had changed.

With a wave from Dorfeuille, two officers dragged the corpse back down the hall, leaving a trail of black sludge like old motor oil from its wound.

Everything tilted. That gunk had taken down more of Hooper's men than the things themselves.

The two officers disappeared through the heavy doors that led to the parking lot. Eyes in dead faces watched them go—some holding fear, others anger. The doors slammed shut.

"Okay, everyone wait here," Dorfeuille announced. "I'm going to make sure they're set up." He locked eyes with Hooper. "I don't want any more incidents." He had to lean into the fire door that led to the school's gymnasium to get it to open. For a moment, Hooper caught a glimpse of terrified staffers—a mix of Canadians and locals—behind a registration table.

Last time Hooper had been down here three years ago, he'd been trying to keep the peace after their presidential elections. Canadians, Poles, French—plenty of men and equipment but no will to use them as groups fought and burned and looted. He'd rotated home after three months.

The virus had hit less than a year after that. Without an organized government to fight back, casualties on this island—and other unstable countries—had hit almost forty percent.

When it was all over, the countries that were still standing decided that rather than sending peacekeepers and aid, the best way to deal with the chaos was absorb those countries. The American flag now had fifty-seven stars and Canada had four new provinces. New provinces where the "human rights" of these things needed to be protected.

"You had no reason to . . ." the same voice that had called for calm began, now speaking unaccented English, ". . . kill Georges." It emerged from the crowd of decaying bodies to stand before Hooper. Make-up, trying to hide what looked like a grenade's shrapnel wounds on its face, cracked around its ruined jaw as it spoke.

The wounds told Hooper why it looked familiar. Its name had been Jean-Henry Marcelin. A fringe politico in life, now it spoke for the things' rights. Not just voting, but the right to marry, adopt kids, run for office. It had organized bus rides to voting stations all over the city. And when threats of violent protests had started, it had been the one to call for police protection.

"It crossed the tape," Hooper replied.

"It was an . . . accident—"

"What, you want *more* special treatment?" Hooper gripped his prod tighter. "Bad enough we got to let you in here."

The thing moved forward, feet dragging through the deadly black sludge, making Hooper's guts clench. Didn't matter that scientists—in their labs after it was all over—said ten seconds' exposure to air killed all trace of the virus. A bite or scratch, even splatter in your eyes or mouth, would turn someone. The toes of the thing's well-polished shoes stopped inches from the yellow tape. "The Canadian Supreme Court has . . . ruled that we have the same rights—"

"They didn't see what I saw." Hooper's head swum with the memory of three things yanking loops of guts from his partner's clawed-open belly, still alive and screaming for a bullet in the head. "What your kind can do."

"We regret our actions in . . . the grip of the rage," the thing said in French. The crowd muttered its agreement. "Yet we have committed . . . to nonviolence. You must have known Georges . . . was no threat."

Hooper felt the other officers' eyes on him. In English, Hooper replied. "It knew the rules. It broke them."

"And what of the rules . . . protecting us? The courts declared *les revives* . . . equal and yet we are . . . segregated in camps . . . and denied jobs. In the countryside . . . we are hunted down and . . . executed. Where are you to enforce . . . your laws?"

Hooper brought his prod across his chest. "You telling me how to do my job?"

"Hoop," Chen, to his left, said. "Stay cool, man."

"No, I'm not taking shit from one of these things."

"We commit to the . . . betterment of our home," Marcelin said, again addressing the crowd. "Yet we are called 'it' and 'things' by . . . those sent to ensure our . . . safety. O Canada, indeed."

A few of the things sniggered—dry, hacking gasps.

"I'm not here for you." Hooper shoved the thing with his prod, knocking it back a step. "I'm here to keep the living from killing each other. A president leaves and you riot. You hold elections and riot again. You blame America, the UN, anybody but yourself."

The thing raised its skinless hands. "And now you assault me . . . violate my rights on . . . a day—"

Hooper whipped the prod up, setting the butt against his shoulder and taking aim. "You want to see your rights violated?"

"Hoop," Chen warned, his tone communicating what he left unsaid—he didn't have Hooper's back.

The think stepped back, moving out of the prod's range. "I'm behind the line. You . . . have no right to threaten . . . me with lethal force."

Hooper advanced, stepping back in range. "Lethal? Lethal! You're already dead."

Another officer: "Hooper, man, be cool."

Retreating back another step, it said: "You cannot—"

Hooper followed. "Can't? Can't what?"

"He talks," another thing—right to Hooper's left—said in thickly accented English. "Just talks."

Hooper glanced at it. At the things on either side of it. And behind it.

He'd moved right into the middle of them.

Fear snatched at him and he went with it. He dropped the prod, reached for the submachine gun—

Chen: "Hoop, don't!"

Safety off—

"Hoop—"

Stock in shoulder, barrel up, finger—

Two gunshots cracked. Something slammed into his chest, knocking him back. Stumbling, he squeezed the trigger, a burst of gunfire arcing up through the things and into the ceiling. Sparks flew. Pain blossomed in his chest under his body armor.

The things scattered, panicked, knocking into him and bouncing off.

"Hooper, drop the weapon!" Dorfeuille had his pistol aimed at Hooper.

The son of a bitch had shot him.

Hooper brought the gun up again, fired at the crowd of fleeing—

His left leg collapsed and he hit the ground on his back. A white-hot sting shot through his thigh, hot warmth gushing down his leg. Panic spread above him, bodies moving, voices shouting in fear and confusion. Through scissoring legs, he glimpsed things on the floor, unmoving, holes in their skulls leaking black sludge.

Looking behind him, he found a path clear of the poison to get against the wall. Shoving with his good leg, he left a smear of blood.

Gun up, searching for a clean shot through—

Pain seared through his wounded leg. A thing—jaw gone and sludge leaking from an empty eye socket—lay on its belly, twisting its finger into his leg. Hooper screamed in pain, hate, fury. He swung his gun around—

Gloved hands snatched it. A boot on his chest pressed him flat. "It's over Hooper!" Dorfeuille stood over him—*on* him—pistol trained on his head. Behind Dorfeuille, Chen slung Hooper's submachine gun over his shoulder before yanking the thing away by its feet. Its finger popped out and Hooper screamed. Two more officers knelt, ripping open his pant leg. "Jesus, you nicked something, Captain," one said. He pulled his radio from his vest and shouted 10-codes for a downed officer.

With an order from Dorfeuille, the second officer took Hooper's pistol and passed it to the captain. Dorfeuille removed his foot to let his men work. Hooper grit his teeth against the pain as the officers pressed their gloved hands to his wound. Blood seeped through their fingers. Chen appeared with an aid kid. Up and down the hall officers had the things up against the walls and under control. The thing that had jabbed him was on its feet, lined up with the others against a bank of lockers. It spotted Hooper, held up its finger—still smeared with Hooper's blood—and pointed to its empty eye socket.

Panic seized Hooper. He grabbed Dorfeuille' ankle.

Dorfeuille, who'd been telling Chen to check on the civilians in the gym, looked down at him. "Settle down, Hoop."

"Shoot me!"

"Hoop—"

"Shoot me, you numb fuck! I'm infected." He waved a hand at the one-eyed thing. "You—" An officer at his leg poured pure agony into the wound. Hooper roared, hands balling into fists. "Shit! If you're any kind of real cop you'll take me out!"

Dorfeuille glanced down at Hooper's leg, at the thing against the wall. The other officers had gone quiet, watching.

"Do it!" Hooper screamed. The exertion made him dizzy, his vision cloudy. He was running out of time. "Ain't one of you cops man enough?"

"I cannot do that," Dorfeuille told him. "Regs say—"

Hooper aimed a fist at Dorfeuille' boot but missed, striking the floor. "I won't be one of them!"

From the crowd, the deep voice: "There's a program to help with . . ." a wheeze ". . . the transformation."

"No—!"

It continued: "We can help—"

"You said you were nonviolent, you liar! Your follower killed me!"

Doors burst open at the far end of the hall. Two local paramedics rushed in, a portable gurney clattering between them.

"Over here," Dorfeuille called. "Possible infection." Dorfeuille stepped away to make room. Hooper reached after him, but Chen held him down.

"Lie still," one the medics told him as he began to work.

"Shoot me, man," Hooper begged Chen, spittle flecking against Chen's face shield. "Do it!"

"There's jobs on the force," Chen told him, hands on Hooper's elbows. "You can still be a cop. Or take your pension—"

"No!" Hooper wanted to tear out Chen's throat with his teeth. He fought to jab a finger at Dorfeuille, strength waning. His eyes failed to focus. "If I come back, I'm coming"—he had to stop and take a breath—"for you. I'm gonna"—another breath into lungs that refused to fully inflate—"fucking *feast* on you."

"Wound is discoloured," the paramedic said. A bright light shined in Hooper's eyes. He tried to swat at it, but his arm just flopped across his chest. "Pupils not responding. He's infected." He said something in Creole to his colleague. Hooper caught enough to know it meant not to bother treating the wound on his leg.

"Cut it off," Hooper gasped. "Might be time."

"Book him," Dorfeuille said, motioning to the one-eyed thing. "Aggravated assault on a cop."

"Assault?" Hooper managed to get out. "He's killed . . ."

"I am disappointed . . . in you, Max," the deep voice—Hooper couldn't remember its name—said.

"You're not going to die," Chen told him. "It'll be different, but it's not the end."

"Can I borrow your cuffs and a gag?" the other medic asked of Chen. Chen reached for the equipment on his tactical belt.

An arm free, Hooper tried to reach for him, but his arm merely twitched.

Chen—fading to a blue blur—said: "You'll get through this, Hoop."

Colour drained from the world as Hooper felt more than saw the medic fit restraints around his hands—which refused to obey Hooper's commands to fight, punch, claw—like he was some perp. Then his feet. Fingers pried open his jaw for the gag and Hooper could smell the sweat on them. He tried to lunge and bite, but his jaw refused to move.

He had to fight back. Fight something. Kill something.

Consume something.

Because those fingers . . . so close to his mouth . . . so hungry . . .

ONLY AT THE END DO YOU SEE WHAT FOLLOWS

Arthur hadn't set foot in his house in over three years. He knew what waited for him within.

The closest he came was parking down the street in the shade of the oaks overhanging Ridgeline Crescent. From that anonymous distance, he'd watch his sister-in-law, Connie, meet the potential renters on the porch steps. She'd do her real estate agent thing—telling them the features of the house and how great the neighbourhood was before leading them inside. Connie had told him owners shouldn't be at a showing, but he'd explained he just wanted a glimpse of the people who might end up living in the house where he and Jacqueline had spent seven years of marriage. And where Jacqueline had died. Connie had agreed to the compromise, admitting at least it got Arthur out of the small apartment where he lived now.

But the truth, which he couldn't tell Connie, was rather than waiting for her call, he wanted to see the reactions of the potential renters. The ones Jacqueline hadn't named usually left with a shrug and handshake. But some stumbled down the steps, looking to one another and back at the house. One might be crying. Or screaming. Connie doing her best to console them.

And, so far, the couples whom Jacqueline *had* named emerged all smiles and enthusiasm, gesturing excitedly at the house.

Sweat trickling down his sides, Arthur now waited for Connie to come out with Bronwyn, the latest potential tenant.

But it's Bronwyn and Owen, Arthur told himself, not sure if he'd said it aloud or in his mind. *"Bronwyn and Owen."* When Connie had called two days ago telling him a Bronwyn Lumley had moved to the city and wanted to see his house, he'd asked about a husband or boyfriend.

"Nope," Connie had replied. "Heigh-ho, the derry-o, the Bronwyn stands alone." She'd verified Bronwyn had a good job, good credit, and good references, so no need to worry.

But he did worry. It wasn't just the five months without a tenant nearly depleting his modest savings. Each passing month without the appearance of "Bronwyn and Owen" shook his faith in what Jacqueline had told him. Put his future more and more in doubt. She'd named "Bronwyn and Owen" between "Lynette and Francis," who'd moved out suddenly after only a month, and "Anna and Jorge." If Jacqueline had said "Jennifer and Owen" or "Sarah and Owen," he wouldn't have been so worried by a single woman with that name wanting to see his house. Plenty of Sarahs in the world.

So when the crimson Mercedes had pulled up and the forty-something woman in the stylish pantsuit and heels had emerged, he'd still expected a man to step out of the passenger door. Instead, the two women had gone inside.

He knocked against the steering wheel, waiting. Even in the trees' cool shadows, the bright summer morning baked the car. His own stink from not showering for three days mixed with fresh cut grass, the jasmine and wisteria erupting in the late summer's heat and humidity. He checked his watch: fourteen minutes since Connie and Bronwyn had gone inside.

A good sign, in its way. Those who weren't interested didn't stay more than ten minutes. The ones who left screaming lasted even less. Once they'd gone, Connie's professional demeanor would fall away like a puppet's strings being cut: head bowed and shoulders hunched, unbuttoning the jacket of her tailored suit. She'd stomp to Arthur's car and explain what had happened. "They heard voices in the bedroom," she'd told him after the first incident. Other problems had followed.

Something about the place made them uneasy.

The wife or girlfriend got a sudden, fierce headache.

The husband or boyfriend smelled blood.

After the third squabble, Connie had explained: "Our good, young netizens research homes. Check police records. Find if there's been trouble. Then use it to try to negotiate the rent down. Sickos."

She'd asked him if it upset him and he'd replied he was fine, which was true. Jacqueline hadn't named those people. They didn't matter. Bronwyn and Owen did.

So if Bronwyn—just Bronwyn—rented the house, what did that mean for everything that was to follow?

A pair of joggers passed by on the sidewalk. Desperate to focus on something, he watched their outfits wink from vibrant to muted as they passed in and out of the trees' deep shadows. A low aperture stop with a fast shutter would capture them mid-stride. He cast about for other shots. Something to fill the time. The wrought-iron railing of his front porch. Its intricate detailing that Jacqueline had loved. A higher stop, then, to preserve every angle and curve.

But thoughts of picking up his camera again just reminded him of the three unheard voicemails from Reggie waiting on his phone. Maybe just letting Arthur know about some touch-up work heading his way, but no doubt Reggie wanted to know if Arthur had thought any more about partnering with him to buy the studio now that the boss was retiring. Reggie had raised 70% of the cost, so Arthur would buy in as a junior partner. That meant business decisions would rest with Reggie, but that suited Arthur fine. He'd never been one for responsibility.

No more mindless anniversary and family portraits, Reggie had promised. A real studio and gallery, like they'd dreamed about for the ten years they'd worked together. Arthur just didn't have the money. He could go to the bank, putting the equity in his house up as collateral, but if the business failed, he'd lose the house.

Lose Jacqueline.

And they were supposed to be together in the end.

But if Jacqueline was mistaken about Bronwyn and Owen—

The front door opened and Arthur leaned forward. Down the street, the two women emerged from the house. After shaking hands, Connie passed over an information slip and business card. Bronwyn strode to her Mercedes and drove off. Connie waved until the car turned the corner, then walked the half block to Arthur's car.

Arthur white-knuckle gripped the steering wheel.

"She says she'll think about," Connie said, getting in the passenger seat. "But I don't have a good feeling."

Arthur's stomach dropped.

"So," Connie continued, "we've got some tough choices. The market tells people 'buy,' not 'rent.' We need to lower what we're asking. Make it competitive." She explained a lower rent would mean extending his mortgage's amortization period and a likely penalty for renegotiating, but Arthur barely heard her. He'd follow any advice Connie offered.

Except Jacqueline hadn't mentioned changing payments. Just to rent the house. Rent it, right now, to a couple named Bronwyn and Owen.

"And if that doesn't work," Connie went on, "and I hate to say it, but it might be time to think about selling. You have enough equity in the house that you'll be okay for a while."

"I'll think about it," Arthur replied, not knowing what else to say.

Connie took his right hand in her left and squeezed it, not seeming to mind its sheen of sweat. She said, "Why don't you come by for dinner tonight?"

Arthur had no plans. He never had plans. But his older sister had never liked surprises. "Will that be okay with Laurel?"

Connie grinned. "I'll make sure it's 'O,' 'K,' and the other twenty-four letters with Laurel."

They discussed when he should arrive and what he could bring, settling on six o'clock and a bottle of red wine. Arthur made a mental note to pick up a bottle of the Argentinean Malbec Jacqueline had been fond of. Connie went back to her car and Arthur drove away, but circled back to Ridgeline Crescent and, seeing Connie had gone, stopped in front of his house. Bored by condos in the Central Business District and row homes' homogeneity, Jacqueline had fallen in love with the house's ironwork railings, wide porch and the master bedroom's gabled dormer windows. And some years from now, after the income from the renters she'd named had allowed him to pay off the mortgage, Arthur would move back in to be with her.

Unless, for the first time, she'd been wrong.

Or, more likely, he'd misunderstood what she wanted from him.

He tapped the steering wheel, telling himself he could face what was inside. Not just the memories.

He had to hear it again. Had to be certain.

He got out of the car and hurried around to the side door. Unlocking it, he swallowed and stepped inside.

The house seemed a parody of its former self. Even after three years, he didn't realize he'd been expecting potpourri and the votive candles Jacqueline had loved. Instead, a faint citrus smell hung in the air. On the walls, neutral tones covered the bright and flamboyant colours Jacqueline had selected. The abstract black and white photos she'd hung, including some of his work under her tutelage, had been taken down. All traces of Jacqueline—the unbearable reminders of the hollow spaces her death had carved in his life—had been stripped away. Like he was an intruder in a stranger's home. Like he didn't belong.

He turned and climbed the back staircase, the steps' familiar creak filling the silence, to the upstairs hall where a pine-scented air freshener replaced the citrus. All the doors stood open, except the master bedroom's, sunlight spilling from the south-facing bedroom across the polished hardwood. He approached it and reached for the curved, brushed nickel handle, but paused. He hadn't been in this room—the bedroom they'd shared, where she'd betrayed him, where she'd died—in three years. Empty now, except for some part of her that awaited his return. A return she'd foreseen happening years from now.

He grabbed the handle, turned it and pushed the door open.

Alone. Her voice. So perfect. So alive. She might have been standing beside the doorway.

Tears welled, cold creeping along his skin. "Yes, I'm alone." He swallowed, not sure how to begin. "She—Bronwyn, I mean . . . I don't think she's taking the house."

Echoing in the room's emptiness: *Bronwyn and Owen. Arthur, alone.*

Arthur considered moving into the room. Instead, he remained at the threshold. "But there's no Owen. Were you wrong? Should I do something different?"

Lynette and Francis. Bronwyn and Owen. Anna and Jorge.

"Jess, please! Tell me what you mean."

Arthur, alone.

"What should I do?"

She remained silent.

A familiar lump settled in Arthur's throat. The kind when he pushed too hard and provoked her icy silence.

He turned, went back down the stairs and out the side door. She'd said what she would say, repeating what she'd already told him. Even in death, she remained unwavering in her certainty.

He tried to take comfort from that, yet reaching the car his unease still clung to him like his shirt to his sweat-soaked back.

He parked in the narrow lot wedged between the apartment building and a beige low-rise office complex, the sky a narrow strip of blue five storeys up. During the ride from his house, he'd promised himself that he'd return to the apartment, grab his camera and spend the afternoon taking shots. Maybe shadows crossing the Gardener Building's gothic façade. Or slow shutter-speed shots of tourist-filled squares, rendering people as blurry ghosts but the buildings sharp and eternal.

In the elevator, Arthur played Reggie's voicemails. The first two asked for an update. The third told Arthur that someone else had expressed an interest in the partnership. If he didn't hear from Arthur by the end of the week, Reggie would accept the other offer. Reggie finished by inviting Arthur to come by the studio, regardless of his decision. It had been too long since he'd seen him.

Arthur deleted the messages and went searching for his camera, not certain where he'd put it, fighting the momentum of his usual daily routine. He wouldn't pass this day like every other—torturing himself with other photographers' Flickr, Instagram, and Tumblr accounts. He had to do something to fill the empty hours between now and when he'd go to Connie and Laurel's. When he'd been with Jacqueline, he'd rarely had idle time.

They'd met at the studio, her looking for help with some Nikon auto-everything that they didn't sell. She was an attractive woman, so Arthur played along. She returned twice more to speak specifically with Arthur, which puzzled him until Reggie clued him in that she must like him and he should ask her out. When Arthur reminded Reggie of the policy of not dating customers, Reggie reminded Arthur that the woman had never actually purchased anything.

So the next time she came in he asked for her number. Smiling, she wrote it on the back of a business card and handed it to him, adding, "Took you long enough."

She managed an art gallery in the Central Business District, so they talked photography and toured exhibits. He integrated into her circle of friends, meeting artists, gallery owners, and agents. She got him into the *nouveau avant garde* movement sweeping the city, saying his own work tended to veer into the pedestrian the more expressive he tried to be. Bookings and showings became so frequent he had to quit the studio to keep up. She took over organizing his shoots and showings, saying he didn't have it in him to be his own boss.

Though his place was bigger, he moved into her Garden District condo. Sometimes, he returned from a shoot to find the short-sleeved, plaid collared shirts he liked gone from the closet. In their place hung Tommy Hilfiger polos. Or Diesel and Guess jeans occupying the drawer where his Levis had been. It was all part of the image he needed, she told him, if he wanted to succeed.

He proposed to her after two years and Jacqueline arranged her dream wedding.

At some point, a suspicion of infidelity had grown. Late nights at the gallery, always a given, grew more frequent. At parties or openings, she laughed at other men's jokes and touched their arms or chests.

He wondered what he had done. If she wanted to vacation in London, they went to London. He let her pick the restaurants to eat at or which friends to meet up with after work.

It had been a Tuesday in June when a shoot in the Garden District ran an hour late. The ringtone for his home line chimed on his phone and he held his breath when he answered. Instead of Jacqueline asking where he was, a police officer told him there had been an accident and he needed to get home right away. Details would be lost in a blur of grief, but by the time Laurel drove him to her place for the night, he'd learned Jacqueline had tripped, fallen, and fatally struck her head. The police had informed him a man had been with her, but refused to release his identity. They had no evidence of foul play. Learning the man's identity would only make the situation worse.

Days and nights at Laurel and Connie's flowed together. Laurel, always the big sister, dealt with the lawyers and funeral home's paperwork, presenting him with things to sign. She hired people to clean up his house. Connie sat with him, listening as he alternated between blubbering and ranting.

The funeral came and went, memories of tears, hugs, and condolences blurry and vague, like an amateur photographer not knowing how to set a focal length.

Then Laurel, still the big sister, moved him back into his house, telling him he needed to get on with his life. Thankfully, Connie convinced Laurel that they should spend that night with him.

And so the first night in what had become his—not their—bed, Jacqueline's voice roused him from a fitful sleep: *Find my camera*.

"Jacqueline?" he asked the darkness before turning on the bedside lamp, revealing the empty bedroom. Thinking it a dream, he rolled over, clutched the pillow and sobbed into it.

Her voice came again, repeating the message. He jumped out of bed, searching the closets and en suite bathroom before moving into the hall. Laurel found him in the living room and told him he'd been dreaming, which she repeated the next morning when Arthur told her he had heard Jacqueline twice more that night.

Connie was a bit more accepting, telling Arthur maybe Jacqueline had something to tell him. "Like apologize," Laurel added.

Once they left, he searched for the camera. Laurel had probably been right. Or he was going crazy. In the haze of sleeplessness and fatigue, either was acceptable.

He eventually found the camera between Jacqueline's dresser and the wall. A massive video file took up almost all of the memory. Transferring the file to his computer, he sat stunned as the video's opening shot showed Jacqueline in their bed pulling the covers over her bare breasts. She gave the camera a familiar icy stare.

"Put that down," she said.

"Come on, relax," a man's voice Arthur didn't recognize replied. "I'll take the vid card when I leave. Something to remember you by."

"Bullshit you are." Jacqueline threw back the covers, revealing she was naked, and defiantly got out of bed. She closed on him, reaching, but the image lurched back. The image stabilized on Jacqueline grabbing a pair of black lace panties from the floor.

"This was a mistake," she said, pulling them on. The image lingered on her as she put on a black lacy bra Arthur hadn't seen her wear in years.

"You still trying to make him jealous?" the man asked, keeping his distance. "Hoping he'll finally man up? Jesus, Jess. He'll never grow a spine. Either be honest with him or leave him."

Grabbing her skirt from the floor, she said, "He's got talent. Unlike you. He needs guidance. He'd fall apart without me." She stepped into her skirt.

The camera moved closer, focused on her breasts. "But do you love him?"

In response, she reached out again. The image rolled, panning across the ceiling before returning to Jacqueline in mid-fall, skirt twisted around her ankles, arms extending in a vain attempt to halt what gravity demanded. It followed her fall. Her head made a soft, anticlimactic knock against the footboard, then she lay still on the floor. The man screamed profanity and the camera fell, landing on its side with Jacqueline's head and shoulders visible in the lower part of the frame.

Arthur stopped the playback, biting back the urge to vomit, and staggered away from the computer. A sharp edge of rage pressed like a knifepoint against his breast bone, propelling him from room to room, cursing and screaming accusations until hoarse. Exhausted, he had collapsed on the couch and faded into sleep. At some point during the night, he had roused himself and climbed the stairs, head thrumming in a post-rage hangover. He found the bedroom door closed. Upon opening it, Jacqueline's voice said: *Watch the video. Listen.*

He'd screamed and nearly backpedalled down the steps. Breath hitching, he approached the open, dark doorway. "Jess?"

Watch the video. Listen.

He burst into the room, equal parts wanting to embrace and throttle her. He flicked on the overhead light, finding the room as he had left it—bed unmade, clothing scattered. A condition Jacqueline would never have tolerated.

"Where are you?!"

Her voice, from all sides of the bedroom, like he was within her: *Watch the video. Listen.*

Her calm authority soothed him. "What is this? Please, Jess." He waited, emotions ebbing and flowing, until the realization dawned that either he had lost his mind or some part of Jacqueline had never left this room.

With sleep far off, he did as she told him. At his computer, he fast-forwarded through her death and then listened as the man tried to rouse her and finally called 911. Beneath this man's pleas for an ambulance to come quick, Arthur heard Jacqueline mumbling.

He rewound to the beginning of the file and slid the volume selector to maximum. The sound of her skull striking the footboard shot bile up his throat. In the moment after, her eyes staring, Arthur heard Jacqueline's voice: "Find my camera," and, after enduring the man's scream at full volume, "Watch the video. Listen."

Rewinding and zooming in on Jacqueline's face, Arthur saw her lips moving in time with the words. While her lover whined "ohmygod" somewhere out of frame, Jacqueline mumbled: "Rent the house." As the video wore on, he could make out a few more words and phrases, but most were lost in the man's frantic screams.

When the paramedics arrived, the camera was knocked into the corner, the unmoving image of the side of the dressed filling the computer screen. The paramedics exchanged questions and instructions offscreen while Jacqueline's lover begged her to wake up. The clatter of what must have been a gurney. Then the voices retreated, fading, and silence from the video file.

Arthur put his head down, processing that he had watched his wife's death. Fatigue stole in and he let it take him. But her voice said: "Find my camera." He shot up. The screen still showed the side of the dresser, the timer continuing to run. "Watch the video," Jacqueline said from the computer speakers. "Listen." A few moments later: "Rent the house."

Pairs of names followed, all of them the coming tenants. A few times, there would be a few words in addition to the names. Like "James and Mary, the baby" or "Colette and Henri, the fight." The names ended with "Midori and Yoji" and her next words were "Arthur, alone." After this came terms Arthur assumed would make sense once he had moved back into the house: "glass," "northeast," "bus driver," "scar," and ten others. After a few minutes of silence, she began again with "Find my camera."

He stopped the file and moved into their bedroom. The sun had come up by then, golden light chasing dark shadows into corners.

She spoke him, her voice coming from everywhere: *"Rent the house,"* and listed the names and notes for the tenants to come, then the fourteen words and finished by repeating *"Rent the house"* over and over. He'd asked her questions, pleading, but she never wavered. Even as he left the room and shut the door, she continued to tell him what she needed him to hear.

He called Connie later that morning. By the end of the week, he was in the small apartment she'd found for him and arranged for movers to put the rest of their—*his*—things in storage.

Laurel used her older sister's privilege to harass him to call some friends, get back to work and get on with life. But he could barely find the energy to get dressed most mornings.

Some of Jacqueline's friends invited him out for dinner, but he declined. He suspected some of them knew Jacqueline had been cheating on him. Besides, he'd always felt they merely tolerated him as Jacqueline's husband who sat quietly while Jacqueline held court.

It hadn't taken long for the calls and texts to stop and, along with them, contract offers.

Fortunately, Reggie passed along editing and touch-up jobs Arthur could do at home. Between that and his dividend from the rent, he made ends meet. Still, there were lean times between tenants. In three years, two of the four sets of tenants had moved out without warning. James and Mary had accused him of planting a speaker in the bedroom. Mary said a woman's voice would wake her saying "the baby." Connie denied this on Arthur's behalf, but it didn't stop James from doing several thousand dollars in damage punching holes in the walls looking for a speaker when Mary miscarried the child she hadn't even known she'd been carrying. Lynette and Francis had left five months ago without any explanation.

Now he waited on Bronwyn and Owen.

He gave up on locating his camera. "Tomorrow," he promised himself, sitting on his couch and grabbing his laptop.

He roused himself, not knowing when he'd fallen asleep, and showered.

He arrived at Laurel and Connie's promptly at six. Laurel greeted him at the door wearing a red silk top, but shorts and bare feet. The comforting smell of jambalaya made his stomach grumble. Connie appeared from the kitchen, her suit replaced by a T-shirt and shorts. He passed over the wine, feeling awkward and foolish in his collared shirt and slacks.

After hugs of greeting they moved inside, Connie pouring him and herself a glass. Laurel mixed a four-olive martini and settled on the couch next to Connie, Arthur on the loveseat.

"So," Laurel began, "how's work?"

"Good," Arthur replied, feeling the same way he had when his mother had asked about his grades. He sipped his wine to be polite. He'd never cared for malbec.

"What are you working on?"

"Nothing," Arthur admitted. He hadn't shared the news about Reggie's offer, not wanting Laurel's interference. She'd used her retirement savings to open a boutique grocery in the University District after quitting as the manager of a supermarket. "Not at the moment, anyway."

Laurel leaned toward him and Arthur waited for another of her lectures. Instead, she simply said: "We're worried about you."

Connie nodded and Laurel took her hand. Laurel continued, "Connie told me the showing today didn't go well and it hit you hard. I'm scared you're putting too much faith in renting the house and not enough in yourself. Our wedding photos are beautiful. And I've had friends who wanted to hire you, but I didn't know if you were up to it. And maybe that was a mistake. Maybe I've been too hard on you." She looked to Connie, who nodded reassurance.

"I can convert a small corner of my shop into a studio for you," Laurel continued. "I'll show you how to set up accounts and keep books. Hell, I can keep your books for you."

Before Arthur could process this, Connie added: "It's not just having something to do. I ran some numbers. About lowering the rent? A competitive rent, after mortgage and taxes, would leave you just enough to buy a cup of coffee. I mean gas station coffee. And that's assuming the bank will renegotiate. To do that, they'd want you working full-time. And if you're working full-time, it's better to move back into the house instead of carrying a rent and a mortgage in this uncertain market."

Arthur's shifted in his seat. Jacqueline had intended that he move back into the house, but only after the last tenants—Midori and Yoji—had moved out. But there were five more sets of tenants between now and then, including Bronwyn and Owen.

Unless this was how Owen would appear. "If we're lowering the rent, let's call Bronwyn and offer it to her."

"I did," Connie said. "I floated the idea. She thanked me and told me it's not right for them."

Arthur's heart skipped beat. "Them?"

"Oh, forgot to tell you. She has a son named—"

Owen.

"—Owen. Just turned eighteen. To teach him some responsibility, she wants to put his name on the contract. But she says a house that size is just too big."

Arthur's breath left him.

Laurel took his hand and said: "I know it's a lot to think about. And maybe selling the house is the smart move. Let it go. Start something new."

Head going light, Arthur asked: "She's certain? Bronwyn. She's *not*—"

"She told me she's signing with Century Gate condos in the morning," Connie replied.

"Excuse me." Arthur stood and stumbled to the bathroom, falling to his knees before the toilet.

A new future unspooled before him. One without the comfort of Jacqueline's predictions. He'd need to make decisions, their outcomes unknown.

Arthur, alone.

He'd always assumed she'd meant that when he moved back into the house after Yoji and Midori, he'd be by himself. But perhaps she meant that when he returned, she'd be gone, the bedroom silent. They could both be at peace because by then he'd have finally figured his shit out and wouldn't need her anymore.

He was far from that place now.

But if he accepted Laurel's offer and returned to his house, Jacqueline would be there to motivate him. He could keep up with the mortgage. Keep his house. Keep his Jacqueline, even if her predictions were no longer accurate.

And finally he'd have a camera back in his hands.

Certain he wasn't going to vomit, he stood and returned to the living room.

"Was about to come and check on you," Laurel said, standing. "You okay?"

"Yeah," he replied. "Okay, I'll work at your store. Let's figure out how to keep my house."

Laurel embraced him. Connie joined a moment later.

All the doors stood open except to the master bedroom. Had he left it open or closed yesterday? Maybe Connie had been by. She'd left him three voicemails that morning. Once he'd told Jacqueline what he needed to say, he'd listen to them. Then call Reggie to decline.

Trembling, he stepped forward, twisted the handle and entered the bedroom.

Alone.

His heart skipped a beat. Arthur wiped the sweat beading on his forehead. Sunlight had warmed the room hotter than the day outside.

He swallowed and told the emptiness what he had spent the entire night preparing: "You were wrong about Bronwyn and Owen. So I'm opening a studio at Laurel's shop and moving back here. I don't have a choice."

Her voice from everywhere: *Arthur, alone. Alone.*

"Yes, I'll be alone."

Bronwyn and Owen. Anna and Jorge.

"Damn it, Jess, I listened. Did what you asked. But you were wrong. Now I might lose the house. Lose you. I have to—"

Arthur, alone.

"Alone. Because I can't grow a spine, right? Can't man up? You *wanted* me to find you with him, right here, wanted me to get angry. But the shoot ran late. And all this time I thought this was you trying to say you were sorry for cheating on me. Make it easy for me by telling me what to do. But if I'd had to make tough decisions after you died, I wouldn't be here. So I'm making tough decisions now."

Alone.

"Why tell me these things over and over? You're wrong. But you've never been willing to change or admit you were wrong."

Bronwyn and Owen. Arthur, alone. Bronwyn—

"Shut up!"

—and Owen. Arthur, alone. Bronwyn—

"Connie thinks I should sell this house."

—and Owen. Arthur—

"But maybe she's right."

—alone.

"Sell it and let some else deal with you!"

The front door opened downstairs and Connie called out: "Arthur?"

Jacqueline's voice: *Bronwyn and Owen.*

Arthur froze. Soft voices conversed downstairs. Footsteps moved across hardwood. Outside, Connie's Prius and a familiar red Mercedes were parked at the curb. Realization tingled that Bronwyn had changed her mind.

He hurried across the upstairs hall and tried to descend quietly down the creaking back steps.

Footsteps moved up the front staircase. “Arthur, are you up there?” Connie called out.

Feeling foolish, he replied, “I’m up here.” He turned and met Connie in the upstairs hallway. “Was trying to sneak out. Didn’t want to be here for a showing.”

“No, that’s fine,” she said. “Didn’t you get my messages?”

“No, not yet. I wanted to . . .” He couldn’t finish.

Connie embraced him. “I know it’s hard. But I’ve got great news.” A grin curled at the corners of her mouth. “Bronwyn called me this morning. She had a long talk with Owen, who said he’s old enough to take care of a house. So she wants to take another look. The kicker is Owen is going to school here. So I floated a four-year lease for the lower rent and she seems agreeable.” Her grin became a wide smile. “For four years, the bank will have to go for it. That means we don’t have to worry about the mortgage while getting the studio off the ground.”

“Yeah,” he agreed.

She half-turned toward the staircase. “Do you want to meet them?”

“I . . .”

“I know it’s not your favourite, but it would be a bit Howard Hughes if you left right now. I’ll keep it short.”

“I’ll be down in a second.”

As she descended the stairs, Arthur moved back into the bedroom. Numb, his voice trembled: “You knew.”

Alone.

“Damn it, don’t tell me that!” he hissed. “Stop punishing me! You cheated on me so don’t tell me I’ll be—”

But that’s not what she’d said. Never had been. This whole time she hadn’t been saying “alone.” She’d been saying—

“A loan.” The pieces fell into place. “A loan against the house to buy in with Reggie?” *Arthur, a loan.*

Tenants would keep coming. They’d pay off the mortgage. Partnering with Reggie would be a success, letting him pay off the business loan against the house without having to make hard decisions. And after Yoji and Midori, Arthur would move back in and find how “glass” and “northeast” and “bus driver” figured into his future.

All he had to do was just let it happen.

He left the room and went down the front stairs to find Bronwyn and a young man with a strong resemblance to her chatting with Connie. They turned and Connie made the introductions.

"It's such a lovely house," Bronwyn said. She placed a hand on Owen's shoulder, who flinched at the motherly contact. Arthur sympathized. "I didn't think Owen would be able to handle helping me care for a home, but he convinced me."

"Yes, well," Arthur sputtered. He looked at Connie, then back to Bronwyn. "I know you're new to the city, but do you have any interest in *buying* the house?"

Sometimes Arthur parked in the shade of the oaks across the street from the house where he'd lived with Jacqueline. Paint flaked off the porch, leaving a patchwork of rotting bare wood. With several of the panes broken, the city had slapped plywood over the lower floor windows several months back. Since his last visit, a section of iron railing had collapsed into the yard.

Most days he'd just look before continuing on to a shoot. With Laurel's help, he'd used the profit from selling his house to set up a small shop in the Garden District where he specialized in architecture. Working first with Connie and then her connections, his stylized photos made listings stand out. And sometimes, through personal referrals, he did the occasional wedding. When he could, he sent business to Reggie, who'd been successful with that other partner.

But today, he grabbed his camera off the passenger seat and got out. According to Connie, a young Internet millionaire had bought the property. On Monday, demolition would start to make way for a new, modern home.

Pacing the sidewalk, he searched for the perfect angle to capture the yellowing, overgrown grass sticking up through the railing's rusted lattice. Close up, narrow field—a symbol of the inevitable fall of people's constructions to the passing of time and nature.

Bronwyn and Owen had lived in his house for nearly six years. He never knew if the Lumleys heard voices, but suspected the next occupants—Caroline and Michael Deveraux according to the city records Connie had checked—had. They'd lasted three months before moving out. Watching the housing listings, he'd seen his house up for sale three more times in the space of two years before it had become abandoned.

He looked up, backing away until he found the perfect angle to shoot the master bedroom's shattered windows for the last time. Whether Jacqueline still spoke her string of broken predictions to the empty room, he didn't know.

THE WALL OF GLOVES

The second most terrifying thing is the wall of gloves: winter ones, thick and heavy; a white leather golfer's; multicolour woolen mittens; a lady's white, silk elbow-length. All lovingly tacked to the barn's walls. So many.

Too many to be from . . .

"Where do you get them all?" I pant.

"Some I find. On the street or bus. Others"—his gaze flits to the white, elbow-length—"I keep." He raises the cleaver, focusing on my hands shackled to the table.

I turn away, shutting my eyes so I won't look on the most terrifying thing: the wall of hands.

OF THE ENDANGERED

"You can see the town from here," Baako, the messenger who'd led Noah from Charlotte, called back over his shoulder from the crest of the hill.

Noah urged his horse to a trot, eager to finally reach the town of Dean End. Despite the joy of spending time in the pristine forest, the basic furnishing and simple meals Baako had described now sounded like heaven. Ironic, Noah mused, considering Baako's belief that they were headed for the border of Hell.

As they reached the crest, the green canopy gently descended into the valley below. Opposite, the forest rose up the far side before giving way to bare, rocky peaks. The sun setting behind them, they cast dark, pointed shadows like the teeth of some ancient, massive predator across the town in the valley's heart. Three stone bridges straddled narrows in the river. Hugging the far bank, a long, grey, low-slung building stretched for almost a half a kilometre. Columns of smoke rose from chimneys before being dispersed by the valley's winds. The peaks of its black roof reached six or seven metres high. Four water wheels, each taller than three men, turned in the river's current.

Small farms nestled in the lowlands, filling the open terrain. But on the far side of the valley, a score of massive farms—some over a thousand hectares—had been carved from the forested slopes.

"Pendore's factory," Baako said, naming one of the town's elders. He pointed to the massive farms. "And those are his people. Salvation and resurrection, we should let him deal with it." He spurred his horse to a canter and Noah followed, thinking he caught a whiff of sulfur on the breeze.

Two weeks ago, Noah had been in Charlotte, rounding up a pack of six-legged, beagle-sized lizards. While making arrangement to transport the creatures he'd caught to Philadelphia, word reached him that a man had come east from the wilderness, looking for a monster hunter from Pix. Curious, Noah agreed to meet him. Charlotte sat on the frontier of civilization, as far as Noah knew, and aside from a few tiny settlements everything to the west remained the realm of monsters.

The man from the east, Baako, described how a demon was attacking his town. While Pendore, one of the town Elders, wanted to hunt the demon along with the Riders, the local constabulary, the other two Elders sought Pix's expertise. Noah had been happy to oblige.

During their two-week journey west, Baako had explained there had always been rumours of some Hellbeast in the forest to the west of the river. But five years ago, when Pendore's people had moved across the river to begin clearing land for their massive farms, rumours had become sightings. Then small farm animals had been attacked or taken. Now the whole town lived in fear. For generations, Dean End's faith and devotion had held Hell's power in check, Baako had told him, but Pendore threatened all of that.

Noah hadn't understood the animosity or blame directed at Pendore, but suspicion buzzed like an itch he couldn't reach at seeing the factory. The skill and knowledge required to build something so complex shouldn't have existed. Not this far east, not anywhere. To say nothing of maintaining the massive farms.

An hour later, the forest gave way to sloping farmland and a strong stink of sulfur. In open ground, Noah could make out details—simple clapboard houses and buildings with sides and windows smudged grey. What he thought had been a rock formation along the riverbank resolved into a slag pile running down from the factory, explaining the stink. Soot and ash nearly obscured "THE DEAN END FORGE" painted in white on its roof.

The path widened into a thoroughfare headed toward the town centre. Residents eyed Noah as he passed. They'd probably never seen anything like his leather duster, denim pants, and six-shooter. When Noah had first met Baako, the younger man's breeches, tunic, cloak, and tricorn seemed an anachronism in Charlotte. Now Noah was the one out of place.

Elder Livingstone asked, "So, is it sufficient compensation for killing this demon?"

Noah forced himself not to stare at the contents of the simple chest.

Reflected candlelight cast dancing golden shapes across the room's ceiling timbers and stone walls. A moment ago, Noah had wondered why it had taken two men to carry in the small wooden box. Coins, rings, an elaborate sconce, a pocket watch—all gold. He could accept goods or services as payment where the banks had not reached, but he'd never seen so much. He took a sip from his mug, ignoring the water's sulfuric smell, and grabbed a coin whose imprint had worn smooth.

"Interesting," he said, estimating how much he could take with him. The encumbrance of the equipment he'd brought in his saddlebags already taxed his horse. He'd had no choice but to leave the bulk of his equipment back in Charlotte, locked in his wagon. It never would have made it through the wilderness.

Across the table, Elder Hongtu alternated between twirling the long hairs of his neckbeard and picking at the red vest pulled taut over his belly. Elder Livingstone sat still, narrow hands flat on the rough-hewn table, owl-like eyes locked on Noah. Candlelight reflected off the silver thread woven into his vest.

Noah cast the coin into the box, clanking as it landed. "Yeah, this'll do."

Across the table, Hongtu blew out a breath of relief. Livingstone simply nodded, one hand rubbing his stomach.

"Couple of conditions." The simple wooden chair groaned as Noah shifted his weight. He longed for the overstuffed couches back in Charlotte. "Room, board, care for my horse. All provided."

"That sounds reasonable," Hongtu said.

"No one questions what I do," Noah continued. "And no one touches my equipment."

Hongtu looked to Livingstone and they nodded. "Agreed," Livingstone said. "We have heard some of what you utilize is rather . . . unconventional."

"Only I kill this thing and take the body when I'm done."

"We have no objections," Livingstone said. "So long as we have proof that the demon is dead."

"Last, I'll need a small wagon or cart. Somethin' that can make it through the forest goin' back east."

Livingstone and Hongtu shared another nod of agreement.

"I am sure we can provide you with something," Livingstone said. "We have an agreement."

The whole time, Noah had wondered at the absence of Elder Pendore. Or if he even knew about the meeting. "Ain't there three Elders?"

Hongtu leaned back, but Livingstone said, "To take action, the Elders require a majority vote. We do not need Stefen's accord."

"Stefen?" Noah asked.

"Elder Pendore," Hongtu explained.

"Tell me," Livingstone said, leaning forward and fixing Noah with his owl-like gaze, "do you know the story of Pastor Dean?"

"A bit," Noah replied. When Baako had told Noah the name of the town, Noah had suspected—and Baako had confirmed—it had been settled by the Western Dean Expedition, a group of three hundred who'd disappeared into the wilderness a century earlier and been considered lost.

"Pastor Dean fled Salem, fearing Philadelphia's 'progress' had weakened the causes of devotion, hard work, sacrifice. They travelled far, fortified by their devotion, and when they climbed the mountain to the west they found Hell itself burning in the next valley. It is clear that providence called Pastor Dean and his congregation here to hold back the tide of evil through faith.

"We have maintained those ideals. Until Stefen. He left here still a boy and returned a young man with a mind full of heresy. His machines take the sweat from a man's brow. They can clear the forest in a season where it would take a man years. He insists on finding new ways to do things and destroying our traditions. He has built the stables and boarding house to attract traders from the west. Built that monstrosity of a factory. He even allows women to work there and wear breeches like they were men."

"We share some of the blame," Hongtu admitted, looking to Livingstone, but the other Elder scowled. Apparently, Livingstone did not enjoy this subject. Hongtu continued, fingering his beard. "When Elder Livingstone was elected, Pendore approached him at his orchard. Offered him a device made of glass like a pitcher with a long, narrow spout. Except it was half-full of liquid and had no mouth to add more."

"Stefen said it could predict the weather," Livingstone continued. "The higher the liquid in the spout, the worse the weather. As a new Elder, I was eager to curry favour with other farmers. I accepted it much too quickly."

"Elder Livingstone shared it with me," Hongtu added. "I was most excited. With that, we welcomed more of his contraptions, not seeing until it was too late the damage they did. These things that reduced our efforts made some men crave larger farms, which meant time and money to keep the devices running."

Livingstone's hand returned to his abdomen. "Seduced, we were, away from Pastor Dean. Yet Stefen's influence grew until finally he was elected an Elder. Emboldened, his followers built their farms on the western slopes, ignoring

Pastor Dean's edict that it would be seen as a provocation.

"So you understand it is because of him that this demon was sent from over the mountain. I was content when only Pendore's people were affected, but now devout men are punished and the whole town seethes with fear. Our devotion is not enough. This demon must be stopped and the people must see it was Elder Hongtu and I who set things right. Even if it means embracing a servant of Philadelphia. So now that we three—"

The door to the small room opened and a man older than Noah, but far younger than the two Elders, stepped in. A jagged scar cut a deep groove in his left cheek. A simple cotton shirt covered his muscular frame, contrasting Livingstone's and Hongtu's white blouses and vests. He said, "Seems I'm missing something."

"Elder Pendore," Hongtu said, "we've just concluded our negotiations with Noah to find this monster."

"Yes, I heard he'd arrived," Pendore said, taking a seat at the table. "Didn't know you were talking to him."

Livingstone explained Noah's conditions and compensation. "Elder Hongtu and I are in agreement, so it is binding on you as well."

Pendore looked at the chest before Noah, opening his eyes wide in mock surprise. "With this kind of money, why not *buy* a cart?"

"Like I said," Noah said, trying to keep the upper hand, "don't question how I do things or I'll be on my way."

Pendore faced the other Elders. "How about this? The man's here and the deal is done. He can have the best room in my place, best meals I can offer. But if he hasn't stopped this thing in a week, you let me go after it. For free. It's a better deal than we're getting here."

"There are others—reverent gentlemen—who could billet Noah," Livingstone said. "We don't require your cooperation."

Pendore turned toward Hongtu. "How about it, Zian? All those farmers you represent get to keep their gold."

Looking to Noah, Hongtu asked, "Is a week enough time?"

"Don't know what I'm dealin' with," Noah replied. From what he'd first learned from Baako and then from the Elders, the creature was covered in black or brown fur. Some claimed it lumbered on four legs, others said it walked on two. It stood as tall as a man's belly or twice his height. Regardless of the contradictions, nothing like it existed in Pix's records. "Ain't no way to say."

Hongtu glanced between Livingstone and Pendore before saying, "I believe a week is reasonable."

"Motion carried," Pendore announced, slapping the table.

Across from Noah, Livingstone scowled and resumed rubbing his stomach. Clearly, he was a man unaccustomed to not getting his way.

Noah knew the feeling. His instructors had told him that Pix's reputation would earn him near reverential treatment. For well over a century, others like him had wandered the frontier, using equipment with abilities that defied explanation to deal with the monsters encountered by the western expansion of civilization. No one had reacted the way Pendore had with his counter-negotiation.

Pendore faced Noah. "You kill this thing before the week is out, you get your gold. You can have my best cart with an adapting axle system that'll keep the bed smooth and level. Even throw in a couple of my own horses. But I think all you got is a bunch of hox-pox tricks."

Noah kept his face impassive, contemplating. The creature was clearly a predator and hopefully territorial. If he could learn its patterns, he could trap it within a few days and show the Elders its lifeless body, claim his reward and be on his way back east. He said, "Just remember: no questions. And no one touches my stuff."

Pendore grunted. "You sound like a stage trickster I saw once in Winchester."

"It's agreed," Livingstone said, standing. He extended a hand to Noah.

Noah stood and shook.

Livingstone asked, "What do you require to begin?"

"A meal and a rest," Noah replied. "Long ride. Come mornin', I wanna talk to farmers who're hit."

"I can see to that," Hongtu said.

"And Elder Pendore here," Livingstone added, gesturing, "can show you to your accommodations."

"Sure." Pendore led Noah into a narrow hallway and out a side door into the gathering dusk. Outside the town's meeting hall, the sulfuric odor stung his nose.

"I'll see to your horse," Pendore said, untying its lead from the hitching post.

"Thanks," Noah replied.

They moved down a wide street. Storefront windows blazed orange—a general store, a jail, a barber. But no doctor, druggist, or even an apothecary. No school that Noah could see.

A few men hurried past, each carrying a weapon of some form. Across the river, the factory's massive roof obscured all but the mountains' peaks and the crimson sky above. Tendrils of smoke twisted up from chimneys while the water wheels cranked and splashed.

"I gotta know something," Pendore said. "You *really* think you can stop this thing? Not some performance, not telling us what Philadelphia says we should do. But put it down."

Noah dropped a hand to the butt of his six-shooter. "Yup."

"Nice iron. Any chance I could get a look at it?"

"Nope."

"Look," Pendore said. "All respect to the reputation of you Pix monster hunters, you're one man"—he canted his head toward the horse—"with limited equipment. You have that gun. Fine. Shows me you're serious. So come to the factory. See what we've been making. It's got to be better than what you brought with you."

"Doubt it."

"We're making rifled barrels. Shorter, lighter weight with better accuracy. And almost have a mechanism for breech-loading worked out. Man could get off six shots in a minute." Pendore motioned to the rifle clipped to the saddle. "How's that match up against what you've got?"

Though Livingstone and Hongtu had told him their version, Noah needed to know Pendore's side of the issue. "All respect to your factory, why *ain't* ya huntin' it?"

"Let's get inside."

They walked in silence to a large tavern. Noah expected music and voices to spill from a social gathering place, yet only the low murmur of conversation drifted out the set of doors. Noah grabbed the saddlebags off his horse before Pendore passed the reins to a young man with instructions for it to get the best care. Moving through the tavern's front door, the tang of tobacco and sour stink of spilled beer almost covered the town's rotten egg odour. A scattering of men and a few women clustered around large tables, sizing up Noah from under the brims of tricorns.

Pendore grabbed a lantern from behind the bar and led Noah into a back room.

"Why aren't I hunting it?" Pendore began, shutting the door. "Because Livingstone and Hongtu forbid it." He motioned to a table and chairs. Noah set the saddlebags on the floor, glad to be free of their weight, and sat while Pendore lit more lamps. "They say this creature is from Hell and I'm to blame. You hear that story?"

"Yup," Noah replied.

"So they say I wouldn't stand a chance. Livingstone doesn't like doing business with Philadelphia, but would like me killing the thing even less."

Pendore sat opposite Noah. "See, if I bring this thing down with my equipment, it'll bring more people over to me. I've already got most of the Riders' loyalty. They're supposed to serve the Elders as a whole, but with my equipment they're more effective. If we stop this thing, Zian—Elder Hongtu—might keep going against Livingstone like he did just now. Livingstone's family has always had it comfortable, so he can afford to be devout. But Zian's a farmer. Practical. Didn't like it much when Livingstone had the few Riders still loyal to him round up all that gold from farmers trying to scratch out a living.

"But with more people behind me, and Zian on my side, we'll have bigger farms and can stockpile food against droughts and hard winters. I'll bring in doctors and medicine and banks. Open a school so boys can learn more than their fathers' trade and girls can learn more than having babies." Pendore leaned across the table. "Progress. Knowledge. That's why I'm offering anything I have at the factory."

"'Preciate it," Noah replied, "but got what I need."

Pendore stood, chagrined. "Good enough. Because either way works. I want to move into the next valley. Some crops grow better on an eastern slope, so if you stop it people won't be afraid to move west. If not, I'll kill it." He moved to the door and turned. "I'll have a meal brought in and arrange for you to have the best room in the place. You need anything, ask for me personally. In the meantime, good night." He doffed his tricorn and left.

The Riders, Pendore leading, led Noah across one of the stone bridges and up a road twisting west through the wooded foothills. Beneath Noah, his horse's pace began to slow. He sympathized with it, but spurred it to keep up with the group. For five days it had carried him up these slopes, burdened by the saddlebags, as he'd interviewed farmers who'd seen the beast. This time, speed was essential.

The forest road opened onto hectares of rolling farmland, dusk muting the colours. Wheeled machines dotted the fields, only shapes in the failing light. Towering above the vegetation, windmills spun slowly atop wooden frames. The Riders headed straight for the main house, where a figure in the doorway stood surrounded by men bearing lanterns and torches. Nearby, sheep bleated in a simple wooden pen.

"I shot it!" the man shouted, hoisting his musket above his head. "I killed the beast!"

The crowd murmured, not quite convinced. Still, Noah reflected as he dismounted, they must believe the creature didn't pose a threat for them to be out while the sun set.

Ahead of him, the Riders tried to cut through the crowd. "Easy, Yoji," Pendore shouted above the din. "Let's put that musket down."

Noah ignored the commotion as he slung the saddlebags over his shoulder and, after a moment's consideration, grabbed his rifle before moving as fast as his encumbrance would allow. He doubted a single musket shot could kill it, but it would make the beast dangerous. Noah silently cursed these primitives, their superstitions and willful ignorance. This farmer was fortunate that the creature hadn't turned on him.

Rounding the pen, the sheep packed tighter together, their bleating growing panicked.

A trail of blood smeared into the dirt and grass led away from the pen. Several paces on, a rust-coloured liquid joined the blood. The trail ran into a crop field, twisted and broken stalks showing the creature's path. Noah found a three-clawed paw print wider than both his hands put together, pressed several centimetres into the soft, brown earth filled with the dark liquid. Moving deeper, a slaughterhouse stink filled his nose and the drone of insects reached his ears. Pushing into the next row, a cloud of flies surrounded the scattered entrails of a blood soaked sheep carcass. The remains he'd examined so far had been several days old, rotting in barns or dragged into the forest by the creature before being worked over by scavengers. Here he had his first chance to examine fresh remains. Farther on, the creature had trampled a path through the orderly stalks. The field continued to rise, giving way to open land and then the forest, just shapes of shadow and darkness, rising up the mountainside.

A snatch from an ancient poem came to him: *The woods are lovely, dark and deep*. He couldn't recall the rest but had the impression the next few lines dealt with promises and covering long distances.

He considered pushing ahead, but with the sun setting, he had only ten or fifteen minutes before dark. With all attacks coming near dusk or dawn, the creature was clearly crepuscular and adept at hunting in the low light. Wounded and in pain, it would no doubt be dangerous and unpredictable. It might even be circling back to finish its meal.

Noah hunkered down next to the remains, waving away the flies. He'd return tomorrow at first light and try to pick up the trail. For now, at least, he had a place to leave a trap.

Pendore and a Rider pushed their way through the crops behind him. "Why are you stopping?" the Rider asked.

"Wanna see how it kills," Noah replied, noting the three parallel slashes in the throat that had nearly decapitated the animal. If shock hadn't killed it, blood loss would have in a matter of seconds.

"Why's that matter?"

"Let the man work, Bartholomew," Pendore said.

Noah squinted, wishing he had more light. He shifted to the sheep's belly, which had the same three parallel slices as its throat.

"Let's go get it," Bartholomew said. "We got a trail—"

Noah removed a flat, quarter-circle of metal from his bag. Flicking the trigger, it unfolded once to a semicircle and again to a full circle, twenty centimetres in diameter.

"What's that?" Pendore asked, leaning in.

"Trap," Noah replied. "Case it comes back."

"*That's* a trap?" Bartholomew asked.

Noah turned the severity selector on its base to the lowest setting before placing the disc on the ground. "Touch it," he challenged.

Bartholomew snorted, leaning forward, hand extended. "Buncha hox-pox n—" His fingertips made contact and his body fell limp to the soft soil.

Pendore shouted, "Resurrection!"

Noah ignored Pendore and checked Bartholomew's carotid pulse—strong and steady.

Pendore kneeled. "Is he dead?"

"He's fine," Noah replied. "Be up and 'round in 'bout ten minutes." He gripped the disc by the nonconductive thirty-degree wedge and adjusted the severity dial to a setting he hoped would bring down the creature based on what little he knew.

Pendore tried to shake Bartholomew awake, then pried an eye open. "How can something so small do this to a man?"

"Call it 'hox-pox,'" Noah said, standing. "Told ya: my tools, my way. Don't ask questions."

Pendore rubbed his chin, eyeing the disc.

Noah grabbed Bartholomew under his arms and hefted him up. "Grab his feet? Thing might come back. Don't feel like waitin' ten minutes."

Pendore nodded and together they carried Bartholomew out of the field and into the glow of the lanterns and torches borne by the men still gathered around Yoji's dooryard. After setting Bartholomew down, Noah elbowed his way through the crowd toward Yoji. He needed to know what the farmer had seen.

Above them, the mountains' peaks glowed scarlet.

Pendore entered the empty tavern and sat opposite Noah. "How's your meal?"

"Fine," Noah replied, washing down the last of the rabbit stew with water. Noah wished he had an analyzer to check the level of carcinogens it held. Likely not enough to be worry about with limited exposure, but over a lifetime it could cause problems. Perhaps it explained Livingstone's stomach ailments.

"Two more days," Pendore stated.

Pendore's gloating chilled Noah. In his three years, every town had regarded him with awe and respect. None had questioned his rule that only he could kill the beasts that tormented them.

Yet tonight, he'd endured accusing gazes. Heard the conversations that some farmer had almost killed the creature while the expensive monster hunter hadn't come close to even seeing it. Livingstone had come by to communicate his displeasure with the lack of progress. Noah shuddered to think how much damage Pendore and his allies might do in trying to find this beast if Noah failed.

"It'll turn up. Either the trap or someplace nearby. Wanna ask ya to have Riders ready to go if somethin' happens."

"Why do you say that?"

"That farmer must've hurt it. Couldn't get to the forest. So it stopped and ate what it could. Probably ran when we showed up. Now it's hurt and hungry. It'll strike again."

"That sounds like an animal feeding. Not a demon punishing."

"Ain't no demon. Came 'cause the forest's getting cut down." Noah looked at Pendore. "Your big farms 'cross the river are where it used to hunt. What it ate left, so now it feeds on pigs, sheep, anything it can find."

Pendore leaned forward. "Maybe I was wrong about you. I thought you Pix types were pretenders. Come in, wave around some trinket, saying it'll stop a monster."

"Took ya this long to figure I'm really here to stop it?"

"Took this long to figure out you *can* stop it. I just don't mean that trap. You're learning about it, studying it."

"So?"

"Livingstone and men like him claim to have all the answers. You're thinking. Learning."

"And?"

"Do you know how rare that is? Even to the east, towns are idle in their knowledge. They wait for a new man or new book to arrive from Philadelphia to tell them about better ways to construct a building or treat disease. Doling our knowledge. We are pushing ahead, fearlessly, in expanding what we know and can do. You could have a place here."

"No thanks."

Noah imagined that as he headed east from Dean End with the creature, Pendore would go west over the mountain to establish a larger factory, another slag pile spilling down into another river, more heavy metals polluting the ecosystem.

Still, with a rational mind and scientific approach, Pendore had a chance of coming to realize the harm he was causing. Unlike Livingstone and his zealotry.

He blew out a breath, hoping Philadelphia could hem Pendore in when they learned what he was doing. "I'm gonna get some rest." He stood.

Pendore did as well. "I have some things to attend to myself. Good night, Noah."

Moving upstairs and into his room, Noah removed his outer clothing, extinguished the lamp and climbed between the coarse wool sheets. In the last few moments of consciousness, as thoughts drifted, he saw his career before him, rushing to find these creatures before the inevitable future where cities covered the continent and the beasts he sought were wiped out from history.

He must have slept because pounding on the door pulled him awake. After a moment of disorientation in the dark, the door opened, spilling in light from several lanterns.

"Noah!" Pendore said, Riders surrounding him and his hand on a sobbing boy's shoulder. "Get up. It's killed a man!"

The group emerged from the forest into a large yard. The boy steered his horse around a series of barns and outbuildings to a simple stone farmhouse. In the side yard, a woman knelt in the dirt, wailing. She clutched a man, twisted and still, to her chest as she rocked. Smears of blood, brown stains in the dawn's light, covered their simple clothing. Pigs, wandering freely from what was left of a smashed pen, scattered in a squealing wave before the halting horses.

The boy leaped from his horse and ran toward the woman. "Ma! Ma!" He collapsed at her side, throwing his arms around her. Nearby, several pig carcasses lay in the dirt.

Elder Pendore waved the Riders into a semicircle. "Spread out. Look for any signs of where it's been or could have gone."

"Be careful," Noah added, positioning himself next to Pendore. "Thing's probably hurt and dangerous. If ya see it, tell me. *I'm* the one who kills it."

The Riders galloped off, rifle in one hand and reins in the other.

Noah and Pendore dismounted and approached the woman. Secretly, Noah hoped the man had been killed by some accident. Anything but an attack by the beast. Several metres away, a pitchfork lay discarded in the dirt, tines thick with a dark liquid; a sickle lay farther still. Near the pen, Noah spotted a musket with a snapped stock.

Noah struggled to keep his face neutral as he knelt in front of the woman. The stench of copper-hot blood and outhouse-stink of bowel filled his nose. He asked, "Can I see him? See what it did to him?"

The woman looked up, eyes blazing. Blood smeared her cheek. "*Chutia!* You were supposed to kill it. All I hear is you talk and talk. Now my Sanjeev is dead."

"Please," Noah repeated.

"Kavita." Pendore knelt, tricorn held over his heart. "Please, it could be important."

The woman, Kavita, nodded and slowly lowered the body to the ground. The boy, who had been crying into his mother's shoulder, shrieked.

"Salvation and resurrection." Bartholomew, recovered from earlier, had joined them.

The faint hope Noah held that this had been some accident, or that the farmer had been trampled, evaporated. The farmer's simple white tunic and breeches had been ripped to tatters. His right arm nearly severed below the elbow, attached only by bits of skin and tendon. Slice wounds, all of them the familiar three parallel cuts, scored the torso and abdomen. Grey-purple loops of bowel bubbled from the belly. The man's throat had been sliced open.

"I'm sorry," Noah said.

Kavita hugged the body of her husband back to her blood-soaked dress.

Noah stood and moved to the smashed remains of the pigpen. Bloody tracks—man, pig and the three-clawed impressions—led away.

"So what now?" Pendore asked.

"We pick up its trail and go after it!" Bartholomew said.

"*I* go after it," Noah said, returning to his horse. Grunting with the effort, he lifted the saddlebags and set them on the ground. "'Fore someone does somethin' stupid."

"Maybe you're not all hox-pox tricks," Bartholomew said. "But it's not sheep and goats no more."

Noah bit back a retort that the reason this man had been killed was that he had recklessly confronted the creature. Instead, he unclipped a rolled-up backpack from the saddle and opened it. Only the passing seconds mattered, not debating with these primitives. Still, he wondered if this farmer had been among the crowd gathered to listen to Yoji's boasting. Emboldened, had he rushed out when he heard it attack? A convergence of two species that never should have met. Silently, he selected supplies from the saddlebags and loaded them in the pack.

A Rider, not much older than the boy now sobbing over his dead father, galloped up to them, breathless. "We found a blood trail and some tracks. Starts by the pen"—he motioned with his head—"cuts through the fields toward the tree line." He pointed up the sloped terrain, finger trembling. A kilometre distant, the farmland ended abruptly in dense forest. Above, the trees clung to the mountains' slopes before giving way to rocky peaks tinged pink by the rising sun.

"Good work," Pendore said.

"There's more. Elders Livingstone and Hongtu are here."

Noah turned, looking down the broad path that curved out of sight into the forest. A team of horses pulling a cart carrying Hongtu and Livingstone approached. Noah finished transferring the supplies he needed to the backpack. He slung it over a shoulder, snapped the saddlebags' clasps shut and replaced them back over his horse. As he pulled his rifle from the saddle, the cart stopped before him.

"Faith and charity," Elder Hongtu greeted Noah, descending to the ground. Livingstone followed.

Noah nodded.

"We understand a man is dead," Livingstone said, owl-like gaze fixed on Noah.

"Yeah," Noah replied. "He attacked it. The thing—"

"Sanjeev had been devout." Livingstone absently rubbed his abdomen. "Perhaps this demon sought to punish him for being seduced away from the teachings of Pastor Dean to the supposed effortlessness of Pendore's weapons. Or serve as a warning to us for our dalliance with you. That is to say, with Philadelphia."

Hongtu's fingers twisted in the white strands of his neckbeard.

Noah rested the rifle across his shoulders. "Every second I spend here jawin' is a second I ain't huntin' it. Got a point?"

Livingstone drew himself up. "If you stop it, you are to bring back its head. We will mount this Hellspawn's skull in the town square as a warning to never stray from the teachings of Pastor Dean."

Resentment bloomed in Noah's belly. "Ain't the deal. Thing's mine. All of it."

"I am altering our agreement."

Noah forced a laugh. "And if I leave 'cause ya broke the deal?" he bluffed.

"Then we'll keep your horse and equipment," Livingstone replied. "It's a long walk back to Charlotte."

Resentment flared to fury at the realization that Livingstone had backed him into a corner.

"Resurrection," Pendore cursed. "You can't make a decision like that on your own. I vote 'nay.' Zian?"

Hongtu looked down, stroking his neckbeard. "We do require proof it is dead. This seems a simple way. I support Elder Livingstone."

"Return without its head," Livingstone added, facing Noah, "and we will throw you in the stocks for three days and three nights. If someone else is hurt, we will visit that injury upon you. If someone else is killed, even if you kill the creature, you will be put to death."

"Salvation!" Pendore screamed. "We never talked—"

"It is the law of Pastor Dean." Livingstone glanced at Hongtu, who reluctantly nodded his agreement.

Noah held Livingstone's gaze. "I'll need bait."

"What real hunter needs bait?"

"Resurrection," Pendore cursed. "If the man needs bait, let him have it." To Noah, he said, "What do you need?"

Noah motioned to the pig carcasses.

Pendore nodded. "I'm sure Kavita wouldn't object."

"Such little respect for personal property, Stefen?" Livingstone said.

"I believe," Hongtu began, stroking his beard, "Elder Pendore is correct, Elder Livingstone. Time is short. Killing this thing matters more than other concerns."

Livingstone looked at Noah. "Bring me its head." He turned and headed for the cart.

"I will pray for you in the wilderness," Hongtu began, but Noah moved to a narrow wood-framed tower with a multi-bladed rotor at its top. Belts and pulleys ran from the rotor's axle to a series of pipes and valves at its base, a spigot emerging from it, several empty buckets surrounding it.

Pendore followed. "Let us come with you. I know it's important that *you* kill it, but one man alone—"

"Bunch of you, makin' noise?" Noah placed a bucket below the spigot and turned the handle. Water rushed out. And with it, a hint of that sulfuric smell. "More of a danger than help."

"Then just me. Look, you can keep the gold. But the two of us stop this thing, bring its body back? We show people Livingstone's piety doesn't mean anything. It's progress that'll stop it." Pendore put his hand on the network of pipes. "Knowledge."

"I work alone." Noah turned off the spigot and carried the bucket to the nearest pig carcass, knelt and shrugged off his pack. After rolling up his sleeves, he drew his knife and carved into the pig's belly.

"Here," Pendore said, hunkering down next to Noah. "Let me. Don't want the smell on your clothes or this thing'll mistake you for a meal."

"Thanks," Noah said, genuinely grateful as he handed over his knife. He dipped his hands into the shockingly cold water, rubbing them clean, and passed an empty tin to Pendore, who sliced meat into it.

Filling his waterskins from the spigot, Noah watched Livingstone kneel with Kavita and her son, their heads bowed. Two Riders wrapped Sanjeev's body in a thick cloth. Hongtu stood alone and surveyed the land, probably wondering what would become of this farm with the man of the family dead.

After cleaning his hands and wiping off the tin with his tunic, Pendore passed the metal tube and knife back to Noah, who loaded them into his pack.

Pendore extended his scarred, calloused hand. "Good luck."

Noah shook, shouldered his pack and crossed into the field where the Rider had found the blood trail. Cries of grief resumed as Noah followed rust-coloured smears through the broken stalks toward the forest.

Inside the tree line, Noah hunkered down and swapped out the period-appropriate rounds in his weapons for stun charges in the rifle and high-velocity explosive rounds in the pistol.

Once he'd found the creature, he'd arrange an evacuation with Philadelphia and be done with this place. It meant leaving behind his horse and some equipment, but without his thumbprint no one would be able to open his saddlebags. And when Noah didn't return, these primitives could believe whatever they wanted about the creature and its fate.

Inhaling the comforting smell of pine, peat and damp earth, he followed the thinning blood trail and the occasional three-clawed track in the soft brown soil up the mountainside. His ears filtered out the soothing, familiar forest sounds—birdcalls, small animals moving in the branches—listening for anything out of place. Around him, thick trees—wider than a man could reach his arms around—towered, blocking the midmorning sun.

After an hour, the upward sloping forest floor gave way to dry, crumbling soil—impossible for tracking. And with the blood trail dried up, he'd come as close as he would get.

He climbed to a rock outcropping that provided a view of the forest below and removed several containers from his pack. One was the tin of pig meat. Another, a small vial containing an enzyme to break down proteins. The last was an aerosol cylinder, thick as his forearm and nearly as long. He unscrewed the top of the cylinder, set it upright on the ground and cut pig hide into the open end. After pouring in the enzyme and screwing the top back on, Noah carried the container down from the outcropping, set it among the rocks and thumbed a switch on its top. Thirty seconds later—enough time to get clear—a small nozzle emerged, silently spraying the pig's scent into the forest below.

By then, Noah had returned to his perch. He dug in his satchel for scentless, freeze-dried rations and waited. He considered what other unknown and unrecorded creatures might still roam this forest. And what had been here a thousand years ago, long before people had arrived.

Movement drew his eyes to the forest below—shifting shadows lacking a breeze to explain them. They shifted again and Noah slowly brought the rifle's scope to his eye. His breath caught at the sight of it—mammalian, bilaterally symmetrical, quadrupedal, brown-fur with streaks of white. Measuring four metres from snout to tail, it resembled a cross between an *Ursus* and a member of the extinct *Macropus* genus. Using its front legs, it pushed itself up, balancing on its strong rear legs, using its long, thick tail as a counterweight. Its triangular, rodent-like head swayed at the end of a serpentine neck.

The creature lowered to all fours and moved out of the tree line. Taking slow, measured breaths to calm his thudding heart, Noah lined up the creature's head in the crosshairs and squeezed the trigger. The tip of his rifle glowed orange and the creature let out a low moan before collapsing.

Adrenaline surged. He had it. A creature unrecorded in any text and he'd brought it down. Noah grabbed his pack and scrambled down the slope toward the beast.

A few metres from it, he drew his six-shooter and forced himself to advance slowly. The stun charge should have rendered it unconscious, but with its size and unknown biology, he could not be certain. Approaching from the rear, he extended his left hand and stroked the firm, wiry fur of its flank. The creature's only movement was its slow, deep respiration. Gun trained on its head, he gave it a sharp shove, but it remained still.

He stifled a cry of joy, already thinking twenty-four hours ahead when he'd be in a modern lab beginning his documentation.

He reached into his pack and removed his communicator. Using his thumbprint to activate it, he keyed in the emergency code.

After a moment, a voice said, "Noah, this is Hollister."

Noah grinned hearing the voice of the Institute's director. The emergency code must have caught the director's attention. "I've taken a creature alive, sir, and need immediate evacuation."

"What manner of creature?"

Noah described the beast, what had happened since his last update and his situation in Dean End.

Silence followed his explanation. Then: "Noah, our budget is thin as it is."

"This is the first apex predator we've ever found, sir. We could ask the Directorate to extend our funding—"

"The Directorate is considering *cutting* our funding. With the declining rate we're finding undocumented species, we might not be around in ten years. To say nothing of those creatures you had transported from your Charlotte excursion. Sixty-three specimens? Think of the costs. We euthanized all but two, which are in stasis."

Noah's chest constricted. He'd spent a week tracking the six-legged creatures. Clearly intelligent, they'd adapted to his strategy to trap them. They'd dart away, rush back, dart away again, chattering and hooting as if playing. Eventually, he'd trapped as many as he could, forced to use lethal means on the rest. It hardly seemed fair—these creatures had been there for millennia. To them, these invading bipeds were the monsters. "They're pack creatures, sir. Two of them can't function—"

"You're speaking like you expect them to live out their lives."

Noah eyed the creature before him, fear unspooling. His gaze fell upon dried, near-black blood congealed around a wound in its left shoulder. Noah knew his next few words could do more harm than Yoji's musket. "Sir, what's happened to the other specimens I've collected?"

A sigh. "We're not a zoo. We've learned what we needed to about them. Some of the small herbivores we can deal with. But the others, no."

Noah shut his eyes, jaw clenched. He'd honestly believed others at the

Institute, once they had beheld these wonderful creatures, would come around to his belief that they deserved to live. "Sir, this will be the last one."

"No, Noah. I've been patient with your little menagerie. Do your job: put it down and destroy the remains."

Noah played the one card he had. "I told you I need to bring its head back. I can't return to Dean End—"

"Then we'll pull you out. I'll send coordinates for the rendezvous. Is there anything else?"

"No," Noah admitted. The thought of killing this animal and reducing it to ashes with incendiary charges made him feel ill.

"Stand by for evacuations details." The line went silent, but the interface indicated data download.

Noah shoved the communicator in a pocket and stroked the creature's thick fur. If he could find a way to transport the creature out of the forest in stasis, he could present it to Livingstone. Try to shame him into honouring the original agreement. Livingstone would resist, but Pendore might be able to pressure Hongtu. Yet how could he move several hundred kilograms—?

"You killed it."

Noah spun toward the voice. Pendore, a rifle in his hand, emerged from the tree line. He wore a fresh tunic, a satchel hanging at his side, a saber on his waist.

After a moment to get back into character, Noah asked, "What're ya doin' here?"

"Isn't it obvious?" Pendore asked, moving toward him, slinging the rifle over his shoulder. "I followed you."

"I need something to move this thing," Noah said. "Go back to the farm. Get the Riders to bring a small cart or wagon up here."

"Why?" Pendore replied, moving closer. "The beast is dead. You fulfilled your contract."

"Keep tellin' ya not to question how I do things."

Pendore stopped next to the creature, watching its sides expand with each breath. "So you didn't kill it." Pendore's reached for the sabre at this hip, drew it—

Noah dropped a hand to the butt of his six-shooter. "No!"

Both hands gripping the hilt, Pendore raised the sword above this head.

"Stop!" Noah pulled his gun.

The blade slashed down, slicing deep into the creature's long, slender neck.

"No!" Noah screamed, the barrel tracking Pendore while his eyes were drawn to the convulsions wracking the creature's body.

Pendore brought the blade down again, blood splattering his tunic, and the severed head fell away from it neck, landing in the soft soil. "We hire you to kill this thing," Pendore said, looking at Noah, "but you draw a gun on *me*?" He slashed his sword to the side, spraying blood across the forest floor.

Noah glanced at the creature. A spasm shot through its form, then a weaker one. A third, just a twitch. Blood leaked, but didn't spurt, from where its neck has been severed. A desire, base and low, urged Noah to pull the trigger.

But the damage was done. Noah holstered his gun. "It was mine."

"You're a mystery to me." Pendore pulled a rag from his satchel and cleaned his sword. "I'd heard the monster hunters of Pix could track any creature, kill it without touching it. I thought it was hox-pox nonsense. But it's not enchanted amulets or spells." He sheathed the sword and motioned to the pocket where Noah had dropped the communicator. "You use machines."

"I'm not telling you anything," Noah spat, his cover breaking. "Get the hell away from me or I'll show you just how far hox-pox nonsense can go."

"Since I was a boy, Noah," Pendore said, "I was told not to question the ways of Pastor Dean. We live on the borders of Hell, men like Livingstone would say, our devotion the only thing holding it back. I'm not the first to question it, but I did something about it. Travelled to Salem, Winchester, and Charlotte. Learned what I could, but didn't wait for progress to come from Philadelphia.

"And now we have stronger blades, better guns. In a few years, a system that can pump human waste out of buildings instead of digging outhouses. A friend thirty miles north of here is working on a wood-fired furnace where steam would move a cart without a horse. Another believes we can catch rising steam to ride into the sky.

"We're making a better world. Not held back by men like Livingstone, but not held back by Philadelphia's slow pace. Not afraid to pursue knowledge. You and I are alike—"

"We're nothing alike!"

Pendore knelt, removing the satchel from his shoulder. "Then why do you Pix types wrap yourself up in legends?" He reached into the satchel and removed something the size of a dinner plate wrapped in heavy canvas. "You want to hide the truth that these are just machines." Unwrapping the fabric revealed the trap Noah had left at Yoji's farm the night before.

"Ya need to leave."

"Where are you from Noah?" Pendore pressed, standing and moving closer. "*When* are you from?"

"You're crazier than Livingstone."

"I've heard in Philadelphia there are giant machines that can travel so fast you could go from Boston to Atlanta in days. *Days.* Soon, it will be hours. It's not much more for machines that could transport us to tomorrow. Or yesterday. Are you from tomorrow, Noah? Is this your yesterday? Is that why you insist on killing these things yourself? You don't really kill them, but study them. Creatures that no longer exist in your time?"

Noah dropped his hand to the butt of his pistol. "Go."

"I'd hoped we could be allies, Noah. So be it." Pendore knelt, pulling a large oilcloth from his satchel.

"The hell ya doin'?"

"I'm going to bring its head back to town and mount it above my factory's door," Pendore said, maneuvering the head into the cloth. "Remind people it was *me* who finally stopped the creature."

"Remind folks ya broke the deal. Livingstone and Hongtu ain't gonna—"

"I'm not worried about them. I don't think Livingstone has that much time left. You can have a horse of mine. Leave with whatever you please. You just have to tell the Elders the truth: I killed it."

"Not gonna happen."

Pendore paused in his preparations. "I'm sorry to hear that." Pendore dropped the oilskin's edges. Then sprang up, a flintlock pistol pointed at Noah, and fired.

The shot struck Noah in the chest, knocking him flat, but his underarmour held. He looked up, seeing Pendore drop his pistol and pull the rifle from his shoulder. Still down, Noah drew his revolver. In the second it took Pendore to cock the rifle, Noah had his gun up. The revolver twitched, tracking its target. Noah squeezed the trigger. The gun *buzz-clicked* and fired, catching Pendore in the sternum. The round exploded, ripping Pendore in two. His lower body dropped, upper torso spinning away, spraying blood and viscera across the clearing. It crashed to the forest floor five metres distant.

Noah gulped air, pain flaring where the slug had hit him. He got to his feet and approached Pendore's upper half, gun still up. While his hand trembled, the weapon's internal workings stayed steady on its target.

Thoughts collided in his head—

—He'd killed a man—

—It had been self-defence—

—Pendore wanted to kill him—

—No choice—

—Had Pendore survived—

—He was now a murderer—

Pendore—what was left of him—lay face down in the soft dark soil. Severed below the solar plexus, blood oozing around bones and organs cauterized black. Noah bent and grabbed a wrist, checking for a pulse. Finding none, he pulled the body over onto its back. Pendore's lifeless eyes stared up at the sky, blood leaking from a slack jaw.

Noah collapsed to the ground. Each painful breath inhaled the tang of charred flesh and ozone of the spent shell. He'd been trained to fight creatures, kill them if needed. He carried the guilt of every creature he'd euthanized. But never a person.

Pendore would have killed him, Noah repeated to himself. Probably would have told the Elders he'd found Noah dead deep in the forest. And if anyone ever found Noah's remains, scavengers would have picked clean any evidence of what had killed him. Scavengers that would do the same to Pendore.

He'd had no choice.

He was still a murderer.

And the creature. He looked over at its lifeless form.

To hell with this place, he thought, getting to his feet and holstering his gun.

Trying not to think, Noah pulled the communicator from his pocket and found blood on his fingers. He wiped them on his coat before scanning the topographic maps of the mountain Hollister had sent him. They traced a path up to a small plateau near the top.

Maybe Noah would see Pastor Dean's Hell.

Loading the trap into his pack, Noah began to climb, grateful to leave the scene of carnage behind. He made it a dozen steps before falling to his knees and retching.

Out of breath, palms raw, he reached the plateau. Crossing to the far side, he found the mountain swept down into lush green forest and open meadows before rising again, ten kilometres distant. From there, more peaks and ranges continued almost as far as he could see. Behind the last range, the red-gold terminus of the terraforming wave shimmered like hellfire as orbiting platforms rained down the biochemical mixture.

Noah stared, his aches forgotten. In his training, he'd studied its biochemical process. Even now, he could recite the engineered compounds from memory.

But he'd never seen it. Few who had never been in orbit had. Past the wave lay the planet's original, unspoiled biosphere, one so similar to Earth's that the planet's indigenous creatures that had not fled before the wave could survive and adapt to the re-engineered environment. Yet kilometre by kilometre, the wave's ceaseless advance destroyed the natural biosphere. A hundred years earlier, it likely had been raining down into the valley below. In twelve hundred years, it would collapse on the far side of the planet.

Settling in the shade of a boulder and sipping from his waterskin, Noah cursed the Directorate. The first generation of settlers had wanted a new Earth unspoiled by centuries of pollution. They'd set the satellites in motion and established the Directorate on a cloaked island twelve kilometres off the coast. Once cloned vegetation and wildlife had taken hold, they'd built the first city, which they'd dubbed Philadelphia in the hope of forming a harmonious society, using ancient construction techniques.

Within a generation, Philadelphia had grown, the frontier expanded and new cities established. Fearing too-rapid expansion, the Directorate had enacted a long-debated policy to forbid sharing knowledge of their location. It established institutes in Philadelphia to control the release of technology and the flow of information, including the Philadelphia Institute of Xenobiology—the "Pix" of legend—with its mandate to eliminate indigenous life forms that had passed through the terminus. Six generations later, no one outside the Directorate or its institutes knew they inhabited a planet circling a G-type star in the galaxy's Perseus Arm.

Noah took his communicator, still sticky with Pendore's blood, from his pocket and entered his codes. Hollister's voice said, "We have your location. The shuttle should arrive within two hours. We'll approach the western slope."

"Okay."

"Have you eliminated the creature's remains?"

Noah surprised himself by saying, "I killed a man."

"Can you repeat that?" Hollister asked.

Noah did, describing his encounter with Pendore. He resisted the urge to retch again.

"You couldn't handle a primitive?"

"That's what I'm trying to tell you, sir. They're not primitive. Not out here. Philadelphia has lost control." Noah considered the others Pendore had spoken of. Men—and perhaps women—determined to expand, destroying the pristine world the founders had envisioned.

"I'm sure the Directorate can make arrangement to regain influence,"

Hollister said. "Noah, listen to me. You did the right thing. Not allowing primitives to gain proof of an indigenous specimen is worth killing over. You destroyed the carcass, right?"

"Yes," Noah lied.

"The shuttle is on its way. When you get back, I think you could use a temporary break from field work."

"Yes, sir." Hollister was lying. Noah would be taken out of the field, assigned to another institute.

"I'll see you soon, Noah."

Noah stared at the terminus, imagining his future spent among the sterile glass and steel towers on the administration island that he'd fought so hard to escape. Cut off from the sounds and smells of the wilderness. And in Dean End, Livingstone would never know what happened, just that the attacks had stopped. He'd turn the situation to his advantage, increasing his hold, reinforcing the superstitions.

But Pendore's followers? Without their leader, would they fragment or would someone take his place? Without more attacks, would they move over this mountain into the next valley? Build another factory? Keep spreading? And as they did, their weapons would slaughter whatever "monsters" they encountered.

Noah hurled the communicator. It arced away and was swallowed up by the foliage below. Without it, the Institute couldn't find him. He imagined the shuttle circling, maybe dropping someone in to search for him, before giving up and returning to Philadelphia.

By then, he'd be back in Dean End, presenting the creature's head to Livingstone and collecting his reward. He'd tell the Elders that Pendore had died trying to kill the beast.

He'd head east and recover his equipment in Charlotte. With the gold, he might be able to establish a preserve to send the animals he saved, where they'd be secure from the wave of settlers that would soon spread west into this wilderness.

Noah turned and headed east down the mountain.

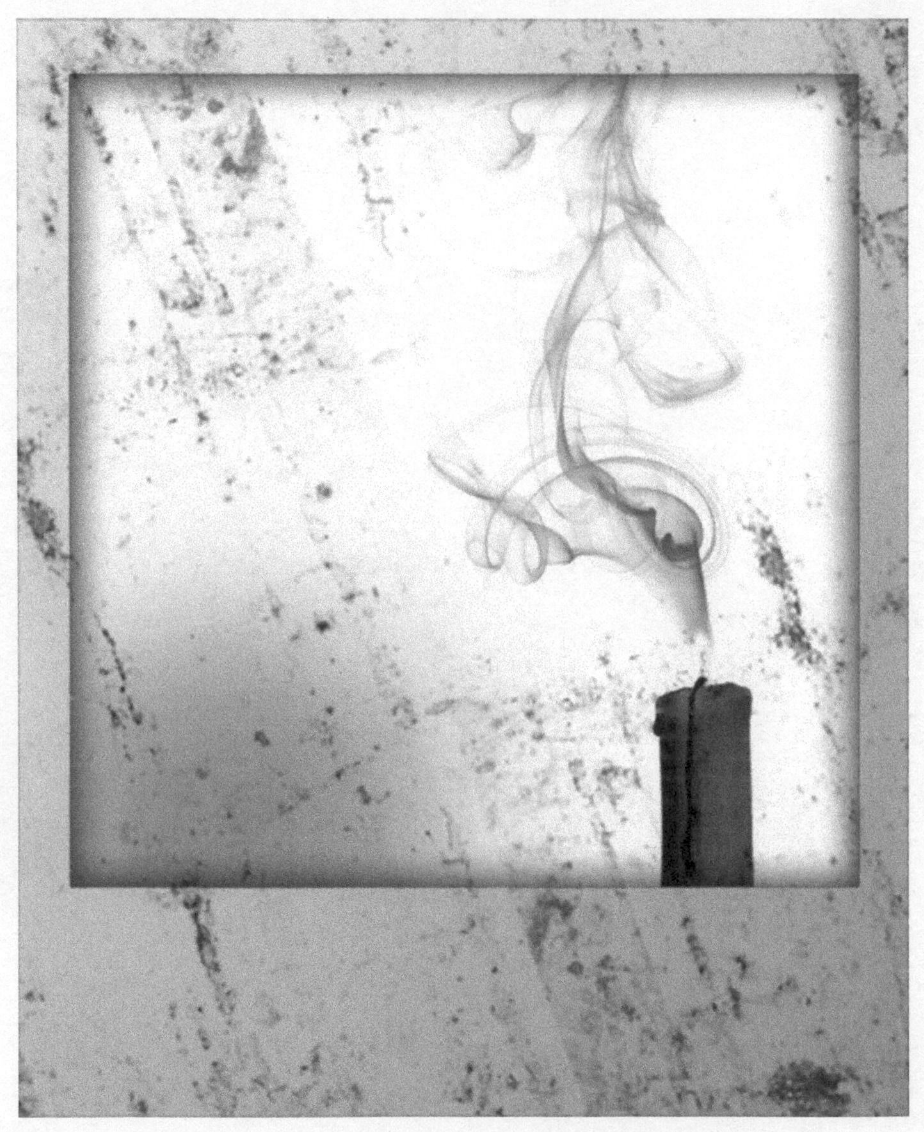

BRIEF CANDLES

With another set of neighbours talking to James at the end of the driveway, the doubts crept again along the edges of Mary's mind. Doubts that moving out of the city would improve things with James's parents. Doubts that she and James should have moved to this new neighbourhood without a flame burning in a translantern.

Outside, the mom pushed the stroller back and forth to soothe the sleeping infant wrapped in a pink blanket while the dad held his toddler daughter's hand as she twisted and pulled, bored by grown-up talk. And James smiled and chatted, motioning to the house and street, while he no doubt tried to hide that it all just reminded him that they didn't have anyone they could ask to die, so they could have a baby.

Snatches of the conversation drifted through the open bedroom window while Mary organized the clothes scattered across the bed from one of the last unpacked boxes. ". . . great schools . . ." "Love it so far . . ." ". . . safe . . ." ". . . good neighbours . . ." ". . . away from the half- and quarter-souled coloureds." Mary kept her head down, folding his shirts into a pile, socks and underwear in another, her skirts and blouses on the opposite side of the bed. Yet the emptiness ached in her belly with thoughts of the other neighbours they'd met during the first three weeks in their new home. It was a gorgeous start to summer, with young families pushing strollers and guiding toddlers while moms-to-be glowed with their beautiful bellies. At backyard barbecues or cocktails parties where they'd meet their just-moved-in neighbours, it was almost as if some of the moms intentionally taunted her. Their accents hinting that they came from up the valley or down east, these women told Mary about a sister back home who felt too old to have a second child, or the tragedy of a young niece or nephew passing away suddenly. Regardless of the details, these women had received a flame and, with it, the rare blessing of a third child. "The Cycle turns," they'd beam, absently stroking their bellies.

Not fast enough, Mary wanted to, but couldn't, reply. Five years of marriage and still using condoms and tracking her cycle like couples who already had their two children. She envied, and in darker moments even hated, her girlfriends whose letters exclaimed that they were pregnant and, a few months later, described the hardships as their bodies swelled and changed.

She hadn't expected the wait to be so trying. They'd been married less than a year when she'd urged James to give up the flame holding the soul of his paternal grandmother to his brother Leonard so they could maintain peace in the family. She'd believed Vivian, James's mother, would find another flame for them soon enough. But the short wait she'd envisioned had stretched over four years and now the emptiness of this house, with its two other bedrooms still primer-white instead of baby blue or soft pink, pressed in like night air before a storm.

A storm she hoped to avoid this evening with James's parents coming for dinner for the first time since moving in.

Everything sorted on the bed, Mary began placing things in their proper drawers. Glancing outside, she saw that the couple had left. But James had crossed the street and was heading down the sidewalk for a house near the end of the block where an older man awkwardly yanked a lawnmower's pull cord. After a moment, Mary realized the man was left-handed and the right-mounted cord gave him trouble. Another moment still and, taking in his white hair and stooped posture, she realized he wasn't just older but *old*.

James greeted the man and they began to talk, motioning to the mower, the man's house, James's house and then back to the mower. After a minute, James gave the handle a sharp yank. The engine's roar filled the mid-afternoon summer air. Rather than returning home, the two men let the mower run for a few seconds, shut it off and disappeared into the garage.

Clothing put away, Mary descended to the kitchen to start on dinner. She wondered why an old man had moved to a new neighbourhood filled with young families and if he felt as out of place as she did.

"Just met a new neighbour," James announced, coming up the stairs. "Name's Alvin Rusk. Interesting guy."

"Was he the one you were helping with the mower?" Mary replied. He'd been gone over an hour, enough time to put dinner in the oven and have a quicker shower. "Yeah. Moved in a week ago." James stripped off his shirt and tossed it into the hamper.

Mary buttoned up the dress she'd bought for that night. "How old is he?"

"Seventy-two." His jeans went next. "Can you believe that?"

Mary could. Her parents' letters described a commune up the valley with inhabitants in their eighties and even nineties. The younger residents revered, respected and cared for them rather than waiting for, or even urging, them to die.

"No kids, though," James added, filling in a missing piece. "That he knows of. Sounds like he had his fair share of company in Europe during the wars." He stood naked in the bedroom, looking around. "Where are the towels?"

Even after five years, the sight of him thrilled her. The effort of moving in and setting up had left them drained most nights, but right now they had time. If they were quick. To be with him, his arms holding her, inhaling the smell that was his. "I don't know," she said, teasing. She began to undo the buttons up the front of her dress. "Come find them."

He looked at her, then the bedside clock, and his shoulders slumped. "Not now, okay? Are there towels in the bathroom?" He didn't wait for an answer before moving into the hall and shutting the bathroom door behind him. A moment later, the shower spit a few times before the flow steadied.

Mary redid her buttons, forcing her thoughts away from James and onto what was left to do that evening. It would have been a mistake, anyway. It had been two weeks since her period, her most fertile time.

What would she do if she got pregnant without a soul for their baby? In another letter, after Mary had told her parents about giving James's translantern to his brother, they'd suggested she get pregnant "by accident" and force James to confront his beliefs. Would he side with his mother, who'd no doubt pressure Mary to end the pregnancy, or support her in finally starting a family?

But the scheme never took into account what she believed. *Which was what?* she asked herself.

Mary pressed the heels of her palms to her eyes, forcing back the building tears. Thoughts like those didn't help. She had to be strong and calm tonight. It had been her suggestion to host James's parents for dinner. James had resisted, reminding her they'd moved out to the suburbs to put some distance between them, but she'd insisted.

The truth, she admitted to herself but could not admit to James, was she was terrified to face pregnancy and childbirth without her mother. Yet her parents had settled permanently in that commune. Their letters were cordial enough, but Mary hadn't seen them in years and didn't honestly know if they would leave after the horrible things she'd said to them. So despite James's feelings toward his mother, Mary had no other choice than to rely on Vivian when they finally had a flame and could start a family.

The shower shut off. Knowing James would be in a mood and seeing her so upset would make it worse, Mary went downstairs to check on dinner.

The doorbell rang.

In the living room, James let out a groan Mary could hear over the boiling pots. With her hair done up and new dress fitting perfectly, she felt ready. She hoped James was. At least he had thawed a little as they had finished tidying, cracking jokes and his hand "accidentally" brushing her breast or bottom.

But hearing James move to the door, a familiar fear twisted in Mary's belly—that tonight would be the night James's simmering anger would boil over at Vivian and he'd vent the four years of rage he'd been carrying. Just as she'd driven away her parents, James would drive away his, leaving them alone and without any hope of getting a flame except buying one.

And, Mary feared, would James's anger turn on her for putting them in that situation? Her breath caught. At twenty-seven, the time where they could start a family was slipping away. Another fear crept cool and tight up her neck that James might leave her for a younger woman with a flame who could give him a child.

"Hello, sweetie!" Vivian boomed, breaking Mary's thoughts. Wiping her hands on her apron, Mary moved into the hall and toward the door. "Hello Mary!" Vivian cried, shrugging out of her coat and pressing her bright reds lip to Mary's cheek. Thomas, James's father, followed silently behind, offering James a handshake and a barely audible "Nice to see you, son." Mary pecked him on the cheek and, after a few words of greeting, returned to the kitchen.

Vivian followed, lifting pot lids and looking in the oven. "Make sure to baste that," she offered. "Need to turn this down," she added, changing a jet's dial. After "Make sure that doesn't burn" and "use butter, don't use oil," Mary said, "Thank you, Vivian, but I think I can handle the rest. Why don't you go sit and enjoy yourself?"

"Oh, I don't mind." She looked over her shoulder at the doorway and took a step closer to Mary. Voice low, she asked, "I really wanted to ask: have you talked to your doctor? About 'the pill'?"

Mary's breath caught. "He's not sure it's the best," she lied. "For me. Who still wants children."

"Well, I hope you and James are careful," Vivian replied. "You especially. It'd be a shame if . . . well. It would be shame." Her bright red lips curled up into a smile. "If you need any help in here, just let me know." She turned and left, saying, "Now what are you men talking about?"

Mary shut her eyes, letting out the breath she'd been holding.

Having time to let things simmer, she untied her apron and moved into the living room where she found a gin and tonic waiting. She sipped at it as Vivian went on about how much faster the new highway made the ride out from the city. She shifted to how she wanted Thomas to close down his practice so they could get out of the city and move to the suburbs themselves. With so many young families out here, a doctor would be in high demand. "And with that latest Negro riot," she added, "who can say where it will happen next?"

Mary looked to James, worried he'd take the bait and correct his mother that most "riots" began as peaceful marches for the equality Negroes had been promised by following the Cycle. They became riots when police turned fire hoses on the protestors or sicced attack dogs on them. Or perhaps he'd remind her of the Negroes he met every day who were as smart and reasonable as any fully ensouled follower of the Cycle. Working in settlement services for new immigrants, James's job brought him into contact with Negroes, Orientals, and Hispanics from all over the world seeking a better life in this country. At least once a week he described a family, or sometimes a young man on his own, who only wanted to work hard and make their own way. Hardly the savages that Vivian believed anyone who didn't follow the Cycle had to be.

But James sat on the couch, swirling the ice in his glass. He resembled his father so much, silent and letting Vivian ramble about how well Leonard was doing with his new auto dealership. To say nothing of his three wonderful children who were growing up so fast. Thomas spoke about his practice when Mary asked him directly, but Vivian would interject, steering the conversation back to one topic or another.

By the time coffee had been served and cleared, Vivian's musing had veered from Vietnam ("Their resistance to accepting the Cycle only shows how badly they need it") to President Johnson ("More trustworthy than that Orthodox Kennedy") to elderly distant relatives ("Your second cousin Stanley still lives alone up in that shack"). Mary despised herself for how her attention had been piqued at the mention of James's cousins and aunts and uncles, hoping that someone's health had taken a bad turn, or worse, so that when they died James and Mary might receive a flame and finally start their family. She debated casually suggesting to Vivian that these distant relatives consider not waiting for a natural death and do the honourable thing by cycling on. If they were all as devout as Vivian claimed, they'd consider it an honour for their soul to live in the newest member of the family. But the news was of good health all around, leading Vivian to assure them that the Cycle does indeed turn, to have faith and be accepting of a flame in its due course.

When Vivian and Thomas left around 9:30, James shut the door and leaned against it, head bowed and mouth set in a thin line.

"I'm sorry," Mary began. "I shouldn't have—"

James held up his hand. He didn't look at her. "This buys us some time. She's wanted to see the house. She's seen it. I don't need to see her again. Unless she has news on a flame."

Bringing plates into the kitchen and wanting to take her mind off Vivian, Mary said, "Tell me more about Alvin."

"More fun than my parents," James replied, sorting clean silverware from used.

"Oh?" She carried in more, placing everything on the counter.

"He's lived quite a life. A man constantly in motion." As James sorted plates from bowls, cups from glasses, his movements softened, his anger draining. "Played baseball. Fought in the wars. Ran his own store for a while."

Mary said, "I'd like to meet him."

"Yeah," James said, moving behind her and wrapping his arms around her waist. "We need some friends around here."

Mary stripped off her rubber gloves and placed her hands over James's, knowing what he'd left unsaid. That it would be good to have a friend without kids or translanterns reminding them of their home's crushing emptiness.

"It's a pleasure, Mr. Rusk," Mary said, balancing the plate of hors d'oeuvres on a hip and taking Alvin's offered hand. The gentleness of the older man's grip surprised her.

"No need to be so formal," he replied. "It's Alvin. Here, let me grab that." He reached out and took the tray from her, holding it in his left hand before sweeping his right into his home. "Come on in."

Mary stepped past Alvin into the living room where faded black and white photos covered the wall behind a simple, plaid couch. An old, wingback chair with worn fabric faced a tiny television. Through the archway into the dining room Mary saw a small circular table with two wooden chairs.

"Simple, I know," Alvin said, setting the tray on a coffee table. "But it's all I need. What can I get you to drink?"

James asked for a beer and Mary did as well while examining the photos. As Alvin milled about in the kitchen, she spotted younger versions of him in photos of muddy fields and dense jungles, or looking dashing in a baseball or postal uniform.

"I was quite the handsome young devil," Alvin said. When Mary turned to take her drink, he winked. "Always the active sort. Thought France would be a big adventure, but . . . well." He waved his hand, clearing away the subject and moving on. "But when the Japs bombed Pearl I re-enlisted. Forty-two and could still fit in my uniform." He patted his barely there paunch. "I could out-run, out-fight and out-drink those young sprouts. And those overeager jackrabbits didn't know how to treat a lady." He chuckled and Mary noticed how the left side of his face curled up, while the right remained still. "But hell, listen to me, rambling on. Mary, my dear, I've met James. Let's hear about you."

Mary told how she was born and grew up in the city's west end. She mentioned her older brother, David, and how she'd been twelve when he'd been killed in Korea. Not wanting to ruin the mood, she didn't tell Alvin that no one had been with David to light a flame and capture his soul when he'd died. She recalled vividly, but did not describe, their priest explaining how David's soul would not be lost. Instead, it would have entered into a Korean newborn, saving the child from the wild, uncivilized life of a quarter- or eighth or even no-souled who were so common over there. Which was why, the priest went on, that part of the world was constantly beset by things like wars and famine, and susceptible to dictators and communists.

She skipped over the change in her parents, who'd never been faithful in attending church, as they attended fewer holiday services and decorated less for equinox celebrations. And by the time she started high school, boys and clothes and music filled her life, not how long her father's hair had grown or that they visited unnamed friends some evenings, leaving her home alone.

So there was no need to tell Alvin about coming home from school on the Friday after the Vernal Equinox to find her father home from work. With her mother, they sat her down in the kitchen and told her that they had converted to Christianity. She couldn't breathe, trying to process that her parents had joined this new religion, though they insisted it was two thousand years old, that rock musicians had brought it back from visits to the Middle East. It was people in their twenties who were growing out their hair, quitting respectable jobs, moving to remote camps and reproducing like Africans or Orientals because they believed their all-powerful god could create as many souls as it wanted. And because those souls returned to this god after death, the idea that one could trap a soul in a flame when someone died and release it into a newborn baby by extinguishing the flame was ridiculous.

It was that realization that made her leap from the kitchen table and run to the living room to find the candle in each of the two translanterns on the mantle extinguished. Smoke still curled from the candle in the fourteen-inch high octagonal translantern, which her mother brought into the marriage and would have been Mary's. She snatched it up, its brushed chrome sides still warm. The squat, cone-shaped translantern with circles stamped into its copper sides, which would have gone to David, was cool. Her legs nearly gave out with the realization that she'd had gone from the enviable position of bringing two souls into a marriage, the one thing that could get some boys' attention over her friends' pretty faces or curves under their sweaters, to none.

She's wheeled on them, unleashing hateful rants about blasphemy and heresy, spouting conservative politicians' rhetoric on how breaking the Cycle would lead the country down a path of depravity, hedonism and idleness. She didn't know if she believed it, just that she wanted it to hurt. And lastly, the one thing she *did* know, is who would marry her if she could not bring a flame to the marriage?

They told her God loved her, would love her children and place souls within them, but by then she was halfway up the stairs. She slammed the door and flopped onto her bed, sobbing into her pillow with the knowledge that the life she had imagined had been wiped away by something as simple as two breaths. Men without a flame could still succeed in life, but women grew into crazy old spinsters or, sometimes, prostitutes. Now she'd be one of them. And she found that this realization fuelled her grief, not that her grandparents' souls had been let loose to wander until they entered a newborn who might otherwise have been soulless. Because, in that moment, she realized she didn't believe in the Cycle. There was comfort in the traditions and the notion of a population that wouldn't explode out of control, but the idea of trapping a soul in a flame was as unbelievable as a single god who could create souls from nothing.

But others did believe and would judge her for what her parents had done. Whispers behind cupped hands followed her through the halls at school. At home, her parents' overtures to follow Christ ended in screaming fights with her storming out and spending hours alone at the library since she wasn't welcome in her friends' homes any longer.

And when high school ended, she moved out and told them she never wanted to see them again.

Of course, she told Alvin none of this. Not even James knew all these details. With his parents so devout, she didn't dare risk telling him of her own lack of faith. A pang of guilt still soured her stomach over how she had lied to him when they had first met that her father had been killed in WWII and so she was eligible for the Potsdam Dispensation of having a child without a flame. By the time she'd confessed, they'd been so deeply in love he had forgiven her and told her if they only had one child they'd have to love it twice as much.

Instead, she told Alvin that she and her parents had had a falling out after she'd finished high school, so she'd moved into an apartment with three other girls. She'd worked as a secretary at an insurance company, met James through some common friends, fallen in love, and then married. And once married, of course, quit her job to take care of the home in preparation for children.

"Well. Quite a story," Alvin said, finishing the last of his can. "So who's ready for another?"

Head buzzing but not quite spinning, they thanked Alvin and headed for home. Past midnight, the night air was still warm.

"What's so funny?" James asked, slipping his arm around her waist and slowly tracing a fingertip up her side.

"Just that Alvin is not what I expected," she said, giggling and then realizing she'd been giggling for some time. James's finger tickled and teased and her giggles became squeals. She put her hand around his waist. "And not full of baby talk or how great it is not to be surrounded by Negroes."

They reached the front door, Mary having just enough self-control for James to open the door for her, follow her inside, and shut it before grabbing him, pressing against him, kissing him. "Upstairs," she breathed and turned, awkwardly mounting the steps, flying into the bedroom and flopping on the bed on her back. A moment later, James's was above her, lips on her neck, hands everywhere.

She let James strip off her clothes, her hands too clumsy and drunk. Her fingers stroked the swell in his pants. "Hurry. . . ." she said.

Voices from teachers in those all-girls classes in high school piped up in her mind as clothes fell away and cool air licked her skin. ". . . boys can't help themselves, so girls must be in control." "We have our own cycle to track and protect . . ." ". . . a woman's hips and breasts are curves to remind her of the Cycle's endless curve . . ."

"Oh, shut up."

"Huh?" James asked, confusion in his voice and suddenly still.

"Nothing," she panted. She caressed his face, his neck, his chest. "Nothing." When he remained unmoving, she slapped his shoulder. "It's nothing, now come on."

"Okay," he grunted, leaning to the side. She heard the bedside table open, his hands rummaging through contents.

"Oh, just do it," she begged.

"Without—?"

She reached out in the dark, following his body down and guiding him inside her. "Yes."

James obliged, thrusting forward.

A noise woke James out of a restless sleep. After a second, he shut his eyes and tried to doze back off. A dull pain coated the front of his head.

Stopping by Alvin's after the Autumnal Equinox fireworks had seemed like a good idea. Alvin had had some beers in the fridge, tomorrow was Saturday, so why not? Besides, it was better than going to the Sutherlands' or Atwoods' and listening to the dads talk about little league, new school year schedules, or what a pain setting up a swing set could be. Sure, he kept a smile on his face, but sometimes he wanted to shake one of them. Didn't they read the paper? Watch the news? Who cared what their kids were doing when kids were dying in Vietnam. And for what? Or the hypocrisy of the so-devout southern governors claiming Negroes could never be fully ensouled no matter how hard they worked, despite scripture saying the opposite. The country was changing. Hell, the whole world was.

And they knew he and Mary wanted kids but didn't have a flame. Talking about little Michael on the swing or Jennifer losing a tooth just twisted the dagger a little more.

That's why he and Mary had spent so much time with Alvin over the summer. They could talk baseball, movies, politics. Crack some jokes. And his opinions surprised James. The first time watching Walter Cronkite report on a Negroes' equal rights march, James had braced for comments like his mother's. A century after slavery, his mother would have started in, Negroes had more babies than they could support. Got mixed up in crime. No better behaved than their no-souled ancestors brought over from Africa. At least under slavery, his mother had once said, they had a chance to become fully ensouled through hard work and following their masters' teachings.

But Alvin, more than fifteen years older than his mother, sided with the protestors. As for 'Nam, Alvin kept repeating it was a mistake.

And unlike the young families that turned in early, Alvin was game to stay up until midnight or later.

"You awake?" Mary asked again, pulling him from his drifting thoughts.

"Yes."

"I've been thinking," Mary said after a moment. "What if we asked Alvin to cycle on?"

James let the idea roll around his head. He'd never considered going outside the family. Or, he had to admit, feared his mother's reaction to it.

But lying there, staring at the ceiling, the idea gave him hope.

Over the summer of getting to know the older man, Alvin's happy veneer had slipped at times. He'd talked about playing baseball or walking his route. Being young and strong. Endless energy. But he'd given up the route when the winters got too hard. Tried his hand at running a plumbing store owned by an army buddy, but the demands of lifting heavy boxes proved to be too much. So did his fourth floor walk-up in the city.

He'd thought a house in the suburbs would be easier but found its upkeep taxing. Even one flight of steps seemed too much at time. And he didn't always trust his eyesight to drive.

"I don't know how much time I got left," he'd said once, empty beer cans covering the patio table. "When I'm gone all that'll be left are some army records and old box scores."

Alvin didn't speak much of friends. Said he and his sister didn't talk. So it didn't seem there would be anyone wanting his soul when he passed. With some luck, Alvin might consider it an honour to cycle on. To take his own life before the last of his strength faded and have his soul go to someone he knew.

James would miss his friend, but the Cycle taught that Alvin had had his time. A pang of selfishness at using scripture he didn't even believe to justify asking Alvin to cycle on weighed on him, but the thought of finally holding his own child pressed back.

Next to him, Mary continued, "I know your mother won't approve at first, but over time—"

"We don't need to tell her," James said, hoping the hangover didn't put too much anger into his voice. "We say it's from your family. A second cousin or something. Someone distant."

Her hand found his. "The guilt I have, even to this day, over lying to you about the Potsdam Dispensation," she said. "It eats me up. I don't want another lie—"

"It's none of her business."

"Okay," she said again, squeezing his hand.

"Yeah, let's ask Alvin," James said, squeezing Mary's hand back. "Should we . . ." He paused, not sure what to say. His mom would be a natural at asking Alvin to cycle on, but James didn't know where to start.

"We could have him for dinner," Mary suggested, like she could read his mind. "I could make something nice, tell him how much we want kids. What it would mean to us."

"Alright." He gave her hand another squeeze and she slid closer to him. He wrapped his arms around her, grateful. Mary went still, her breathing deeper. But thoughts of what lie he would tell that would satisfy his mother's curiosity kept him awake. When his sister-in-law, Sharon, learned she was pregnant for the third time, Leonard had wanted to go to a publicly funded hospital. Find some poor, old person and buy their soul when they passed.

Neither Leonard nor James had expected this to be a problem. The church encouraged it. Better a soul be born into a middle-class or wealthy family than again into poverty. Less of a drain on social programs. One less fully ensouled person in menial work. Let a Negro take that job to work toward becoming fully ensouled.

But Vivian had called James, demanding he give the flame of his grandfather on his mantle to Leonard. She'd hear no other alternative. When James asked for an explanation, she described her life as a girl in Germany after World War I, telling him things he'd never heard before. The war had caused havoc with the Cycle. The peace treaties' conditions had broken the people's spirit. Flames were used as currency. Women without flames bought counterfeit translanterns. Souls split and split again as babies without flames were born. Who else but a half- and quarter-souled people would fall under the thrall of a madman? Her family had barely escaped when the country had fallen into war again.

So, she'd declared, this baby would have a flame from inside the family. Not a homeless beggar who'd ended up on the street because he probably wasn't fully ensouled to start. If James didn't give in, she'd convince his father to cut him off. And Leonard. At the time, Leonard's car dealership still needed their father's backing. And James and Mary would need help when the time came to buy a house. Not finished, her voice like ice, Vivian promised to wear Sharon down. Force her to have an abortion. And he'd be to blame. His sister-in-law wasn't strong like Mary. James knew his mother could do it.

Before he could tell his brother about the threat, Mary had said he should give up the flame to keep the family together. They'd only been married a few months. They'd find another way. A fight like this wasn't worth it.

James knew Mary's parents were Christian. Though he and Mary didn't attend church regularly, he suspected Mary's faith ran deep if she'd estranged herself from them due to their conversion. So he'd given in. And spent four years hiding his jealousy of coworkers' photos of their kids on their desks and pretending seeing dads playing with their kids in the park didn't cause an ache in his heart.

Mary shifted in his arms, her breathing slow and steady. James released her, shifting farther to his side of the bed. Staring at the ceiling, he kept thinking how he'd tell his mother.

His parents arrived fifteen minutes early. "Are we early?" his mother asked, looking at her watch. "Why, I guess we are." His father silently handed over his hat and coat.

Mary called out greetings from the kitchen but stayed there.

While James mixed drinks, Vivian started in on the young women out in San Francisco she'd seen on the news. Dressed in leather and denim, showing off their swollen tummies for the television cameras. "They seem so proud to be pregnant and not have a flame for their poor babies." James handed out the drinks and mixed a new one for himself having had two already.

They'd already fought it out, but his anger at Mary for inviting his parents to the dinner when they were going to talk to Alvin still boiled. Didn't it make sense, Mary explained to James, that his parents at least meet Alvin? If Vivian and Thomas liked Alvin, she and James might not need to endlessly repeat some lie of where the flame came from. Since Thomas and Vivian always left early, James and Mary could talk to Alvin after.

He could have refused. Told his mother they needed to reschedule. But in the end, he gave in. Like always.

The doorbell rang, cutting off Vivian. James stood and answered the door to find Alvin with a bottle of wine.

"So, Alvin," Vivian said after introductions had been made, "tell us about yourself."

Alvin talked about his life and asked about Vivian and Thomas. Vivian told him about herself, about Thomas, his practice, their life together. She was her usual self, but Alvin held his own. They got into it, politely, over 'Nam and Negroes and the changing times. James watched, sipping his drink and getting refills. This would not end well. Meeting Alvin wouldn't affect her opinion of asking Alvin to cycle on. But he wanted a child more than his mother's approval. And with that realization, a calmness that even the booze couldn't provide settled over him.

It was like a schism in his mind cleaving his life in two. Before, his mother controlled whether he would have a family. After, he would make the decision. There would be no lies about some distant cousin of Mary's or worrying over whether his mother would forgive him for going outside the family. Whether or not his mother would be a part of her grandchild's life was a decision she would have to make.

He waited until after dessert. As his mother transitioned from one story to another, James took Mary's hand and interjected: "Sorry, Mom, there's something I've been meaning to ask Alvin. A favour."

"Certainly," Alvin replied, taking a sip of coffee.

Mary squeezed his hand, though encouraging him or wanting him to stop, he didn't know. "You know Mary and I want to have a baby."

"Of course he knows," Vivian said, sitting at the table. "We've been talking—"

"And," James went on, "we were hoping you'd do us the honour of cycling on."

"What is this?" Vivian asked, suddenly still and voice icy.

Alvin held James's gaze for a moment, then delicately set his coffee cup down.

"You said you don't have any children," James went on. Mary squeezed his hand again. "What you said about not being remembered really struck us. And how hard things are for you. So . . ."

"No," Vivian said. "No, I forbid this. I *forbid* it."

"Mom," James said. And for the first time, put some threat in it.

"I will not have some stranger's soul in my grandchildren."

"I, um . . ." Alvin began, dabbing at this mouth with his napkin. "That is to say . . ." He folded his napkin, folded it again. "I'm a Christian, James. Mary."

Mary's grip loosened.

"I wondered if you might be, too," Alvin went on.

"How dare you?" Vivian said.

"Mom—" James started.

"Young couple like them?" Alvin said, facing Vivian. "No translanterns? I wanted to ask. Wondered if you've given your life to Christ, but if I was wrong . . . Well . . ." He cleared his throat and stood. "Thank you for a lovely dinner."

James stood as well. "Alvin, I'm so sorry—"

"People like you," Vivian started, "would have us breed like animals. Souls dividing. People spreading too far. Using up our resources."

"People like me?" For the first time, James heard anger rise in Alvin's voice. "You watch the news? The population is increasing faster than the number of immigrants we got coming in. But it's not Negroes doing it." Alvin grimaced and his hand rose to his temple.

"Foreigners sneak into this country," Vivian replied. "Dirty, no souls with no respect—"

"Take a walk around this neighbourhood," Alvin continued. "Some families got three kids. The Sutherlands? They got four. Good, proper families." He gesticulated with his left hand, emphasizing each word, but his right hung by his side. "Sure, maybe they had flames for their kids. Maybe. Or maybe between here and wherever they came from they lit a candle. Tell folks here it's some distant cousin back home. But they tell folks back home they got it from some homeless guy here." Alvin paused, placing his left hand against the side of his head. The left side of his face bunched up, but the right hung limp.

James expected his mother to explode, but she sat stunned, mouth set in a thin line.

Instead, his father asked, "Alvin?"

Alvin waved his hand at Thomas. His voice shook with barely contained anger, but the words came out slurred. "And resources? How many more roads out of the city and houses with huge yards we goin' to build? One of the reasons more people are followin' Christ is they're seein' the Cycle for what it is. A way to get rid a old people 'stead of takin' care of them. Justify centuries of slavery. Justify racism and 'bortion. But people 're—" He shook his head and forced out: "People 're livin' . . ."

"Well," Vivian said. "Nothing more to say?"

"Alvin," Thomas said, his voice steady as he rose to his feet. "You need you to sit down. I think you might be having a stroke."

The word struck James. The son of a doctor, he hadn't noticed the symptoms. He moved around the table to Alvin. "Let's get you into the living room."

Alvin stumbled back, the right side of his face frozen. "God pr'tect me." He limped down the hall, left hand up, right arm lifeless. "Pastor Dean warned me 'bout this." He bounced off a wall, unable to keep his balance.

"Call an ambulance," Thomas called over his shoulder, following Alvin, a hand out. "Alvin, please."

James followed his father as Mary reached for the phone. Behind him, Vivian snapped, "Don't you dare! The Cycle turns."

"Shut up, mother," James said, motioning for Mary to call and following his father after Alvin.

"And no one is getting a candle?" Vivian remarked, still seated. "A coloured family could benefit from his soul."

"I didn' believe 'im," Alvin was saying. "That desperate Cyclers 'd poison someone t' get their soul." By then Alvin had reached the front hall. He groped for the handle, opened the door and stepped outside onto the porch.

James and Thomas followed. The sun had set, but the streetlights had not come on. As Alvin descended the front steps, James said, "Alvin, we didn't do anything."

"Alvin," Thomas added, "we need to get you to a hospital."

Alvin's legs wobbled stepping off the curb and into the street. "Leave me 'lone."

Headlights caught James's eye. In the dimming evening, he made out a big Ford Fury convertible, its top down. It barely slowed for the stop sign at the Fuller Avenue intersection and roared down Ridgeline Crescent toward them.

James charged at Alvin. The headlights swelled, massive. The engine deafening. He wrapped his arms around Alvin and they tumbled, wind from the passing car whipping his shirt and hair. Together, they landed hard on the opposite sidewalk.

The car skidded, clouds of grey smoke flying from its squealing tires, and came to a stop. Rock music from some British band blared from the radio.

"Sorry, pops!" the driver shouted, standing in his seat. His dark hair reached his shoulders. "Didn't see you there."

"You could have killed us!" James shouted.

A teenaged girl in the passenger seat, a tie-dye T-shirt draped over her and sunglasses so large they covered half her face, stood. "Hey man, Jesus forgives us. So should you."

She sat down and the car sped away.

"Alvin?" James asked, gently shaking him. Alvin, eyes closed and jaw slack, didn't respond. Thomas appeared at their side. He put his ear to Alvin's mouth and chest, then ran his fingers along the back of Alvin's head. To James he said, "Back inside, son. Get me your First Aid kit. Flashlight. Some ice and a wash cloth."

James ran back to his house, noticing neighbours gathering on their front walks. His mother waited at the bottom of the porch steps. "Is he hurt bad?" she asked, an unlit candle in hand. James snatched it and threw it down the street before mounting the stairs.

Mary waited on the porch. He explained what he needed. They gathered the items quickly. On their way back out, James and Mary passed his mother, rigid and fuming. The ambulance arrived moments later. In a blur of motion and shouted instructions, the paramedics loaded Alvin into the big, white vehicle. Its siren wailing, it rushed off down the street.

The spectacle over, neighbours retreated back inside. James, Mary and Thomas returned to the house. Vivian waited, scowling.

"People saw you save him," Vivian said. "The Cycle turns. It was his time. What are they going to think about you now?"

"I don't care," James said.

She glared at him for a moment before saying, "I thought I raised you properly. In the church."

"A church that says it's okay to leave a friend to die because he's old isn't one I want to be part of!"

Vivian took a step back, shocked. Gathering her composure, lips pressed white, she turned to Thomas. "Get our coats. We're not welcome in this home."

James let her go.

His father called to let him know Alvin was awake and asking for him, but the prognosis wasn't good. "His attending told me he's had a series of small strokes over the years," Thomas had explained. "This one was bad. The hospital's keeping him comfortable. But they won't treat him."

"The Cycle turns," James had said.

"Indeed it does," Thomas had replied.

James asked about his mother. Thomas told him she was still mad but would settle down in time. She loved her sons too much to hold that much of a grudge. James wasn't so sure.

Following the coloured lines on the hallway floor, James wondered what Alvin wanted to talk about. Finding the right hall, he heard voices coming from the open door of Alvin's room. Peering in, a dozen people stood around the bed. The youngest was a teenager, the oldest older than Alvin. Half were white, the others Oriental, Negro, and Hispanic. Their heads bowed, a woman his mother's age recited some kind of poem. The language was difficult to follow, but ended with ". . . dwell in the house of the Lord forever. Amen."

A prayer, James realized. He'd just heard a Christian prayer.

Alvin's eyes met James's. "James," he said. He lay propped up on pillows with bandages wrapped around his head. His left eye glistened, but the right was lifeless. The entire right side of his face drooped. The group turned to look at him. Voice still slurred, Alvin explained: "Friends, this is the young man who saved me."

A murmur went through them. James felt paralyzed, not sure what would happen next.

The woman who had led the prayer said to him, "God bless you, James." She motioned for him to enter. "You are welcome to join us."

"That's okay," James said. "I just wanted to see how Alvin was."

"All are welcome to hear the word of the Lord."

"Let 'im be, Ellie," Alvin said. To James he said: "We won't be too long."

James found a chair and waited. Finally, the group left, most smiling at James as they passed. He stood and went into Alvin's room.

"'Lo, James," he said, left side of his mouth curling up in a smile.

"How are you feeling?" James sat in a simple chair next to the bed.

"Comfortable as I can, I s'pose. Docs say it won't be long. A big 'un'll come and get me." He cleared his throat. "Thank you for, um . . . Well, f' saving my life. I'm sorry. For what I said, that is." He tapped the side of his head. "Brain wasn't workin' right."

"Apology accepted," James said, smiling. "And I'm sorry for asking you like that. And my mother . . ."

"You can't help that. Don't think there's any man who can keep your mother from sayin' what's on 'er mind." He swallowed. "I have t' ask, though. I've been thinkin' 'bout it. Why save me? Why risk your own life? The Cycle says th' old die so th' young can live. That stupid kid would've run me down and you and Mary could be parents in nine months."

"Because . . ." James said, "it was the right thing to do."

"That's very Christian of you, but not th' Cycle."

"I guess . . ." His mind spun. "Sometimes we get mixed up in what our religion says and not what it means. I could have let you die and said 'the Cycle turns,' but it wouldn't have been right. The Cycle's about having the best world we can. Don't take too much from it. Work hard. For me, the best world is one with you still in it. Even if it means waiting a little longer for a baby, it's too selfish to ask you to die."

Alvin nodded, sunlight catching tear tracks on his cheeks. "I've been thinkin', James. 'bout that night. If I'd been home when th' stroke hit." He swallowed. "I'd be dead right now. God wanted me at your place. I'm sure a it. He moved through you so I'd live." He wiped at his tears. "There's some message in this. Some meanin' t' m' life."

James remained silent, not sure how active a role Christians believed their God had in their lives.

"I should have discussed this with you man to man," James began, frustration creeping up. "Mary invited my parents over. I should have said 'no.' Or talked to you first."

"Too late for that, James. God works His will. Or 'the Cycle turns,' you might say." He reached out and took James's hand. "Don't be mad. You an' your mom; your feelin's run deep. You got that from 'er, but you got your dad's soft-spoken side. Your mom knows what she believes. I think you get into fights with 'er 'cause you don't. And Mary. She's a keeper. She's got no family but you. I know what it's like t' lose family. When I gave my life t' Christ my sister cut me off. Just like that." He wiped at his eyes again. "Hey, listen t' me ramblin' on."

"It's okay," James said and meant it.

Alvin cleared his throat and asked, "So, you think the Sox are going all the way?"

James passed the letter to Mary. He'd read the shaky writing twice at the hospital.

Dear James and Mary,

The doctors have told me my chances are not good, so I am going to write this while I can.

We believe different things, but I've come to see there's no harm in someone lighting a candle when I die. My soul belongs to God and I'll face His judgment, but if you take comfort from a candle and it reminds you of our friendship, it's a blessed thing. And if you choose to blow it out when your first child is born, where's the harm?

My church doesn't agree. They say it's blasphemy to consider it. But I think about what you said. That sometimes the words of our faith get in the way of what they're trying to teach us.

And I think that's what God wanted me to realize. With everything I've done in my life, I don't think God will mind one candle. It's an act of Christian charity.

I hope you'll tell your little boy or girl about me. That I tried to live a good life. I did some terrible things in the wars, but I hope I've made the world a better place. And I hope your son or daughter will learn that lesson from me.

That's what I want to leave to this world. The meaning of my life. We can make the world better even with small actions.

I hope you never see this letter and we can go back to drinking beers and watching the ball games. But if not, I thank you for giving me this time so I could see what God had to show me.

Sincerely,
Alvin

As Mary read, James placed the simple translantern that the nurse had given him on the mantle. Through the few round holes in the thin metal frame, a candle burned with Alvin's soul.

At least, that's what he'd been taught to believe. What his mother believed and what Mary believed.

She finished reading the letter and hugged him.

"Does this mean . . . ?" she started, her words slightly muffled with her face against his chest. "Your mom—"

"Alvin was more like family than some cousin I've never met. My mom will have to accept it."

She squeezed him tighter and began to cry. He held her for a few moments, then she asked: "Did you mean what you said to your mom? About not wanting to be part of the church?"

James went cold. After his parents had left that night, James had been terrified of Mary's reaction. That night, in bed, he'd stared at the ceiling, wondering if his marriage was over, his mother would disown him and Alvin would die.

In the days since, she'd never mentioned it.

But now here it was. He picked his word carefully. "It's her insistence on being right. On following so many rules. So many of them are hers. They're not even the church's." He glanced at the translantern, the flame burning inside. It didn't hold a soul for his child, he admitted to himself. Just permission to have one. "It's not her decision. Why should she—why should anyone—get to say when we can start a family?" Frustration flared now. "Like our kids would be . . . ? What? Monsters killing small animals? People new to this country act like they're fully ensouled. But downtown, white people who should have been fully ensouled live on streets, break into cars." Mary shifted against him, pulling away, and his anger collapsed to fear.

She looked up at him, tears in her eyes. "I've wondered," she said, "why is it that a Negro or Oriental, even as an adult, can become fully ensouled through hard work and accepting the Cycle, but a white baby *must* have a soul when it's born?"

James nodded, fear melting to surprise—shock even—at Mary's question. He told her of the time as a teenager when he'd asked his mother something similar. "She wouldn't answer. Said only a half-souled person would ask."

"I think about what Alvin said," Mary went on, "about abortion and slavery. The Conklins and Sullivans with their three kids."

The night when they'd made love without a condom after returning from Alvin's house came to mind. "Do you believe in the Cycle?"

Mary was still for a moment, then shook her head. "I don't think my parents are right, either, but I don't think I believe. Not anymore. It doesn't make sense." She hugged him tighter, her face against his chest. "I've been so scared that you'll lose your parents like I lost mine. I said such terrible things to them, things that your mother would have said. I—I didn't want you to lose your parents, but I see now."

"My mom won't risk losing touch with her kids. And grandkids. Things will have to change. But we have a flame now and . . . and I don't even care about that. It's our decision."

They held each other for a while.

Not everyone Alison invited came to her birthday party. Only about half the girls who'd gone to Jennifer Conklin's party and Karen Sullivan's party went to Alison's. It made Alison sad, but Mommy told her to be happy about the girls who did come.

There were games and presents and cake. They listened to music on Daddy's radio and sang along with the songs they liked.

At least Rebecca Okafu came. Alison had never seen Rebecca at other birthday parties. Sometimes Rebecca would play with the girls in the neighbourhood, but Alison didn't know anyone who'd been to her house. And some of the other girls said mean things behind her back. Alison thought it was just because Rebecca was black.

After everyone had gone home, Mommy said it wasn't Alison's fault that some girls hadn't come. Alison wanted to play with her presents, but Mommy sat her down and Daddy sat down, too. That meant they were serious.

They told Alison that some of the parents didn't like that Mommy was going to have another baby, but didn't have a translantern. That's why some of the girls hadn't come to the party. It wasn't that they didn't like Alison, but their parents had told them not to go. Some people, they said, believe you had to have a special candle before you could have a baby. That was the Cycle, Alison knew. Daddy's mommy and daddy believed that. But Mommy's mommy and daddy believed anyone can have as many babies as they wanted. They were Christians, Alison also knew.

What Mommy and Daddy believed was somewhere in the middle. They said even if people believe different things than you, you had to do what you thought was right. They told her again about their friend Alvin. She was named after him, she knew, even though it was funny to be named after a boy. Alvin had done some things some of his friends didn't like. But he did them because he thought they were right and could make the world better. Even a small thing can make a difference.

Alison asked if Alvin's friends stopped being his friend.

No, they told her. His friends forgave Alvin because he was a good man. When he passed away, they followed their traditions to remember him and show him respect.

Alison thought about that, then asked if some girls didn't come because she'd invited Rebecca. Alison said her friends said black people weren't fully ensouled. They said their parents said the Okafus were going to wreck the neighbourhood. "Next thing you know," Alison said, imitating Karen's daddy, "there will be coloureds all up and down the damn street." Alison giggled, imagining Ridgeline Crescent on top of a dam. She hoped her backyard would be on the water side, not the side with the big wall going down.

Mommy and Daddy didn't laugh.

"They're 'black,' sweetie," Daddy said. "Coloured isn't a nice word."

Alison thought about that for a second. "But black is a colour."

"Alison," Mommy said. Mommy only needed to say her name like that for Alison to be quiet.

They asked her if she understood and she said she did. She helped Mommy and Daddy clean up from the party and had a small supper. She was stuffed from the cake and chips. Mommy helped her get ready for bed and tucked her in.

Lying awake, she heard the older kids yelling and playing outside. Downstairs, Mommy and Daddy watched television. For a little while, she thought about her presents and the great day she'd had playing with her friends. Especially Rebecca.

She thought about Alvin. He'd been a brave man. A soldier. And brave enough to believe something different than other people because he thought it was right. And he thought it would make things better for other people.

She wanted to be brave like Alvin. And Mommy and Daddy. She didn't care what some of the other girls thought. Rebecca was nice and fun and smart.

Tomorrow, she'd go to Rebecca's house to play.

THE PACK

DOCUMENT 1: COMMUNIQUÉ

SENDER: Dr. C.-L. Ibarro, Medical Director, Advanced Soldier Enhancement and Survival Program (ASESP)

RECIPIENTS: Brigadier General Douglas Stern, Advanced Weapon Systems Research, Development and Engineering Centre (AWSRDEC)
Clark Bernshaw, Assistant Deputy Undersecretary of Defence

I have completed assessments of the six surviving members of the ASESP.

The nanites now constitute between 2% and 3% of the men's body weight. This represents an unanticipated 300-fold increase from initial dosage.

There is another complication. Each man was injected with a unique nanite model. Each man now hosts an identical hybrid model which appears to be the result of cross-contamination and replication.

I cannot explain the periods of prolonged silence reported among the program's survivors.

I cannot predict what other side-effects may occur.

I will repeat that I warned that field testing could result in unexpected consequences.

I recommend the nanites be removed immediately.

DOCUMENT 2: COMMUNIQUÉ

SENDER: Brigadier General Douglas Stern, AWSRDEC

RECIPIENT: Clark Bernshaw, Assistant Deputy Undersecretary of Defence

Sir—
Dr. Ibarro was unable to remove the nanites. She is unsure how to proceed.

I'm worried by these men, who took on the nickname "The Pack" during their training. The few times I've talked to Sergeant Calabrese, it's like he's looking right through me.

I haven't heard one laugh, seen one smile, get mad. When they're together, they'll go hours without saying a word. It's eerie. Makes me wonder how far Dr. Ibarro went with having those things play with their brains.

The only outsider they retain any respect for seems to be Colonel Holding. If it wasn't for her, I don't think they'd follow chain of command. I have increased Holding's security clearance. We will need her fully informed on the nature of the program if we are to have any hope of working with these men further.

Honestly, I think something happened to them in the desert.

—Doug

DOCUMENT 3: COMMUNIQUÉ
SENDER: Clark Bernshaw, Assistant Deputy Undersecretary of Defence
RECIPIENT: Brigadier General Douglas Stern, AWSRDEC

Doug: I know you opposed early discussions of extreme ASESP termination measures, but I ask you to look to the safety of your command and the American people. Consider the changed behaviour of these men and the capabilities this program was designed to instil. I have come to believe they could pose a significant danger.

The men volunteered. They were aware of the risks. It seems Dr. Ibarro's technology did not undergo a thorough shakedown on their last mission; perhaps a more dangerous mission is called for.

DOCUMENT 4: TRANSCRIPT
(Audio file on cellphone recovered from Assistant Deputy Undersecretary Bernshaw's basement. The voice has been confirmed as Sergeant Calabrese.)

CALABRESE: Good, you're awake. Didn't mean to hit you so hard, but couldn't have you screaming like that. It could draw attention in this nice Arlington suburb.

Stop struggling, Under Secretary. The straps are too tight. No one is coming to save you. Your bodyguards? Dead.

You know who we are, right?

BERNSHAW: Sergeant Calabrese. From—

CALABRESE: Good. Now, you're going to tell us what the hell you did to us. Then, how to fix it. And I'm recording this in case anything happens to us.

BERNSHAW: Let me make a phone call. We can sort this out—

[SOUNDS OF A STRUGGLE; MUFFLED VOICE]

CALABRESE: No. No calls. Going to tell someone where we are? We'd just kill them, too.

[SEVERAL SECONDS OF SILENCE]

CALABRESE (cont'd): My friends say to kill you. But you're going to understand, Under Secretary. What we've been through. What we've become.

Colonel Holding had three hundred volunteers that first day. Three hundred men and women willing to put their lives on the line. We didn't even know the risks. "Become better, stronger soldiers," they told us. No more bulky exoarmour. Win these damned wars and get our boys and girls back home. And after people got screened out or flunked out, you had ten of us. We put up with injections and drinking crap that looked and smelled like motor oil past its prime.

Some quick shakedown missions. Then the big one. Dropped deep behind enemy lines to hit a supply depot. We pulled it off, then waited for an evac drone that never came. Heard about the double agent, the drone getting shot down, in debrief. All we knew then was that we had strict radio silence orders and a fifty-klick march through hell.

We reported minimal enemy contact. But that's bullshit. We got hit on the third day.

Small arms fire and mortars. We'd been holed up, catching some sleep. Had some of our gear off. Shrapnel cut Bailey across the middle, guts spilling out. Screaming, thrashing. I held him down and Gündersen got a pressure bandage on. Over Bailey's screaming, Gündersen said she felt something moving. I told her to shut up and dug for a fentanyl tab in my kit. But Gündersen lifted the bandage.

The rip in Bailey's skin looked like scorched, ragged lips pulled back over a mouth of blood-smeared meat. But the bleeding had stopped. And I thought I was seeing things, but the organs were shifting, putting themselves back where they belonged. Should've shit my pants. Or puked. Or something. Instead, I put the tab in Bailey's mouth, calm as can be. Knocked him out a few seconds later. The organs kept moving. Then two feet of ripped-up bowel got shoved out of the wound. And I'll be damned if the skin didn't pull together on its own.

Next second, a mortar threw me into a rock, head first. I didn't have my helmet on. Just remember the sound of my skull breaking.

When I came to, the enemy had broken off. Gündersen was down. Caught five rounds in the chest.

Five rounds I saw get pushed back out of the entry wounds.

The next day, the three of us were up like nothing had happened. We knew the program would make us tough, but this? I felt like nothing could stop Bailey, Gündersen and me. We were tight. And I don't mean because we'd been through the shit together. We acted as one. Like we knew what each other was thinking.

Two days later, an RPG took Nawaz's arm and half of Pratt's face. And then they were Pack, too.

Soon we all were.

But we lost people. Whatever you did can't fix an artillery shell taking your head off.

Or Danielson. Cut in half by an IED. Chest level. Could see the bottom of his lungs inflating. Still alive, dragging himself through the sand and rocks, begging for us to kill him. But we couldn't do it. Knew we had to, but couldn't. He finally offed himself.

Ever lose anyone close, Under Secretary? A parent? A child, maybe? That's nothing. Imagine your happiest memories torn away. A healthy tooth ripped out of your jaw. A ragged, bloody wound that will never heal.

And then those things we did to the locals. Soldier, revolutionary, counter-revolutionary. Even civilians. Cutting them, beating them, killing one while another watched.

It wasn't payback. It just needed to be done. We needed the intelligence: enemy size and location, passable routes, places where we could get food and water.

I figured we were getting frosty.

But the truth is, I could murder a hundred infants with my bare hands. To protect the Pack. You bastard, what did you do to us?

Damn it, a good soldier needs to know when to stop.

So after three weeks, six of us walked out of that desert. All Pack. Even Depardieu, who hadn't been hit. And with Lieutenant Carter dead, I was its leader.

We lied to Holding during the debriefing, of course. Didn't tell him we'd survived shit that should have killed us. He's a good officer, but we lied to his face. Figured if we didn't, you might start poking and prodding us. Maybe split us up.

And we couldn't handle that.

Wasn't a surprise when Colonel Holding told us we had a new mission. More dangerous than the first. We knew a suicide mission when we heard it.

So we tied Holding like we got you tied. Worked her over. Following orders, she said. Came down through a General, but started near the top. You.

Don't know why we let Holding live.

So we got off the base. Quick, clean. When six men work as one there's not much we can't do. But our pictures were all over the news within hours. So we cut up our faces. Used hammers on our jaw and cheek bones. Just enough to not be recognized. It healed, of course, so we'd do it again.

Day after day.

Think about the pain, Under Secretary.

Think.

About.

It.

Now do you get it? We didn't volunteer for this. To be dead inside. You made us, so you're going to fix it. Turn us back into the men—the soldiers—we used . . .

One of my friends has found something. He's . . .

Who's . . . ?

[SILENCE]

This is you.

[SILENCE]

You're Pack.

[SILENCE]

[To Recorder] Colonel Holding: If you're looking for us, we're going back to the desert. Call off the search. We're not a threat. We understand now that we can never go back to our lives. But we can make peace.

DOCUMENT 5: COMMUNIQUÉ
SENDER: Colonel R.C. Holding
RECIPIENT: Brigadier General Douglas Stern, AWSRDEC

Sir. Thank you for forwarding me that transcript. I've found their trail. Ramstein, then Blackjack Air Base. Looks like transport was authorized by Assistant Deputy Undersecretary Bernshaw himself. It seems the Pack took him with them.

I'm healed up and ready to go. Arthur Neech can assume command while I'm gone.

DOCUMENT 6: COMMUNIQUÉ
SENDER: Dr. C.-L. Ibarro, Medical Director, ASESP
RECIPIENT: Brigadier General Douglas Stern, AWSRDEC

I have reviewed Colonel Holding's medical files from the exam following her interrogation by Sergeant Calabrese.

She has nanites in her blood at levels comparable to those in the program. I believe she is now a member of the Pack. This would explain her rapid recovery.

I believe the transmission vector is simple exposure. Hospital conditions allow containment, but outside those the nanites might spread. I believe that when a serious wound is inflicted, the nanites replicate at an accelerated rate to repair the wound. Anyone so exposed will be Pack.

I have also reviewed the audio file from Undersecretary Bernshaw's basement.

We must first assume Undersecretary Bernshaw has become infected given the head injury inflicted by Sergeant Calabrese that rendered Bernshaw unconscious.

I also believe Sergeant Calabrese's reported lack of emotion is caused by the nanites' modifications to the amygdala. The modifications' original purpose to reduce stress reactions caused by critical injuries has become amplified. Members of the Pack may be incapable of emotional reactions or attachments, similar to psychopaths. They do, however, possess a strong bond with one another.

I am further beginning to suspect the shared hybrid model allows some form of wordless communications. The recording and Colonel Holding's reports include moments of prolonged silence. Each nanite model communicates using a unique wireless network. This hybrid model would have a single network. This network may allow the only emotional attachment these people can feel. Further study will be required.

I recommend Colonel Holding be found and detained immediately.

DOCUMENT 7: COMMUNIQUÉ

SENDER: Brigadier General Douglas Stern, AWSRDEC
RECIPIENT: Maj. A. Neech, Officer Commanding (Acting), ASESP

Arthur—
We tracked Holding to Forward Air Base Blackjack, but lost her. We've got reports she headed into the desert. We think she's going to join Calabrese and the Pack. Fighting is down in that sector, so I want you to find Holding, Undersecretary Bernshaw and all surviving members of ASESP. Neutralize them. Ibarro thinks killing the host will cause the nanites to shut down.

We've got to contain this, Arthur. There's no way to know what'll happen if this gets out of hand.

—General Stern

DOCUMENT 8: COMMUNIQUÉ

SENDER: Major A. Neech. Officer Commanding (Acting), ASESP
RECIPIENT: Brigadier General Douglas Stern, AWSRDEC

General Stern: This will be the last communiqué you'll receive from me.

Despite daily patrols these last few weeks, there's no sign of Bernshaw, Holding, Dr. Ibarro, or any other member of the Pack.

We've had no enemy contact, either. In fact, there's been no fighting across eighteen sectors for five weeks.

It must be the Pack. They're spreading. These heartless killers are spreading peace. Just by their presence. Just by being here.

But desertion rates have passed 35%. Soldiers are wandering off from patrols or in the middle of the night. Somehow the Pack has breached our walls, the infection spreading.

I imagine the deserters are feeling the pull of the Pack the way Holding must have, despite being tortured by them. The way Calabrese must have, realizing some of the people he'd tortured had become Pack and he'd left them behind.

They can't stand being away from those like them. To feel like you belong instead of the slow stripping of anger and joy and fear. To be at peace.

And General, I want it, too. Dear God, I don't think I can fight it anymore.

ponse.data[0]['create
tetime.strptime(ltdat
time.now()
today-ltdate2).days
daywindow:
.screen_name,
len(response.d
response.data:
j.entities.urls:
for k in j.entities.u

THE THING THAT KILLED HER

During their handshake, Alejandro got right to it. "I'm looking for Lydia."

The thick fingers of Cedric's left hand covered Alejandro's right, giving a sympathetic squeeze. "I'm sorry to hear she's missing." He motioned to the two wingback chairs beside his desk and sat.

Much fancier, Alejandro thought as he took the seat opposite, than the ones in his small office at the state capitol a few blocks west.

Cedric leaned forward: elbows on broad thighs, palms together, fingers steepled under his chin. His *I'm really listening* pose. "So how can I help you find her, Alejandro?"

"Get me into the camp at Yale."

The lines in Cedric's face pinched in confusion. Then his eyes went wide with realization.

Before Cedric could speak, Alejandro pushed on. He hadn't rehearsed, always better off the cuff. He explained how on the day of the Ascension he'd been on his way to the state capitol before Lydia had woken up. Then his rush to get home. The chaos. The hell of not finding her and the last month of not knowing what happened. "If she'd turned that first day," he said, words flowing like they came from some other, perfect place, "she'd have become lucid before the military moved in and starting slaughtering Second Chancers." So far, he'd been telling the truth. For the lie, he let his anger slip loose. Voice trembling and letting go of the tears that always seemed near, he said: "I've been hearing rumours from the Yale camp. A woman Chancer who'd organized others during the Ascension. Kept them hidden and safe. Doesn't that sound like Lydia?"

"Alejandro . . ." Cedric leaned forward, resuming his pose. "Lydia could be—"

His head went light. "Don't say dead," came out faster than he wanted.

Cedric said, "I was going to say 'she could be anywhere.'"

"She'd have contacted me if she could. But not if troops locked her up." Alejandro's hands balled into fists. "Get me into the camp. Let me look for her."

"I assume you've tried to gain access?"

Alejandro grunted and outlined how Governor Trumbell's office had rebuffed his requests with terms like "ongoing threat" and "uncertain situation." "But he might listen to you."

"I understand, Alejandro, but Trumbell owes me no favours. He and I both know it, so my asking him to grant you access would be seen as provocative."

Alejandro's hands balled up again. Cedric's calm, rational manner had helped vault him from the Connecticut General Assembly to the U.S. Senate last fall, becoming the state's first black senator, but also meant he'd never climb higher. To move up, you had to be a fighter. "Then provoke him."

Cedric leaned back, smoothing his blue tie over a paunch he'd gained during the campaign. "Look, Alejandro, Trumbell is walking a fine line trying to prove his GOP *bona fides* at the national level while not alienating the blue state Republicans who elected him. But if pressed, we may not like his reaction."

"Where do *you* stand?"

"I'm not sure what the Second Chancers are, but I will take the time to find out. Once we have a better understanding of their nature, we can determine their legal rights."

"How long you been rehearsing that line?"

If the provocation had any impact, Cedric didn't show it. "We're still counting bodies, Alejandro. We must take the time to let ourselves come to grips with what has happened. For now, compromise is necessary on a number of issues."

Alejandro stomach dropped. Cedric didn't consider this a meeting between friends, but something political. Back in the state Senate, Cedric had acted as Alejandro's mentor. Only twenty-four when he'd won his first election, Alejandro had gravitated towards Cedric's lack of pretense in private talks despite his outwardly calm persona. They both came from rough parts of Hartford and fought bare-knuckled in the back rooms for programs to help kids liked they'd been escape gangs, poverty and unemployment.

But now the *I'm really listening* pose, repeatedly using Alejandro's name and saying "Second Chancer"—the sympathetic term for those who lacked all medical indications of life yet continued to move and speak. Cedric was treating him with the care and politeness one used with a constituent, not the honesty of a friend. Perhaps Cedric viewed Alejandro as too controversial. Since Internet access had been restored, Alejandro had gained a small following on social media in demanding Governor Trumbell release Chancers from the camps.

Yet Cedric had used the more pejorative terms in his public statements—"infected" instead of "Chancer" or "Second Chancer," "outbreak" instead of "Ascension." He hadn't objected when Trumbell ordered the National Guard to confine the Chancers who'd survived the military's near-extermination to large outdoor stadiums—exposed to the elements, no beds, no food or water. Not that Chancers needed to eat or sleep, but some states—Oregon, Maine, Massachusetts—had been more humane in putting Chancers in schools or government office buildings. Yet in other states, stories, photos, and videos streamed out of National Guard units hunting down and executing Chancers. Instead of segregating Chancers, as the President had ordered, the soldiers wanted payback.

"If Lydia is in the camp," Cedric continued, "and Chancers are indeed the same people they were before the Ascension, we have to wait." Cedric stood, declaring the meeting over.

Alejandro got to his feet.

"I can't imagine how difficult this must be for you," Cedric went on, "but I promise you, we are on the right side of history." Cedric stepped forward, but as Alejandro extended his hand Cedric embraced him, saying, "Remember, you're one of the good guys."

Caught off guard, Alejandro returned the hug.

In the hallway, Alejandro jabbed the down button and paced. This meeting had been a long shot, but he'd hoped Cedric would let something slip. A rumour, an upcoming bill, anything he could leverage against Trumbell to get into the camp. He'd bring a video camera—or smuggle in his phone—in with him and interview as many Chancers as he could. Show that despite their ruined bodies and horrific appearance they were the same people as before the Ascension. Build support for their freedom. Bring down those who'd advocated their extermination—

—Chancers' faces, motionless, skin taut and tinged deep-bruise purple. Endless piles of them, burning—

Things wobbled. He put a hand against the wall to steady himself.

The elevator arrived. Getting in, Alejandro cursed Cedric. The Governor's office had stonewalled him. The majority leader said they could take no action until the legislature sat. The dozens of court challenges would take years. With four-term U.S. Senator Martin Burnaby missing, Cedric was the state's *de facto* senior senator with the power to get things done. But Alejandro, only in his third term as a state senator, feared he'd end up as he always had—acting the firebrand while senior party members consulted, negotiated and eventually compromised.

He had nothing left. Except return to his too empty home.

Stepping out of the lobby's revolving door, a hint of the acrid burning fuel scent still hung in the hot afternoon air. With a breath—

—panicked sprints between houses—

—gunfire—

—shapes moving in shadows—

—Lydia at the back gate—

"Oh God." The city street pitched beneath him. Cold sweat broke out despite the afternoon heat. He leaned against a bus shelter, shoes crunching the shattered remains of its Plexiglas sides that still needed to be cleaned up.

The morning when the Ascension had started, he'd meant to leave a note telling Lydia he loved her and he'd miss her during her visit with her family in Santa Monica. The time apart would be good, though. He could work late without feeling guilty. He'd been on his way to the capitol, merging from Route 9 onto I-91, when he realized he'd forgotten to write the note.

He'd been in some committee meeting, checking his phone for word from Lydia that she'd reached the airport when he saw the e-mails. An emergency in New Haven. Then Hartford.

Boston.

Santa Fe.

Tokyo, Johannesburg, Bonn.

Still no word from Lydia.

A page appeared and whispered to the chair, who'd gone pale and adjourned the meeting, saying: "We're under some kind of attack."

Rumours had filled the halls. The State Troopers had urged everyone to sit tight, but that told Alejandro he needed to get out of there. Lydia didn't pick up. The radio reported flights were grounded, airports in lockdown.

Possibilities raced through his mind as he'd headed south for Middletown: she was safe at the airport; stuck in traffic; never left the house. The trip from the capitol building in downtown Hartford, normally thirty to forty minutes, took over three hours on the jammed highways.

Finally reaching Middletown, he weaved around accidents and abandoned roadblocks. Motion surrounded him. People running—some fleeing, others pursuing. A lone police officer stood on the sidewalk, firing at people in a grocery store parking lot, the store itself ablaze.

The sun setting, Alejandro reached home. Getting out, the roar of traffic mixing with random gunfire contrasted with the stillness of his deserted street. Scanning, he spotted a neighbourhood teenager—Kyle, he thought his name was—several houses down, running along the tree-lined street toward him. *At* him. Kyle's long black hair had gone grey. Skin taut purple.

Instinct propelled Alejandro into his house, slamming the front door and throwing the deadbolt just as Kyle clambered up onto the porch. The teen pounded on the door.

"Lydia!" Alejandro had screamed. The door holding, he'd searched the house. Nothing. No cell signal. Landline dead. Indecision rooting him in place, his mind traced the futile Mobius-strip logic of needing to go find her, not knowing where to start, needing to try, but how—

A man's voice pulled him to the present. "Hey, you're Alejandro Gutiérrez?"

Alejandro pivoted, shoes grinding the Plexiglas shards, to find an older Hispanic man, hair streaked white and a fresh scar from ear to collar bone. "Yes."

The older man extended a hand and said in Spanish: "Bless you for your work. My wife, Mariana. Soldiers, they took her. She said the Blessed Virgin sent her back. She had a message for the world, but those *cabrónes* took her."

A buzz grew in his chest. Pumping the man's hand to accentuate his words, Alejandro replied in Spanish. "I'm never going to stop fighting until our wives are free. Now excuse me, I have another meeting."

He fought to hang on to that enthusiasm as he headed for his car. Across the street, bullet holes pocked a building's brick-red façade and plywood covered its shattered windows. Ragged scraps of yellow police tape tied to streetlights lay limp in the still air.

Southbound on I-91, most of the highway had been cleared of abandoned cars, the few that remained pushed onto the grassy shoulder to be towed. On the radio, the anchor ticked off good news stories: flights had resumed at Bradley Airport, cell phone coverage had been restored to most of the state, schools were scheduled to reopen in a few weeks.

No mention of Second Chancers. No concern for thousands held without due process. Desperate to stay riled up, he flipped over to what had been a pop station, but the owner had found God during the Ascension. "Only one man has risen from the dead. They are here to tempt us with lies of what comes after death. No judgment, they say. We are all connected, they say. Folks, these things don't eat, so how can they be walking around? Well, what supernatural force could impel them? I can think of one."

Spotting flashing red-blue lights at a checkpoint ahead, Alejandro slowed.

A white-knuckle grip on the steering wheel, Alejandro took the curving exit ramp faster than he should have. "Legislature's not in session," the checkpoint's lead cop had responded when he saw Alejandro's legislative ID. "That makes you nobody." It had been evident they'd known who he was and the cause he advocated. That's why they made him step out of his car while they searched it. "Can't be too careful checking for Chancer smugglers." After half an hour, they finally let him go.

Mounting the porch, his rage steeled him against the paradox of his home. Lydia's essence filled its spaces. Photos of her, of them. Mementos from their eleven years together that she'd insisted they save—movie tickets, sea shells from Hammonasset Beach, a two-dollar bill a clerk had given as change on their second date. He'd mistake the house settling for her footsteps. Late at night, he'd awaken having thought he heard her voice. Her smell lingered in her pillow. And yet every room seemed too empty, too still.

Too silent.

Tears threatened to push up again. They'd seemed to do nothing but fight in the months before the Ascension. She'd tap her lower lip, a tic when she grew frustrated. Then she'd unload on him about his job, about a baby, about how much housework fell to her. She had her own pursuits, administering a women's shelter and studying law. But when they needed to sacrifice, she gave in. Where did his priorities lie? Being with her or always out fighting for some cause?

How had it come to that? They'd met in student government fighting the administration's rules that could bar students with juvenile records from residence halls. From there, they'd pushed to restrict campus security's ability to frisk or search bags. They'd demanded an easier appeals process for student who's violated conduct codes. His love for her had grown into an aching thing. Sex had left him exhausted but craving more. She made him roar with laughter and pushed him to be better, smarter, craftier. How in all that—

Bodies. Flames. The putrid, sweet charcoal sink. That goddamn arrogant captain who'd turned intersections and lawns into infernos—

"No," he hissed, teeth gritted. There had to be something. He scanned the three computer screens on his dining room table. Conversations flew past. He clicked on a video generating considerable discussion. A physician in St. Louis claimed she had replicated the results of the researchers in Quebec City, showing Second Chancers maintained a consistent mass down to the gram. Though using different terms, she asked the same question as the radio station DJ: where did the calories that moved Chancers come from?

"Are Second Chancers perpetual motion machines?" a commenter asked. "Does the first law of thermodynamics not apply to them?"

Another comment about harnessing Chancers as a source of labour descended into a debate about slavery.

Farther down, a comment stated the physician had been arrested, the Chancers executed.

Alejandro nearly shoved the monitor off the table. He shot to his feet, knocking the chair back—the video, the camps, the propaganda about getting back to normal.

He looked at his cell phone and the idea struck.

He sat in front of the webcam, cleared his throat and—without rehearsing—hit record, letting the words flow.

A car horn woke him. An everyday sound slowly returning to normal.

Half-asleep and eyes gritty, he checked his phone. Almost ten in the morning. The icons for e-mails, social media messages and voice mails all showed "100+."

Excitement propelled him to his feet. He turned on the TV on his way to the computer. A local station showed an aerial shot of Yale Bowl, the university football stadium converted to one of Connecticut's camps. Small crowds had gathered in the parking lots. They waved placards with slogans demanding the release of Second Chancers. A few wore purple make-up. The image zoomed in on something that looked like a small tower.

His fingers flew. In seconds, he found a news report from that morning about three groups of Yale engineering students competing to see who could build a functioning trebuchet, but police had shut them down. A subreddit discussed how to protect launched phones so they wouldn't shatter on impact. Another news story reported someone with a T-shirt cannon firing phones wrapped in shirts into Rentschler Field in East Hartford while drones buzzed in and out.

The governor's office had released a statement urging people to stop.

Alejandro smirked as he read how their actions "risked destabilizing public safety." The state senate majority whip distanced the party from Alejandro. But the suggestions that he run in the election to replace Martin Burnaby in the U.S. Senate made Alejandro smile. "If the courts do the right thing and give Chancers the right to vote," a comment said, "it will be a landslide."

Subsequent comments said voting was a God-given right and God had forsaken Chancers.

He kept searching, finding articles from the previous night. His simple message had grown and spread: with coverage restored, find a way to get cellphones into the camps. Since the military had concentrated Chancers into outdoor arenas in urban areas, phones didn't need to be smuggled into closed facilities or risk being rendered useless in rural dead zones. He didn't know how to do it but had been certain others would figure it out. And, he'd concluded, to let him know if anyone found his wife.

He'd meant it only for Connecticut, but Alejandro saw comments from across the country and into Canada.

Opening his e-mail, he found interview requests mixed with messages of support and condemnation. He played a voicemail from Cedric. "Do you know the shitstorm you've created?" That was the Cedric Alejandro remembered. "You need to tell these people to stop."

"Not gonna happen," Alejandro muttered. He clicked on a video from Nova Scotia, keeping the sound off but enabling auto-transcription. MY NAME IS PETER COUNTING WOOD, the captions stated, a small bay behind him with a city farther on. IF MY WIFE SEES IS TELL HER I MISTER AND I LOVER.

Cedric's voicemail continued: "I know you're trying to find Lydia, but this won't go how you want. Trumbell will feel he needs to push back. And people will support him. They're scared and confused. They want a strong leader. Someone who says 'there's the problem' and goes after it."

"What do you think I'm doing?" Alejandro muttered, flipping through local TV stations.

"Look, call this off and I'll make some calls. Get back to me, okay?"

"You could have made those calls yesterday." Most stations covered the camps, but the local Fox affiliate showed clips of the U.S. House Majority Leader reacting to a video of her twenty-year-old Chancer daughter recorded at an abandoned impound lot in Phoenix. "That dead thing is not my girl," she said. Alejandro knew bluster when he saw it. This wasn't it. It was terror. "It's the thing that killed her. Something that will not stop unless we stop it." The scroll reported "TheThingThatKilledHer" was trending across social media. The next item reported that while the president called for calm and patience, quoting First Peter and the Gospel of John, the governor of Idaho urged a return to mass extermination, citing Revelations.

So much like that Army captain, justifying the piles of bodies—some burned, some burning, some waiting to be ignited. Bragging about his men's ruthlessness—

The room swayed, his chest tight. He pitched forward, head between his knees, heart thudding at the memory of Lydia's voice, yanking him awake during the fifth night of the Ascension. He'd been dozing, fading in and out of not-sleep.

Alejandro had nailed boards he'd found in the basement, left by the previous owner, across the front door. Luckily, the front of the house sat high on its foundation, putting the windows out of reach, and an eight-foot cedar fence around the backyard protected its rear. Though secure, food was running low. What had been in the fridge had spoiled and he'd almost run through what little had been in the pantry. At least the water pressure still held.

Several times, he'd tried to get to a neighbour's house. During the day, he'd never made it past his driveway before someone soundlessly pursued him back behind the fence's safety. At night, shapes moving in the darkness wore down his courage.

With nothing but time, he'd reflected on how selfish he'd been. She'd been right, of course. He'd come to take her for granted. A fear tickled the back of his mind that her trip to see her family might have been an opportunity to reconsider their marriage. What if, on the other side of the country, she told him she wasn't coming back? Even if she were still alive somewhere, would she return to him?

From time to time he'd heard gunfire. And voices. The first time he'd gone outside and called out. A man, voice gruff and distant, had replied: "It's okay! Don't be afraid! We're all connected! The universe itself is alive!" Then something had pounded on the other side of the fence.

But on that last day, alone with his thoughts: "Alejo? Are you there?" The front door.

He flew from the couch, barking a shin on the coffee table in the darkness. "Dee?" He put his hands on the door. "Sweetie?!"

"It's me—"

She'd made it. Somehow she'd made it. "The front door's boarded up. Come to the back." Right shin throbbing, he felt his way through the darkened house. Outside, moonlight cast deep shadows, everything silver-white. The cool April breeze carried the harsh scent of fires. Orange-pink glows dappled the horizon. He undid the lock holding the gate shut. He pushed it open an inch, saw her waiting, threw it open and pulled her inside. He yanked the gate shut before wrapping his arms around her and crying out in joy.

And with his arms around her, rocking back and forth, the hairs on the back of his neck stood up.

She must have sensed it because, her voice raw, she said: "Alejo."

Her cheek, pressed against his, felt cool as the night air. Her skin seemed brittle under the pressure of his fingers. He pulled away and tripped over his feet at the sight of her: bruise-coloured skin, hair gone grey, eyes cloudy. A chunk of flesh had been ripped from her right shoulder, dark stains spattered across her clothes.

"It's me, Alejo," she said, making an *it's okay* gesture.

He tried to crawl back, strength draining from his limbs. "You're . . ."

"I know how I look and can only imagine what you're thinking. But I'm not going to hurt you. I love you and have so much to tell you."

After she'd changed into clean clothes, they sat entwined on the couch. Gradually, he grew accustomed to the coolness of her skin. Lydia explained how she'd been stuck in traffic when a wave of people had washed across the highway. Their skin purple and eyes white, they'd smashed their ways into cars, yanking out and attacking drivers.

She described fighting off a young woman, but not before she'd bitten Lydia in the shoulder. Lydia had tried to run and here she paused, tapping her lip and Alejandro wanted to embrace her. She'd described becoming "lost in others' thoughts"—connected to people all over the world, unsure if she'd been attacked or the attacker. As she tried to make sense of this, she watched helplessly as her body pursued and attacked the living.

Then, something—some *force*—pulled her up and out, taking her someplace "higher" dominated by a beautiful light. A light that had created everything. Connected everything. "Not God," she clarified. "At least, not the God of the Bible." Infinite. Peaceful. She came to understand the Ascension *needed* to happen. Whatever illness or infection that corrupted the body also elevated the mind. "Almost like a soul," she added, though Alejandro had never known her to be religious. "Something . . . eternal."

But the light had sent her back. Her consciousness returned to her body, finding it smeared with gore. As she made her way back to Middletown through the carnage and destruction, she gathered others like her—lost, but filled with hope—with similar stories: after being attacked, they went to someplace "higher," but the light had sent them back to their bodies. Comparing their timelines, they found two days had passed from the time of the attack to when they returned.

Those still in its grips ignored Lydia and her growing group, but relentlessly attacked the living. A lone scavenger stood no chance, but military patrols had moved in, turning Hartford into a war zone, cutting down anyone infected. She told how she had lost half her group as they'd approached a Humvee, begging for help.

So they moved at night and hid during the day. Seeing flames, the group had refused to enter Middletown and remained in the woods off Route 66. Alejandro hadn't been surprised Lydia had continued on her own.

Her story caught up to the present, she'd took him upstairs and opened a window. After a moment, he heard it: the low rumble of vehicles. "The military," she'd said. "Those poor men are terrified and don't understand we're not a threat. If they find my group, they'll kill them. I have to bring them here."

In his memory, their argument went on forever as the distant sounds of vehicles growled and sputtered. Going out there would be too dangerous, he said. Bringing others like her to their home could make it a target.

She'd countered that as an elected representative he was obliged to protect them. The chaos would end, she'd promised.

By then the sun had risen, making it too dangerous to go out. Overhead, inky cloud wind-driven smoke floated south. Lydia told Alejandro to go to sleep and when he awoke a few hours later, he found canned and dried food in the kitchen. From the neighbour, she explained. The house was empty, but she knew where they kept a spare key.

Alejandro had wolfed down the food, realizing he didn't even know their neighbours' names while Lydia knew where they kept a key. While he ate, Lydia spoke. "The world is going to change. The light sent us back to deliver the message that everything is connected. We're part of something greater. Together we can be a part of that."

It had been her appeal to them being "together" that made him give in. He'd change, prioritize her, listen to her. They'd be the unstoppable team they had been.

The *thwup-thwup-thwup* of helicopters and rattle of gunfire had echoed in the river valley as the day wore on.

When night had fallen, she'd kissed him, her lips cool and dry. "I love you so much," she told him.

The emotion choked him. "Me, too. I love you." He wanted to say more, but the words would not come before she slipped out the back gate into the darkness.

She never returned. He stayed up the whole night, the stench of fires carrying on the night breeze.

An hour past sun up, military vehicles roared into the city. Checking the radio, he found stations back on the air with Governor Trumbell bragging about the relentless forces retaking the state. They'd ended the crisis and were restoring order.

"Lydia," Alejandro whispered, tears dropping to the dining room floor at the month-old memory. The television had moved on to mounting claims threatening to cripple the insurance industry.

He had to be strong. Had to see this through.

He dialled the local CNN affiliate to accept their interview request. He wanted a large audience for the next step: rally people to get the Chancers freed. No negotiation, no compromise.

His phone buzzed again. The caller ID told him it was another of the television stations that had set up outside. Alejandro set the phone down and resumed watching the fire-filled images.

It had started in Ohio. A group of college students, arms linked, had tried pushing through a cordon of National Guard troops surrounding a camp. They'd met batons and rifle butts, resulting in rocks and bottles. Tear gas brought Molotov cocktails. Then gunfire, killing twelve.

Montana and Pennsylvania had followed. The group in Lancaster had been pushed back with few injuries. In Billings, station KTVQ reported the Highway Patrol had shutdown I-90 on either side of the city while local police hunted for a doomsday militia blamed for the attack. No word on causalities, but a spokesperson expected them to be high.

It hadn't stopped there. The scroll reported that, at last count, twelve camps across nine states had been stormed, resulting in countless Chancers escaping and over one hundred deaths. Alejandro had wanted to throw his remote at the TV when the anchor had reported the number of dead could include Chancers' bodies, so the actual number of deaths might be lower. Still, she continued, officials worried that with so many loose they might start attacking the living again.

And every few minutes, Alejandro's name went by in the crawl as the possible author of the destruction.

All this following a six-minute interview earlier that evening with that attractive, brunette host on CNN. They'd discussed his search for Lydia and why he championed the unpopular cause of defending Chancers' rights. She'd wrapped up by asking what came next. He'd shrugged and let the words flow, smooth and precise: "The government has turned against its people, violating its essential duty to reflect our will, and therefore negating its mandate to govern. Therefore, we the people must do whatever it takes to see that our loved ones are liberated."

In the short time it had taken to drive back home, his supporters had taken his words to mean storming the camps. As the coverage repeated the clip every ten minutes or so, he'd been amused by how much he sounded like Cedric's public persona.

He hadn't been home for long when trucks from local stations had set up outside and reporters had knocked on his door. Cedric and senior party officials had phoned, demanding he call it off. Even the governor's office had offered a meeting to settle things.

But he didn't want to comment, call it off or settle things.

Let it burn, he kept thinking. *All of it*. The afternoon when the army had rolled into the city, the police had arrived at his house and brought him to a staging area at city hall. That smug army captain had taken him, the mayor and city council members on a tour of the city in an army transport. With pride, he'd shown them the corpses piled haphazardly on lawns and side streets, milky eyes in bruise-coloured faces staring out. The stink of burning fuel had burned his nose, oily black smoke curling into the sky.

"Let *them* deal with the fire now," Alejandro said as some Fox anchor reported an increase in the body count.

Knocking roused him from a sleep he hadn't intended to fall into. He ignored it and rolled over on the couch. His cell phone buzzed and the knocking resumed. The process repeated a minute later. Checking his phone, he found it was just after midnight with several texts from Cedric: "It's me. Open up." After debating for a moment, Alejandro got to his feet and opened the front door, letting in the cool night air and revealing Cedric. A Hawaiian shirt and cargo pants had replaced his usual suit.

"You in disguise?"

"You should come with me," Cedric replied.

Alejandro rubbed grit from his eyes. "Where?" Past Cedric, the TV trucks had left.

"Get your ass in the car."

At least Cedric was being straight with him. Alejandro grabbed his keys and phone and followed Cedric around the corner to his car.

"Take the battery out of your phone," Cedric said.

"Why?"

"They can track it."

Unsure whether to be amused or worried, Alejandro complied. Cedric started the car and took a twisting route toward the south side of downtown. Finally, Cedric pulled around the back of a small strip mall only a few blocks from Alejandro's house. Alejandro wondered why they didn't just walk. Then fear, cold and slow, crept up his spine at the fear they'd been followed.

Once parked, Cedric led Alejandro through the weed-choked lot behind the buildings and into a thick copse of trees that blocked out the building's floodlights. Arriving at a chain-link fence, Cedric pushed open a flap and led Alejandro into the gloom of a parking lot in back of a small, one-storey building. It took a moment to realize they'd come out behind the church on Fuller Avenue that had been shut down since the Ascension. No lights inside or out illuminated the lot. The building itself blocked light from the Fuller Avenue.

Cedric led him to the building and knocked on a metal door. It opened a crack, then swung wide. Cedric led Alejandro into the darkness. A third person moved in the small space that smelled of dust and crumbling wallpaper. The door slammed. An overhead bulb popped on, illuminating a narrow hall with a staircase to his left descending to a doorway. Ten feet away, the hall ended in a door where a middle-aged woman wearing a clerical collar stood, hand on a light switch. She smiled at Alejandro and said, "Welcome to our sanctuary."

Alejandro nodded, wondering what she meant but saying nothing. He wanted to get on with this. Cedric and the minister exchanged a nod, then Cedric led Alejandro down the stairs, the minister following.

The space had been a storage area, but shelves and boxes had been pushed to the walls to make room for an assortment of mismatched cots, chairs, and tables. About twenty Chancers and half as many living sat or lay on the furniture, talking in low tones, reading or just waiting. A woman Chancer knelt by a cot, stroking the hair of a living little girl and urging her to go to sleep.

Cedric walked through the room to a small cluster of Chancers, saying: "Martin."

A portly Chancer dressed in slacks, blazer and collared shirt turned. It took a moment to recognize the missing Senator Martin Burnaby, his curly copper hair now dull pink, a ragged gouge taken out of his left cheek.

"What is this?" Alejandro asked.

After excusing himself from the group, Burnaby said, "Follow me so we can talk in private."

Alejandro followed Cedric and Burnaby into a janitor's closet. Burnaby said, "We've brought you here to ask that you use your new-found notoriety to diffuse the situation."

"Diffuse it? People are finally doing something to help you. To free you."

"At what price? For all your advocacy, you do not understand Second Chancers." Burnaby paused. "Have you considered that Chancers do not eat, eliminate and only breathe in order to speak?"

"Yeah, perpetual motion machines," Alejandro replied.

"In a sense. You see, in space bursts of energy appear and disappear at random, seemingly coming from nowhere. There are many theories to explain it, but what if this energy comes from the fabric of existence itself? A living, conscious energy which permeates all matter that some might interpret as a light." Burnaby paused again.

Alejandro waited, impatient with Burnaby's theatrics.

"That energy is what propels Second Chancers," Burnaby finally said. "We are the living universe made manifest. One month ago, humankind reached some critical mass that triggered the Ascension. A transformation of living tissue into something else while our minds ascended to where we learned that all humankind is near a new plateau of being. Very soon, everyone's minds will no longer be dependent on a corporeal form but be integrated into the fabric of existence. Become eternal."

Alejandro clenched his jaw against tears. Lydia had said something similar on their last day together. Under control for the moment, he asked: "Why am I here?"

"To stop the violence. We are all connected and violence done to another is no different than violence done to oneself. Using violence to free us is no different than using it for our extermination. It provokes fear and panic, which are base, animal reactions. It must be through rational thought that our message is understood and our true nature revealed. All humankind can reach the plateau that we Chancers have and become beings of mind, but only if you love and accept one another. That is what the Ascension is meant to bring. It is a trial. A crucible. Yet if both sides are governed by their fear then the promise of the Ascension will have been for nothing."

Alejandro refused to let the obviously rehearsed words sink in. They wanted him to back down, to compromise. "Even if we stop, the people who want to kill you won't."

"We have to take the first step," Cedric said. "Take the long-term view. People won't get over their prejudices easily but—"

"Why are you here, Cedric?" Alejandro asked. "You said you didn't know what Chancers were. That you needed time."

"I could not take the risk of revealing my knowledge of this place to anyone," Cedric replied. "Martin contacted me two weeks ago. We've been strategizing about whether he should go public and take his seat in the Senate. I knew some of these Chancers are from Lydia's group, but I was afraid—"

Alejandro's hands balled up. "You knew? You knew and you sat there—"

"I know what they told me!" Cedric interrupted. "That Lydia kept them safe, like you said. She went to find you and disappeared. I couldn't tell you that because you've been pushing too hard and I didn't know what you'd do. But now I do and I was right not to tell you. And if Lydia is in that camp, she's in danger—"

"She's dead!" Alejandro exploded. "She found me and went out to bring back others and they killed her!"

Her face, motionless. Lips slightly parted. A blackened hole the size of a quarter above her right eye. One of dozens in a pile. The flames hadn't reached her yet.

It had taken two soldiers to pull him off that smug captain.

Alejandro doubled over, sobbing. Cedric put a consoling hand on his shoulder, but he swatted it away. Straightening, he said, "I don't care if we're all connected or there's some higher power because we *are* stupid, fearful animals."

"Alejandro," Cedric said, face soft in understanding. "I'm so sorry. This whole time, I thought . . . I didn't know she'd reach you."

"You claim to care for us, but you are motivated solely to work against those who killed your wife," Burnaby said. "You are simply a contrarian. But know this: your wife exists. She is all around you, watching, and you can join her—"

"To hell with you," Alejandro said. "And this place. You want to wait to be killed, that's on you." Alejandro passed between Burnaby and Cedric, opened the door and headed for the stairs. The minister's shocked expression told Alejandro this hadn't gone as planned.

"Bye!" the little girl said, waving. Her mother shushed her.

Alejandro stormed up the steps, plugging the battery back into his phone to find if any more camps had been stormed.

Gunfire ripped Alejandro from sleep. He rolled off the couch and flattened on the floor. After a few moments of silence, he grabbed his phone and searched for what was happening but found lots of questions and no answers. After a few more moments of silence, he pulled on pants, a shirt and some shoes, shoving his phone and legislative ID into pockets. Running out the front door, a few more shots echoed, coming from the direction of downtown.

Rounding a corner, strobing blue and red light painted houses and buildings. A fear gripped him that bloomed as he turned onto Fuller Avenue. A Middletown PD cruiser, lights flashing, blocked the intersection, holding back a small crowd of onlookers. Past the cruiser, a mix of state and local cruisers crowded the street out in front of the church. Bodies lay from the street, up the steps and to the Church's double doors. Cops, guns drawn, stalked among them. The crowd flinched as an officer, a dark shape in the red-blue lights, fired a round into a Chancer's head.

Alejandro sprinted a block east, lungs burning, and ran behind the strip mall and through the flap in the fence. Emerging, he found two patrol cars' lights illuminating about a dozen bodies sprawled, unmoving, across the parking lot. His vision wavered, things swaying.

A girl shouting "Mama!" focused him. Two officers conversed while a third sat on the ground, helmet next to him, head hanging between his knees. A fourth, his or her face obscured by lights reflecting of the helmet's face shield, tried to lead a little girl from the carnage. "Mama!" she shrieked again, one arm extended back while the officer tried to pull her by the other.

Alejandro recognized the girl from the basement, the one a Chancer had been trying to get to sleep. He yanked his ID from his pants and approached. "What the hell is happening here!"

One of the cops wheeled and headed for Alejandro, hand out in a *Stop-Right-There* gesture. The other hand rested on his gun. "This is a crime scene!"

"I'm a state senator."

Closer, Alejandro could see the sitting cop's shoulders spasm. He was sobbing.

"I don't care!" the approaching cop bellowed.

Alejandro scanned the bodies—shirts peppered with holes, parts of their heads shot away. "How many did you kill?"

The officer managed to bundle the girl into the back of a patrol car.

"'Kill'?" the closer cop replied. "They're already dead."

Cold horror twisted through Alejandro as he spotted the minister who had greeted him lying motionless near the rear door. Farther on, Cedric lay in a pool of blood turned black in the cruisers' lights.

Alejandro fought to keep from buckling. But in the pause, the cop stepped forward, inches from Alejandro's face. "You don't get it, do you? Probably holed up in some bunker while guys like me fought these things." The cop's right eye began to twitch, his body trembling. "Do you know how many of my friends they got? My wife?" Tears leaked down his cheeks and spittle flew from his lips. "My kids? They're animals! Just 'cause they're talking animals doesn't mean I'm not gonna put 'em down like animals!"

Alejandro bit back the response bubbling up his throat when he spotted a news van parking in the alley that ran alongside the church. He held up his hands in surrender and moved for the alley.

He'd get his message out, laying these deaths at Trumbell's feet. Everyone would know about this senseless brutality. And not just the dead, but that little girl was a victim, too.

And that sobbing cop. Who knew what he'd been through. He shouldn't be out there. Same with the one who'd confronted him. They needed help.

Everyone did. So lost, so broken.

Pulling out his phone to check what else might be happening, panic shot through him. He hadn't taken Cedric seriously when he'd said "they can track it." He'd put the battery back in while leaving the church. He tried to reject such paranoia, but how else to explain the attack? Reaching the end of the alley, guilt pressed in on him. For the carnage here. The people in Ohio and Montana. Who knew how many more?

And Lydia. If he'd let her go that first night before the military had reached Middletown it would have been different. But he'd had to fight her, to resist.

He just wanted to go home. To wrap his arms around Lydia. Tell her he loved her. Tell her how sorry he was. Ask for second chance. He'd change. Put her—put *them*—ahead of his work.

"Senator Gutiérrez!" A reporter he recognized moved from working the crowd and headed for him. Behind her, a cameraman set up.

Less than a minute later, they were live. Alejandro barely heard her describing the scene, wondering if Lydia was somewhere, watching him. The reporter touched his arm. ". . . and I am here with State Senator Alejandro Gutiérrez, who witnessed the event. Can you tell us what happened here?"

Alejandro opened his mouth and waited for the words to flow from their perfect place.

And waited.

THE LEAVING

The tinkle of the bell above the door drawing her eyes, Georgina blew out a relieved breath—Paul. At his feet, just before he closed the door, a scattering of leaves—black and curled like burnt scraps of paper—blew across the old, faded linoleum.

Aside from Mrs. D'Angelo wiping down some tables, they had Georgina's small diner to themselves.

Good. Just how she wanted it.

Late afternoon sun through the big front window illuminated his grin, the stubble on his chin. The undone buttons at the neck of his flannel shirt revealed dark curls.

Smoothing down her apron and hoping she looked better than hideous after a day's work, Georgina moved to the counter and said, "Hi, Paul."

"Good afternoon," he replied, grin growing.

Then the barnyard stink struck Georgina, overpowering the diner's salty, deep-fried smells. That decade-old memory of Colin pounding on the back door.

But Paul was here. Now. Safe. Four days ago, when the Leaving had started, she'd looked up every time the bell rang, wanting it to be Paul. So far, there had only been word of that one boy being killed. But no matter how many times she assured herself that someone must've told Paul by now, she worried over whether anyone would know if something had happened to him.

He sat on the stool opposite her.

"We're closing in about fifteen," Georgina said. "Kitchen's shut down, but I could get you a beer."

"Yes, please. I'm just here to say hi."

Halfway down the narrow aisle, Mrs. D'Angelo looked up and cocked an eyebrow.

Georgina grabbed a mug and poured his favourite draft. "Haven't seen you around. Began to worry something had happened." He *had* to know, she told herself, setting the mug on the counter. Word would've gotten around—new man in town, all alone, cleaning out his newly inherited grandmom's farmhouse.

"I've been working on the barn," he replied. "There are so many things to sort through." He took a quick sip. "So what is with the notice from the police on the door? A coyote attack and curfew? Is it related to the smell and leaves turning black?"

Georgina's stomach dropped. He didn't know. But if he was in the barn last night . . . ?

Georgina realized she'd be the one to tell him. That was okay. She'd prepared for it, rehearsed what she'd say. Been prepared since Jefferson Hollow had awoke to find the leaves on all the trees fading from brilliant green to matte black, a month earlier than their usual transformation to fiery brilliance. She'd explain the smell, the leaves, and the rules everyone in Jefferson Hollow knew—you stayed inside once the sun had set.

Georgina waited for Mrs. D'Angelo to come round behind the counter. The older woman had lived all her sixty-two years in the Hollow and explained the Leaving to others, including her late husband. Between the two of them, Paul would have to believe.

Georgina opened with: "A boy was killed last night. Out in Sunrise Village. That new housing development?"

Paul leaned forward. "Oh my God. What happened?"

She'd expected he'd want details. Paul worked as a medical examiner in the city. Taking a deep breath, she began: "We don't know—"

Mrs. D'Angelo laid a hand on Georgina's shoulder.

In the parking lot, two pickups turned into spaces. Brawny men wearing reflective orange vests over sweat-stained T-shirts climbed out of the beds and cabs.

Mrs. D'Angelo gave a squeeze. *Hurry.*

Paul looked at Georgina, waiting.

She'd wanted to take her time, explain it, answer his questions. She sputtered: "At night—"

Loud, deep voices on the steps.

"Should I tell them we're closed?" Mrs. D'Angelo asked.

Paul turned toward the door.

"No," Georgina said, head bowed. She needed the customers. "But one round."

The bell clanged as the men came in, heavy boots thumping, black leaves blowing in on a breeze carrying the animal smell.

Mrs. D'Angelo let out a frustrated snort, readjusted the clasp holding a bun of silver hair in place, then set her shoulders in her *I work for tips* posture before approaching the booths where the men settled in.

Paul touched her hand and said, "You were saying about that boy?"

Georgina hadn't rehearsed it like this. As Mrs. D'Angelo explained that the diner was closing, Georgina scanned the men's faces, not recognizing a one. Not locals. They'd call her story of leaves and smells and death crazy. And might convince Paul.

"Coyotes caught him as he was walking home," she said, echoing the police chief's official statement. A statement that newcomers in Sunrise Village would accept. "Best to keep indoors—"

"You closin' early 'cause a *coyotes*?" chuckled one of the men, turning to face Georgina.

"To a pack a them, you'd be a tasty morsel," Mrs. D'Angelo spat over her shoulder, passing the order pad to Georgina. "Grab the beers, sweetie?"

Smiling at Paul, Georgina moved to the cooler.

"They're from the construction crew working Highway 32," Mrs. D'Angelo muttered to Georgina as they assembled the order. "Far enough south of Fellow's Point now it's almost the same distance to get here. We'll be seeing more like them soon."

Georgina couldn't blame Mrs. D'Angelo for her resentment. Despite its dangers, despite her children leaving decades ago, the older woman loved Jefferson Hollow. Said she'd die here. Felt the Leaving forced a hardy, self-reliant character on its residents that most small towns had lost. But Highway 32 would change all that and this crew symbolized that inevitable change.

"It looks like you have your hands full," Paul said while Georgina placed bottles on a tray. He stood, reaching for his wallet. "I'll come back tomorrow."

"Stay inside after dark," Mrs. D'Angelo said, carrying the tray to the men.

Paul grinned. "I'll be okay. It's just twenty feet to the barn."

Panic leapt up—icy, sharp. "Paul," Georgina began, not sure what to say. "Really, you should . . ."

His eyebrows knit.

"What are you doing for dinner?"

"The same as usual," he grinned. "Something in the oven or the barbecue. Did you have other ideas?"

Heart thudding. "You could come to my place."

His grin widened. "I would love to. What can I bring?"

"Just yourself," she replied.

"When and where?"

"Six o'clock?" Georgina gave directions to her house.

He handed over some bills covering his beer and a generous tip. "I'll see you soon."

Georgina watched him go.

"You're glowing, sweetie," Mrs. D'Angelo said, coming behind the counter with the empty tray. "Are you planning on having supper in an hour and sending him on his way before sunset? Or . . . ?"

Georgina grinned, heart still a heavy beat in her chest. It had been a while since she'd had a man in her life. But all of them had pursued her, asked her, made the moves. And they'd all been happy here in the Hollow. Farm kids. Sons taking over their dads' stores. Tradesmen servicing cottages up and down County Road 625. High school educated or dropouts. None wanted something better. To get out.

Not since Colin.

"I don't know," Georgina said. "But I've got to get something for supper and showered—"

"Then go. I can handle these guys."

"Are you sure?"

"I've done this plenty of times when your mother got sick. Go."

Georgina kissed Mrs. D'Angelo on the cheek and hurried to her car.

From the parking lot, Georgina turned right onto County Road 625 and drove south toward town. This far outside town centre, only a few trees were bare. Someone passing through would hardly know anything was wrong.

Ahead of her, it was different.

But behind her, 625 followed a twisting path north into the city, over an hour away. Highway 32—straight, smooth, four lanes wide—would cut that time in half. Already it had transformed the small towns along its route into bedroom communities. Sunrise Village was the first step toward monotonous, vinyl-sided neighbourhoods, restaurant chains' neon signs, and massive box store parking lots.

Though she understood Mrs. D'Angelo's feelings, Georgina welcomed the change. Since she'd been a girl—hell, since Mrs. D'Angelo had been a girl—the town had remained the same. Even her girlfriends were the same ones from high school. The ones who hadn't found a way out. Georgina envied them. Hard work in school, despite after school shifts, netted scholarship offers. But her mom's condition got worse. So she'd stayed, working the diner and taking classes at the community college up in Fellow's Point.

Then Colin—

Then her mom—

In town, oaks, maples, and elms stretched bare grey branches to the sky. Cars hurried up and down Main Street, people finishing errands before sunset. Black leaves blew through the parking lot behind the grocery store as Georgina got out and rushed inside.

The same store, Georgina reflected, run by the same family. Only the high school kids at the cash changed.

But Paul was new. When he'd first arrived, intent on cleaning up the farmhouse and selling it before going back to his life, she'd allowed herself impossible little fantasies of city life—managing a small restaurant, visiting little boutique shops, going dancing. And dating Paul.

But after a week he'd taken a liking to the town. "Never been here," he'd said. His grandmom always visited them. "Might keep the house for weekends and vacations. Maybe ask a friend in the county office up in Fellow's Point if there's any open positions."

That's when she started shaving her legs again and wearing make-up to work.

An announcement that the store would be closing in five minutes on account of the curfew pulled Georgina from her thoughts. She got in line at the checkout, rehearsing what she'd tell Paul about the Leaving. Reaching the cash, she didn't recognize the girl tallying up her things. Probably another kid from the Hollow starting an after-school job, but what if she was a newcomer living in Sunrise Village? Had someone warned her? A teacher? A friend?

Paying, Georgina wondered how many others wondered the same thing across Jefferson Hollow.

Heading for her car, black leaves crunching under her feet, she considered what would happen when Highway 32 finally passed through Jefferson Hollow and hundreds—or thousands—moved here? When the next Leaving started, it wouldn't just be one boy the first night.

But she'd tell people like she'd tell Paul. And after tonight, Paul would help spread the word.

Tonight. Even with what she had to tell him, the thought of what else might happen tickled her all over.

Georgina' stowed the vacuum in the closest just as the door bell rang. Opening the door revealed Paul, slacks and a polo replacing jeans and work shirt, a bottle of wine in hand. Beyond, daylight was a marmalade stain on the western sky, painting everything in a fiery glow through the bare trees.

"You look fabulous," he said, smiling.

She wore a simple white blouse, jeans, and flats. No time for anything else. And not like she had anything nicer. "So do you."

Georgina shut the door against the shifting leaves and animal smell.

Wine opened, brie and crackers set out, they sat in the glass-walled sun room off the den, watching the black leaves stir and chase themselves across the lawn. They talked, debated, bantered. He asked about the boy in Sunrise Village, which led to how rare, puzzling deaths motivated him. Seeing justice done. Fitting seemingly unimportant pieces together. Like unravelling the full life his grandmom had lived by her books and photos and mementos.

He asked about Georgina's life in Jefferson Hollow. She explained how her mom had died before Georgina finished college, leaving her the diner and the house. Plus a mortgage, student loans—Paul could sympathize—and staff. Because her mom had used her savings on drugs and experimental therapies, Georgian had nothing. Except the diner. Thankfully, Mrs. D'Angelo knew the business inside and out, but for seven years Georgina barely made ends meet and had been unable to find a buyer.

With the sun down, the sun room's glass walls became black mirrors. Georgina admired how the two of them looked together—cozy, comfortable. Sunset also meant he was spending the night.

She had to tell him.

Then Paul's stomach rumbled. They laughed and he apologized. While Georgina put the finishing touches on dinner—a simple chicken recipe—Paul browsed her bookshelves, commenting on titles they had in common.

Dinner served, he raved about it, wondering why it wasn't on the diner's menu. "Because," Georgina replied, "the Hollow's a deep-fried chicken kind of town." The conversation shifted and flowed. Wine poured. Georgina repeatedly took a deep breath, preparing to explain the Leaving, but every time she came close Paul described some outrageous memento he'd found tucked into a closet or crawlspace and had her laughing.

More wine opened. Georgina's head—and other things—tingled pleasurably. He was smart, confident, funny. The way his eyes lingered on her.

Dishes in the sink, they moved to the couch. Logic born of wine and lust concluded that since Paul was spending the night, there was no need to ruin it with talk of the town's curse. She straddled him, kissing him, feeling him swell beneath her. His hands—warm and right, cupping her neck, stroking her skin. She slid off, reached for his pants, undid them, teased him. She kissed his neck, nipped his earlobe and said, "You'll need to come down *every* weekend."

"Georgina . . ." He pulled her hand away. "I should . . . I need to tell you something."

She pulled back. "What?" A wife? Kids?

Straightening up, he said: "I'm selling the house. The Sunrise Village developers approached me. They're buying up everything past Fuller Avenue. They offered me . . . quite a lot. I couldn't say no. These past few days I've been working out the details. Last night, I was in the city signing papers. I wanted to tell you earlier, at the diner . . ."

Georgina stared. "So what does that mean?" *For us*, she wanted to add.

"With the money," Paul continued, "I can repay my student loans and pay off a good chunk of the condo. I still want to buy another place in the country. It would probably be smaller and closer to the city—"

"Closer . . ."

"That doesn't mean . . ." He shut his eyes. Shook his head. "I'm not explaining myself well."

Alcohol and shock and the longing to be touched coiled and spun. She wanted to scream at him to get out.

Just like she'd screamed at Colin. Right in this room.

He was standing, adjusting his belt. "I should go."

"No," she said, fighting back an irrational rage that wanted him to go out into the darkness. "You've been drinking—"

He was down the front hall. Georgina followed. He opened the front door. The animal stink flooded in.

—slamming his hands against the backdoor, flaps of skin hanging from his face—

Georgina grabbed Paul's arm. Turned him around.

"Don't—"

Outside, a ripple moved through the black leaves blanketing the lawn.

"My car is right—"

—His motorcycle steps away. He could make it, he'd promised—

"It's not coyotes," she blurted.

Paul shifted his weight. "I don't—"

"The kid. In Sunrise Village. It wasn't coyotes."

"What are you saying? You know what killed him?"

She'd prepared for this. Rehearsed it. But not after two bottles of wine and every bit of her aching for him. "We don't know what it is. We call it the Leaving. Every couple of years, in September, the leaves turn black over a couple of days and then, overnight, fall off the trees and this smell comes. When it happens, you don't go out at night until the smell fades. Usually a few days."

"Don't go outside . . . Why?"

"You end up like that little boy."

Paul rolled his eyes.

"I'm serious!" She clenched her jaw, straining to keep it together. "Eleven years ago. Someone found a teenager under a porch out 'round your grandmom's place. Every inch of him had been sliced up. Turns out he'd run away from home and was trying to reach his uncle who lives here."

Expression sceptical, Paul opened his mouth to say something. Before he could, she said: "A few years before that . . ." She paused for an instant, letting her nerves settle. He wouldn't take her seriously if she lost it. And if she lost it and he left, Paul was dead. "A drifter . . ." she continued. "Out where the train tracks used to be . . . throat sliced so deep he'd almost been decapitated."

"What were the causes of death determined to be?"

She had him. At least enough to keep him inside. Shutting the front door, she shook her head. "During a Leaving, no one asks too many questions."

"There must have been coroner's inquests or police investigations."

Georgina crossed her arms, hugging herself, wishing Mrs. D'Angelo were here. She'd have explained it better, had the answers. Damn it, Georgina scolded herself, she should've told Paul at the diner. Brought him in the back or something. "I don't know. This is just how it is. The stories go back over a hundred years."

He took her by the shoulders. "Georgina, my grandmother left me a letter in the will. Told me if the leaves went black and a smell came up, to ask someone in town who I trusted about it. You're telling me it's a spook story?"

"It's not a story!" she shouted with a venom she didn't expect, pulling away.

"The leaves are likely some cyclical disease," he continued. "As for the deaths, some psychopath or cult could be using the legend—"

"But I've seen it!" she screamed. "Nine years ago. It killed my boyfriend in front of me!" She wanted to stop. No one knew this. But a momentum had her, yanking out the words, hurling them so they hurt. "My mom was in the hospital again. So Colin was spending nights with me. Like revenge 'cause Mom hated him. Long hair and drove a motorcycle. Worked at a garage. Always talking about getting out. Mom told me I could do better. 'Men like him, like your father, are unreliable,' she said. She said if I kept seeing him, she'd kick me out. Cut me off. All my money for school gone. I'd have nothing. But I loved him. So we kept it secret. And when he had enough money, he'd get me out of here." Tears welled up. "But the Leaving started. It was afternoon and Colin was over. Said he'd made a pile fixing up this old Mustang. Wanted us to take off the next day. But I couldn't leave my mom in the hospital. So he asked 'When?' and I didn't know and he said I'd never stand up to my mom. I yelled at him and he said he was going to leave without me and tell my mom about us anyway. I told him to get out." She couldn't quite catch her breath, holding back the tears. Paul's arm was around her shoulders and somehow they'd wound up on the floor. "He—" Her breath caught and a sob escaped.

Words tumbled from her about Colin opening the back door. And the smell. Georgina had been too proud to take her words back and Colin too manly to show fear. It was just dusk—probably safe. Colin ran across the small porch and down the steps, disappearing from sight. There had been a moment of nothing—just the small wooden porch and growing darkness.

Then screaming.

"I called the cops in the morning. Not sure what I did for the rest of the night. Said he tried to break in at sunrise."

"Did they believe that?"

"I guess. My mom never asked me about it." She wrapped her arms around his neck. "Do you believe me?"

"Yes," Paul replied.

Silently, they held each other.

Eventually she led him upstairs. Without a word, he disappeared into the spare bedroom.

Georgina sat on her bed, holding her pounding head.

Something pulled her up and out of sleep. A siren, far away. Pale grey light illuminated her small bedroom.

The front door opened. Clicked closed.

Paul, Georgina realized. Leaving.

She flew to the window. Trees—dark grey angles against light grey dawn. Below, Paul got into his car, started it, backed out of the driveway.

After a moment to be thankful it was bright enough, she wondered if she'd see him again.

At least, she told herself, he knew. He'd be safe.

Unlike whoever that siren was for.

By the time Mrs. D'Angelo arrived for the breakfast shift, the usual crowd had assembled at the counter. Rumours drifted over coffee and eggs and toast. Two boys in Sunrise Village. Camping in their backyard. Parents discovered them come morning. Tent shredded, boys cut to ribbons. House had a fenced-in yard. Probably thought they were safe.

Mrs. D'Angelo tied on her apron. "How was your night?"

Georgina over-poured a mug, coffee slopping over the edges. "I told him about the Leaving."

"And?"

She'd known Mrs. D'Angelo would ask, tried to prepare for it. "He sold the house, Mrs. D. Getting some place closer to the city." She grabbed a rag to wipe up the spill.

"Oh. Well." Mrs. D'Angelo's hands went to her bun of hair. "I've been meaning to tell you this, sweetie, so maybe with this news, now's the time. I'm moving to Austin."

Georgina almost dropped the cup.

"One of my boys got a job with Dell. He can pay for the move. And I've enough stashed away to afford my own place."

"But . . ." Georgina sputtered.

"I know what you're going to say. But the town I love is gone, sweetie. People like Paul, selling it bit by bit. And this place won't last when they open an Applebee's or Fuddruckers right off the highway.

"And I don't want to be here for the next Leaving. With all the new people, we'll either warn them and word'll get out. Or we won't and there'll be too many deaths. Then what? The army? Guys in lab coats?" Mrs. D'Angelo shook her head. "Time for me to go, sweetie. Maybe for you, too." She went onto the floor to take an order.

Georgina placed the coffee before a local plumber. "Terrible tragedy," he said to the man next to him. "Should've listened to the police," the other replied. "Might be someone else tonight," someone offered. Going to be worse next time, they all agreed.

But someone would tell them. Sure, someone.

Headlights arced across the walls of Georgina's living room. She moved to the window, feet aching from a long shift. Paul's car sat in her driveway. Finally. She'd been trying his cell all day.

She hurried to the front door and pulled it open. Almost sunset. Paul moved up the walkway, black leaves crunching.

Georgina held the door open. "Come inside."

"I'm not planning on staying."

"It's almost dark—"

Paul rolled his eyes. "It's a *legend*, Georgina."

"You said . . . you believed me."

"I believe something happened, but not that some mysterious force killed your boyfriend. And I'm going to stand here and prove it.

"I spent the morning at the library scanning the town paper going back twenty years. There's no mention of 'The Leaving' or the smell or black leaves. No articles on drifters or teenagers being killed. But I did find an obit for a Colin Keenan. Was that him, Georgina?"

"Yes. Paul—"

"So I went up to the county coroner's office in Fellow's Point. There are no records of mysterious deaths in Jefferson Hollow. In the case of Colin's death, the police and a local doctor signed off on natural causes, so no coroner's investigation. Family declined an autopsy. You said Colin was killed at dusk, but you told the police he tried to break in at dawn."

"I didn't want my mom—"

A ripple passed through the leaves out near the road.

"Paul, *please* come inside."

"Even a rookie can tell a freshly deceased corpse from one that's been out all night by skin temperature. So I looked into that boy from Sunrise Village. Those wounds were clearly not from an animal attack. I have to ask myself: how can these errors be made repeatedly by the police?"

Georgina held up her hands. She didn't know how it worked, just that—

according to Mrs. D'Angelo—for over a hundred years they'd been able to avoid attention. Keep outsiders from turning their town upside down. Staying inside a few nights every couple of years was a small price to pay to keep their town from becoming another anonymous suburb. "What do you want me to say?"

"I then recalled that you said no one asks questions about deaths during the Leaving. And that no one would go out after dark. So I have to ask, Georgina: rather than Colin leaving, did you kill him?"

She went cold. "No."

"You two had had a fight. He said he was going to reveal your relationship to your mother, which would have ruined your future. So in a heated moment, knowing you could get away with it, you somehow got the better of him, killed him, and said it was the Leaving."

The leaves in the yard shifted without a breeze to stir them.

"That's insane!" But she'd left him out there. After Colin had screamed, he'd charged back up the stairs, bloody gashes in his face. Seeing him, she'd locked the door.

"Help!" he'd screamed, yanking on the door. "Please, Georgina!"

She'd froze.

He'd slammed his palms against the heavy glass door. "Georgina—!"

She'd backed away. A flicker of darkness and his cheek flapped open—gums and teeth visible. Had she screamed? She must've shut her eyes because a sound made her open them to see the porch, empty. Maybe a flicker of motion going over the railing? Then nothing.

She hadn't wanted him to die. But if she'd opened the door they both would've been killed.

Was that true? Could he have leapt inside, then slammed the door? They might've talked it out, forced to stay inside all night.

"Then explain it," Paul said.

The leaves rippled, sliding towards them.

Georgina charged down the steps, taking Paul's hand. "Paul, please. I'll explain the best I can. But we have to get inside." She pulled.

He set his feet. "The sun is down, Georgina. It's a *story*." He shook his head. "I have no choice. I have to refer this to the chief medical examiner."

She yanked his hand hard enough to pull him off balance and up a step. "Listen to me—!"

With a roar, the leaves exploded into an obsidian cyclone, engulfing them. The animal stink assaulted her. Paul's hand yanked out of hers. She threw up her arms to protect her face, leaves whipping past.

Paul's scream reached her through the noise. Eyes shut, face buried in the crook of an elbow, she reached out. Pain, razor-fine, crisscrossed her arms, her legs, her body. The sound deafening. "Paul—!"

The top of her ear separated and fell. Pain blossomed. The panicked, animal need to flee turned her round, propelled her up the porch steps and into her house. She slammed the front door, stood for a stunned moment and then wandered into the living room. Thick, warm wetness dripped from her fingers.

The light in the living room was wrong. Like it came sideways. From outside. She had an instant to realize it was car headlights through the sun room windows before the glass exploded. She dove behind the couch, chunks of glass falling around her. After a few moments, she pulled herself to her knees, shards sliding off her back and hair, and looked over the couch. The crumbled hood of Paul's car poked into her living room through the remains of the sun room.

Georgina found herself next to the car. Within, Paul slumped back, a grimace frozen on his face, eyes flat, dark leaves choking a wide, blood-smeared gash in his neck.

Something black shot by her. Warmth trickled across her scalp.

The stink filled the living room. She'd an instant to realize the barrier between her and the outside had been breached before thundering blackness enveloped her.

Arms wrapped around her face, she ran for the bathroom, pulled open the door, and tumbled in. She kicked the door shut, but not before leaves flowed through the closing gap—spinning, diving, slicing. She dropped to her knees, grabbing for a towel. It fell from her grip. Reaching for the other, she saw her right hand was missing all but the pinky finger. She snatched the towel with her left hand and snapped it upward. Fragments of leaves rained down like ash, releasing the barnyard musk.

She leaned against the vanity, panting. She pressed the towel to her ruined hand.

Cold. Clammy. The world—cock-eyed grey.

Something made her open her eyes. Scratching. In the space between the door and the floor, tips of black leaves wriggled against each other, fighting to get through. Strength leaving her, vision going dark, Georgina pressed the towel, swollen with blood, into the gap. She tried to brace it with her heels, but her legs felt heavy, far away.

Something pushed back.

On the other side of the door, a sound like a thousand tiny claws trying to dig through.

And ringing. A high, sweet sound swelling in her ears.

Like the bell at her diner. Its cheerful tinkle making her look up to see Colin, safe and handsome, coming in. His bike was out back, he'd tell her. Just a short walk and he'd take her away from this small town. Untying her apron, she'd tell her mom she was starting her own life. With Colin.

They'd be together.

They'd be leaving.

YOU'RE A WINNER!

Squeeze the pump again. Nothing.

The fuck?

Knocking.

Takes a second to tell it's coming from the station's convenience store. Somebody knocking on the window. Head's so goddamn—

Sorry, Lord.

So fucking fuzzy. Can't think straight.

Guy behind the counter's looking at me. A dark smudge against the yellow light inside. He's pointing at a poster in the window. Lights are so bright. Everything's got a blue-white glow. The poster's red letters waving like hot blacktop on a July day. I squint. Think it says:

PRAY INSIDE UP TO LORD

Heart thudding. Oh Lord, is this a sign? Telling me what to do after sending me to the middle of fucking nowhere. Ain't nothing out here but trees and lakes and towns smaller than the block I grew up on. But how's praying going to make it right? Mufi don't let debts go. Even if it's just two hundred bucks.

But back in rehab, Father Molina told us junkie losers you're always showing us the way if we pay attention. If we look for signs.

So it must be your will that's had me going more than a day without sleep to get me out here. Thy will be done, Lord.

Just wish I knew what the fuck it was.

All right, take a deep breath. Give my head a shake. Pull it the fuck together.

I look up again, focus this time, and read:

PRE-PAY INSIDE AFTER 10PM

Fuck. So I *am* going inside. No pump and run. Barely had fifty bucks when Ortega lost his shit. After this, I got nothing. How am I going to keep running with no cash? Can do some stick-ups, but sooner or later they'd catch me. Then they wouldn't send me back to rehab but the joint. And Mufi's got people on the inside. After what happened with Ortego? I'd be dead for sure.

Oh, Lord have mercy. This is where it all goes down, ain't it?

Through the window, counter jockey shrugs, like he's saying, "What's it gonna be?"

If this is your will, Lord . . .

Thy will be done.

I head for the door. Legs are heavy, feet a million miles away. Ground's shifting back and forth. Pistol's huge against my stomach.

So I gotta ask, Lord: The counter jockey, he seen my mug shot in the paper this morning? Read that shit about "armed and dangerous"? Least he's the only one inside. And ain't seen another car for fifteen minutes. Out into the blackness, just an empty road. One way going back the way I came, the other going someplace else. A long line of streetlights light up the bottom edges of pine trees far as I can see.

Can't tell if the lights are swaying or I am.

A bell above the door tinkles. Light in here's so goddamn—

Sorry, sorry.

So fucking yellow. Tiny place. Two aisles. Ten feet end to end. Racks of chips and cookies. Motor oil. Deodorant and razors. Big cooler of drinks on one end. Coffee station next to the check out.

But there's also cameras behind the counter.

I tug my ball cap low.

Counter jockey's watching me. Greasy black hair, few days' stubble. Least he don't look the paper-reading type. Lord, why'd my photo gotta show up so quick? That your work, telling me to give it up? Or keep running? And shit, I didn't do nothing. Ortega went nuts when Mufi's people started hassling us. When 'Tega got hit, you made his gun land right at my feet. And put that rusted out car in my path when I'm hauling ass down Fuller Avenue. Some dipshit leaves it running outside a KFC in that neighbourhood? Gotta be you telling me to run. Least then I knew what you wanted.

So what's it going to be now, Lord?

Coffee smells like shit, but I grab an extra large cup and pour. Need the caffeine. Besides, the extra large's got two of those peel-off game pieces instead of just one. Who knows, right?

I take a sip and wait for the kick. One of the tabs looks a little loose. What the fuck. I pull it. Got to read it twice to make sure it says:

YOU'RE A WINNER! Shoot Clerk & Empty Register!

I drop the tab, hands trembling. My knees almost give out. The fuck is this? I ain't no killer, Lord. Doing stick-ups is one thing, but kill this man? Why you asking me to do this? If this is your will, thy will be done, but they got cameras. I won't make it too far. Then it's life in the joint for sure if Mufi's people don't get me first.

I put the coffee on the counter and drop to my knees, looking for the tab. Couldn't have said that.

Floor's covered with those things. Spilled coffee and crap from people's shoes ground into them. They all say "Sorry! Try Again!"

"Yo, man, you win something?" counter jockey asks.

I get up before he thinks I'm some psycho or something. Heart's a jackhammer. "No," I tell him, turning. "Just . . ."

Need a second to think.

Oh Lord, this is why you led me here. This man needs killing and I get the money to pay back Mufi.

Thy will be done, Lord, but the cameras.

"Um, okay," counter jockey says. He hits a few keys. "Coffee's $1.29. How much gas you gonna put in?"

I dig in my pockets. Need a second. Lord, just one more second to figure this shit out. Father Molina never said nothing about something like this. Said to trust you, talk to you, watch for signs—

"And you got 'nother chance on that cup, ya know," counter jockey says.

Oh Lord. What else you got to say? Hands shaking, I almost knock over the cup pulling the second tab. I blink a few times before I can read:

YOU'RE A WINNER! Cameras Are Broken!

"Anything?"

The world's spinning.

"Hey, man, you okay?" counter jockey asks. He's reaching slowly to me with this right hand, like he's worried about me. But his left is moving under the counter. For a silent alarm?

Or a gun?

Oh Lord, Thy will be done.

THE WEAK SON

Am I dead? I must be.

I think I've been in this house for a couple of days now, but I can't remember where I am or how I got here. Funny, I should be bothered by all this, but I'm not. This place seems familiar.

I always end up down here in the basement, looking at one of the floor joists. It has a bunch of wires and pipes snaking through a hole drilled in it. Something tells me it's important.

The front door just opened. In an instant—with just a thought—I'm there.

Two men are coming in, dressed in jeans, T-shirts and windbreakers. One is in his late teens or early twenties, the other old enough to be his father. Behind them, in the gravel driveway, is a pick-up truck.

I think they've been here before.

The older one surveys the room while my brother—

My brother.

They're my brother and father.

"Dad?" I ask, moving to him. "Dad, what happened to me?"

A chill washes over me, full of fear, anger, regret.

It's my father's emotions.

No, more than that. Memories. I see them—*feel* them—all around me.

He was surprised and angry as he read—

He forces the memory away, telling himself he's almost done. After this, he'll never need to come back.

He's afraid.

He's afraid his guilt will keep building every time he comes here until he cracks and confesses what he did. But more than that, he's scared there's some evidence he's missed. He's checked everywhere he can think of, but what if, when he left me, I wrote another note describing what he'd done and hid it for Ken in some secret hiding spot?

Ken. My brother's name is Ken.

"I think we can get all this in one last trip," my father says.

All this?

Last trip?

Ken is still for a moment, then picks up a cardboard box. I move to his side. "Ken! What's going on? What happened to me? What did Dad do?"

Ken heads out the front door, thinking how much he hates this.

My dad grabs a bundle of blankets and follows.

The floor.

It's covered with boxes full of books, plates and cups, old board games. Blankets and sheets are folded in neat piles. There's an old coffee table, some folding chairs and a small shelf.

This stuff has been here the whole time.

Ken and my dad return from outside, their boots echoing sharply.

The echo. It's wrong for this room.

I see why: the hideous green carpet is gone. So are the couches and chairs, the tables, the paintings on the wall. All that's left is what's on the floor.

What about the other rooms?

With a thought, I'm in the bedroom Ken and I used to share. Empty. No pictures or posters on the wall. Our bunk beds are gone. The books and games and trophies that filled the shelves my grandfather built when he bought this place are missing.

The main bedroom. Nothing. I move into the closet. Empty except for a few hangers.

The kitchen. Nothing in the cupboard. The microwave, toaster, coffee maker—the pale green countertop is bare.

This is our cottage. It's almost empty and I hadn't noticed.

I couldn't even remember where I was.

The living room. I'm at Ken's side as he and my father carry out the coffee table. "Ken, why are you moving everything out? Is it because I died here?"

Memories, sick and putrid:

—a phone call—

—screaming his rage—

—a frantic three-hour drive—

Ken slams his mind shut as he walks backwards to the truck. He can't stand how the memories bombard him when he's here.

I've done this before.

Every time they come here, I ask them what happened, but they can't hear me. They work in silence, only speaking to ask for help carrying something or how to arrange things in the truck.

But in their silence, they remember. Their memories scatter and ricochet around me, their quiet a storm of thoughts and regrets. I try to get them to remember what happened to me so *I* can remember.

And then they leave. And I forget again.

"Dad, what are you scared of?" I ask as he enters the room, knocking a dead leaf from his boot.

I was standing on the workbench—

He scratches the back of his head, digging fingernails so deep the pain obliterates the memories.

"Ken," I say as he passes through the front door. "How did I die?"

A hospital. As the doctor talked, my father—a stoic man whose only emotions are anger and disappointment—held back tears. Ken couldn't hear what they said, but saw our father's grief as a performance and began to suspect our dad was covering something up. That maybe he was to blame.

"I don't understand," I say. "What did Dad do?"

Ken thinks about standing in the basement weeks later—silent, shocked—Dad watching from a few steps away.

He rubs his eyes and picks up a box full of old plates. Memories spark to life:

—Mom in the kitchen cooking Thanksgiving dinner—

—Ken and I quickly doing the dishes so we could go back outside to play before dark—

—Ken bringing a plate of leftover pie down to the dock as we fished in the early morning—

As Ken tries to hold these back, I remember more:

Ken and I catching fireflies in the dusk of hot summer evenings . . .

Watching shooting stars on cool autumn nights . . .

Ken teaching me to fish—teasing but patient, laughing but kind . . .

"But why are you leaving?" I ask.

He promises himself he'll return. They just need to shut the place down for while. When he can deal with the pain that I'll never be there, he'll be back.

"But I *am* here!"

Ken lifts another box, grunting to cover what could become a sob, as he realizes the future he thought he would have—where we would share this place and bring our kids here—is gone.

My father looks up from rearranging a box of pots and pans, and asks "What?" with a threatening edge in his voice. Immediately, he regrets speaking. He wants to keep the silence of the last few trips. He's been able to deflect Ken's questions and doesn't want to get him talking again, but his instinct is to see the sound as some kind of protest or exaggeration. Some kind of *challenge*. And his immediate reaction is, and always has been, to deal with *anyone* who challenges him.

Words swell inside Ken . . . just like they have before. He wants to turn and demand to know what really happened. But he's already done that and every time he's asked for details, my father reacts with anger or dodges the question. "Dad, we've been through this," he replies, headed for the pick-up.

"I guess we have," my dad responds, willing himself to be calm. Let Ken have his little rebellion.

"Don't let him shove you aside like that," I say to Ken, tree branches overhanging the driveway, crisscrossing him in dark shadows, as he sets the box in the back of the truck. He goes cold and jagged, looking back inside the cottage. "What question *haven't* you asked?" I demand.

Random snatches of conversations with my friends shoot through Ken's memory.

My friends.

I used to have a lot of friends.

And I was on a team. A sports team.

Memories of my friends' tears and regrets and anger about missing the warning signs coalesce into a single idea. As Ken comes back inside, he asks, "How did you not see it coming?"

Something—like a memory but not a memory—surfaces in my father. He stays focused on the box of pans as he gives it voice. "We *all* missed it, Ken."

It's a rehearsed answer.

Rage blooms within Ken, sharp and scalding. "I was at school, Dad! Don't give me this 'we all missed it' crap when *you* were here."

He has another reply ready, fighting to control the fury at being challenged once again. "What could I have seen?" He stands. "That his grades were slipping? High school was almost over, so he backed off a little bit. You did the same thing at his age."

He's lying. I didn't back off. I just didn't care. But my father did. This rage he can barely control is the same he unleashed when I starting bringing home "F's."

"Slipping, maybe," Ken says, "but he was *failing*, Dad! And skipping school. And he quit the track team. Did you know I talked to Coach Abernathy? Do you know what he said?"

The track team. I ran track.

Ken continues. "Coach said he quit because he thought he wasn't good enough. Coach almost dropped dead when he heard that. Second best kid on the squad thinks he's not good enough. Now where do you think he got that idea?"

Fear of what else Ken might know coils deep and numbing-cold. He knew Ken had suspicions, and he kept a close eye on him to see if he went looking for some hidden note the one time he was here, but had no idea Ken was asking around about me. Where I was weak and a disappointment, Ken is strong—a worthy son. Is he so strong, my dad wonders, that he came here to accuse his own father of having a hand in his brother's death? Could he even be considering avenging his brother?

"Well?" Ken demands.

My father's rage and fear entangle each other. He takes a slow, measured breath, telling himself he is in control and Ken is grasping at straws. Still, my dad notices the handle of a heavy iron skillet within easy reach in the box at his feet. "If he wanted to quit track, that's his business. He was always weaker than you, Kenny. He was the one who would quit."

Mike, my captain on the track team, jumps into Ken's mind. "It wasn't just his grades or track, Dad. Mike Fitzgibbons told me how he started pulling away from everybody, that he was tired all the time, he never talked anymore. You didn't see *any* of that?"

Mike. I lied to him so many times. Told him I was fine and could handle how hard my dad rode me.

My dad thinks of the basement again, and guilt rises, but he pushes it away. It's not his fault. But it *is* his fault, even though he believes he did nothing wrong. And now for Ken to question him. To doubt him. "He's a teenager, Ken!" my father shouts, his rage starting to break lose. "He—"

"He *was* a teenager, Dad," Ken says. "Was."

"Do not correct me!" my father bellows, his voice echoing in the empty, darkening room. He looks down again at the skillet's handle, anger blooming into violence, wanting to strike out, the desire to break and bloody, the need to show he is in control.

He thinks of the basement, his fingers working a knot.

I want to ask about that knot, but his wrath vibrates around me—through me—familiar and terrifying. But Ken is the focus of his rage this time.

Ken holds his ground. His mind is empty—waiting, expecting a blow. Almost wanting one. Wanting the excuse to unleash years of pent-up anger for everything he—we—went through after our mom died and our dad twisted into the man he is now.

As they stare at each other, a small bit of my father's mind realizes that if he lashes out, he could be the one getting hurt. Ken is taller, leaner, younger, faster. Ken can beat him and there's no way in hell my father would suffer that humiliation. Finding out just how weak I was—how I wouldn't even fight back—had been disgraceful enough.

I find my voice and ask, "What happened in the basement?"

My dad turned from me and headed up the cellar stairs, disgusted, knowing I'm too much of a coward to—

He has to get out of here.

I need to keep pressing him. I won't be weak. Not this time. "If you didn't do anything wrong, then tell him. Did you kill me because I was weak?"

His guilt and certainty collide. He pushed too hard, but he needed to push me.

He breaks Ken's stare, picks up the box, angles around him and heads to the truck.

Ken just watches him pass. Again, he flashes on a future without me, but now I see more: plans to get a job at school, find an apartment, never come home. It's more than resentment—Ken is scared what he thinks happened to me might happen to him.

"Ken," I say, "he's scared of *you*. He almost remembered. Don't stop."

My father returns, his mind whirling with something new. Something he's been holding back but can use to distract Ken from asking about me. "Look, I don't want to talk about this. Next week I sign the papers and this will be over." He picks up two folding chairs, waiting for Ken's response.

Surprise and dread—glacier-like in their enormity and cold—seep from him. "What papers?" Ken asks, suspecting what I just learned: my father is selling the cottage.

"Don't let him distract you," I say. "Find out what happened to me!"

My father replies, "With the new owner."

"You sold this place?" Ken asks. Emotions spiral from him: anger, surprise, revulsion.

"We both made the decision to sell." A lie.

"No, bullshit," Ken replies. "That's not what we talked about." Ken's memory is a shattered mirror. Strained phone calls about if he could enjoy being here

. . . coming here only once after I was dead and Dad never leaving him alone for a moment . . . the pain of my absence . . .

"We gave it three months."

Three months?

"And you said you didn't want to come here anymore."

I've been here for three months?

"Yeah, but I never said I wanted you to sell the place."

"What else am I supposed to think?"

Ken is speechless.

"Think about the basement, Dad," I say.

He came down the stairs after getting back from town and saw my feet—

He shakes his head at Ken and heads back outside.

"He's lying," I say to Ken, and Ken knows it. "Stay on him. He'll crack. He'll confess. And then you can keep this place and not leave me here alone again."

But Ken is disgusted. He feels like the world has fallen away and he is alone to face it.

With nothing else he can do, Ken picks up the shelves and heads for the truck.

This can't happen. If this is the last time they'll be here, what will happen to me?

I think of when Ken and I were kids and those memories fill Ken. He pauses, the shelves almost forgotten, unable to hold back tears. Random memories tumble from him, filling the space around me. I snatch one—Grandpa teaching Ken to fish when he was a little boy—and hold it, twining it with the memory of him teaching me to fish. "This was *mom's* cottage," I say. "Dad has no right to sell it."

Ken's sadness solidifies, turning to sharp-edged anger. He slams the shelves down and says, "Ya know, maybe you could think—maybe hope—maybe fucking realize—that I would want to come back some day! Bring my kids here. Keep this place in the family."

My dad swallows his rage. "You never said you wanted to own this place."

"I didn't think it needed to be said."

"It's too late." My father remembers relief at the buyer's offer. And enthusiasm a few weeks earlier as he gave the buyer a tour of the cottage. During everything, my father never mentioned me, even as I followed him, peppering him with questions. But the memories those questions brought up only strengthened his determination to sell.

"You didn't think to ask me what I thought before you sell it to some stranger?" Ken asks.

The buyer asked about spending a weekend here and my dad agreed. "I thought I knew."

Some time ago, there *were* sounds and movement here, but I ignored them. Was that him? Did someone spend a weekend here and I didn't even notice?

"Well, Dad, you didn't."

"There is nothing I can do."

"Ken, don't let it end here!" For the first time in my—for the first time ever, I shout at my father: "Tell him what you did if you're so fucking certain it was the right thing to do!"

As he came down the cellar stairs, he saw my shoes on the workbench and realized I was standing on it. Then he noticed a piece of notebook paper on the steps—

Satisfied he's won the argument, my dad grabs the shelves from Ken.

"He almost remembered!" I shout at Ken. His mind is a deep-red cyclone of thoughtless anger. "Nothing is signed yet!"

The cyclone evaporates. "Just tell the guy you changed your mind," he says. "If nothing is signed, it's not too late."

My father spins and fixes Ken with a stare, furious that Ken has found a new point to argue. He's in charge, he makes the decisions. He's not some coward who needs to be told what to do.

My father thinks of that floor joist in the basement.

I'm down there, looking up at the large hole in it.

Upstairs, my dad says, "Your brother died here! I cannot stay here anymore!"

There are small strands of something caught in the hole's rough edges.

"Then don't sell. I thought you were going to rent it or let it sit empty. Do that. But don't sell it!"

They look like fibres from a rope.

"It's done, Ken. The paperwork is a formality, but it's done."

I don't remember my dad ever stringing a rope down here.

"You know," Ken says, "you talk about quitters, Dad, and it seems like you're the one who's quitting now."

In my father's memory, was he tying a knot . . . or untying one?

"Don't *ever* talk to me like that."

But there's a laundry line outside. Why—?

"Or what?"

Oh God.

"What are you going to do, Dad?" Ken continues. "Ignore me like you ignored—"

Oh God no.

"I did not ignore your brother!" my father bellows. His unbound fury slashes dark crimson, but beneath it is the truth: he didn't ignore me. He focused too much on me. "He was a selfish quitter! Don't lay his bad decisions on me!"

"He needed help! God, how could you have been so blind? Did everyone see it but you? Did you *want* it to happen?"

"Kenneth—" my dad begins, but can't say anymore. His will breaks and memories surge up. I'm pulled upstairs into the deepening darkness of the room.

He was headed into town for groceries and figured he should get a new seal for the hot-water tank while there, but needed to measure it. He came in the side door and down the cellar stairs, finding me standing on the workbench, motionless, one end of a rope around my neck, the other through that hole in the joist.

"He loved this place," Ken continues, his voice breaking. "Loved it so much he chose to die here. And I love this place. But none of that matters because you're going to give up on something that belongs to the family. Or what's left of it."

My dad, pulled back from the memory, says: "We. Are. Done." He heads for the truck.

"Ken!" I scream. "He could have stopped me."

I thought he had gone into town and I was alone. As I stood there, I wasn't sure if I was going to do it. I couldn't stand him anymore, couldn't stand being such a disappointment, but was this the only way? I wondered if Ken could help me. Maybe get an apartment together.

Then I heard the side door open. I froze, terrified, unable to move even as he came down the cellar stairs.

He just stared at me.

"You quitter," he finally said. "Are you really that weak? I've see you moping around and this is your solution?" He picked up the note. The note where I explained how angry I was, how he made me feel like a failure. He read it and said, "Well, if you're going to do this, then *do* it. For the first time in your life, do something right. But no one's going to see this." He crumbled my note—a note I spent weeks writing—and stuck it in his pocket.

"And then he turned around and went upstairs!" I scream.

My father appears in the doorway, his face a kaleidoscope of shadows in the gloom. His mind is all right-angles with the certainty of his victory. He will sell this place. Ken knows nothing.

"Ken, don't let him go!" I scream. But Ken is done, his mind on someplace past here. "Don't give up."

My father says, "You coming?"

"You let me do it!" I scream at him. I stood for hours before stepping off the workbench, my heart empty, my mind filled with my father's words. "Tell Ken what you did, you coward!"

When he returned from town, he'd expected me to be sobbing in the living room. Not finding me there, he put away the groceries and went into the cellar, new rubber seal in hand, certain I would be down there, crying. He first saw my feet again, but this time they were swinging freely in the air.

Seeing this through his eyes, I remember. I circled him, asking him questions, wanting to know what had happened. But all I did was build his anger—anger that I gave up, that I didn't stand up to him.

He cut my body down, untied the knot, and checked for a pulse. Not finding one, he put the rubber seal on his workbench, then called 911.

"Yeah," Ken replies.

"Don't leave!" I scream as Ken walks out into the fading light. "Don't leave me here alone!" I think of us as kids again, but it makes Ken feel ill. "Don't let him sell the cottage!" The door swings shut, leaving me in darkness. "Don't be weak and give up!" A key slides into the lock, the tumblers turn, the bolt clicks home. "Or just kill him!" I move to a window and see the pick-up head along the narrow, tree-lined driveway. It reaches the end, turns, and disappears up a forest road.

They have to come back. They've got to. Then I'll get my father to admit what he did. I was so close. They must have forgotten something. Or forgotten to *do* something. At the end of the summer, we used to have a ton of things to do to close this place, like turning off the water pump or . . . something. We had a list of chores, but I can't remember them. I guess that's why we had the list.

But they were moving things, so they need to come back for more, right? Sure. Even though the living room is empty, there are other rooms in this place. They must have stuff in them.

They'll be back, whoever they were, and that'll be good because things seemed better when they were here. I could remember things, like where I am. But right now, I'm okay. Funny, I'm not lonely, even though I think I've been here for three or four days by myself.

I go down into the basement and look at that joist again. The one with the hole in it. I think it's important.

Am I dead? I must be.

PROG
P
LNR/
CDS
ABC
DEF
1
2
3
GHI
JKL
MNO

WHILE GABRIEL SLEPT

Pray: Deliver Your strength to my loved ones. . . .

—soul spirals away like wisps of smoke shredded to nothing. reclaimed by darkness. like i belong to it. strength, love, feeling. gone. this place takes all i am. only certainty remains: must *do something*—

Was in kitchen, now in nursery. Don't remember getting here.

Been like that a lot lately.

Pain a white hot needle twisting under my left temple. My wife—

—can't think of her in any other term—

—just a description—

—the liar doesn't deserve a name—

—looks up, gives a look like *Why am I doing all the work?* then makes *gootchy gootchy goo* noises, tickling the baby's feet. The baby—

—also undeserving of a name—

—giggles.

Dry, sweet smell of baby powder, formula, wet wipes—overpowering. Stomach clenches and does a slow roll. Should run to bathroom, but can barely move my feet.

"So that's that" is Mom's conclusion to a topic I don't remember. Phone's heavy as a brick. Struggle to keep it to my ear. She asks, "And how's my granddaughter?"

Look at the baby. Needle twists harder. Hope to keep pain from voice. "Fine," I lie. Baby is fine, but don't have the heart to tell Mom she isn't her granddaughter.

"I do hope you and"—my wife's name—"can bring her up and visit some time soon. I can't wait to meet her."

There is power in what Mom didn't say: bring her up and visit some time soon *while I still have time*.

"Sure, some time soon."

My wife pulls a blanket over the baby, shushing her to sleep. Sings a lullaby.

Needle punctures something. Fury sprays hot like arterial blood.

Should smash her head with the phone. So tiny, so small. Rage-fuelled strength to crush, to pound . . .

To . . .

Pray: Please God, tell me I don't need to do this. . . .

—not darkness. darkness is the absence of light. no concept of light here. a realm god passed over. heaven and earth, light and life, created elsewhere—

Outside on balcony. Wind has picked up, cold against face and arms. Smells clean. Mom is talking about visiting Dad this afternoon.

Turn, see wife bent over baby, smiling.

Safe.

Needle now an ice pick, jabbing inside skull.

Phone bad idea, anyway. Just shattering plastic, a welt, some blood. Then cops. Cuffs. Comments about what kind of monster could do that. And Mom wondering why the phone cut out.

"Be nice if you could make it out to see your father," Mom hints.

Look down at street, nine storeys below. "I know. But it's hard with the baby." Jump would kill me, but my priest said I'd go straight to Hell. No chance to tell God what He will not hear in prayer: that my wife and mother and father need His strength and grace. He may not act, but He must hear.

And I will not escape the pain of my wife's betrayal through death. Not if she's still alive.

But after . . .

Barely lift feet to step back into living room. Like moving through syrup. Pain quivers with each footfall, wringing the back of my neck.

"Sound good?" Mom wants to know.

No idea what she said. "Yup."

She might hear indifference in my voice. Might ask: "What's wrong, dear?"

How to respond? "Not really, Mom," I could say. "I got the results this morning. Amazing what technology can do. Swab my cheek, then the baby's, and mail them off. A week later, some lab tells you your wife got knocked up by some other guy and didn't even tell you."

"That's horrible, dear," she might reply.

"Did I mention she tried to make it out like it was my fault? When I asked her about the credit card charges at lingerie and 'adult toy' stores, she doesn't deny it. Like she wasn't trying to hide it. She tells me I'm boring and shallow and she'd hoped she could change me, but it never happened. So she sought out other men."

And Mom might say "No, dear, you never mentioned that" but instead says: "You sound tired, sweetie."

Soft footsteps. Small, bare feet on hardwood. I turn. "I am." Truth for once.

"You should—"

Lose the rest. My wife is saying something.

Hear neither of them.

Ice pick scraping inside my skull, scoring jagged grooves.

"Hold on, Mom." Hand over mouthpiece. Look down at my wife. So tiny. Not even five feet tall. I played fullback in college. Making love, I had to be careful. Could have crushed her.

Maybe that is how I could do it. Make it look like an accident.

But thought of my hands on her repulses me, like handling human filth. Only way I would touch her is hands around throat.

"Sorry?"

She rolls her eyes, looks back up. "What I said was 'I'm going to take a nap. Make sure the baby doesn't cry.'" She motions to the door of the bedroom we made the nursery—

—No, not "we" made—she picked everything, I did the work—paint, assemble furniture, hang pictures. Barely had the strength for it. My wife's role was to find the flaws, tell me our child deserves the best.

Envy Dad. Unable to remember anything—his name, where he is, who Mom is. "I'll try."

"Do more than try. I did the work for nine months. Least you can do is keep her quiet for an hour." She turns, heads for our bedroom.

Wish phone wasn't cordless. Phone cord looped over her head, pulled tight around throat until she stops moving.

What would Mom hear? Gasping, struggling, cartilage cracking.

My wife shuts bedroom door and for a moment I can believe she's gone for good.

—never here in the first place—

—never met her, fell in love, confronted her about the credit card charges.

She confessed and vowed she was done. Stopped trips, late nights. But resisted counselling.

Six months passed. Started getting home an hour later than normal. Then two. Sometimes not home until midnight. Wondered if cheating again. Prayed she would remain strong and faithful, but felt nothing. Only darkness. Darkness that filled me. Headaches clouded thoughts. Unfocused at work. Tired all day, but could not sleep at night. Strength gone. Trouble making love.

Told me she was pregnant. Should have been happy—a baby would bring us together—but suspicions remained. We had not been together often and sometimes I could not finish.

Was baby mine?

Ice pick pries something lose. Thick as my pinky finger, it squirms deep in my skull.

Break into a sweat. "Sorry, Mom. What were you saying?"

"Are you okay, sweetie?"

"Far from it," I could answer. "Do you remember teaching me to pray, Mom? How to clear my mind and open myself? You used to tell me God cannot answer all prayers, but He hears them. So praying brought me peace, Mom, because I knew God heard me. But I don't think God hears me anymore. Everything's dark when I pray."

"That's terrible, sweetie," she might say.

"It's worse than that," I'd continue. "I could kill her. But my priest said God does not hear prayers of sinners unless they repent and ask forgiveness. I do not know what sin I committed so God will not hear me, so how can I ask forgiveness? And I would never be sorry for killing her. But I think I have found a way."

Talked to another priest on other side of city. Lied and said infant son had heart defect. No hope. I asked: Can he hear me and understand when gone? Priest said while alive, infant cannot understand, but can as spirit.

Had found way for God to hear me. Tell baby my prayers—my wife needs God's strength to remain faithful. And my mother needs strength in the face of the illness that will take her life. And my father needs God's grace while his mind slips away.

"And then if I kill the baby," I might tell Mom, "she goes to heaven as my messenger."

"Sweetie?" Mom asks, waiting for answer.

"Just tired, Mom." Thing in my head wriggles, borrowing deep. Hold back a gasp of slashing pain.

"That lasts another ten years, dear." Trying to be funny.

Look back toward bedroom door. How would it feel to put hand over her mouth and pinch her nose? Imagine her struggling—surprisingly strong—arching her back and awkwardly kicking and punching, pivoting her head, desperate for breath? Would I have the strength and resolve to hold my hand in place until she stops fighting?

For that, I do. If I have sinned so that God does not hear me, I am lost. What is one more sin? Or two?

Approach the door. Soft, gentle sounds of sleep. "Gotta go, Mom."

"You take care now."

"I will."

"Kiss"—the baby—"for me and tell"—my wife—"I said 'hello.'"

Open door. See her sleeping. The serpent in my mind stills, waiting. "Okay."

Open myself again, searching.

Pray: Show me a sign I am heard. . . .

—cold, boundless nothing. not indifference. indifference would mean something was there. here is the void—

Wind carries sirens through open patio door. Living room is cold, clean-smelling. Phone on floor by bedroom doors, both of them open.

Tires squeal to stop outside.

Mind is free. Twisting, wriggling thing is gone.

Pick up phone. Feels light, like it should. Strength in my hands and arms. I can move. I could run if I wanted. Rapid beeping from earpiece like forgot to hang it up. Voicemail light blinking. Dial in code. Mom's voice: "What was that?! What just happened?! Is everyone okay? It sounded like . . . sweetie, I'm . . . I'm calling 911." Message ends.

Pounding on front door. "Police. Can you open the door, please?"

Drop phone and step through patio door. Cool breeze on skin. Inhale. Look down at street. Crowd has gathered around something.

Pray: Forgive me. . . .

TOUCH THE SKY, THEY SAY

Four steps up onto the observation platform and the sky is barely a foot above my head. Featureless, grey—a morning headache after a bad night's sleep. Same as it looks from the street, forty-one floors down.

Up here, the wind is July-hot and attic-dry, switching directions, rippling our clothes. The group is a mix. A couple of business types on lunch. There's a middle-aged guy in black jeans and a sleeveless Harley Davidson shirt. A teenager with spiked hair despite his school blazer and tie.

The last one up is a girl in her twenties with peroxide-blonde hair and a Ramones T-shirt. She doesn't hesitate—fingertips stroke the sky. I see my own uncertainty mirrored in her expression. Once in a while, the stories go, someone collapses to the planks of the platform, sobbing.

Not her.

She lowers her hand and descends the wooden steps to the elevator, heavy boots clopping all the way. A pudgy man with crescents of sweat in the armpits of his suit presses his palm against the sky for an instant, then follows the blonde.

There's six of us left, trying not to make it too obvious we're all waiting to see who will go next. The Harley shirt turns and leans against the wooden railing. We're at the highest point in the city; you can see for kilometres. See straight across to where the sky cuts through the CN Tower and the truncated columns we used to call skyscrapers. Maybe he's just here for the view. I join him at the railing and look south. The lake's calm today, reflecting the sky's perpetual flat, grey light. I jam my hands in my pockets, fingering the folded-up rejection letters.

Far below, a car horn sounds, echoes, fades. The familiar quiet resumes. Since the sky fell, we're all so polite. A quick toot of the horn used for caution, not a weapon, not a complaint. Years ago, waiting for one tutor or another in a music room lit pure-gold by the afternoon sun, I used to focus on the constant blare of rush hour, picking out horns not tuned to F major.

The kid with the spiky hair appears next to me, hands on the railing. He leans far over and, for a second, I think he's going to jump. But he rocks back, curls his hands into fists and drums them on the railing. A complex beat in 3/4 time.

The man in the Harley shirt straightens up and shoots a fist against the sky. His knuckles crack and he grimaces. The stillness broken, two others reach up. A moment later they're down the stairs.

The kid watches them go, then moves to the other side of the platform.

Wiping sweat from my forehead, I check the clock above the elevator doors. I've been here for eleven of the fifteen minutes my ticket allows.

The career woman in her expensive pantsuit and hairdo raises her hand, eyes shut. On contact, she shudders and lets out a small sob. But that's it and she's gone, high heels clicking down the steps.

Just me and the kid, now. I wonder what his story is. Maybe he wonders about mine. We probably both wonder if it's true what they say. That when you touch the sky you accept it's all real. That no one is climbing Everest or Logan again. That Calgary, Mexico City, and Madrid are just gone. That whoever was in a plane or penthouse when the sky fell is never coming down. That no more planes are ever going up. No more sunsets or starry nights or full moons. No more night or day. No more summer-fall-winter-spring.

Touch the sky, they say—the people who have—and you can let it all go. Let go of twenty years of daily piano and violin and clarinet practice. Let go of that desperate dream of making a living in the arts. Let go of any hope of attending one of the last remaining Fine Arts schools. Any hope of one day having your own orchestra.

Just touch it. Accept it. Accept there's no longer a place for passion or grief or heartache or joy. The world is what it is. There's no need any more for creation. The sky fell and we survived the year of panic and wasted effort and now we know better. We know there's nothing we can do or control and we know that nothing means a goddamn thing anymore.

I reach in my pockets for the letters, hold them out before me and open my fingers. The hot wind catches the pages, spreading them across the wooden deck, to the edge, over it.

The teenager watches them go and then yanks loose his tie. "Fuck this," he tells no one. He balls up the tie and pitches it over the railing. Without once looking skyward, he stomps down the steps.

The staffer who escorted us up appears at the steps, her uniform as grey as the sky. "Time is up," she announces flatly and motions for me to come down. I obey. She takes a place by the elevator doors, hands clasped before her, impassive. The others wait—calm, docile.

I begin to whistle low, a composition of my own in E flat. The kid nods along, tapping his legs with his palms. He follows the rhythm through its asymmetric 5/4 metre, his beats growing increasingly complex. I have a moment to admire his talent before I catch the glare of the man in the Harley shirt, the irritated shuffle of the business types, the frown of the peroxide blonde.

My instinct is to stop out of politeness. I look away and force myself to keep whistling.

The elevator pings, ready to take us back down to the street.

PUBLICATION HISTORY

Δπ ("Delta Pi") first appeared in *Torn Realities*, Post Mortem Press, 2012

"Ascension" first appeared in *AE: The Canadian Science Fiction Review*, 2011

"The Machinery of Government" first appeared in *Tesseracts Fourteen*, Edge Science Fiction and Fantasy Publishing, 2010

"Full Moon Hill" first appeared in *On Spec*, 2007

"Silverman's Game" was published by Damnation Books, 2010

"They Told Me to Shuffle Off This Mortal, Infinite Loop" first appeared in *Title Goes Here* #12, 2012

"That Which Does Not Kill You" first appeared in *Fear the Abyss*, Post Mortem Press, 2012

"In the Shadow of Scythe" first appeared in *Leading Edge Magazine* #62, 2012

"Balance" first appeared in *Postscripts to Darkness. Vol. 5*, 2014

"But It's Not the End" first appeared in *Undead Tales 2*, Rymfire Books, 2012

"Only at the End Do You See What Follows" is original to this collection

"The Wall of Gloves" first appeared on *The Drabblecast* #162, 2010

"Of the Endangered" first appeared in *Leading Edge Magazine* #65, 2014

"Brief Candles" is original to this collection

"The Pack" first appeared in *AE: The Canadian Science Fiction Review*, 2012

"The Thing That Killed Her" is original to this collection

"The Leaving" first appeared in *Blood Rites: An Invitation to Horror*, Blood Bound Books, 2013

"You're a Winner!" first appeared in *Night Terrors III*, Blood Bound Books, 2014

"The Weak Son" first appeared in *Tesseracts Thirteen*, Edge Science Fiction and Fantasy Publishing, 2009

"While Gabriel Slept" first appeared in *Night Terrors*, Blood Bound Books, 2010

"Touch the Sky, They Say" first appeared in *AE: The Canadian Science Fiction Review*, 2010

ACKNOWLEDGEMENTS

Thanks must first go to my wife, Kate. Sharing your spouse with his make-believe friends, fiends, and foes requires an extraordinary level of patience, understanding, and love. If you're reading this, my love, thank you. But it's not going to stop anytime soon.

My undying gratitude and love to Sandra Kasturi and Brett Savory at ChiZine Publications (CZP). When they first started CZP, they took a chance on handing me—a new writer whom Brett had met at Ad Astra (a Toronto SF convention)—the responsibility of marketing their new publishing house. Through them, I not only learned about writing, but the business of publishing. I've had the chance to work on so many amazing projects, meet extraordinary people, and gain insights into this business that have been invaluable in navigating some complex waters. While other demands have taken me away from my role as CZP staff, it's a thrill to be joining their ranks as an author. I'm eternally grateful to count Brett and Sandra as such dear friends.

Of course, hats off to everyone at CZP, including the incredibly talented Erik Mohr, whose cover adorns this book. Honestly, when Sandra told me they wanted to publish my collection, my first thought was: "I get an Erik Mohr cover!"

As to the stories in this collection, thanks must go to my writing group, the East Block Irregulars: Derek Künsken, Peter Atwood, Marie Bilodeau, Hayden Trenholm, Liz Westbrook-Trenholm, Geoff Gander, Kate Heartfield (who has also joined the CZP family with *Armed in Her Fashion*), and Agnes Sobiesiak. All of these talented authors have made these stories better through careful analysis, helpful suggestions and unflinching criticism.

Speaking of authors, there is not enough room to thank every author who has influenced and inspired my writing as an art, but I would like to thank those who have influenced my identity as a writer. These are friends I have made over my ten-year journey from newly published author up to this book's publication. I've learned how to do readings, conduct panels, interact with fans, juggle projects, and handle praise, pressure, and rejection. Even though many of them had established careers when we first met, none of them ever treated me as below their notice since I was a new author. I'd like to thank, in no particular order, the following for sharing friendship, wisdom, advice, taxi rides, reading slots, panels, bar bills, and random stories late into the night: Bob Boyczuk, Brent Hayward, Gemma Files, Claude Lalumière, Helen Marshall, Robert J. Sawyer, Sèphera Girón, Michael Kelly, Suzanne Church, Madeline Ashby, Liz Strange, Craig Davidson (and his punk-ass doppelgänger Nick Cutter), Samantha Beiko, Tony Burgess, Peter Halasz, Ian Rogers, Charles de Lint, Michael Rowe, Ellen Datlow, Matthew Johnson, Lydia Peever, and Douglas Smith.

A very special thanks to David Nickle, whose introduction begins this text. I met David almost a decade ago when CZP published his debut short story collection *Monstrous Affections*. Many know this book for its cover—the disturbing Sloan Man face that has become CZP's mascot. But the work within *Monstrous Affections* was transformative for me—chilling, emotionally raw, stylistically confident, and utterly disturbing. "The Mayor Will Make a Brief Statement and Then Take Questions" from that collection is an unquestionably perfect short short story. (And made all the better if you've ever heard Dave read it in person.) I have often joked that David Nickle is the author I wanted to be when I grow up. His introduction to my debut short story collection brings things around, closing one circle and opening another.

Then there are the editors and publishers I have come to know and work with. Again, in no order, my thanks and respect go to: Duff McCourt at *AE: The Canadian Science Fiction Review*; Diane Walton and Susan MacGregor at *On Spec* (who purchased my first short fiction sale "Full Moon Hill," which appears in this collection); Sean Moreland at *Postscripts to Darkness*; Eric Beebe and Paul Anderson at Post Mortem Press; Marc Ciccarone and crew at Blood Bound Books; and Christopher Jones, Nanci Kalanta & Tony Tremblay at HW Press. I hope to work with you all again!

A special paragraph for writer, critic, and friend Adam Shaftoe-Durrant. Adam and I met over his review of my short story "Touch the Sky, They Say" (first published on *AE: The Canadian Science Fiction Review* and included in this collection). His review was not kind, but not unfair. Somehow this set off a long friendship of bonding over *Community*, *Rick & Morty*, pop culture, and internet memes. Adam is one of the sharpest, most insightful critics I have read, and I hope he will be able to turn his laser-sharp focus to this work.

Second to last, my thanks to the Ottawa speculative fiction writing community. Since I first started writing seriously ten years ago, our little city that fun forgot has assembled a powerful speculative fiction writing community. I am honoured and humbled to have been welcomed into your ranks.

Lastly, thanks to you who is reading this. I know acknowledgements can be self-indulgent or dry or in-jokey, but if you've read this far: thank you! You are invaluable to the process of storytelling. Some think a story is complete when an author finishes writing it, but it's not. A story can only truly exist in the mind of the reader. While every reader sees the same words on the page, each experiences a unique story. So I acknowledge you for letting these people, places, times, and events live within you. Even for a little while.

ABOUT THE AUTHOR

Matt Moore has been writing stories since he could clutch a pencil and carve block letters into handwriting practice paper. His nonfiction, poems, and short fiction have appeared in a number of magazines and anthologies. *It's Not the End and Other Lies* is his first full-length work. When not writing, he organizes the Ottawa Chiaroscuro Reading Series, a professional reading series of speculative fiction.

Raised in New England, a place rich with legends and ghost stories, he now lives in Ottawa, Ontario.

Learn more at mattmoorewrites.com.